THE FOURTEENTH POINT

Other Books by John Ball

Last Plane Out
The Van: A Tale of Terror
A Killing in the Market
The Kiwi Target
Rescue Mission
Phase Three Alert
The Fourteenth Point
Mark One: The Dummy
The Winds of Mitamura
The Murder Children

Virgil Tibbs Mysteries

Five Pieces of Jade
The Eyes of Buddha
Then Came Violence
Singapore

Chief Jack Tallon Crime Novels

Police Chief
Trouble for Tallon
Chief Tallon and the S.O.R.

**For more exciting
eBooks, Audiobooks and more visit us at**
www.speakingvolumes.us

THE FOURTEENTH POINT

JOHN BALL

SPEAKING VOLUMES, LLC
NAPLES, FLORIDA
2014

THE FOURTEENTH POINT

ISBN 978-1-61232-994-9

For Bob and Gloria Blacka, the best of companions

THE FOURTEENTH POINT

CHAPTER ONE

The Most Reverend Frederick Danford-Smith leaned forward and laid his thin hands carefully on the table before him. With his dry voice and the authority of his seventy-eight years he held the full attention of the others who were seated with him. "I must remind you," he said, "of the extreme importance of the occasion. In addition to other considerations, it is very likely to be reported extensively by the press — not only here, but also on the Continent and in America as well."

A substantially built, ruddy-faced churchman who looked like a former Rugby star, and was, replied from across the table. "You are completely correct, of course, but can you question the fact that Philip Roundtree is, without quibbling, one of the most eloquent voices in the entire Church of England?"

"I will certainly grant his gifts," said Danford-Smith. "They have been recognized for some time. He always preaches well and sometimes brilliantly. I will also acknowledge his distinguished success as an administrator. The problem is that I don't entirely trust him. That is, I'm never quite certain what he is going to do."

A quiet bishop at the end of the table felt called upon to speak. "Gentlemen, there is a very grim and unwelcome fact we are ignoring. Within the last few years the influence and authority of the Church have been in retrograde. That's the bare bones of it. We can't expect this unhappy trend to correct itself unless we find ourselves plunged into another war, and God forbid that. If we hold Convocation and say essentially the same things we always have, you know what will happen. We will continue to go downgrade and we will have missed a major opportunity."

The ruddy man was quick to follow that. "You are in favor of Roundtree, then?"

"I'm in favor of someone who will be vital, even challenging. I wouldn't have taken this position twenty years ago, now I fear that I must."

The bishop was a much younger man, but the archbishop sensed that he spoke for the assembled company. And what he had said had behind it the force of logic. Danford-Smith deliberately put out of his mind reminders that Philip Roundtree had once delivered a sermon on abortion and that he had described one of the most august personages within the Church as having had more embroidery than common sense, and gave his consent to the common will. "We shall invite him, then," he concluded. That done, he spoke an inward silent prayer. With Philip Roundtree in the pulpit, unless God took a firm hand, almost anything might happen.

It was very late in the afternoon, so late that dusk had already settled over the city and little pools of light were becoming distinguishable under the streetlamps. The thickening shadows were already in command of the quiet confines of the study, where the narrow windows never admitted a full complement of sunlight. Behind the heavy oak desk, which had seen more than three generations of service, Philip Roundtree sat in deep, silent thought. He had been there for some time, all but motionless in his high-backed chair, ignoring the growing darkness, making up his mind. He was preparing himself for what might be the most venturesome event of his life.

At fifty-six he was firmly established and in a secure position. His administration of his diocese was a major success; there were material factors which testified to that. Most of his sermons had been very well received, granted that a few had not been so enthusiastically welcomed. His personal life, both as an individual and as a family man, was exemplary. It was not an easy thing for him to contemplate risking all this, especially since it was too late in life for him to live down what might be a serious mistake.

But he kept recalling something Shaw had said about there being two kinds of people: the reasonable, reliable ones and the difficult ones who were never satisfied with anything. Therefore, Shaw had concluded, all progress depended upon the difficult people.

Philip Roundtree would never be "difficult" in that sense, but he was facing a decision from which there would be no turning back. To tamper with the entrenched structure of the Church at all was dangerous; he was seriously considering upsetting it completely.

He stirred himself and was surprised to discover how dark it had become. He could barely see the dim outlines of the windows and the shape of the desk before him. At the same time a second realization came to him — that subconsciously he had already made his decision. He could, and undoubtedly would, give it some more thought, but it would end up the same way. For a moment he pressed his hands hard against the arms of his chair, then he rose to his feet.

As he washed and prepared himself for dinner, he wondered how he would tell his wife, Janet, and what she might say in return. The boys were concerned, in an indirect way, but neither of them was old enough to grasp the implications of what he proposed to do. He decided it would be best to come right to the point — gently, but without preamble.

He entered the dining room smiling, as befitted his role as husband and father, seated himself, and gave thanks. That brief ceremony concluded, he laid his napkin in his lap, looked up, and announced to Janet, "I've made up my mind, I think."

She knew, almost at once, that from her viewpoint the news was not good "Are you certain that this is something you want to do?" she asked. She had to be careful because the boys were there, but the intonation of her voice should tell him much.

"Yes, I think so." He helped himself to mashed potatoes and took careful note that his younger son Geoffrey did not neglect the carrots.

Janet thought very carefully. She could not tell him what to do, of course, particularly in ecclesiastical matters, but every feminine instinct she possessed told her that potential trouble, possibly even disaster, was in the air. She loved her husband profoundly, and for that very reason felt that she somehow would have to help him and perhaps point out to him what others might think. That was so important to a man in his position. Actually she knew little about what he had in mind, but she could sense much.

"When are you going to start on the sermon?" she asked.

"The first thing in the morning," he answered, and then became aware that another decision had shaped itself. For a moment or two he wondered if it was by any chance inspiration — a possible indication of what was wanted of him; then he dismissed that idea on the grounds that he was unworthy of any such attention. He was prepared to accept the entire responsibility for his own actions. And, he knew, there would be plenty to accept.

"Quite a large shipment of books came in for you today,"

6

Janet told him. "From Foyles. I didn't want to disturb you, so I had them left in the front hallway."

That was precisely the piece of news that he most wanted to hear. "Excellent," he said. "I do hope they were able to find *The Opening of the Wisdom Eye*."

Janet was puzzled. "What is that?"

"It's a very interesting discourse on certain aspects of the Buddhist faith. It's of particular interest because it was written by His Holiness the Dalai Lama."

"I see." She responded automatically, quite unaware that it was actually a lie. There were so many excellent works on Christian thought and purpose, with new ones being added all the time, she did not quite understand how her husband had the time to go dabbling into Oriental beliefs.

"Is it in English, Father?" his elder son wanted to know.

Philip smiled at him. "Yes, Peter, and one of the translators is British."

That, of course, made everything quite proper; Peter returned to his plate confident that his father was, as always, on firm ground.

For the next several days the Right Reverend Philip Roundtree, Doctor in Divinity, was for all practical purposes available to no one. As the news of the great honor he had received filtered through the diocese, his self-imposed isolation was fully understood. Almost anything that he could have undertaken would have been approved by most of his spiritual constituents. Some few, of course, held other views. For the most part they shielded themselves in the armor of their venerable seniority and carefully concealed their collective expectation that one day he would fall flat on his face. To all of the rest the vital, admittedly handsome man who was their bishop deserved the highest honors that his church was able to bestow. They admired him for his imposing presence in the cathedral and they loved him for his warm humanity outside of it.

7

All of which was fully known to the highest authorities within the Church. Had he been a shade more predictable, their enthusiasm would have been much greater.

None of these considerations bothered Philip Roundtree himself as he plunged into a paroxysm of work: he began by carrying the large carton of newly arrived books into his study and unpacking them with brisk efficiency. After that he created a systemized disorder, with volumes scattered almost everywhere and notes covering every available spot on his desk. Janet saw very little of him except at mealtime, and she worried because he was so very late in coming to bed. She could not remember when he had worked so hard for such an extended period of time. It was the sermon, she knew, but her husband seldom required more than an hour at the most to put together a discourse that would be talked about favorably for days. His schooling was so sound, and he had a tremendous knowledge of Christian doctrine literally at his fingertips.

When Sunday came he was, as always, a commanding figure in the pulpit, his delivery full-bodied and genuinely inspiring. Among the congregation only she knew that the sermon was an old one which he had originally written before he had been elevated to the episcopate. Never before had she known him to draw on the past like that; it was not like him. She guessed the reason — that he simply had not had time to prepare something new — and once more she wondered if he wasn't applying himself too hard to the task he had been assigned. After all, these big church convocations did come twice a year, and while the Sunday sermon was the high point, and being invited to deliver it was a great honor, there had been many such meetings in the past and many many more would follow in the future. The Church made very few changes and it made them slowly.

She got her husband back, so to speak, four days after that. He emerged from his study one afternoon, dropped into his favorite armchair, and settled himself down as though all the energy had been drained from his body. She was immediately concerned; this was another new symptom she had never encountered before. Her first thought was to call the doctor, but she knew that that suggestion would be vetoed. He was simply exhausted, that was all. She got down on her knees to comfort him, at the same time wondering if *any* sermon was worth taking this much out of a man.

Then he smiled at her and she knew that everything was going to be all right. The hand that had been in his lap found hers and through it she let her own strength and devotion flow into his body. At that moment her reservations fled and she was only aware that her man needed and wanted her. In her feminine world that took precedence over everything else, even the hierarchy of the Church of England or the sermon over which he had been working so intensely.

"It must be a very *fine* sermon," she said.

Her husband looked at her, his face thoughtful and reflecting the fact that his mind was still fixed on something far away from that moment. "It had better be," he told her, "because no one has ever preached one like it before."

CHAPTER TWO

Arthur Gravenstine pulled open the door of the Sherlock Holmes and stepped inside with a comfortable feeling of expectation. The pub was not unduly crowded, which pleased him; he was in a reflective mood and he had no desire to participate in a mob scene before the bar. He glanced at the giant rat of Sumatra, preserved in a suitable jar, hung the hat he still chose to wear on a convenient peg, and then addressed himself to the business of getting a drink. When he had been served he sat down and sampled the warm beer, which was precisely to his taste. Then he relaxed and allowed himself to forget the trials and tribulations of the day.

He had been by himself for some ten minutes when a colleague came in. He knew Felix Wyeth, the music critic, sufficiently well to be glad to see him; they were fellow sufferers to a degree and Felix was an understanding type.

When Felix had joined him with his own beverage, Arthur made appropriate small talk of the kind that newspapermen share the world over. Wyeth spoke of the concert of avant-garde music which he would be compelled to listen to that evening and of the audience likely to attend.

"Any news in it?" Gravenstine asked. It was a pretty hopeless question, but he put it nevertheless.

The music critic consoled himself with his beer. "Not a chance. Four new composers, all of whom beat on washtubs and score their stuff in thirteen flats."

"Grim," Arthur said.

It meant another day of oblivion for the talented and deserving man who had probably heard more string quartets than anyone else in England.

"You have the big Convocation coming up, don't you?" Felix asked. He even allowed a little hopefulness to come into his voice.

"Yes. Twice a year, sort of an airing of the mothballs."

"I don't think that I could cut it as religion editor, no matter how much homework I did."

"Of course you could. You write wonderfully well, and that's the best asset you could have. The rest you could pick up in any library. Music takes a lifetime."

"Not necessarily." He paused to consult his beer once more. "You know, as long as I've been with the *Times* I've never appeared on the front page."

"Yes, I know," Arthur said.

"Nothing ever happens in music that rates it. I thought I had it once with the Flagstad return concert after the end of World War II, but it turned out to be a bright news day and I was back somewhere inside along with the society column."

"You'll just have to wait for the second coming of Ludwig von Beethoven."

Felix became gloomy. "That wouldn't help either, they'd just call him an imitator." He drank a little more beer. "You had a good one once — the Peter Townsend business. That story went all over the world."

Arthur shook his head. "It did, of course, but it was considered a political matter — great personages, all that sort of thing. The religious angle was important, but secondary."

"What would happen if the Archbishop of Canterbury were to assault someone in Westminster Abbey?"

"The crime boys would handle it. They *own* the front page, the PM gets on only when they relinquish the space — you know how it is."

Felix leaned closer. "I heard a rumor, just a thin one, but there might be some substance to it. Let me ask you something: Could a sermon, any sermon, ever make news?"

"Well — there was *The Scarlet Letter*."

"A bit far back, and what happens in America doesn't really count. I mean today."

Arthur Gravenstine searched his memory. "There have been occasions," he conceded. "Very rare ones. If Frederick Danford-Smith were to preach on the spiritual worth of free love, that would be noted."

"But he hasn't."

"And he won't unless he loses his mind."

Felix strengthened himself with the remainder of his beer. "I have some relatives scattered about; good church-goers, some of them. Have you encountered a man called Roundtree?"

Gravenstine reacted visibly. "He is my one and only hope," he said.

"Well, he's to preach the keynote sermon, or whatever they call it, isn't he?"

"At the Convocation — yes, he is. Brilliant fellow. Bit of a rebel, enough so that he might forget himself some day and say something really important."

Felix probed. "What if he did?"

A dreamy look came into Arthur Gravenstine's eyes. "The front page," he murmured softly.

"Could he do it?"

Gravenstine nodded. "It's a possibility. He's so good they couldn't bury him even though they tried to. His people adore him. And he *did* preach on abortion once. I did quite a piece on it."

"For what it's worth, here's a clue. I get the word that His Lordship is behaving a little like a man who might be up to something. Are you going to cover his discourse?"

Arthur looked at him. "The *Times* expects me to be there; it will be one of the major religious events of the year in England. I shall attend."

"Take some extra paper with you."

A bit of stray light came through the etched glass windows at the front of the pub and caught Arthur Gravenstine right in the eyes. He took it as a sign. "Felix," he said, "let me return the favor. I shall pray that England's greatest symphony conductor, whoever he may be, is discovered to have three wives and a whole orchestra of illegitimate children scattered about. And that he subsequently performs the Beethoven Ninth with all of his bastards as the chorus."

Felix shook his head. "Bigamy is a crime," he said sadly.

By ten in the morning the sun was comfortably high in the sky, but it provided only a thin and watery radiance. The ocean-tempered wind steadily eroded what little warmth there was while a high entrenched overcast filtered the limited comfort that the sun was providing and kept much of the British Isles in the grip of a continuing chill. However, it was Sunday, and the Church of England did not permit its massive dignity to be undermined by the weather. The formal procession formed on schedule and with a certain tottering magnificence began to thread its way into the cathedral. The organ raised its mighty voice as the Church dignitaries slowly filed in and began to fill their assigned pews, row after row.

Janet Roundtree watched them carefully, searching their faces and trying to read signs or portents that might be some guide to her. She knew that there was nothing she could do, but she was still concerned. When the narrow, somewhat ascetic features of Frederick Danford-Smith caught her attention, she had a sudden tightening feeling in her breast and wondered if her husband could really cope with all of this. Then her confidence came back; they were, after all, only human men and they too had their weaknesses. She would have been terrified if she had been required to stand before them and say anything as simple and certain as "Let us pray," but Philip had great moral courage and even before such an august congregation he would be brilliant. He had certainly worked hard enough, even to the point of insisting on typing the final draft of his sermon himself. She had no idea what he was going to say, but she did not want to miss a word of it.

Her inner tensions stayed with her as she entered the vast nave and quietly took the place that had been allotted to her. Presently the Litany began, fixed like a great granite boulder that had withstood the erosion of wind and water for ages, and would for ages yet to come. As the familiar words and responses filled the cathedral, she found comfort in their sameness and the stability that they represented. She knew when to rise and when to sit down, when to sing (softly, for she had no voice and she knew it) and when to remain silent in momentary prayer.

Voices conducted the service and moved it inexorably forward. Voices she did not recognize, but voices that revealed they had done the same thing hundreds of times before. The epistle was read and then the Gospel, all according to the established forms that had come down through the centuries virtually unchanged to tell her that literally God was in his heaven and all was right with the world. Not every single thing, perhaps, but the foundations of the Church, Philip's and her church, were built upon bedrock and they offered her a great and vaulting protection.

Her attention had been wandering a little as it did sometimes; she came back to reality when she realized that within a few moments it would be time for the sermon to

14

begin. And then she saw Philip, wonderful in his Convocation robes, looking poised, serene, and confident. She said a quick little silent prayer for him and then watched with hopeful, proud eyes as he climbed into the pulpit.

At that precise moment the lighting in the whole cathedral appeared to change. By some apparent miracle the clouds parted to allow the full power of the sunlight to stream in through the stained-glass windows. Somehow that lent a special magic to the moment beyond all that she had expected and her reservations evaporated. Philip looked marvelous as he stood waiting; his splendid strong face, his firm resolute shoulders. At that moment her body cried out for him and she wanted to be far away with him somewhere, locked in the safety and comfort of his arms.

Then she heard his voice, the splendid voice he had, and his first words were full of richness and meaning.

" *'The true light that enlightens every man that is come into the world.'*

"As we assemble here today in this service of worship, we join in spirit millions of other Christians who throughout the centuries since Calvary have gathered also to pray, to glorify God, and to give thanks for the grace they have received. And we have all received grace far beyond our limited powers to understand. For how often it is that today's misfortune proves to be tomorrow's great blessing. Let every man praise God for whatever happens to him, for by so doing he acknowledges and accepts the infinite wisdom of the Divine."

Responding, perhaps, to the increased light which enhanced the richness of the great nave, the Most Reverend Frederick Danford-Smith felt slightly better. He had heard rumors that had disturbed him. But Philip Roundtree was off to a good safe start; if he could somehow manage to hold that pace, all would be well.

"And never before in history has so much happened to so many in so short a time. We, and all of the people of the world, within the past few short years have been brought into unprecedented closeness by means of almost instantaneous communications and giant jet aircraft which bridge the vastest oceans in a few brief hours. Medicine and other sciences have advanced by quantum jumps. Men have stood on the surface of other worlds and have returned; the Holy Scriptures have been read to us from the vast void of airless space. We have also been brought under the fearful shadow of nuclear holocaust and other means of mass destruction too appalling even to contemplate. Our need for closeness to our Creator was never more acute."

Janet knew then that this would be a great sermon, that her husband would step down from the pulpit with a new aura about him, and that the inspiration of his words and thoughts would echo throughout England.

Less emotionally, the quiet bishop who had urged that Philip Roundtree be invited to preach knew that whatever was to follow, he was not going to be disappointed.

"It is essential for us to remember that the church is a living entity, a vital and indispensable one, that must not only keep pace with the progress of mankind, but also lead it and guide it as we have been charged to do."

The ruddy-faced clergyman who had been the strongest advocate of inviting Philip Roundtree to be heard unconsciously nodded his head in agreement.

"Before this august company, and upon this solemn occasion, I direct your attention to the twenty-second chapter of Matthew, verses thirty-seven to forty — words which summarize our Christian faith. 'And He said to him, "You shall love the Lord your God with all your heart, and with all your soul, and with all your mind. This is the great and first commandment. And a second is like it, you shall love your neighbour as yourself. On these two commandments depend all the law and the prophets." ' "

Philip Roundtree looked about him. He remained silent for a bare moment and then added, "And Christ also said,

'In my Father's house are many mansions; if it were not so, I would have told you.' "

He consulted the manuscript before him and the timbre of his voice changed. "I direct your attention now to the first of the four sacred books of the Hindus, the Rig Veda, which was written approximately twenty-five hundred B.C. I quote from chapter ten, verses one hundred and ninety-two to one hundred and ninety-four:

> " 'One and the same by your resolve
> And may your mind be one accord.
> United be the thoughts of all
> That all may happily agree.' "

At that moment the quiet bishop looked up, a new expression on his face. It was compounded of surprise, a measure of concern, and a fragment of fear. For he had an intimation of what Philip Roundtree might be going to say, whatever words he chose for the purpose.

Frederick Danford-Smith sat motionless, listening and waiting.

In the press section Arthur Gravenstine felt a mist of sweat break out on his brow.

In the pulpit Philip Roundtree was poised and confident. His hands gripped the carved railing, not in urgency but with the power of a decision made and now being implemented.

"I next turn," he continued, "to one of the outstanding leaders in the world of Islam. I refer to His Imperial Majesty Mohammed Reza Pahlavi Aryamehr, the Shah of Iran. I quote His Majesty: 'The ideal world we all hope to create is a world in which all of the constructive and creative thoughts and powers of men, irrespective of geographical, racial, and religious differences, will work harmoniously together to bring about a society fit for the whole of mankind.' Surely all of us can subscribe to that."

Roundtree consulted his prepared text for a moment or two before he continued. "This same message rises in the hearts of good men everywhere, and it has done so through-out the ages. Some six hundred years before the miracle of Bethlehem, Confucius set down a similar principle, as also did Gautama Siddhartha, who became the Buddha, and Zoroaster, more properly Zarathustra."

Then Philip Roundtree looked up from his notes and faced the Convocation of the Church of England.

"It can thus be seen that the needs not only of our cur-rent age, but also of this very day, impose a challenge greater than any we have ever been called upon to answer before. And we are not alone in this; throughout the world men of good will, within the structure of their churches and outside of them, call for us to follow the same path that our Savior Himself pointed out."

It was deadly quiet. The ruddy-faced churchman swal-lowed hard and knew that he might have to answer in part for the thing that Philip Roundtree was doing.

The voice from the pulpit went on, full and strong. "Christian unity is a topic about which we have heard a great deal and toward which many men of surpassing talents have given much of their lives. And they have made great progress, for the constant divisions and separations have been halted, and in such places as the Church of South India we have seen the wonderful fruit of their labors.

"But now we must address ourselves to the greater task — the beginnings of the unity of all mankind under the banner of a single common faith. There are multitudes to say that this cannot be done, but there are multitudes more who attest that it can."

As though he was unaware of the startling nature of his words, he once more consulted his manuscript. "I have read with great interest a small book by a young man of our own faith, C. G. Lewis, whose *Tibetan Venture* recounts his experiences while a volunteer teacher in the refugee communities of present-day India. In this work he states, 'I felt more convinced than ever of the essential unity of all of the major religions. Through some greater measures of revelation granted to them than to others, all are groping toward the same Godhead, and all have experienced the mystery that lies within life and beyond it, and all are seeking to explain or to reach this mystery.'

"It is not my intention to spend these few precious minutes with you this morning indulging in an overabundance of quotations, but so great a topic, so mighty a mission, must find support in many areas if it is to succeed in its divinely ordained purpose. I find it of great importance, therefore, to lay before you the words of a spiritual leader of the highest rank who is known to everyone here, although I doubt if any of us have ever been privileged to meet him face-to-face. Let me give you first what he has written.

" 'Just as a particular disease in the world can be treated by various methods in medicine, so there are different religions that bring happiness to human beings and others. Different doctrines have been expounded by different exponents at different periods and in different ways. But I believe they all fundamentally aim at achieving the same noble goal, in teaching moral precepts to mold the functions of mind, body and speech. They all teach us not to tell lies, or bear false witness, or steal, or take the lives of others, and so on. Therefore, it would be better if disunity among the followers of different religions could come to an end. Unity among religions is not an impossible idea. It is possible, and in the present state of the world, it is especially important. Mutual respect would be helpful to all believers, and unity among them would also bring benefit to unbelievers, for the unanimous flood of light would show them the way out of their ignorance. I strongly emphasize the urgent need for flawless unity among all religions.' "

Philip Roundtree looked up. "*Thou shalt not kill, thou shalt not steal, thou shalt not bear false witness* — these admonitions were given to us by the finger of Almighty God himself through his servant Moses. And consider for one moment the overwhelming result if a unanimous flood of light could indeed show the unbelievers of the world the way out of their ignorance! These are Christian purposes, these are Christian ideals to which every one of us can subscribe. To bring the unbelievers into the fold of God — to what greater purpose could we dedicate ourselves! For the benefit of those who, like Thomas, may doubt, for those who feel that such a magnificent purpose is predestined failure, let me state that the words I have just read were set down for us by a man not of our own faith, but the leader of another great world religion. I refer to His Holiness Gejong Tenzin Gyatsho, known best to the Western world as the Dalai Lama."

The Most Reverend Frederick Danford-Smith closed his eyes and allowed his head to sink until his chin seemed to touch the top of his robes. Those who sat closest to him were unsure whether he was in pain or in prayer.

For ten more minutes the voice of Philip Roundtree filled the mighty cathedral, never rising above the level of controlled discourse, but ringing with challenge and the conviction that had impelled him to attack the single greatest problem known to the faiths of mankind. As the sermon went forward Arthur Gravenstine realized frantically that he was running out of paper and that he would have to stop his rapid shorthand to concentrate on the more significant passages. Then he almost missed the one thing he needed most; only a slight shift in the speaker's intonation put him on his guard in time.

"I say to you," he heard Philip Roundtree declare, "that when we who are gathered here today refer to ourselves as the Church of England we are employing a misnomer, for the Church we comprise belongs to God; it is not England that we worship, but the Almighty.

"We have been given a mission we can no longer ignore, one which our urgent present age demands if the Church as a great and powerful force and entity is to survive at all. It is the work of God to which we are called, and in His service we can recognize no obstacle.

"And now unto God the Father . . ." The congregation rose.

As soon as he was able, Arthur Gravenstine made his escape from the cathedral and rushed to his typewriter. He would have liked to have waited and talked to some of the senior Church personages who might have been persuaded to comment, but he was desperately anxious to commit what was in his mind to paper. He knew and understood that Philip Roundtree had all but destroyed himself, for what he proposed was patently impossible, but by God he had stood up like a man and had declared himself without equivocation on the hottest topic that any churchman could face. And that, Arthur Gravenstine knew, was front page news.

CHAPTER THREE

Sir Cyril Throckmorton Plessey emerged from his bed-chamber and began to make his way down the hallway toward the staircase. That in itself was noteworthy, for at his age the ability to wake up in the morning was an achievement. Sir Cyril was perfectly aware that he had outlived the biblical three score years and ten by a considerable margin, and delighted in ignoring it. In fact he had given specific instructions that the housemaids he employed be comely wenches and, whenever possible, of at least somewhat dubious character. "Should I decide at any time to resume one of the more enthusiastic activities of my youth," he had explained, "I would like to have the necessary means close at hand and available. I see no point in wasting valuable time in needless persuasions."

As he made his way down the long curved staircase Sir Cyril held the oaken handrail only lightly. He had been urged to install a lift as a concession to his years; it had given him considerable satisfaction to reject that idea forthwith. Unlike many who lived in the venerable manor houses of England, Sir Cyril felt no pinch of funds; his investment skills were legendary and he had not yet chosen to let up on the traders who tried to live by their wits on the floor of the exchange. The extent of his holdings was unpublished, but whenever his name was mentioned in financial circles there were those who felt impelled to remove their hats and face Threadneedle Street.

As he entered the morning breakfast room with its pattern of inviting sunlight provided by the many windows, he found waiting for him the standard arrangement he had decreed. Beside the chair he was to occupy was Ames — Ames, who had been with him for more than thirty years and who knew him better than his mother ever had — with two young ladies in starched uniforms merely to improve the view, and the *Times* properly folded beside the service plate. He glanced toward it and read from a distance the single word *strike*. He could have done without that, but otherwise the arrangements for his reception were beyond cavil.

Sir Cyril seated himself with a tactful slight assist from Ames, spread his napkin, allowed himself a few seconds to study the two housemaids, who were delighted to receive this attention, and then nodded. Having thus ordered his breakfast, which was already cooked and waiting, he unfolded the *Times* and prepared himself to discover what lesser men were doing about the world. With an eye that a foraging eagle would have respected he scanned the most urgent news and then halted abruptly. He was so absorbed he all but ignored the presentable female who placed his eggs before him.

Someone had had the profound nerve to hand it to the Church of England straight between the eyes.

Fascinated by this wonderful discovery, Sir Cyril read with avid attention; Ames, who had anticipated his reaction, left him strictly alone.

Sir Cyril had never heard of Philip Roundtree that he

could recall or of Arthur Gravenstine, whose name did not register on his consciousness. The article was a long one which continued on the inner pages, but the initial three paragraphs were meaty enough to make him reread them. The details of when and where he brushed aside, but what the speaker had said riveted his attention. Paragraph two was the best of it:

"In his stirring and uncompromising discourse Bishop Roundtree stressed the urgency of the times. He declared that religion would see its strength withered if it failed to keep pace with the vast and rapid advances in other fields of endeavor. In particular he declared, 'When we call ourselves the Church of England we are employing a misnomer, for the Church we comprise belongs to God; it is not England that we worship, but the Almighty.' This challenging viewpoint is not known to have been previously expressed from the pulpit on an occasion of equal importance."

"Ames," Sir Cyril said, "have I ever heard of this man Roundtree?"

"If I recall correctly, sir, I believe that you took note of the occasion on which he delivered a sermon on abortion. It was mentioned in the local press."

"So that's him!" Sir Cyril, fortified by this new knowledge, consumed the entire article along with his three-minute eggs. He then looked up.

"This fellow Roundtree seems to have documented his case well. He quoted the Hindus, Confucius, and an Arab. On second thought I don't think the Shah is an Arab."

"I couldn't say as to that, sir, but since his name is Mohammed, I would presume that he is a follower of Islam."

"Sound conclusion. He quoted the Buddhists and cited Zarathustra. He covered about all the bases there are, as the Americans say. Who else is there? The Jews perhaps."

"I noted, sir, that he also made reference to Moses."

"Smart boy, Roundtree, he ought to be in business."

24

"It appears that he does have a business, sir, and from the article I would gather that he's doing quite well at it — to this point. His future prospects, I would venture, are somewhat clouded."

"I presume," Sir Cyril said as he accepted tea, "that old Freddy Smith was there."

"If you are referring to the Archbishop of York, sir, I would be inclined to regard it as a certainty."

"Great," Sir Cyril said reflectively. "I'm only sorry that I missed it. Freddy must have had apoplexy, at the least a mild stroke."

"I have seldom heard you refer to His Grace before, sir — are you acquainted with him?"

"Acquainted? Hell, Ames, I knew him long before he was sanctified. Freddy was a little odd even in those days — not much wenching, very little constructive hell-raising suitable to a young man. Sort of a holier-than-thou type."

"If I may say so, sir, subsequent events would seem to bear out that he was on reasonably firm ground in that."

"True, Ames, true. Still, a good shaking up is good for a man every now and then, it keeps the sediment from sinking to the bottom. When that happens the wicket falls and for all practical purposes the party's over."

"Very wisely said, sir. Would you care for anything else?"

Sir Cyril shook his head and then spoke once more. "Ames, how much money do you think it would take to, shall we say, attract the attention of the Church of England?"

"I would say about five pounds ten."

"That will get you a good prayer on the local level, but I'm thinking now in larger terms. This boy Roundtree has started something; what do you think is going to happen to him?"

"I would say nothing, sir, for a period of four or five months. Then I would expect that it would be announced that he is retiring from his present high responsibilities for reasons of health. It will be added that it is his wish to step down so that he can apply his well-known energies to writing a new and expanded study of the life and teachings of the Apostle Paul."

"Ames, how are your investments coming?"

"Under your guidance, sir, I have been able to achieve some quite satisfactory results."

"I'm not surprised, you have the head for it. Look ahead, that's the secret, look ahead."

"Absolutely, sir."

Sir Cyril rose to his feet with some slight help from the arms of his chair. Ames would not have offered to assist him except in case of dire emergency. "Ames."

"Yes, sir?"

"Gifts to the Church of England are completely tax-free, I believe."

"I am quite certain of that, sir."

"So whatever I might give to the Church, the Crown will pay a good part of it."

"A very large part, sir."

Sir Cyril arrived at a decision. "Freddy Smith once favored me with a lecture on morals which I did not require — at least not from him at that stage of the game. I've waited some time to square that account. Get me the *Times* — the same man who wrote that piece if you can. He writes as though he has some life in him, whoever he is."

"A Mr. Gravenstine, sir. I will notify you as soon as he has been located."

Arthur Gravenstine was reached at his desk, where he sat spending much of his time answering the telephone. The UPI had just called him from New York for further details concerning the life and activities of Philip Roundtree. He had supplied the information gladly, withholding the sad fact that the career of this distinguished churchman was undoubtedly already in rapid retrograde.

26

On his desk Gravenstine had a memo with a quote from the Most Reverend Frederick Danford-Smith which confirmed his worst fears on that point. "I had no previous notice," His Grace had said, "of the context of the sermon which Dr. Roundtree delivered. In view of the circumstances, I have no comment to make at this time."

The beheading ax which was so carefully preserved at Madame Tussaud's was about to be limbered up once more.

Arthur wondered if there was anything he could do — the power of the press and all that. He began to shape in his mind an editorial that would offer at least cautious support of Roundtree's bold move. The *Times* could not be committed too strongly as supporting a foredoomed failure, but a word of quiet encouragement might not be amiss. He had it! For his regular weekly column he could comment that whatever the obstacles, England had again led the way in pointing out a great human need. The need was firm reality, there was no question of that — it was simply that it was beyond human reach within the current time frame as far as most rational men could see. But Roundtree saw further and eventually, in a century or two, his words might be recalled as prophetic.

Then the phone rang once more. Arthur picked it up and was informed by the operator that Sir Cyril Plessey was calling.

To have one of the richest men in England take notice of him was an event, but he greatly feared that he was about to be nobly chewed out. His rebuttal would be simple; he had not written the sermon, he had only reported the facts as any responsible journalist would be expected to do. He had already used that same speech several times that morning.

When the connection had been completed he was informed that Sir Cyril would be with him momentarily. Seconds later a voice that was known almost as well as its owner came on the line.

"You're the fellow who wrote that piece about Philip Roundtree?"

"Yes, Sir Cyril; Arthur Gravenstine here."

"Well, first off, I thought it was damn good reporting."

That threw Arthur a wicked curve, but he was equal to it. "I'm very honored, sir, to have you express that opinion."

"Good. Now a question or two if you don't mind."

"Not at all, sir."

"In your opinion — and give it to me straight, mind you — how serious do you think he was?"

"Sir Cyril, if he wasn't serious, then God wasn't either when He told Noah to build the ark."

"He really meant it then."

"You're damn right — I mean yes, sir."

"Not for quotation, how good is Roundtree?"

"May I speak confidentially to you, sir?"

"Totally."

"Roundtree is probably the best mind the Church has. Mind, that is, combined with initiative, resourcefulness, and moral courage."

"Then if he was listed on the stock exchange, you'd buy."

"No, sir, I'd sell short with every cent I had. The archbishop was not amused."

"I hear you very clearly, Mr. Gravenstine. I think we should meet."

"I would be greatly honored, sir."

"In the meantime, here's something you might be able to use. I happen to think that Roundtree's right; if we don't get off our behinds we'll be left waiting at the church, and that's literally the case."

"May I quote that, sir?"

"You may, but clean it up a little. Here's something else. Roundtree has proposed something, but nothing gets off the ground without money — right?"

"Emphatically, sir."

"Very well. Quote: Inspired by the glowing words of Dr.

Roundtree, and desiring the greater benefit of all mankind, I propose to present to the Church of England, as it is presently known, a sum of money to be used exclusively to carry this great idea forward. In doing so it is my expressed wish that if at all possible Dr. Roundtree be relieved of his present duties so that he can give his splendid leadership entirely to this project. I want him to be head of it."

Gravenstine's pencil flew over the paper before him. "Sir Cyril, this is a superb gesture and if you'll pardon me, very substantial news in the bargain. The *Times* is proud that you have selected us to make the announcement. You were planning to let us have it exclusively, weren't you, sir?"

"No. In fact, Gravenstine, I'm going to ask you to do me the favor of passing the word along. You won't regret it. For reasons that have nothing to do with me personally, I'd like to see this get a good play."

"Sir Cyril, I believe I understand you perfectly. The archbishop, I presume, will read about it in the papers."

"Exactly! I don't know why you're writing religion, you should be covering crime. Anyhow, there it is for what it's worth."

"Splendid, Sir Cyril. One question, sir, if I may. I don't recall that you mentioned any sum; do you have one in mind?"

"Yes, I have. Glad you asked. For openers I will give one hundred thousand pounds; if I am pleased with the progress made and if my wishes are respected, I expect to increase that sum, perhaps materially. Is that enough to get on the front page?"

Gravenstine could have wept for joy. "I can virtually guarantee it, sir," he replied.

The Most Reverend Frederick Danford-Smith once more leaned forward and laid his thin hands carefully on the table before him. As before, he held the full attention of the others who were seated with him. "It seems," he said, "that we are precisely where we were before except for one thing. The last time we agreed to invite Dr. Roundtree to preach. He has now done so."

"Indeed he has," the quiet bishop said.

Danford-Smith looked at the ruddy-faced churchman who sat opposite him. "Have you any comments?" he invited.

"I am not evading my part in that decision, Your Grace," the big man answered, "but I do note the fact that the Church of England has been considered to be front page news by the *Times* two days running."

"You are impressed by publicity, then?"

"Not for its own sake, sir, but in view of the amount of it that the devil consistently gets, some rebuttal could be considered constructive."

The quiet bishop spoke again. "The sum of one hundred thousand pounds as a direct gift I regard as constructive also."

"True," Danford-Smith answered, a bit tersely, "but it has a very large ring through its nose — we can use it only for this interreligious business of Roundtree's. The ecumenical movement has shown some progress since nineteen-ten, and there was a parliament of religions in Chicago in eighteen ninety-three. Hardly the most likely site, I should think. Now Roundtree wants to get us all involved again."

The former Rugby player drummed his fingertips against the table top; then he realized that it was distracting the archbishop and ceased abruptly. "Your Grace," he said, "we can back away from this thing if we want to. The Church can issue a statement to the effect that we support Dr. Roundtree's conclusions — we can hardly do less than that — but we feel that the matter requires a great deal of further study before it can be carried forward. We could acknowledge Sir Cyril's gift and ask him to hold it in abeyance while plans are being formulated."

"Yes," the bishop added, "and thereby mortally insult

one of the wealthiest and most powerful men in England — Sir Cyril is no fathead, as everyone knows, and he would see through that in a flash."

"Well then, what do you propose?" Danford-Smith asked.

A younger man, who had appropriately remained silent up to that point, ventured to be heard. "Our alternatives are quite clear, I believe," he said. "One, we can accept the gift, appoint Roundtree to see what he can do, and ask him literally for the Lord's sake to watch his footing. Two, we can reject the idea out of hand as beyond the present scope of human capabilities. If we follow that path, then some prior communication with Sir Cyril would be mandatory, of course. Three, we can split it down the middle, advancing with controlled speed and caution until the thing dies a natural death."

"Or Sir Cyril does," the bishop added.

"That's about it, yes, sir."

A brief silence followed.

It was broken when a telephone located in one corner of the conference room rang very quietly. The younger man rose and went to pick it up. He conducted a brief conversation and then returned to his place at the table.

"I trust that it was important," Danford-Smith said.

"Yes, Your Grace, I would say that it was."

"Then in that case suppose you tell us."

"There have been two developments, sir, which might bear on our discussion. It seems, Your Grace, that there has been a great increase in the incoming mail. Much of it has to do with Dr. Roundtree's proposal."

"To be expected, I suppose. I presume most of it is to advise us to keep our hands off the structure of the Church of England."

"On the contrary, Your Grace, the support for Roundtree is overwhelming. Many of the letters contain contributions to be added to the amount Sir Cyril has already offered. No count is presently available, but I was given a quick estimate of several hundred pounds so far."

The quiet bishop tilted his head back and for a few moments stared at the ceiling. When he looked down again the others were waiting for him to speak. "That casts a little new light," he said. "I believe that we now have to consider the possibility that Roundtree was absolutely right — that people, just ordinary people, are tired of denominational and philosophical differences. That they want to see an end to holy wars."

"You mentioned two items," the former Rugby star reminded.

"Yes, sir," the younger man answered. "We have received a communication from the United States; it was originally addressed to Westminster Abbey, but has been redirected on to us. It is from the city of Wilmette, Illinois."

"I was not aware that we knew anyone there," Danford-Smith said.

"The message is addressed to us from the temple there which is, I believe, the headquarters, or one of them, of the Bahai faith."

"Precisely what do they want?"

"The text of the message is being sent to us immediately, Your Grace, but the essence of it is that the Bahai people wish to applaud 'the splendid leadership of the Church of England' in advancing interfaith understanding."

Frederick Danford-Smith mellowed slightly. After a moment's reflection he nodded his head slowly once. "Very fraternal of them," he conceded. "We will have to formulate a suitable reply. Perhaps Roundtree should sign it, as an appropriate gesture."

The younger man had not yet settled back into his chair. "There is a bit more, Your Grace. If I understood correctly, the Bahai people stated that they would like to have the honor of being the first to accept our invitation."

32

Danford-Smith raised his guard. "What invitation?" he asked.

"To the world conference of religions that Roundtree proposed. Apparently they believe that we are going to call one more or less immediately."

CHAPTER FOUR

Despite the fact that his biography in *Who's Who in America* gave his age clearly as sixty-two, Dr. Harley Poindexter walked with a light step and carried his body with the evident enjoyment of masculine vitality. As he crossed the campus from the Student Union, he breathed in the air of the very early spring and let his soul feed a little on the freshly budding trees.

When he reached the administration building, which in an earlier era had been the women's dormitory, he ran easily up the steps and pushed open one of the double doors. A single sweeping glance told him that the main floor business area was, as usual, in good order; then without slackening his pace he climbed the wide staircase briskly and was still breathing without effort as he entered the president's office. His secretary looked up as he came in.

"How are you making out?" he asked.

In response the young woman picked up her notebook and consulted it. "Of the thirty-four active trustees, I've

34

been able to reach thirty. Dr. Griswold is still unable to take calls, but I tried anyway."

"His family will appreciate that. Did they mention any change in his condition?"

"Only that he will be ninety-three next Tuesday."

"I hope he makes it. Go on."

"Mr. Wilkins can't be reached, he is on safari."

"With how many young ladies?"

The secretary pursed her lips for a moment. "They didn't say, sir. My guess would be four."

"A reasonable number. How about the other two?"

"Mr. Inglebrecht is out somewhere on his yacht — he may be en route to Hawaii. But you know that he always approves of everything anyway."

"Yes, God bless him. The last?"

"Dr. Yee is out of the country — his office referred us to the State Department."

"I'm satisfied, we have almost ninety percent of the board. How did they react?"

The young woman drew a breath of triumph. "Every single one of them was for it, sir. Mr. Swenson said that it was the answer to a prayer."

Poindexter was pleased. "He may be right — it was mine. Bring your book and come on in; we might as well get started."

He entered his long office, plopped into the chair behind his desk, leaned back, and began to dictate.

"Dear Dr. Roundtree — that's the right form of address, isn't it?"

"I'd have to look it up, sir, it could be the Most Reverend or something like that. Personally, I like the simpler form better."

"I'll bet that he does too, and since he's a bishop he's bound to be a D.D. O.K., Dear Dr. Roundtree, let that stand."

"Yes, sir."

"I have read with the greatest interest your recent challenging sermon proposing an interreligious confrontation in the context of today's urgent world situation. In my capacity as president of Maplewood College, I take great pleasure in informing you that we may be in a unique position to implement this magnificent idea, and to bring it to reality."

Poindexter paused and looked at his secretary. "Will that grab him?" he asked.

The girl flushed slightly. "It's got to," she said.

"Good. To continue: To spare you the trouble of looking us up, we are a small liberal arts college located in the north central United States. We have a very fine physical plant including a new and splendidly designed chapel auditorium that seats twelve hundred; this facility is equipped with a fully professional, high-quality sound system, many smaller meeting rooms, and a first-rate pipe organ. I indicated, however, that we had something unique to offer and this is very literally the case. Paragraph."

Dr. Poindexter swung his feet up onto the corner of his desk. "In the year nineteen twenty-three this institution was left a very substantial sum of money by our late benefactor, Mrs. Eleanor B. Bixby. Mrs. Bixby's gift carried a singular stipulation: that the money could be used only for the purpose of, quote, furthering religious harmony throughout the world close quote. The exact wording of this phrase was the subject of some legal study; since at that time we were affiliated with one of the major Protestant denominations, several missionary societies petitioned to have the funds released for their work. However, when we sought a court opinion on the matter, it was held that missionary activities, no matter how benevolent, did not meet the terms of the bequest. It was stressed at that time that the money could be used only for the exact purpose stated, namely the furthering of religious harmony, and, most significantly, on a world basis. The words, quote, throughout the world, unquote, in the opinion of the court would have to be taken in their literal sense. Paragraph.

"As a consequence this very generous bequest has been held for a full fifty years while the college has awaited an opportunity to apply it for the purpose stated. I hardly need add that during this time it has increased several times over, so that the total amount now has reached seven figures in U.S. dollars. Less than two years ago we had the matter reopened when our financial situation was somewhat pressing, but, as we expected, the original interpretation of the testator's intentions was again upheld. Paragraph.

"I have this morning had contact made with all of the available members of our board of trustees, approximately ninety percent of the total. Without exception they have agreed that what you have proposed in all respects meets both the requirements and the intention of the Bixby legacy. Our legal counsel is of the same opinion. It is my great pleasure therefore, sir, to inform you that by the unanimous vote of all available members of our board of trustees we invite you to make Maplewood College the site of your proposed conference of the world's religions. I am further authorized to advise you that as soon as our invitation is accepted, if you elect to take this action, the Bixby funds will be made available for the implementation and conducting of the conference. Paragraph.

"In informal conversation with Judge Raymond Wettstein this morning I received his assurance that if he is called upon to rule on the matter, he will support the opinion of our trustees, our attorney, and myself that the conditions of the Bixby bequest are fully met by your proposal. Incidentally, he too had read your sermon and went so far as to state that if the conference is indeed held here, he would like the privilege of attending some of the sessions. Paragraph.

"All of us here at Maplewood await with great interest

your reaction to this proposal and invitation. Very cordially yours."

Dr. Poindexter looked at his secretary. "What do you think?" he asked.

"Don't you want to tell him about our dormitories, library, dining facilities, and things like that?"

Poindexter shook his head. "He'll assume the bulk of that. The point is, the conference will have to meet somewhere. We have a nice place here and a good many of the delegates, I would assume, would enjoy visiting this country. But you know what greases the wheels of industry."

"Money?"

"Right! For this particular purpose we have it — in abundance. Don't forget that churchmen, like college presidents, are always beating the bushes for funds."

"And if he doesn't come, then he'll have to explain why he turned down more than a million dollars."

Poindexter swung his feet back down onto the floor. "Let's see what happens," he said.

The Right Reverend Dr. Philip Roundtree came out from behind his desk to greet his visitor and held out his hand in welcome. He did so for all of his guests, but Arthur Gravenstine did not know that.

Roundtree invited him to sit down and saw that tea was provided. That attended to, Gravenstine got down to business. "My Lord Bishop," he began, "I am eternally grateful to you for an unintended great favor — you put me on the front page for the first time in my career as a religious reporter." He tried his tea and then continued. "Dr. Roundtree, I'm here to interview you, of course, concerning your inspiring call for a world religious conference. I had planned to do this before Sir Cyril Plessey phoned my managing editor to suggest the same thing."

Philip leaned back and considered things for a moment. "Perhaps it might be better," he suggested, "if you were to talk first with the archbishop. I have it on good authority that he might appreciate that."

Gravenstine took a little more tea, but his voice was still dry when he spoke again. "Sir Cyril has been in contact with His Grace, I understand — they went to school together. And the ordinary people have been heard from too — I presume that you are fully up on that."

"To a degree, yes."

Gravenstine leaned forward. "Dr. Roundtree, you can't back away from this now any more than Jacob could have let go of the angel. Your sermon, sir, has literally gone around the world; mail has been coming in from everywhere."

"I don't profess to belong to the fourth estate," Philip said, "but I do realize that this is a news story — I wanted it to be one. I see no point in preaching without purpose. I don't want to be quoted on this, but I knew what I was doing when I delivered that sermon. I knew that I was putting my career on the line with the odds all against me. But dammit, someone had to speak up! Others have in the past when they faced the stake for it."

Gravenstine nodded emphatically. "I grasped that. Now Sir Cyril has put his influence and some of his money behind the project. So have the people who have sent in their pounds, several thousand of them, to help the cause along. And there are Deutschmarks, francs, even yen. You see, sir, you were right! The ordinary churchgoers want this, there's no doubt. You know that Sir Cyril has proposed that you be relieved of your present responsibilities so that you can devote your full energies to this project."

Philip remained careful. "There have been a good many attempts along this line. There's the World Council of Churches and many similar organizations."

Gravenstine waved a hand. "I know that, sir, I've reported on most of them. I don't question the capabilities or good will of their sponsors, but the cold bare fact is that none of them have had the scope of what you have proposed."

"What do your friends call you?" Roundtree asked.

"Art."

"All right, Art, off the record for a moment, I am perfectly aware that the Lord Archbishop was not unduly pleased — I didn't expect that he would be. But he is far from a stupid man, as you well know. I admit that I wanted this thing to have an impact, but candidly, I got much more than I bargained for."

"Understood."

"Good. Now you can quote me on this: I am entirely obedient to my superiors in the Church and will always do as they direct me without any qualifications. If, and I stress that 'if,' the archbishop were to see fit to assign me to implement such a conference, then I would do my utmost, to the limit of my abilities, to follow his instructions. However, at this point I feel that it would be improper for me to press the matter further until my superiors have had an opportunity to reflect on it."

"They have reflected," Gravenstine said. "They've done very little else. Frankly, sir, you have Pandora outclassed right now, but I suspect with the opposite result. By the way, my Lord Bishop, have you received any unusually interesting letters from America recently — say from a small college?"

"How did you know?" Philip asked.

"The Associated Press, sir, is a most efficient organization. And I gather that the publicity director at Maplewood College is no slouch either. We received the news this morning, which is why I phoned you so urgently for an appointment."

"Are you going to print it?"

"Everyone is going to, sir. After all, you hit a rock and out gushed water."

Philip pressed his lips together. "Art, I didn't propose

this thing as a personal venture on my part. You should understand that very clearly. There are many splendidly equipped men who have devoted their lives to the ecumenical movement and who are very up on interfaith matters."

"True, sir, but none of them are, so far as I'm aware, a bishop of the Church of England and one who has made news on that subject literally around the world."

"I have you to thank for that."

"You wanted your words to be heard, didn't you? Well, they were. Shall I add something to that?"

"Please."

"All right, my Lord Bishop — prepare yourself and pack your bags. Because as sure as the sun and Sir Cyril Plessey are going to rise tomorrow morning, you will be going to America to lead that conference." Gravenstine stood up. "I hope, sir, that you enjoy your stay at Maplewood College."

Janet Roundtree had never seen her husband under such pressure, even when he had first taken over his new and heavy responsibilities as a diocesan bishop. That had meant an increased burden for her too in her enforced role as the bishop's wife, but she had quickly become accustomed to that, particularly when she discovered that Philip's new dignity and authority only influenced his public and professional life. When they were by themselves he was unchanged, still the man in her life who held her in his arms for a few minutes after they had gone to bed and made her feel the warm fulfillment of her womanhood. Now, however, things were different.

There was a vast increase in the mail and some additional staff to handle it. More often than not he had his lunch sent into his office and he was frequently late for dinner. When at last he went to bed he always kissed her good night, but then he was almost always asleep in seconds. It was pure fatigue and she knew it, but she was upset by it nonetheless. Her nerves, too, began to show the strain, and at times she had to guard herself against speaking too sharply to her sons when they were guilty of minor infractions.

Her composure suffered an additional small setback one evening when a special messenger arrived with a letter shortly before six. She glanced at the clock and decided that it could wait until the dinner hour; Philip had asked her not to disturb him unless it was important and a few more minutes could not make any material difference.

Her decision made, she hustled the boys through their preparations and checked that the table was fully ready for the evening meal. She had just finished when Philip came in and kissed her gently on the forehead.

"I have something for you as soon as you are ready," she said.

He nodded and went in to wash. When he reappeared the boys were already in their places and it was time for grace to be said. Philip did that and then took the envelope that Janet held out to him. "It came just a few minutes ago," she explained. "I knew that you would be in directly, so I kept it for you."

Philip nodded his approval, glanced at the return address, and then hesitated for a bare moment before he tore it open.

There were two pages inside, closely typed. He looked at the signature and then at his wife. "Frederick Ebor," he said, knowing that she would recognize the official signature of the Archbishop of York. Then with clear calm he read the letter, ignoring the bowl of soup that had been set in front of him.

When he had finished Janet asked, "What did Danford-Smith have to say?" By putting it that way she stripped the archbishop of a little of the aura of his office in case the news was not good.

She waited while her husband quite deliberately tried his

soup and approved of it. "It's all quite formal, of course," he answered her, "but pretty much what I've been expecting."

"Is it bad?"

"No, not at all. Shall I summarize it for you?"

"Yes, please." The boys were old enough, and whatever it was, they would have to be told anyway.

At that moment she had a sudden vision; without her bidding her mind leaped back to the time when Philip had been just a priest with a local congregation — a group of fine people who genuinely esteemed him and every one of whom he knew by name. He had been Father Roundtree then, secure and happy when he stood outside the church every Sunday morning and greeted those who had come to hear him. And her life had been so much less complicated as she had stood a short distance away, speaking with the ladies.

His voice brought her abruptly back to the present. "I have been temporarily relieved of my diocese," he told her. "I'm to prepare it to be taken over by my suffragan with all reasonable speed."

A quick tightening in her throat made her words difficult. "Where are we going?"

Then he smiled at her, that wonderful smile of his that had first won her heart long before he had ever courted her seriously. "I'm not certain of that, dear — there is a possibility that it might be to America."

"America?"

"Yes. The archbishop has decided that for the next year at least I am to devote myself to the project that I proposed."

Janet caught her breath in wonder. "He likes it then!"

Philip hesitated. "I don't honestly believe that he does, but some momentum has been built up and he can't exactly drop it. Some very influential people have indicated their support and a great many of the ordinary folk — who are the ones who count the most, really." He became quite serious then. "You see, pet, I meant what I said — I truly believe in it. I have for a long time. Now I've been given the task of doing the impossible. I'm supposed to call a conference."

"Sponsored by the Church?"

Philip shook his head. "No, that wasn't mentioned."

Geoffrey was heard from for the first time. "That's dirty, Dad, they're asking you to bowl without a team in the field behind you!"

Janet watched as her husband looked at their son. "I might just be able to field a team, Geoff, if I try hard enough. There are a lot of people of good will in the world, and at least I have the blessing of the Church."

"Why are we going to America, Father?" Peter asked.

"There is a college there, a small one, that has offered us its hospitality. And the people there have some special funds they are willing to make available for the conference. More than four hundred thousand pounds."

Janet gasped. "They have such wealth?"

"Not really — it comes from a special endowment that has lain fallow for half a century."

"Is it a good place, Dad?" Geoffrey enquired.

"Yes, as far as I know."

"Why not go and have a look, then?"

Philip answered carefully. "I will first have to write to Dr. Poindexter, the president there, and put some questions. Later I might have to go after we have been in direct communication."

Peter had other ideas. "Don't write him, Father, call him up. It's only two or three pounds, and think of the time you'll save."

Geoffrey looked at his wristwatch and made a mental calculation. "What part of the country is it in?" he asked.

"The Midwest, I understand."

"Then it's midmorning there now. Go ahead, Dad, ring

him up. The Americans are used to that sort of thing and Sir Cyril is paying the bills — you told me that."

It was quiet for a moment.

"I think I will," Roundtree said.

The connection was made with remarkable speed; the operator called back within five minutes to announce that Dr. Poindexter of Maplewood College was on the line and waiting.

Philip took the instrument. "Good morning, Dr. Poindexter," he began, "Philip Roundtree here."

Back came a cheerful, almost buoyant voice on the line. "Delighted that you called, Bishop; what news have you?"

That was certainly direct and to the point. "Only this — that my Church has relieved me of my present responsibilities so that I can devote my full energies for the next year to exploring what might be done to hold a conference of the various world faiths."

"Then I take it that your Church is sponsoring this meeting officially."

"No, sir, I believe not."

"Surprising, I must confess, but in a way good news for us. It means that you are now free, if you choose, to come here."

"That is quite possible," Philip said with due caution.

Poindexter's voice became brisk. "Why don't you run over here next week if you can clear the time and see what we have to offer. There's nonstop service from London to Chicago; you can make an easy connection from there and I'll pick you up at the airport. If you can stay for several days, please plan on it — there is a lot to do."

Philip hedged. "That's very kind of you, Dr. Poindexter, but there is the question of time, and while we have been funded I don't want to create any wrong impressions."

"Perfectly understood, Bishop, but we are your hosts and that includes your air fare, of course. I wrote you about the Bixby legacy."

"But that would be an imposition."

"Positively not. Plan on coming; call me back when you have your reservation. You will come over, won't you?"

Philip made a quick, careful decision. "Yes, I will," he answered.

CHAPTER FIVE

Dr. Harley Poindexter waited with suppressed enthusiasm for the first passengers from the DC–9 to come through the arrival gate. He had no preconceived ideas concerning the man he had come to meet, only a strong supposition that he would be wearing clerical garb. Whatever his proportions and age might be, the fact that he had prepared and delivered the sermon that had been almost literally heard around the world was all that Poindexter, for the moment, needed to know.

He spotted his guest immediately when he saw him and felt at once that an extra dividend had been declared. The well-set-up, definitely handsome man in the round collar and purple vest was all that he could have hoped for. He stepped forward and asked, "Dr. Roundtree?"

"Yes. Dr. Poindexter, I believe."

The voice was richly British as it had been on the phone, but in it Poindexter detected something else — the same kind of spark that had motivated him all of his own life and had kept him reaching for something worth having that was just beyond his immediate grasp. He sensed that he was going to get on with this English churchman very well. "We can pick up your luggage downstairs," he said. "Then we can be on our way. I have a car waiting."

"Quite, I'll follow you."

After a short wait Philip reclaimed a single heavily substantial suitcase and then followed his host through the terminal doors. Once outside, he paused momentarily to look about and breathe the cool clear air of the northern United States.

"Is this your first visit here?" Poindexter asked.

"Yes. I've always wanted to come, of course, but the occasion never seemed to arise."

A sleek black car which to Philip seemed immense drew up and the young man driving it jumped out to take charge of the luggage. After introductions Poindexter ushered his guest into the back seat and then joined him, settling back with a genuine feeling of well-being. Already, it seemed to him, the conference idea was off to a good start. There would be some formidable obstacles, but differences in faith were man-made and therefore subject to revision. He did not quite visualize himself bowing down before an image of the Lord Buddha, but in due time all things could be resolved.

It was quiet for a short while as they entered a freeway, then Roundtree spoke again. "You certainly have marvelous roadways here."

"Thank you. We pretty much regard them as necessities since we travel so much by car."

"So I understand. Your climate is rather like England, you know."

"Yes, I've been there on occasion. Our summers are usually very pleasant and never uncomfortably hot. Good for a conference of many different peoples, I think; not too extreme for any of them."

Roundtree turned to face him as far as he was able. "Now that this thing is actually pending, or so it would appear, I must confess, Dr. Poindexter, that I am having moments of concern."

"Of course, you wouldn't be human if you didn't. I've had the same feeling many times when complicated matters have come up, but remember that religion is in itself a uniting force. The desire to find and serve God is almost universal; as I recall you touched on that."

"Yes, I did. The Muslims preach that there is one Almighty God and so do we. The same one, as a matter of fact."

"Absolutely. On another topic, Dr. Roundtree, I'd be very interested to know what plans you have in mind — in the preliminary stages, of course."

A shadow of concern crossed Philip's face. "I might as well confess my shortcomings immediately; for the past three weeks I have been so snowed under I've barely had time to tie my shoes."

"On the contrary, I completely understand your position. On the assumption that you might elect to hold your meeting here, we have ventured to outline some ideas to present to you."

"I'm most interested," Philip declared. "The American reputation for efficiency is well founded."

His host lifted a hand and let it fall. "All I really did was to appoint a committee to assist you: it's headed by Dr. Hastings, our Dean of the Chapel. On it I put our Buildings and Grounds man, the head of our Department of Political Science, our PR man, and two of our brightest students. I'm quite happy about the results."

Philip was still undecided what to say when Poindexter continued. "You didn't indicate, Dr. Roundtree, how long you will be able to stay with us — we hope at least a week. But to conserve your time as much as possible, subject to your approval we've made a few plans. We hope that you will dine with us this evening. After that we thought that you might wish to retire early in view of the drastic time change."

"That's very considerate, thank you."

"Not at all. Tomorrow morning, at nine, I have a breakfast set up with the members of the committee. At that time we'll show you what we've done and see what you think of it."

That certainly seemed fair enough to Philip. He said something suitable in reply and then once more gave his attention to the gently rolling countryside through which he was traveling at a considerable rate of speed. Presently the driver pulled off onto an exit ramp and went through an elaborate clover leaf onto another road almost as wide as the freeway. Another five minutes on this route brought them to the crest of a low hill; Philip looked ahead through the windshield and had his first view of the city of Winnebago. It matched his expectations — a community of perhaps thirty or forty thousand with ample evidence of green trees and a certain closeness to the earth that gave meaning to its Indian name.

As the car passed through the outskirts he was surprised at the quality of the residences; they were large, elaborate, and each was set in what appeared to be a very generous plot of ground. Presently the newly constructed buildings gave way to older and narrower ones, a majority of which were painted a dull gray. Their roofs were pitched at high angles to shed the winter snows and their ornamentations spoke of generations past. The car climbed up a small grade, the houses disappeared, and the wider expanse of a campus came into view.

Philip had seen many colleges; this one, while not large, had an obvious stability that appealed to him at once. The atmosphere of the buildings and their settings amidst the grass and trees was one of dedication to the restrained pace of learning. In the very center of the campus was a vertically designed old stone structure that had been there at least a respectable century and probably much longer. It was obviously high-ceilinged and inefficient by the latest standards, but it was wrapped with a venerable dignity that clung to it as visibly as the ivy that climbed up its walls.

The car paused for a stop intersection, then moved ahead only a short distance before it turned left into a driveway. There was a house there, large and respectably seasoned enough to be suitable for the presidential residence. As they pulled in, the front door opened and Philip saw a woman waiting for them. He was ushered out of the car and taken up to the doorway. "My dear," he heard Poindexter say, "Bishop Roundtree. My wife Marsha."

Mrs. Poindexter held out her hand with easy grace and warmed him with a smile. "I'm so glad you could come," she said.

"Thank you for having me."

She led the way inside. When they had entered the large living room she turned to face her guest and her husband. "I do hope you had a pleasant trip, Bishop," she began.

"I did," Philip answered. "It was surprisingly brief considering the distance."

"A fortunate combination of six hundred miles per hour and the great circle route," Poindexter commented. "You look as though you had something further to tell us, Marsha."

"Yes, I do. While you were gone, we had several calls from the press."

"I expected that. They want a conference with Bishop Roundtree."

"So they said. Then we had a call from England."

Philip could not restrain himself, a hundred possible disasters flashed through his mind. "Is everything all right?" he asked.

His hostess reassured him with a smile. "Of course. It

was just a request for information about the college. From the office of a friend of yours, I believe. You do know Sir Cyril Plessey, don't you?"

When Philip Roundtree woke in the morning a glance at his watch told him that it was still an indecently early hour. Daylight had come but the city and the college still obviously slept. He lay quietly for a short while, then he arose, put on his dressing gown, and sat down to read. He had brought several books with him for study; as he composed himself in a comfortable chair he chose two of them: *The Path of the Buddha* and the *Holy Koran*. He picked up the latter one first and applied himself diligently to the words of the Prophet. After three quarters of an hour of this exercise he felt that he had absorbed all that he comfortably could at one sitting of the sacred book of Islam. Outside there were the beginnings of early morning activity; a milk truck paused in front of the door while the driver made a delivery. The household remained quiet and still; it was only a little past six.

Reflecting on the fact that he would probably have no breakfast before the scheduled meeting at nine, he picked up the second volume he had chosen and, understandably, found it far easier to read. He already knew the superficial facts concerning the Indian prince who had renounced his position and privileges in order to seek enlightenment, but now he wanted to have a better grasp of the whole philosophy of Buddhism. He was still engaged in reading when a quiet knock sounded on his door.

He opened it to find his host up and fully dressed. "Did you sleep well?" Poindexter inquired.

"Yes indeed." Philip opened the door wider. "I'm very indebted to you for your hospitality."

"Not at all. Why don't you get dressed and we'll have some coffee and rolls in the kitchen. Incidentally, wear whatever you like — formality isn't the keynote around here."

"Street attire would be all right then?"

"Of course, don't wear clericals unless you wish. When you see some of our students you'll understand."

A short while later Philip found his host in the kitchen presiding over a bubbling percolator which radiated an inviting aroma. "I just realized that I probably should have made tea," Poindexter said. "I just didn't think. I can have some ready very shortly. Marsha was tired last night and I'm letting her sleep."

"Coffee will be fine," Philip said, seating himself. He poured out a cupful, added cream and sugar, and tried it. As the hot liquid began to run down his throat and hit his stomach, he could almost feel his whole body respond.

"I very much hope that you're going to like our college, Bishop Roundtree," Poindexter said.

"Why don't you call me Philip — I rather like the American informality."

"Excellent, my name is Harley. About our school here: whenever we do anything important everyone gets into the act — the administrative staff, faculty, students, and anyone else concerned. It works out very well, some students sit with our board of trustees and on every important committee. They really contribute too. I hope that this doesn't disturb you."

"I distinctly recall having been a student myself," Philip said.

"You have a gift; there are some who can't. Our breakfast at nine will be in the Student Union just across the corner — anyone can direct you to the small dining room."

"Fine. Between now and then, would it be all right if I were to just look around a bit?"

Poindexter waved his arm. "The place is yours; go where you like and don't hesitate to visit any of the buildings. I'll

53

get some work out of the way so that I can spend the rest of the day in your company — if you wish."

A few minutes later Philip was outside, on his own for the first time since he had arrived in America. He had on a Harris tweed sports coat that Janet particularly liked and a pair of gray slacks that he often wore for walking at home. The clean freshness of the air appealed to him; it had a tinge of crispness that would probably yield as the sun climbed higher. He noted that there were students about now and evidence of life on the campus. He had no intention of entering any of the halls, but he crossed the street and chose one of the concrete walkways that led across the comfortable green expanse between the buildings. Maplewood College did not appear externally to be an especially formidable institution, but there was a comfortable feeling about it that he could not help but like.

He paused in front of the old stone structure that was clearly the patriarch of the campus and studied its outlines. He was not familiar with American architecture, but its exceptional height clearly showed British influence. Beyond it he saw a low-lying structure of near contemporary design which quite obviously was a library; from its size he deduced that the collection it had been built to contain would be a very good one for a school the size of Maplewood.

Three girls walked toward him, talking among themselves. One of them looked up and spoke a casual "Hi."

"Hi," Philip answered.

The girl stopped. "Where are you from?" she asked.

"England."

She surveyed him for a moment. "You aren't the bishop, are you?"

"How did you guess?" he asked.

"Well — the way you spoke. British accent."

"*With one syllable?*"

"You said 'England' too."

"You're right, I did." There was a question in his mind and he asked it. "Do I look like a bishop?"

"No, you don't, not at all."

He left it at that. "I'm Philip Roundtree, nice to have met you."

"Karen Erickson. I'll see you around — I hope."

He went on his way reflecting that he could not remain anonymous at all if his voice betrayed him so quickly. He had hoped to blend into the background for at least a little while in order to orient himself, but obviously that wasn't going to be possible.

Presently he found himself before an impressive building clearly marked as the chapel auditorium. He wanted very much to see that — enough so that he stopped and considered whether or not to venture inside. He had been told not to hesitate, but his reserve as a guest in unfamiliar surroundings at first held him back.

The door he tried was unlocked and swung open easily for him. As he stepped inside and saw the lobby area, his desire grew even stronger to see what the auditorium itself looked like. Then he became aware that an organ was being played somewhere in the building. It suggested that a meeting of some sort might be taking place, but it could be that someone was just practicing. Very cautiously he opened one of the entry doors slightly and looked inside. He paused to be certain that the vast auditorium he had discovered was indeed empty except for the lone musician at the organ; after that he cautiously stopped inside and drank in what he saw.

It was very large and quite beautiful. The stage was wide and deep with the organ covering most of the rear wall. Long multiple rows of obviously comfortable seats filled the tapered audience area. Overhead sound baffles hung below semiconcealed ducting for the air conditioning system and other necessary piping. But the atmosphere which filled the hall was one of richness, of understanding, and of an ingrained awareness of the culture of humanity to which it was dedicated. The sound of the organ intensified the feeling that was growing within him — the feeling that here, in this place, the dream that had shaped in his mind with such clarity and conviction could become reality.

His imagination took over: the long rows of seats became filled with men and women who had gathered together to acknowledge that there exists something beyond mankind, something beyond the single globe Earth, and something beyond the tombstones in the country churchyard. Here God would be hailed by different names and in different ways, but here He would reign; here His creatures might possibly find common bonds that would help to bring about a better and more peaceful world. He was engulfed by the thought and a strange tingling sensation ran the length of his spine.

His mind rushed forward, ignoring the technicalities and frustrations that might appear in reality, and recognizing only the fulfillment that could come. It conjured up for him the saffron-robed monks of Buddhism who would sit here, the turbaned Sikhs, the followers of Islam, the dignitaries of the various branches of Christianity, the rabbis, the quiet-mannered Hindus, even the representatives of the smaller cults and churches who would contribute their part to the all-over whole. The reality of the splendid auditorium was a starting point, and as he studied it the voice of the organ told him that the conference *would* meet here and that it would, by God's grace, be a success.

He stood, almost transfixed, for some time; when he finally glanced at his watch it was a quarter to nine and time for him to make his way to the Student Union. As he went outside into the open air once more, the vision he had seen stayed with him, and as he crossed the softness of the green grass he seemed to hear the choir of the angels.

CHAPTER SIX

The small dining room in the Student Union proved to be a plain functional facility with little in the way of decor to recommend it. It held four large round tables, each capable of seating eight or nine persons; one of these had been set for the breakfast conference Philip was to attend. As he entered the room at five minutes to nine, he had the uncomfortable feeling that he was unduly conspicuous. Apparently everyone else was already there.

The feeling was momentary, for Harley Poindexter came forward at once to make him welcome. "Please come in, Philip," he said. "The others are as anxious to meet you as I was." He laid his hand on the shoulder of a firmly built man who wore glasses and an open-necked knit shirt. "Dr. Joe Hastings, our Dean of the Chapel. Bishop Roundtree."

Hastings held out a quick hand. "I'm very honored, sir. Whether you know it or not, you preached the sermon of the century."

"A gross overstatement, Mr. Dean," Philip responded as he shook hands, "but I am delighted to meet you."

"Our chairman of Political Science, Professor Moriarty," Poindexter continued.

Philip paused and looked carefully at the narrow, somewhat undersized man he was meeting. "Forgive my rudeness, Professor, but may I venture to ask your first name?"

"It is James," Moriarty answered. His tone of voice told Philip that he was perfectly understood.

"Are you by any chance related?"

Moriarty nodded. "My grandfather, sir, was a most respectable stationmaster in the west of England."

"Still . . ."

Moriarty carefully cleared his throat. "I acknowledge that we once had a very distinguished mathematician in the family — an astrophysicist would be more accurate. He was published not too long before his death. He met with an accident in Switzerland."

"So I understand; the facts are quite well known. I am, of course, delighted." He shook hands gravely.

"If you two have finished, I'll introduce the rest," Poindexter said with a smile. He turned to the only female present. "Karen, Bishop Roundtree. Miss Erickson, one of our student members."

"We've already met," Karen said.

"Mr. Chalmers, in charge of our buildings and grounds."

The two men exchanged appropriate greetings. Chalmers was a quiet type of person whose firm handshake suggested a capability for getting things done.

"Our public relations director, Mr. Quigley."

The PR man seemed to Philip to be very young for his job, but when he took his hand he encountered a confident assurance that he liked.

"Lastly, Bishop, the other student member of our committee, Ned Stone."

Philip acknowledged the introduction and then allowed himself to be guided to the breakfast table, where there was already a scraping of chairs and a general settling down. As soon as the meal was well begun, Harley Poindexter opened the topic that everyone was anticipating. "Bishop Roundtree," he began with no more than a hint of formality, "let me begin by telling you that all of us here have read your great sermon and just for openers, we are all in full accord with what you said."

"Thank you," Philip acknowledged, and then glanced at the plate of scrambled eggs and bacon that was being set before him.

"We've invited you here because we share your enthusiasm and it is just possible that we might be able to be of some help to you. But please understand that as far as we're concerned, it's your show and we want it to remain that way."

The directness of the Americans contrasted with some of the meetings that Philip had attended at home — almost endless meetings as a matter of fact — where he had had to sit for hours looking thoroughly interested and inwardly almost praying for someone to say something that hadn't already been expressed at least three times before.

Harley Poindexter continued. "There is one very important question which we would like to have answered, if you'd be so kind. The best information that we have up to now is that your church has relieved you of your diocesan responsibilities for one year in order to allow you to pursue the matter of a religious conference on a world basis."

Philip nodded. "That's entirely correct," he said.

"Good. Now does this mean that the Church of England has decided to sponsor this meeting formally? If so, then obviously you will want to have it in your own country."

"So far, Dr. Poindexter," Philip said carefully, "my church has taken no position on the matter. It is perhaps too early for that."

"It would seem to me," Dean Hastings added, "that if

they were going to sponsor the meeting, they would have so stated at the same time they announced your sabbatical to pursue the matter."

"Possibly so."

Karen Erickson spoke up. "Maybe I missed something here, Bishop, but it sounds a little like they gave you a pat on the back, cut you loose, but then left you strictly on your own."

"They did exactly that."

The voice was a new one from the doorway of the room. Philip turned, as did everyone else, and saw an elderly man who seemed to be visibly charged with abundant energy. The furrow of his eyebrows and the set of his jaw suggested that he might be prepared to deliver an opinion on any subject whatever with devastating authority. The tweeds that he wore had a very distinct pattern, but their quality was evident as well as the hand of the master tailor who had cut them to perfection. In one hand the visitor allowed himself the concession of a walking stick.

He proceeded to enter the room as though it were a recent addition to his estates and surveyed the breakfast table with a vulture's searching eye. "My name," he announced in a voice which suggested contained thunder, "is Plessey."

Harley Poindexter was already on his feet. "Sir Cyril," he greeted warmly, "we are so delighted! But why didn't you let us know you were coming so that we could have met you?"

"Unnecessary, they had a hire car and driver available. I brought my man with me — do you mind?" The question was in the form of a declaration.

Philip waited for the right moment to greet his benefactor while others were busy making room for a ninth at the table. A student waitress hurried in with an additional place setting while Ned Stone brought a chair from another table.

"You know Bishop Roundtree, I presume," Poindexter said, the immediate epitome of an ideal host as he indicated his other guest.

"No," Sir Cyril stated emphatically, "but I intend to." With that he advanced one additional step and then waited.

Philip shook hands in the respectful manner he had employed so many times when he had been a young priest and said, "I am most honored, sir."

"No doubt." That taken care of, Sir Cyril beamed the laser of his attention toward Harley Poindexter. "The comely wench who directed me here was your wife, I take it?"

"She fits that description. Did she explain about this breakfast?"

"She did — hence my presence."

"Excellent. Please be seated, Sir Cyril, I see that your place is ready." Rapidly he introduced the others and then returned to his own chair. As soon as he was ready he looked around the table.

"Sir Cyril's visit here is most timely and appropriate," he declared. "As you all know, immediately after Bishop Roundtree preached his great sermon, Sir Cyril announced a magnanimous gift, a hundred thousand pounds as I recall, to help launch the program that the bishop had proposed."

There was a momentary pause, Philip was preparing to say something concerning Sir Cyril's generosity, but that gentleman relieved him of both the need and the opportunity.

"I shall now announce the score," Sir Cyril declared with judicial authority. "I rather like that Americanism. His Lordship's sermon vastly annoyed the hierarchy of his church because he made the colossal mistake of saying something pertinent and important. In particular I know that he annoyed Freddy Smith, his archbishop, which was a splendid public service because in times past Freddy has frequently annoyed me."

He paused to inspect the food which had just been placed before him and then gave closer and longer attention to the young woman who had delivered it. "Have you many more like that?" he asked.

"Three dormitories full," Poindexter replied.

"Then obviously my decision to come here was well founded." He paused to unfold his napkin. "To continue: it was patent from the first that Freddy and his boys had found themselves up against a sticky wicket. Some of those people are all right, particularly the younger ones, but in Freddy's case mental rigor mortis has set in and he wouldn't know a good idea if it danced naked in front of him."

He stopped and deliberately surveyed the table, reading the reactions to what he had just said. Philip Roundtree, he noted, had the good sense to remain impassive.

"What Freddy obviously wanted to do was to state, if asked, that the sermon had been a very fine one and then let everything lie where it fell until it started to smell. He was that way in school and he hasn't changed. So I stirred things up a little, but I want it understood that it was in a good cause — because whether you believe it or not, I happen to be aware that Roundtree here was right, totally right, every bit of the way."

"Thank you, sir," Philip said.

Sir Cyril held the floor while he consumed a mouthful of egg and leisurely finished it off with a swallow or two of orange juice. "Now let's get down to cases. You can forget all about the august Church of England sponsoring any all-world, everybody welcome religious conference. It won't happen, one reason being that the Church moves so slowly that glaciers speed by. Roundtree, what's your name?"

"Philip."

"Good — I like that. Now I have the word that all of you here have some substantial funds tied up for just the purpose that Philip has proposed. Also you've got an operating plant. I haven't inspected it yet, but you look sensible and I assume that you know what you're doing."

Harley Poindexter kept his face impassive also; in the doughty Englishman he recognized a doer, and with all his heart and soul he approved of that. If complications arose, he would deal with them in due course.

"All right," Sir Cyril continued. "To put this thing on the rails you've got to have the money and a place for the action, but there's more. You need an inspiring religious leader of real stature and that you have. Also you've got to have a manager, someone of vast experience and unquestioned ability, to put the whole thing together and to keep it that way. He'll also have to be a promoter and a producer; there isn't any room for amateurs at that level."

"Have you any suggestions, Sir Cyril?" Poindexter asked.

"Under suitable conditions, I might be prepared to undertake the job myself. I've trimmed the lambs enough on the exchange this year and I need something else to occupy my mind."

That pronouncement drew an immediate and intense quiet; obviously no one present felt qualified to speak. Sir Cyril took no notice.

"Ames!"

Sir Cyril's man materialized and was at his side with an astonishing combination of speed and decorum. "Sir?"

"Ring up the best hotel here and reserve the presidential suite or whatever they call it. If it's already occupied, mention my name and see that the proper arrangements are made. Allow a reasonable time, of course."

Ned Stone picked up the ball quickly. "There aren't any hotels in town," he declared. "We used to have one, but it's been converted into an old peoples' home."

"Most inappropriate," Sir Cyril snapped.

"Suitable quarters will be prepared," Harley Poindexter declared in a tone of voice which suggested that that concluded the matter. "One question, Sir Cyril. We had not reached the point in our discussion where we were going to take up the possible time of the conference. I would be interested to know what you have in mind."

The elderly Britisher wiped his mouth with his napkin and then looked up in mild surprise. "I see no need for discussion on that point — it's obvious. Time is of the essence. Agreed?"

He scanned the table for signs of dissent and found none.

"No need for delay. I hate delay, all it does is let good ideas go sour. We'll probably hold the meeting right here, and we'll do it this summer."

Philip needed time to clear his thoughts, and he needed solitude. He found both by escaping from the breakfast room as soon as he was able and starting out across the campus. It seemed to him, as he walked calmly and quietly in the sunlight, that it might be the wisest course for him to pack up his things and return home. Thinking of himself in the third person, as he sometimes did, he saw Philip Roundtree as a fish out of water. He had started out to do the impossible and already found himself close to being an unneeded discard somewhere on the overvast plains of middle America. He was not bitter, but he sensed that he was in the same position as a small boy who had wandered much too far from home and who had then discovered that it was rapidly growing dark.

"Philip."

He turned when he heard his name and was surprised to find Harley Poindexter two or three yards behind him; he had been so intent on his own thoughts he had been unaware of his host's approach.

"Yes, Harley." The use of the first name bothered him a little, but he recognized that it was the American custom.

"I wonder if we could have a few private moments together."

"Of course."

"Let's go to my office."

The quiet, controlled tone of Poindexter's voice suggested a return to sanity and Philip was more than ready for that. "What happened to Sir Cyril?" he asked as he followed his guide toward the administration building.

"He's taking a walking tour of our facilities with Karen Erickson. He appears to have quite an eye for the ladies."

"On six continents, I believe," Philip added and then remained quiet until they were in the presidential office. There Harley pulled two comfortable chairs together and motioned him to sit down.

"We had a rather nice little meeting set up this morning," Poindexter began. "Sir Cyril shot it down before it began."

"So I understood. I didn't invite him, by the way."

"Neither did we, but if we make the proper moves, it may work out to everyone's advantage."

"It would be nice if that could come about."

"It may. Meanwhile, Philip, I can understand that right now you must be, at the least, disturbed."

"Sir Cyril does come on a little strong."

"True, and perhaps we did too — telling you that we had gone ahead and made plans. But I do want you to believe that we had prepared some things only to submit them to you this morning. We had a prior agreement among ourselves that anything you didn't like was out — no matter what."

Philip turned a little in his chair. "That was extraordinarily kind of you."

"Certainly no more than your due. Since the others aren't here to lay out their individual contributions, may I summarize them for you?"

"Please — I'd like that."

"If our facilities proved acceptable to you, we planned to make the chapel auditorium the focal point, but we have a considerable number of other meeting rooms available for the use of smaller groups. Our dormitories will accommodate over a thousand — not in luxury, but comfortably. During the summer months, you understand — our offer is predicated on holding the conference during the time that our plant would otherwise be idle."

"Of course, that's most sensible."

"Thank you. I've talked to our food service people; they've agreed to handle the meal problem, and the Student Union dining room should be adequate to handle up to a thousand delegates, if you envision that many."

"To be honest, Harley, I had no specific number in mind, but it should be well less than that."

"That disposes of the food and housing, granted there may be some dietary problems with some of the visitors. Next, we have a good music department and a fine choir. The choir members have already agreed to stay during the summer months if they are needed, and they are willing to learn the music of other faiths as a gesture of respect and regard."

"A good choir can be worth two bishops."

"Not this bishop, but otherwise I agree with you. Next, we can set up a car pool with about fifty good student drivers who would be glad to have the summer employment. We would provide a transportation desk where any authorized person could have a car put at his disposal. Ned Stone would handle that; he's a good boy and you can depend on him."

"All this sounds excellent so far," Philip said.

"Laundry can be handled by a local firm that regularly does the college work. They have for years and we find them very satisfactory."

"You certainly know how to organize things."

"Thank you again, Philip, we try. Now in another vein, we thought it might be a good idea to hold a public lecture series during the conference; each of the major faiths represented would be invited to have someone speak about their beliefs and culture. As a gesture of understanding and also, very seriously, for the public good."

"I had actually thought of having a series of religious services," Philip ventured. "Each faith would present one and the other delegates would be invited to attend. The Roman Catholics could get a dispensation, I imagine."

"Excellent, possibly we might do both. Now the food here is good, but it will never attract any gourmets. One of our trustees owns a famous restaurant where he employs a chef who is supposed to be one of the very best. He has rosettes or something like that. Anyhow, he has offered to have this man take charge of the kitchen during the meeting. That ought to improve the quality considerably."

"A very generous offer."

"Now, Philip, I want you to understand that we aren't trying to buy this conference simply because we have substantial funds available to help it along. I proposed our college to you because we have a good physical plant and because we are on neutral ground, so to speak. America is a land of many faiths; we're not like Spain, for example, where one church has almost total religious control. Here we have significant numbers of almost all of the Protestant faiths, of Jews, Catholics, Buddhists, Bahais, even Muslims, Greek Orthodox, and the Jains. I don't know offhand of any other nation in such a fortunate position. I can think of some where a conference such as you proposed would be all but impossible."

"That is a very telling point," Philip said. "The fact that we are called the Church of England operates a little against us on our home ground when it comes to ecumenical matters."

"True, and this country, Philip, has been noted for religious liberty and freedom since its inception."

"I think the conference should be here," Philip said quite simply. "If it is to happen, few places could be any better."

"Take your time over that decision, Philip, we don't want

67

to rush you into anything. Now about Sir Cyril — I know that he put up something like a quarter of a million dollars and that buys a lot of tolerance."

"Yes," Philip agreed. "It certainly does."

"And despite his years, he obviously has a great deal of energy. Now how does this idea hit you? Sir Cyril wants to get into the act and, frankly, we can't keep him out. Someone in a highly responsible position needs to go out and extend personal invitations, backed by some persuasion if necessary, to get our delegates here. Some might not want too much to come, but if any major group refuses to attend, it will be like the League of Nations when the United States wouldn't participate. I think that Sir Cyril is our boy."

"He travels extensively as it is," Philip said, thinking aloud.

"So I understand — we looked him up after his gift was announced. I have the feeling that if Sir Cyril Plessey can't seine in our participants, then the cause is lost before we begin. And he won't be easily intimidated."

Philip looked at his host with new understanding and respect. "Harley, I'm not quite up on these things as yet, but it seems to me that you have just struck a home run."

"And Philip, since he has declared that time is of the essence, I presume that if he accepts this high responsibility, he will unfortunately be leaving us very soon."

Philip looked at the president of Maplewood College once more. "I'm beginning to like America," he said.

68

CHAPTER SEVEN

Almost two days precisely from the time of his arrival Sir Cyril Throckmorton Plessey departed Maplewood College on his great mission. After an extended conference in the office of Dr. Harley Poindexter he had announced his willingness to undertake the most critical, delicate, and vital task relative to the conference. Further, he had given his opinion that in choosing him for the job those responsible had taken the best possible decision.

After the meeting had broken up, the results were conveyed to Philip, where he had been waiting in the snack bar and recreation area in the basement of the Student Union that was known as the Pit. Flanked by Ned Stone and Karen Erickson, he had been receiving a briefing on student life at Maplewood when the word was passed.

That marked another of the significant events that had crowded his life since he had arrived in America. Within the space of a scant forty-eight hours he had arrived at a decision to hold the conference at Maplewood, he had learned to appear in public clad in a sports shirt and slacks, and he had begun to acquire a mild taste for cola beverages. He had also expanded his vocabulary to include several interesting new words and phrases which he found to be singularly useful. It was, in a way, a considerable relief not to have to wear clerical garb and his purple rabat except on appropriate occasions. He was only troubled slightly by a certain rapid evolution of title that had taken place; he did not wish or expect to be always addressed as the Right Reverend Dr. Roundtree, but he had some difficulty in adjusting to being suddenly known as Bishop Phil. Karen Erickson had referred to him that way during the second day of his visit and the designation had stuck.

On the other hand much of his reception at Maplewood had been both gratifying and comfortable. The guesthouse which the college owned had been turned over to Sir Cyril and Ames; as a result of that maneuver he had remained as a houseguest of the Poindexters, an arrangement that had provided the opportunity for much informal communication with his host. Since Marsha was a fitting match for her energetic husband, the conversation around the dinner table frequently sparkled, and the hesitation that Philip had entertained gradually dissipated. He discovered that he and Harley Poindexter had a great deal in common. Armed with that knowledge he ventured to speak out more freely, and when he did he found his audience sympathetic.

As soon as Sir Cyril had taken his departure, the committee that Harley had appointed met once more and the developing plans for the conference were submitted to Philip for his approval. For three days there was a steady succession of fruitful meetings.

As his host and the rest of the Maplewood committee laid out their plans and ideas, Philip began to accept the realization that the holding of the conference was not only practical and realistic, but also likely to become a reality within a matter of weeks. An ingrained caution that he found hard to circumvent urged him to defer the whole enterprise until it could be given profound and careful study. Yet each time some new facet of the planning was submitted to him for his judgment, he had to acknowledge once more that he was not dealing with ivory tower visionaries, but with practical people who had ample common sense on their side. Gradually his misgivings eroded until, like the steady lightening of the sky before sunrise, the dawning came to him also.

Inevitably his enthusiasm began to grow until he felt a need to keep his feet on the ground. He responded by taking quiet walks through the streets of Winnebago until he fully realized that he had accepted a commitment similar to the one he had made when he had chosen the ministry as his life's work. He had dedicated himself then to God, now he needed only to expand that obligation to include all of his fellow men.

When he was invited to preach the following Sunday morning in the chapel auditorium, he accepted willingly. He had not thought to bring with him the suitable vestments to wear in the pulpit, but he knew that in the United States this would not make a great deal of difference. When the day came he was somewhat surprised to discover that he had drawn a packed house — even the balcony was full. It was immensely encouraging, because while it could have been his rank, he was more inclined to believe that the people of the community were genuinely interested in the proposals he had made.

After the simple order of worship was said, and the excellent choir had sung, Dean Hastings stepped into the pulpit and introduced the Right Reverend Dr. Roundtree with precisely the right degree of dignity and restraint.

Philip preached on his coming to the New World and finding a common unity of purpose in serving both God and man. When he had finished he knew at once that the whole congregation was with him and his own last lingering doubts disappeared. He stood at the door afterward for close to an hour with the dean, greeting those who patiently waited to shake his hand. When it was all over and he was at last free to step outside into the sunlight once more, he felt a fresh renewal as he always did after service, but this time the springs gushed with greater munificence and his spirit dominated his being.

The following day he went home. Both of the Poindexters took him to the airport, which gave him an opportunity to express his thanks for their hospitality. After he had done so, he summed matters up. "We've accomplished a great deal, but now, I believe, we must await results from Sir Cyril. It all does seem to come down to that, doesn't it?"

Marsha agreed. "Yes, it certainly does. But Jim Moriarty dug up an article about him that I found very interesting. Did you know that he has quite a reputation as an explorer?"

"At his age?" Philip asked.

"Apparently so; he's been everywhere and knows hordes of people. I suspect that he earned most of his reputation when he was younger, but I do have to admire the way he never lets his years interfere with his plans."

"When he arrives in heaven," Harley said, "he'll create more stir than General William Booth."

Philip smiled. "I seriously question if Sir Cyril has any intentions of applying for entry into paradise for some time to come."

Marsha nodded as she sat between the two men in the front seat. "I agree with you on that. And he does seem to have a gift for communicating."

"I can guess what it is," Harley offered as he turned off the freeway into the airport entry road. "He strikes me as a man who would be able to meet almost anyone else on common ground — a maharajah or simply a man in the street somewhere. Offhand I don't know of any failures that he's had and certainly he's made a financial success out of life."

"I believe that our cause is in good hands," Philip concluded. "Now I have pressing things to do in view of the decisions we have taken."

Events compressed themselves for him from that moment forward. A short feeder flight took him to Chicago, where he went through the departure formalities before boarding a giant Boeing. When the great aircraft made a clean lift-off he knew that he was truly on his way home. After a lavish meal he slept fitfully and then watched the progress of the foreshortened night until daylight came, and not long after it the coastline of Ireland. Seemingly minutes later he was back amongst familiar things, driving properly on the left, and savoring the other evidences of home. Luncheon was just being put on the table as he opened the door of his home and Janet came running to fling herself into his arms.

He rested during the afternoon and recovered some of the sleep he had lost in the flight. Then, at dinner, he was compelled to recite all his adventures to Janet, Geoffrey, and Peter, who listened with enthusiasm to all that he had to say.

When he had finished, Janet had one small piece of news to report. "The curate you selected to be your new chaplain, I can't think of his name . . ."

"Aubrey Fothergill."

"Yes, of course. I should remember since he's to live with us. He phoned — long distance. He has completed his curacy and is awaiting your instructions."

"Good," Philip said. "I need him and he's a bright one; I've been a little lost since Dan left us. Did he give you his number?"

"Yes, he did."

"Then I'll call him right away and tell him to be here

tomorrow if he can make it. He might as well start immediately."

"Mightn't he think that you're rushing him a bit too much?" Janet asked.

Philip, who understood the authority of his office a shade better than his wife did sometimes, shook his head. "No way," he answered.

The Reverend Aubrey Fothergill had been awaiting his summons to his new duties with somewhat mixed emotions. For a young curate of the Church of England to be selected to serve a term as a bishop's chaplain was a considerable distinction and Roundtree was widely known as one of the best brains in the whole Church structure. The problem lay in the fact that Roundtree had gone far out on a limb with his conference of religions idea. That fantasy was obviously foredoomed to disaster and young Mr. Fothergill had no desire to be associated with such a downfall.

However, since he had no choice in the matter, for the moment he dismissed his reservations. At least the bishop he was to serve was a man of tenacity and conviction, which suited Aubrey Fothergill because he was a naturally stubborn man himself.

Knowing that his call was coming at any time, he had his few immediate possessions gathered and ready to pack. He was unencumbered with a wife; if he had had one he would not have been chosen for his new assignment. As chaplain he would live in the bishop's house, dine at his table, and serve him very much as a military aide looks after the requirements of a high-ranking superior. It would be his duty to filter the bishop's telephone calls, decide which items in the mail should be brought to his personal attention, and control the flow of visitors into his office. On the whole he looked forward to it all; it would have been ideal except for the damning religious conference matter.

He was somewhat surprised when Roundtree rang him

up personally, but of course he had no chaplain to do that for him. As soon as the call was completed, Fothergill notified the rector with whom he had been working and received a blessing in return. That done he made what additional preparations were required and then retired to sleep soundly until seven in the morning. When he awoke he packed his remaining things in the back of his MG and after a suitable breakfast, which he would have eaten if he had been keeping St. Peter waiting at the Pearly Gates, he took his departure. Shortly after eleven he arrived at the bishop's residence and presented himself.

Janet Roundtree received him with a certain concern — he was her new boarder — and without appearing to do so looked him over carefully. He was a bit over six feet, but he had at least stopped growing before disaster had set in. He was quite thin, as so many of the young curates were, although she did not know any reason why this should be so; they seemed to eat well enough as far as she knew. He had a quiet, somewhat reserved manner which was to be expected when he was talking to the bishop's wife. She had him shown up to his room and noted with approval that he did not take too long before he was back downstairs and ready to report to her husband. She saw him out of the door and then decided that he had been about what she had expected. Philip had said that he was bright, so perhaps he would eventually be able to contribute something to the dinner table conversation. That was important, because the boys were just at the age when what they saw and heard would have a considerable influence on their lives.

Meanwhile Aubrey Fothergill was being ushered into the presence of the bishop who would be his mentor as well as his immediate superior during the next stage of his life.

"Good morning, Fothergill," Philip welcomed him. "I'm very glad that you've arrived so promptly. There is a great deal to be done."

"I'm glad to be here, My Lord Bishop."

"Are you prepared to begin more or less immediately?"

"What would you like done first?" Fothergill asked.

Philip leaned back in his big leather chair and surveyed his new acquisition. "How much do you know concerning the religious conference that has been proposed?"

"Only what has appeared in the papers, Your Lordship."

"Do you believe in it, Fothergill?"

"I profoundly regret to say that I do not."

That went with Fothergill's reputation for having his own mind. "Why not?" Philip asked.

"Because it won't work," Fothergill replied.

"You feel, then, that obstacles are too great?"

"Yes, Your Lordship, I do."

"Let me ask you a question. Do you have any reservations based on conscience, or are your objections entirely on practical considerations?"

"Entirely the latter, My Lord Bishop; since you proposed this meeting, it follows that there can be no valid objection on the spiritual side. The Lord Archbishop also was quoted substantially to that effect in the press, I believe."

"You have heard of Sir Cyril Plessey?"

"With greatest respect, I have not been living in a vacuum, My Lord. His gift to the Church for the purpose you proposed was widely publicized; it was on the front page of the *Times*."

"So it was."

"And I understand that the Americans have some vast fortune set aside for the same purpose."

"They have more than that, Fothergill. I was just over there to discuss the matter with them."

"I hope that your trip was profitable."

Philip paused and took his time. "Fothergill, it has pleased the archbishop to relieve me of my diocesan duties for a period of a year in order that I may pursue the conference idea. Since His Grace has taken this action, you will understand that it is imperative that I follow his directive and

76

apply my full energies in the direction that he has indicated." That said, he waited for the reaction.

Fothergill saw the light. "Of course, My Lord, it is the only possible course. And that obviously applies to me also."

"I'm very happy that you see it that way."

The younger man leaned forward. "Very well, Your Lordship," he said. "Where do I begin?"

In the opinion of Arthur Gravenstine the religious story of the century was breaking, and he had no intention of letting it die. Fortunately the usual flow of news was at ebb tide — even the Middle East was, for the moment, peaceful. As long as there was legitimate news value in Philip Roundtree's activities he intended to cover them in full, and by doing so he could also help to keep the flame hot and the kettle bubbling. He therefore contacted Bishop Roundtree with appropriate formality and on behalf of the press corps asked for a news conference.

As it happened, that suited Philip himself admirably; he too knew the value of keeping a good thing in the public eye and his trip to America had provided him with much encouragement. In response to the request he went up to London and took his new chaplain with him. Aubrey needed some seasoning and he might as well begin by smelling the powder and learning how the verbal grenades were handled.

The turnout was more than twice what had been expected and additional refreshments had to be ordered. After shaking hands all around with the accredited press representatives and the photographers, Philip sat down, a cup of tea on his knee, and awaited the barrage.

"My Lord Bishop," Gravenstine himself began, "there are very strong rumors that a decision has been taken to hold the conference that you proposed at a college in America. Could you comment on that?"

"Certainly," Philip responded. "The rumor is quite correct. By an unusual circumstance, a very considerable sum of money — actually in excess of four hundred thousand pounds — has been made available. While no direct strings were attached, as the Americans say, the acceptance of such a sum implies certain obligations."

He paused to permit some hurried writing on press paper. When the air cleared he went on. "Then, as you already know, Sir Cyril Plessey made a magnificent gift to the Church for the purpose of furthering a meeting of the world's major faiths. Sir Cyril personally traveled to America and was there at the same time as myself. When he gave it as his opinion that the conference should be held at Maplewood College, it remained only for me to secure the approval of the archbishop to finalize the matter."

"And did you obtain that approval?"

"Yes, I did."

The conference continued for almost forty minutes; when it was about to conclude Philip pointed out that the success already achieved was due entirely to the great wisdom and foresight of the archbishop. Then, smiling all around once more, he ran for cover.

He was seated in his suite, enjoying a whisky and soda, when the phone rang. Aubrey answered it and then turned. "Sir, the call is from America. Dr. Poindexter is on the line."

Philip got up and went to the phone. "Good afternoon, Harley," he said.

"Good morning, Philip; I have some news for you. We have heard from Sir Cyril. Apparently he tried to reach you, but you were en route to London."

"Where is he?"

"He phoned me from India. He has been to the United Arab Republic, if that's the proper name now, and then to Israel. Apparently with complete success at both places."

"Remarkable!"

"In a way, yes, because there isn't any real hierarchy in Islam, but apparently he saw the right people. At any rate he has extracted firm commitments from both of the major divisions of the Muslims, and they were among those I had frankly expected to hold out."

"My hat's off to him," Philip said.

"There's more, Philip, don't go away. All three major divisions of Judaism are now in the bag — Orthodox, Conservative, and Reformed. How he did that God only knows, but he pulled it off. Apparently it came down to a matter of talking business and Sir Cyril is notably good at that."

"This is absolutely wonderful; I don't know what to say . . ."

"Don't say anything, but keep on listening. It seems that our friend planned his itinerary quite well. He went next to Istanbul and secured an audience with the Patriarch of Constantinople."

"Good heavens!"

"Philip, he lined up the Orthodox Church as though that sort of thing is done every day. All I can say is that you were totally and absolutely right when you declared that people generally are more than ready at least to meet together. When Sir Cyril finished his conversation with me, he was off to keep an appointment with the Parsees. He's in Bombay."

There were some seconds of silence at transatlantic rates. Then Philip spoke with calm conviction. "Harley, it's got to go. It has to."

"Yes, Philip, I agree. We can't back off now, no matter what happens. One point — a general invitation should be issued to all faiths, a sort of 'to whom it may concern' kind of thing. Do you want to do that or shall I?"

"Are you set up for it?"

"Yes, I believe so."

"Then go ahead, Harley, and add my name to yours if you see fit."

"Excellent, Philip, excellent! We'll get on it right away."

"Thank you, Harley. Good-bye."

"Good-bye, Philip. You'll be hearing from me further."

When the connection had been broken Philip sat down and rested his chin in his hand. He remained that way for some time, his thoughts cascading like a multifaceted waterfall. At last he became aware that his chaplain wished to speak to him. He looked up and gave silent permission.

"What was it, Your Lordship?" Aubrey asked.

Philip did not reply for a moment, then, without conscious thought, he found the words to answer the question.

"Aubrey, prepare to march forward. For the second time in recorded history, someone has parted the waters of the Red Sea."

CHAPTER EIGHT

From the moment he returned home, it seemed to Philip that time had suddenly acquired jet thrust and was propelling him down the runway toward a rapidly approaching takeoff. Thanks to his new chaplain the mounting volume of incoming mail was handled with reasonable dispatch, but a multitude of other details kept piling up on his desk. He received frequent criticism and a steady flow of predictions of disaster, but they were mercifully outweighed by a small flood of messages of encouragement.

He heard from Harley Poindexter almost daily, by mail and frequently by phone. If the chill winds of discouragement blew occasionally across the American campus, not a whiff of them could be detected in the writing of the energetic president of Maplewood College. One letter contained a paragraph that stuck in Philip's mind, for its encouragement as well as several other reasons:

We are having an excellent response to our general invitation, but if it isn't irreverent, I'd be tempted to say that some of the organizations that have sent in their acceptances must have come straight out of the woodwork. Many of them don't appear in any of the reference books, but we said 'everybody welcome,' so we'll have to stick by that as far as we can. We've set up some rules regarding the allowable number of delegates and that will help. The latest big catch is the Lutherans. They'll be here in force despite some problems with the Missouri Synod; one of their head men has been kicking up a cloud of dust. That simply goes to prove that no matter how magnificent and inspired an idea may be, inevitably someone will try to shoot it down. But this has no bearing on the success of the conference, which we can now feel and sense everywhere.

When it seemed to Philip that he could not possibly finish everything that he had to do before he left again for America, a summons came for a meeting with the archbishop. In a way he was glad, because no delegation had been named to his knowledge to represent the Church of England and he could not imagine the conference without one.

The Most Reverend Frederick Danford-Smith received him in precisely the manner that Philip had expected: he was cordial, moderately cooperative, and restrained. But he nevertheless put his somewhat maverick bishop at ease and displayed interest in what he was doing.

"By the reports I have been receiving, I take it that your project is now moving forward quite rapidly," the archbishop said. "It is now definite that the meeting will be held in America, is it not?"

"Yes, Your Grace, we have been singularly fortunate. Very good facilities have been made available to us and with them most substantial funding. An added advantage is the fact that the United States are, in a sense, religious neutral ground."

"I see; those points are well taken. And of course, by permitting the Americans to assume a sizable part of

82

the responsibility, we automatically somewhat relieve ourselves."

"That is certainly the case, Your Grace. If I may now speak frankly, I have noted that the permission granted to me to carry on with this effort did not include the official sponsorship of the Church. This I quite understand and accept. My only request now, sir, is that a suitable delegation be named to represent us on the floor."

Danford-Smith folded his thin hands and reflected on that before he replied. When he did so, it was in the form of a question. "Tell me first, Philip, how well are you doing with people . . . of other persuasions?"

"Extremely well, Your Grace. As of right now, thanks to the really amazing ambassadorship of Sir Cyril Plessey, all of the major faiths have accepted, and a great many of the lesser ones as well."

Danford-Smith lifted his chin for a moment. "I confess that I am a little surprised to hear that — and gratified too, of course. Are you getting cooperation from our friends in Rome?"

Philip nodded. "They have agreed to send a team of 'observers.' I'm not concerned with the semantics, Your Grace; the point is, they'll be there."

Danford-Smith let the conversation lapse for a few moments while he gathered his thoughts together. When he spoke again, his words had the weight of an unavoidable decision. "Then certainly we must be listed among the participants. Did you have anything specific in mind?"

"It would reflect the greatest honor and distinction on us if you would consider heading our delegation personally, Your Grace."

The archbishop sidestepped that as Philip had known that he would. "Extremely difficult, I'm afraid, as much as I would enjoy doing so. So many other matters to attend to — you understand."

"Certainly, Your Grace, it was too much to hope that you could be spared. If you could, however, suggest someone else..."

Once more Danford-Smith took his careful time. "How many persons do you believe will be required?"

That was the moment on which everything hung. "Excluding myself and my chaplain, Your Grace, I suggest that four would be appropriate, and I would propose that at least one bishop be included."

The archbishop made a note. "I shall look into it. One more word, Philip, while you are here ..." He sat an inch or two higher as he leaned forward and straightened his spine. "I anticipate that you, personally, will be considerably in the limelight..."

"Not if I can avoid it, Your Grace."

"The handwriting is on the wall in that regard, I fear, and I'm sure that you understand it. Inevitably you will be regarded as a representative of the Church. I trust that in your very natural, and I don't hesitate to add Christian, desire to please those others who will be present, you won't forget your own position. Not that I expect you to get all of the world's religious leaders to agree totally with our doctrines, but try to guide them as close to the truth as you can."

Philip looked at him and in the older man's face read his lifetime of dedication, the depth of his faith and convictions. He understood, and at the same moment wondered how, literally in God's name, his conference could ever succeed in persuading equally sincere persons to abandon their tenets in order to embrace eventually a new and more catholic form of belief. It was manifestly impossible. But if *any* progress could be made ...

He rose to go. "I shall do my best, Your Grace."

The archbishop rose as well. "Then I bid you Godspeed, Philip. I shall pray for your success."

"I am most grateful for that, Your Grace. Good-bye."

Time raced forward also at Maplewood College. The hundreds of details that had to be attended to danced in a frenzied chorus before the overworked eyes of Dr. Harley Poindexter, but that worthy gentleman kept his cool and sorted them out one by one. The matters concerned with the closing of the academic year he turned over to the dean of the college.

From a major car manufacturer he secured a fleet of vehicles on loan in return for the publicity values involved. He arranged to have a press room set up with all the necessary equipment and communications facilities. He contacted the management of North Central Airlines and arranged to have some special flights laid on to handle the incoming delegates. When he discovered that a number of revivalist groups were intending to pitch tents on or near the campus in order to conduct meetings during the conference, he called the mayor of Winnebago.

"I don't want to go on record as opposing or discouraging any form of religious worship," he declared over the phone, "but I'm not going to have this conference turned into a three-ring circus."

"We'll handle it," the mayor promised. "There's an ordinance that prohibits tent meetings within the city limits without special authority. If asked, we'll issue the authority — but we'll restrict the sites to Steele Park. That's a good location, but a long way from your campus."

"Fine, that takes care of that."

Harley was congratulating himself on how easily that matter had been disposed of when his secretary came into his office. The look she give him put him immediately on the alert. "I have news, sir," she reported. "Sir Cyril Plessey has just arrived on campus."

By that Harley understood that his distinguished visitor was already in the outer office. "Show him in immediately," he directed loudly enough to be sure that he would be heard.

The girl turned to discover that Sir Cyril was already

entering under his own authority. "There's no need to shout," he declared. "I have excellent ears."

He crossed the long office and settled himself comfortably in a chair that pleased him. Then he inspected his host and announced, "You've lost six pounds."

"Seven, Sir Cyril. I've had quite a lot to do lately."

"Insufficient regular exercise — you can't keep in shape that way. Take up some active sports, outdoors and in. Some hiking, mountain climbing, and a little wenching on the side — the things a man needs."

"Excellent advice, Sir Cyril, I shall act on it. Meanwhile, let me congratulate you on your superb achievement during the past few weeks. I doubt if another man alive could have done it."

Sir Cyril leaned back. "You're probably right in that — too many dummies running around in striped pants claiming to be diplomats. Most of them don't know enough to keep their left hands to themselves when they're talking with Arabs. *Ames!*"

The reliable manservant entered with a speed which suggested that the Zacchini family might have fired him from a cannon. "Sir?"

"We'll be here for a while. Call up a hire agency and see what you can do about a Rolls, not a black one but some snappy color that the women will like."

"Immediately, sir."

"And lay in some suitable stock for the bar."

"At once, Sir Cyril." He left swiftly but with unshattered dignity, the result of years of diligent practice.

"Who's your public relations man? The young fellow — I didn't catch his name."

"Bill Quigley. He's good."

"Glad to hear it; I'll supervise him personally to be sure that he doesn't make any mistakes. Now another thing — language."

"I don't quite follow you."

86

"About the conference. Apparently no one thought of the fact, but these delegates are going to be speaking a whole raft of different languages."

A sudden engulfing, ice-cold cascade of horror poured over Harley Poindexter; that stupefying thought had never occurred to him. The enormity of his oversight appalled him, and when he looked at Sir Cyril once more, his face betrayed his thoughts.

"Don't worry, Poindexter, I took care of it. Obviously to get anywhere they'll have to use a civilized language and that means English. Most of them know it anyway." He shook an admonishing finger. "Don't believe that old platitude that 'money talks,' it's the other way around. People learn to talk to the money. When tourists have pounds or dollars to spend, the merchants all learn English — they'd better if they want to live. So I required that all delegates be fluent in English. They bought it, of course." He folded his hands on top of his stick and glanced about him to see if perchance there were any additional worlds within view to conquer.

"Sir Cyril, you are amazing!"

"Experience, man — experience! There's no substitute for it."

"I believe you — without reservations. Now for how long may we have the great benefit of your advice and guidance?"

Sir Cyril shrugged. "Can't tell you — I don't know how long this thing is going to last. Roundtree may know, but I doubt it. Too much human nature involved."

Without flicking an eyelid Harley picked up the telephone and asked for Chalmers, the buildings and grounds superintendent.

"Frank," he said when he had his man on the line, "Sir Cyril Plessey has returned and will be staying in the guesthouse for the duration. Mr. Ames is with him to look after his needs. Is everything ready?"

"It will be in half an hour, Dr. Poindexter."

"That's excellent. And incidentally, our usual rules for guests will not apply to Sir Cyril, of course."

"That goes, no matter what?"

"Yes, I'd say so until further notice."

As soon as the college president had hung up, Sir Cyril made his further wants known. "I'll need some offices," he said. "And can you spare a secretary or so to help me out?"

At that juncture Ames reappeared. "Sir Cyril," he reported, "I regret to advise you that the hire car people have no Rolls available at all. They further declared that no one else has one either at the moment this side of Los Angeles. They have a Mercedes six hundred in Chicago they can get, but it's black. They have proposed a Lincoln Continental; it's very spacious and can be made available at once in a color you will approve."

"That's a splendid car, Sir Cyril," Harley ventured.

"Very well, arrange for it. How soon can it be delivered?"

"I anticipated your decision, sir — it is being brought here within the hour."

"And the bar supplies?"

"They are on their way, sir."

"Take care of the other necessities."

"I am doing so, sir. Miss Erickson deeply regrets that she is unable to dine with you this evening owing to a pressing meeting she must attend. She is sending her roommate with a very high recommendation."

Sir Cyril shot a penetrating glance at Poindexter and the college president quickly nodded. "Miss Matsumoto is extremely attractive and should be delightful company."

Sir Cyril arose. "I shall be on my way, then. Time is very short."

Harley Poindexter got up as well. "True — the conference begins two weeks from today. I confess that in some respects it's all a little frightening."

The venerable knight waved a hand in the air. "No need for that," he declared. "Not while I am here."

By common agreement the graduation ceremonies were compressed the following weekend since everyone concerned understood the importance of the meeting that Maplewood was to host. The departing seniors contributed by cleaning up the dormitory rooms, carefully removing all the pinups and putting the parlors in good order.

On Monday morning a transatlantic jet began to let down into the arrival pattern at Chicago O'Hare International Airport; among the passengers were Philip Roundtree, his wife Janet, and his newly installed chaplain. During most of the flight Philip had sat very quietly; while he faced the immediate future with courage and conviction, he knew that he was in relatively the same position as the early Everest climbers who had attempted the summit without oxygen and clad in gentlemen's sports attire. It had been a glorious try, but it had failed and had cost them their lives. He did not want to fail, even though deep in his own heart he knew that he was attempting the impossible.

When the great aircraft had burned its tires on the runway and had settled down, he turned to Janet and said, "This is America, my dear."

She smiled in return, but knew enough to say nothing. Instead she followed as Philip led their way through customs and immigration and then into the vast terminal complex with its stone-hard floors and streams of people hurrying in all directions. He engaged porters to assist with their luggage and then set out toward the North Central Airlines counter to arrange for the last stage of their journey. Aubrey Fothergill carried the hand baggage as he followed quietly, looking about and taking in as much as he could.

Philip found that there was a lump in his throat and tried to swallow it down. It was the same feeling, he sensed, that some of the martyrs probably had experienced when they had been led out to execution, when even at the last minute they could have recanted and saved themselves. He had started all this, and now it was upon him with defeat almost as certain as the stake and the chains that awaited those who had been strong enough in their faith to face death by fire. He was not thinking of himself, he was thinking of Janet and the boys and what he had done to them. And he thought too of Aubrey, a promising, dedicated young man. He had probably ruined his career too by insisting on challenging the one most irreconcilable element in all of human behavior. He looked up to see where he was going and abruptly caught his breath. Before him at the North Central counter he saw two shaven-headed men in saffron robes and knew at once that they were Buddhist monks.

He was aware that they existed; he had seen pictures, but he had never encountered any before.

Almost everyone within range was staring at them. They appeared to be relatively young men, but it was difficult to tell. Their right arms were bare from the shoulder, with the only concession to Western dress the shoes they wore on their feet. At once Philip felt for them; his own clerical attire was distinctive, particularly his purple vest, but few in America would know what that meant and priests were quite common. He quickened his step as he saw one of them turn toward the counter and apparently put a question.

He arrived while the agent behind the counter was still dialing a telephone. "Can I help you?" he asked, looking from one to the other.

There was an awkward moment; he was not sure that his words, or his intentions, were understood. He tried again. "Are you going to Maplewood College?"

That got him a response; the monk who appeared to be the older of the two nodded with the suggestion of a bow. "Maplewood," he repeated. "Yes, please."

Philip turned to the agent who held the phone, waiting. "We are going there too," he explained.

The airline man was quickly responsive. "May I have your name, please, Father?"

90

"Roundtree. Also Mrs. Roundtree and the Reverend Aubrey Fothergill."

"Thank you." He hung up the phone, checked the names on the manifest forms, and completed the check-in process. As he handed over the gate passes he said, "Since you are going to the same place, Father, perhaps you would be kind enough to help these gentlemen. I can call a scooter for you."

"Is it far?"

"Not very."

"Then we can walk. Thank you anyway."

He turned to find that the younger monk wanted to speak to him. "You are Roundpree who call this meeting?"

"Yes, I am." He wanted to introduce Janet and his chaplain, but he sensed a language limitation and the place was much too public. "Where are you from?" he asked.

"Burma."

The exotic spires of Rangoon and Mandalay that he had never seen came into form in Philip's imagination. "You are delegates?" he suggested.

The younger monk answered him. "No. We are to serve. We help."

That brought a sense of relief, one tiny obstacle to free discussion and debate had been removed; hopefully the delegates themselves would have a better command of English. "Please come," he said, and began to lead the way toward the passageway to the loading area. He could almost feel the stares of the other travelers as they threaded through the crowded terminal, but his mind was intent on other things. When they arrived at the gate the aircraft was already boarding and they were able to pass through without any delay.

The seats in the DC-9 were somewhat crowded, but the flight was brief and then he was back again in the terminal building where he had first met Harley Poindexter. Holding

Janet's arm as he came down the corridor, he looked about him for the man he had already come to trust, then he was touched on the arm. He turned to find Ned Stone there.

"Welcome back, Bishop!"

There was real warmth in the greeting and Philip felt it. After introductions he indicated the two monks who were standing quietly by themselves. "Can we make room in the car for these two gentlemen?" he asked. "We'll be glad to double up any way that we can."

Ned signaled to the two Buddhists to join them. "Easy — I've got Sir Cyril's car, so there's more than enough room. Let's get the luggage."

Fifteen minutes later they were on their way, the monks seated in front beside Ned; Philip, Janet, and Aubrey in the back. As the big car purred down the multilane highway, Philip gently took his wife's hand and smiled assurance at her. His mind was suddenly at peace and all was well. Many different emotions had been battering at him during the weeks that had just passed, but they would all have to be put aside. The thing that he had brought about was directly before him now. He refused to allow any forebodings of disaster to enter his mind.

CHAPTER NINE

On the campus of Maplewood College a major transformation was taking place. Instead of settling down into the familiar summer lull, the whole institution was in a steady ascending spiral of activity. Telephone company installers were busily at work setting up the press room. Crews of painters were engaged in freshening up the Student Union and the various other locations scheduled for use during the conference. A linen rental company saw to it that all of the beds in the available dormitories were made ready; even the vending machines scattered about the campus were replaced with newer and more sophisticated models.

In a long caravan the student drivers who had been engaged to work in the transportation pool brought in a fleet of new cars and under Ned Stone's direction set up the operation. The kitchen remained open, providing three meals a day. The well-worn Pit was refurbished and redecorated. After some discussion its food and beverage service was left as it was, catering to the traditional American appetite for hamburgers, hot dogs, and the more popular soft drinks for odd hour refreshment. The library moved all its religious books into the most accessible available locations for the duration of the conference.

As the whole project began visibly to take shape, Dr. Harley Poindexter found himself in his element. Everything was falling into place according to plan. That pleased the college president immensely; it was evidence that the preparatory work had been well done and no more glaring oversights appeared to haunt him. He had a master list on his desk, and as the calls came in to report on progress and specific jobs completed, he kept careful track. Everything was on schedule and not a single serious hitch had appeared anywhere along the line. The news media had been calling steadily, which was also gratifying; Bill Quigley was handling all that.

His secretary interrupted him to say that Dr. Hastings was in the outer office; a few moments later the Dean of the Chapel was seated before his president's desk.

"Joe," Harley asked, "what's the latest on the delegate count?"

"Slightly over six hundred. The first of them are due to come on campus tomorrow, but we're all set up in case any get here this evening — there are still three more flights coming in."

"That's a lot of delegates."

"Amen to that. Apparently there are more ways to worship God on earth than there are harps in heaven."

"And we're still getting requests for admission." Poindexter picked up a letter from his desk. "Tell me, what in heaven's name is a group that calls itself the New Revelations?"

"I've never heard of them."

"Apparently it's one of those one-congregation sects, there seem to be quite a few of them. And all anxious to tell their

94

story, of course. But we simply can't put up and feed the whole religious population of the country, not to mention the world."

"Of course not, Harley. I've been advising all along that we should ration delegate space according to the size of the faith being represented — with some elasticity in order to avoid any unhappy incidents."

"Good. Since we're not out of the woods yet, if any church wants to come in that you can't recognize or find in the literature, issue credentials for one delegate. New Revelations proposes to arrive en masse to show all humanity the way to go."

The dean changed the topic. "We've worked out the housing pretty carefully. In some instances we're putting representatives of different faiths together, but we're keeping the Jews in the north wing of the men's dorm and the Muslims in the other."

"Keep the Bahais away from the Muslims too — the sons of the Prophet martyred one of their founders and that's never been forgiven."

"The Ceylon people are bringing an image of Buddha with them and want a place to set it up."

"O.K., assign one of the smaller chapels or, if the image is too big, pick a suitable classroom and let them convert it into a worship hall." Harley Poindexter leaned back for a rare moment of reflection. "Joe, have we opened a can of worms?"

The dean caught the change in feeling and responded to it. "Yes, Harley, we have. But it's worth it, I think."

Poindexter was still nodding his approval when his phone rang. "Yes?" he answered.

"Dr. Poindexter, this is Paul Jeffreys in the dining hall. We've got a flap going on over here."

"What's the agony?"

"We're in the midst of trying to get lunch ready. A

Frenchman who claims that he's in charge of everything is raising hell and he declines to be thrown out. Do you know anything about this?"

Harley did. "I'll be right over," he said and hung up. Then he explained to the dean. "Inglebrecht, our trustee, promised to provide us with a great chef to preside over the dining room during the conference. Apparently he has arrived."

Upon entering the kitchen in the Student Union, Harley discovered an atmosphere that could have been cut up and used for hacksaw blades. He spotted the visitor at once and was slightly surprised to discover almost precisely what he had expected. The man was smallish, but distinctly plump in the middle. The suit he had on had been cut from Italian silk by an obviously superior tailor. His shoes were mirror-bright, as was the bald spot on the top of his head which reflected the overhead lighting. His face was smooth and pink, but its outlines were overshadowed by a small waxed mustache. These quick impressions were all that Harley had time for, since the man's discomfort was not only obvious but also compelling. Poindexter approached him and asked, "May I help you?"

The reply he received was not precisely what he had expected. "It is here that you prepare fodder for cattle?" The words bristled with indignation.

Harley smiled. "I'm sometimes tempted to think of some of our students in that way, but not very often."

The visitor pressed his palms against the top of a counter before him and leaned slightly forward. "I am Henri Devereux, you have perhaps heard of me?"

That called for an educated guess, which was not too difficult. "The celebrated chef? We're delighted that you're here."

Devereux was slightly mollified, but his body remained tense. "It was promised to me that I would have a kitchen with equipment of the best and a staff to assist me. I arrive

96

and you present me with a scene of horror. There is only unskilled help and the furnishings . . ." It took him a moment to think of something suitable. "It is unfit for an asylum of the insane at full moon."

"If we had had sufficient advance notice of your coming," Harley said, "of course we would have made special arrangements. We were not advised that we were to be so fortunate until the last minute."

He paused just long enough to sense that he was on the right track, then he deftly changed the subject. "Would it be possible to discuss menus with you for a moment?"

"You offer direction?"

"Oh no, sir, I only wish to consult you."

The internal pressure had subsided enough by that time to permit M. Devereux to continue with some display of calmness. "I presume there is to be an opening banquet?"

"Very right, sir, and its success would be a wonderful start for our meeting." As he spoke he noted that his Dean of the Chapel had also arrived and was remaining, for the moment, in the background.

"Success, it is inevitable!" Having given that pronouncement, the noted chef looked about him once more. "What is it that you prepare now?"

"Pizza and salami sandwiches," the dining room manager supplied.

Devereux turned pale, then regained control of himself. "The banquet, when is it to be?"

Dean Hastings moved forward. "We're having some difficulties about that and we're still not sure. Sunday would not be appropriate."

"But obviously."

"Unfortunately Monday falls on the Buddhist sabbath."

"Then Saturday."

Hastings shook his head. "The Seventh-Day Adventists would be insulted."

"Friday?"

"Not after sundown. The Orthodox Jews . . ."

"Which reminds me," Poindexter interjected, "I seem to recall that the Jains will eat only during the daylight hours."

"And I think that Friday is the Muslim sabbath," Hastings added.

"So everyone starves until Tuesday?" Devereux inquired.

"We'll have to check out the date, but I think that Tuesday is all right," Harley said.

"There is then enough time to make things right," Devereux declared. "For this occasion I shall prepare a dinner guaranteed to please everyone who possesses a palate — and enrich those who do not." He placed his fingertips together for a moment. "In this primitive part of the nation there are not available the elegant foods in large enough quantities, so it will be necessary to prepare . . ." He paused to consider. ". . . Chateaubriand with truffles and sauce Bearnaise." He lifted one hand in the air and held it there like a conductor on the podium, savoring his creation in advance.

"Unfortunately, sir, I fear that won't be possible," Dean Hastings ventured to interject. "We are expecting a large Hindu delegation and they won't touch beef in any form. To them the cow is a sacred animal."

"The cow — sacred?" M. Devereux was scornful. "Some, perhaps if it is their faith . . ."

"*All* cows, sir. As a matter of fact, in Nepal, which is a Hindu kingdom, the penalty for killing a cow is identical with the one for murder — fifteen years in either case."

"Whatever we think," Harley said, "we do have to respect the beliefs and convictions of our visitors, particularly during the early stages of the meeting. It wouldn't do to have a major delegation walk out in the first week."

The chef furrowed his brow and consented to try again. "It is a simple dish, in fact ordinary, but I have an orange-glazed ham that is a famous success. With especially prepared yams and . . ."

98

"Unfortunately . . ." Hastings began, but Harley Poindexter took over.

"That would be superb, were it not for the unhappy fact that the Muslims do not eat pork in any form, nor do the Orthodox Jews. It is a tragedy, as I would love to taste your creation."

The rotund little chef turned and faced him, hands on hips. "So is there nothing that will not be taboo by someone? Chicken, perhaps?"

Hastings, unfortunately, was literal. "The Jains can't eat that, they're strict vegetarians."

Devereux worked his lips. "And for these people I am asked to direct the kitchen. It is clearly impossible! Perhaps you wish me only to choose the wines." He gave an excellent performance as a man pushed to the limit of his patience.

"Perhaps you had better tell him," Hastings said, looking at Poindexter. Caution coated every word.

The college president accepted his fate. "There won't be any wines either, I am afraid. You see, the Prophet forbade their use, and there are a number of other religious groups that ban alcohol in any form — even beer."

"It is enough!" His complexion now visibly reddened, the Frenchman swept up his hat with an appropriate flair. "I regret, gentlemen, that there is nothing for me to do here. With pleasure I make my exit to return to civilization and to sanity. Adieu!"

With high dignity he turned on his heel and advanced three rapid steps toward the door. He paused only because Sir Cyril Plessey was entering at that moment and something about the older man's appearance told him that this was not a person to be pushed aside.

Sir Cyril appeared mildly annoyed. "What's the row going on here?" he demanded.

Harley explained. "Mr. Devereux has arrived to take charge of our kitchen during the conference. Unfortunately our equipment is not up to his expectations and he is further upset by the dietary regulations that many of our guests are required to follow."

"I see." That meant that he comprehended the entire situation fully and was prepared to deal with it. He penetrated Devereux with a gimlet eye. "What are your qualifications?"

The portly little Frenchman was ready for that question. It took him almost a full minute to do justice to his reputation, and when he at last concluded he was prepared to be crowned with a victor's wreath.

Sir Cyril surveyed the kitchen for a moment or two before his next pronouncement. "I presume that this notable man must have things his way because he is clearly a master chef of the second class."

"The second class!" Justified indignation raised the Frenchman's voice to a near shriek.

"The second class," Sir Cyril snapped back. "You have heard, of course, of the great Bruno Hoffelmeyer. Once, in the middle of a raging blizzard on the Gobi Desert, he produced for us a soufflé of magnificent lightness with nothing to work with but a yak dung fire and native cookwear. And for dessert his incomparable Piece Olympian with Sauce Patricia — despite the freezing temperature."

The electricity crackled in the air; Sir Cyril gave a convincing impersonation of the Rock of Gibraltar while his adversary vainly sought for a crack in that fortress. Then, despite his temperament, the Frenchman took the prudent path. "The German, but obviously, was trained in France. But since great responsibility has been entrusted to me, I consent — despite the frightful handicaps. It is not possible, however, that I cook separately for everyone."

Sir Cyril agreed. "That would be impossible, or hopelessly impractical at any rate. In view of the numbers eating and the hundreds of different regulations they have, we'll put out the food cafeteria style and label everything. To

100

keep noses in joint we can have two lines, one with no beef and the other with no pork. When they see what you've prepared, they'll eat."

Fortunately Devereux took that as a compliment and almost visibly became more tractable. He mellowed so obviously that one of the young women who was working in the kitchen and who had been keeping quietly in the background out of the line of fire approached him. "Sir," she asked, "have you had your lunch?"

"It is nothing."

The girl did not think so. "Wouldn't you like some nice hot pizza?"

With Gallic courtesy Henri Devereux declined. "I thank you, but no. Also I do not desire any salami." Inspiration provided an afterthought. "It is forbidden by my doctor."

The girl was immediately sympathetic. "I'm so sorry. I know — the spices. How about a glass of milk and a nice peanut butter and jelly sandwich?"

With a tremendous effort M. Devereux restrained himself. "Perhaps later," he murmured.

Calm descended once more. Sir Cyril took his departure, accompanied by Dean Hastings and President Poindexter. When they were safely out in the corridor, Harley put a question. "Sir Cyril, what in the world is Piece Olympian?"

"And Sauce Patricia?" Hastings seconded.

"How the hell do I know," Sir Cyril growled. "It doesn't matter, they got the job done." He planted his walking stick with authority. "I now have an appointment in the Pit," he announced, and departed.

Back in the kitchen Henri Devereux gently clapped his hands. He was understood and the staff gathered around him. "Continue as before," he directed, "for the remainder of the day. Then I shall begin to instruct you. This kitchen, from now on no one enters unless I approve. It is understood, yes?"

Apparently it was.

"Very good. Then even here in this place we shall create a cuisine that shall be part of history."

He noted that some attention was being diverted from his remarks, and turned around to find himself confronted by an intruder — a sad-eyed man clad in long black garments which were in keeping with his flowing beard.

Devereux gestured. "This kitchen, it is a private place. I regret, no visitors. Please to leave."

For almost a long minute the intruder did not appear to understand. He ran a finger across a counter and inspected it. He looked into one of the storage cupboards. Then he turned and spoke in a voice rich with Central European accent. "It will now be necessary for you to follow my orders."

Devereux's jaw tightened. "This, sir, is *my* kitchen, to me has been given the duty and the responsibility. If it is your wish to cook, please to go and do so elsewhere!"

The newcomer ignored him. "I am Rabbi Yasloff. During the length of the meeting all Jewish food preparation will be under my supervision." He lifted his head. "The kosher laws must be followed. All cooking dishes we will now bury in earth for three days, then we shall start again with two different sets of utensils which we will keep separated at all times."

In the morning the influx began. The cars of the transportation pool began to roll before eight in the morning to meet the first arriving flights for the day. Many private cars appeared and several buses pulled into the parking lots. The day was a brilliant one, warmer than might be expected, so that an almost festive feeling pervaded the atmosphere. The Maplewood students who had signed on to help with the conference kept things moving smoothly. In the lobbies of the dormitories the billeting charts aided the check-in process: registration slips were filled out and collected, baggage was handled, and, most happily, not a single incident marred the steady inflow of the delegates and their supporters.

Most of those who came in the morning were from various parts of the United States. Some wore clerical garb, others did not. They arrived and were processed in accordance with standard procedures for delegate reception at any sort of major convention. At noon the dining room put out a meal which was an improved effort by the regular staff and it appeared to go well. Just before he went to have his own lunch, Harley Poindexter received a call from the Winnebago Police Department. The chief himself was on the line and in a way he seemed to be amused. "Harley, when are you going to start serving meals to your religious people up there?"

"We have one going on right now. Why?"

"Well, don't laugh but we had three different calls here quite early in the morning. We saw no need to disturb you at that time, but I thought you ought to know about it. It seems that some of your delegates, apparently Orientals, were out a little after six. As I understand it, they were begging food for the day."

Poindexter remembered something. "Did you get any kind of description of them?"

"Yes, they wore robes; one report said they were yellow, another had them red, the third lady was sure they were orange."

"O.K., I've got it. We had two Buddhist monks who were early arrivals, they came in yesterday. It's their custom to go out at daybreak and beg for their food, so of course they did it here. I'll speak to them about it."

"Fine, no problem. What color *are* the robes, by the way?"

"Saffron. Did they get anything to eat?"

"As a matter of fact, yes — they went into the Dailyland Restaurant with their bowls and Charlie Ferguson who runs the place just happened to be in at that hour. He saw that they had a full breakfast, but you can't expect him to do that every day."

"Of course not, and if you see Charlie tell him I much appreciate his understanding."

At the moment that Harley was hanging up, Philip Roundtree was standing at the window of the office that had been assigned to him looking out over the campus with its increased activity. He heard a tap on the door behind him and turned. Arthur Gravenstine was there.

"Good morning, My Lord Bishop. May I come in?"

"Of course, I'm delighted you were able to come!"

They shook hands. "The *Times* has assigned me for the duration — at my urgent request, of course."

"I'm most happy to hear that. Are you getting anything?"

"I've been out all morning watching the people come. And they really are coming — Methodists, Christian Scientists, Lutherans, the Salvation Army, and it's just the beginning."

There was another tap and Karen Erickson was there. "Are you busy?" she asked.

"No, please come in."

She did. "Bishop Phil, if you're loose, could you join with a few of us this noon? An informal huddle sort of."

He thought for a bare moment. "Yes, all right. By the way, may I present Mr. Gravenstine of the *Times* of London. Miss Erickson."

"I'm delighted," Gravenstine said.

"Sit in if you'd like — nothing classified."

Arthur Gravenstine looked wonderingly at her for a moment. "I don't quite grasp your meaning."

"Would you like to eat with us?"

"Why not; charmed, I'm sure."

"See you." Five seconds later she was gone.

Gravenstine looked at the properly dignified bishop of the Church of England. "How did she address you?" he asked.

104

Philip allowed himself a gentle grin. "Now you know," he answered.

In the main dining hall the Reverend Aubrey Fothergill sat by himself, eating calmly and taking in all that was to be seen. He would have loved to have a glass of stout to assist the meal down his throat, but there was no hope of that. Before him he had a glass of darkish liquid that contained some chipped ice; the concoction had been placed there by a student waitress who had been distributing similar offerings throughout the dining room. He knew he would at least have to try the thing so as not to give offense; he was relatively new in the Church, but he had already learned to proclaim delicious many dishes offered to him that were not to his taste. His resolution made, he picked up the glass and drank a respectable two inches.

It was an odd taste, but apart from the fact that it was far too cold, it was refreshing.

He finished his meal and then returned to the men's dormitory where he had been assigned a room. He had been offered a private one on the strength of his being the bishop's chaplain, but he had refused. He did not particularly want a roommate, but he wanted even less to be a marked man from the beginning. Therefore, within reasonable limits whatever they gave him he would take.

They gave him Jayawardene Thiengburanathum.

The afternoon inflow was at its height; the two o'clock flight had arrived in three sections with a majority of the seats occupied by delegates from overseas. Every available car had to be used to bring them all on campus, including a massive Sikh who stood six feet seven in his socks and without his turban. Among them was J. Thiengburanathum, who was issued credentials, a meal ticket, a seat assignment in the auditorium, and quarters to be shared with the Reverend A. Fothergill.

Despite the fact that Thiengburanathum was an obvious

female, the error was not immediately detected. As a result she went as directed to the North Dormitory, where the student in charge of the desk wisely suggested that she wait in the parlor while he got on the telephone. The only other oversight was a minor one; from the reception center a routine call was put in to the Reverend Mr. Fothergill to advise him that his roommate had arrived. Aubrey received it and went to the lobby so that introductions could be performed.

When he got there, the student on the desk was holding the telephone line. "I was told that my roommate was here," Aubrey said, since no conversation was in progress.

One began at that moment. The student, confronted with the need to handle two things simultaneously, ducked one of them by pointing toward the parlor. Fothergill went as directed, took one look, and fully understood the need for the telephone call. At that point the young woman looked up inquiringly at him; he advanced a few steps and said, "Good afternoon."

"Good afternoon."

At least she could speak English, and apparently quite well. "My name is Fothergill. I suspect that there has been a small mix-up."

"I am not welcome?"

"Very welcome indeed! Pardon me, but were you informed that you would be rooming here?"

"I was."

"Then that's the mix-up. I believe that they are making suitable arrangements for you right now."

He waited, but she offered him no help. He contemplated walking out, then decided to give it one more try. "May I ask your name?"

"I don't think you could pronounce it."

"I'm willing to try."

"Very well, my name is Thiengburanathum."

"First, last, or both?"

"Last."

He was spared having to respond to that by Karen Erickson, who came hurrying in. "I'm sorry," Karen said, then she looked at the Reverend Mr. Fothergill. "You're Aubrey, aren't you?"

"I'm Aubrey."

"Good. Well, when we made out the room charts we fouled up — you understand?"

"Entirely."

"O.K., can you help me out for a minute?"

"Of course."

"Then please take this lady over to the Pit and buy her a Coke or something while we get things straightened out."

Fothergill turned toward the young woman, who was still seated just as she had been. "Will you accept my company for a few minutes?" he asked.

She answered by rising. "Under the circumstances, of course."

Karen spoke. "Leave your gear right here; when we get you lined up, it'll be taken over for you. It won't be long." With that she left.

Five minutes later Aubrey Fothergill entered the refurbished Pit with his unexpected companion. He guided her to a booth and then asked, "Did you have your lunch on the plane?"

"There wasn't time for that, but it doesn't matter."

Aubrey straightened. "I'm afraid that the dining room is closed, but they serve food here and it isn't bad. Let me provide." He had a thought and paused for a moment. "Pardon me, but I'm not sure — what are you allowed to eat?" He meant to put it the other way, but the words were already out.

"Whatever the Lord Buddha provides."

"I must say," he said, "that's the most sensible premise I've encountered."

"We're a very sensible people."

"I'm sure of it. Where are you from?"

"Bangkok. Does my name confuse you?"

"A little," he confessed.

"It's because of Mother," she explained. "My father is a Thai, you know that from my family name." She stopped when a student waitress appeared at their table.

Aubrey took over. "This lady has missed her lunch," he said. "What do you suggest for her?"

"Leave it to me," the waitress answered. "How about you."

"I've had lunch."

"Then to keep her company, how about a dog and a Pepsi?"

That was as clear to Aubrey as the Delphian oracle, but he nodded his assent. Then he looked again at his companion. "You were speaking of your mother."

"Yes. Mother, you see, is from Ceylon; she met my father when he went to Columbo on church business. So she wanted me to have a Sinhalese name, and I got one."

Aubrey was already well schooled in getting names right — it was essential in church work — but now he faced his greatest challenge. "Let me have your name once more," he said. "I want to write it down."

"All right. It's Jayawardene Weerasekera Thiengburanathum, if you want it all. But Jayawardene is enough; in Thailand almost everybody goes by his or her first name — even formally. The telephone directory is that way."

"By first names?"

"Yes, it's easier."

He couldn't think of anything to say after that. Religious discussion might be in order, but it seemed to him that there would be enough of that at the conference. He studied his companion as best he could and decided that, despite her origins, she was very attractive. He noticed particularly her forearm and wrist, part of her anatomy that he could safely inspect without giving offense. Her arm was slender but beautifully formed; her fingers were long and tapered almost to perfection. Her face, when he looked at it once more, was smooth, very slightly dark, and somewhat disconcerting. She had a way of returning his look that was entirely restrained and innocent, but somehow at the same time surprisingly penetrating. He was still engaged in cataloging her when the waitress came back and set a tray down on the table.

"O.K.," the girl said. "Here you are. Since the lady missed her lunch, I brought her a cheeseburger with fries and a malt, that ought to do until dinnertime. And here's your dog and Pepsi. It's a buck forty; you can pay me."

Aubrey surrendered a five-dollar bill hoping that it was enough. The girl took it, promised him his change, and departed. Then he looked at the food she had brought. There was an immense glass of some kind of thick milk, a ground meat sandwich which showed evidence of melted cheese at the sides, chips, a sausage in a bun, and another glass of the dark stuff he had had given to him at lunch. He was not entirely certain that he was right, but he placed the meat sandwich in front of his companion and gave her the milk also. The rest, he assumed correctly, was his.

The waitress came back with mustard, catsup, two glasses of ice water, and his change. As soon as she had left he turned to the girl from Bangkok and asked, "Will it do?"

"Oh, splendidly. It's much more than I need, but thank you."

As Aubrey bit experimentally into his own sandwich, he wondered if it would be suitable later for him to escort a lady Buddhist to a flick. Her English was excellent and perhaps she might enjoy one.

By the time that the long twilight had begun to settle over the campus more than two hundred and fifty delegates for the conference had been received, processed, and provided with quarters. The food in the dining hall, while not up to gourmet standards, had already begun to reflect the presence of M. Henri Devereux; the kitchen staff found him a surprisingly patient teacher once his authority had been clearly established. After some negotiation it was arranged to have the required number of kosher meals catered, which greatly relieved the pressure on the staff.

Sir Cyril's solution to the major dietary problems — to have each dish clearly labeled as to its contents — seemed to be effective. After dinner the parlors in the dormitories and the facilities in the Student Union played host to a wide assortment of different people, and so far as any casual observer could tell, everything was working out splendidly.

The following day was a very long one: it began early in the morning when the drivers from the car pool went to meet the first flight coming in from Chicago. The cars came back full and just in time to leave for another load. Delegates arrived by almost every reasonable means of transportation — in private cars, by rail, and via at least one chartered aircraft, which put down at the small but efficient Winnebago airport. More than three hundred checked in on campus; many had to be kept waiting for their turn to be shown to their quarters and to have their baggage delivered to them. The Pit did a thriving business in snacks and off-hour meals; halfway through the afternoon an emergency call was put in for additional supplies of ice cream and, oddly enough, doughnuts, which everybody seemed to like and to be permitted to eat.

During the evening meal the small Maplewood orchestra provided music. The clatter in the huge room diminished its effectiveness, but it did serve to add a touch of elegance in the otherwise strictly functional dining hall. Philip Roundtree took his evening meal with his chaplain; he was not in a mood to do very much talking, which Aubrey well understood. Halfway through their repast Fothergill saw something and spoke rather hurriedly. "Dr. Roundtree, there is a young lady just coming in. Would you have any objection..."

"On the contrary, I'd be delighted. Go fetch her."

Aubrey departed and soon returned carrying the tray for Jayawardene Thiengburanathum. Then, confronted with the need to perform introductions, he was embarrassed — he couldn't begin to remember her name. It did not help matters that Philip had risen and was clearly waiting to be presented. He took the only way out. "I can't pronounce it," he admitted.

The young woman held her hand out to Philip. "I'm Jayawardene," she said.

"Please join us, I'm Philip Roundtree."

"Bishop Roundtree — who delivered the sermon?"

"I'm afraid so."

She looked at him with genuine concern. "Please don't ever be afraid — seek enlightenment. You must already have come far down the Eightfold Path."

"Thank you." When they were seated, he put a question. "You are a Buddhist delegate, I take it?"

She shook her head. "Not a delegate, I represent the Buddhist press."

During the rest of the meal they talked about Thailand. The girl explained that she had learned her English there and had never before been in an English-speaking country. She was very pleasant and both men derived pleasure from her company.

When they were finished, Philip returned to his office to spend a little time in constructive thought. As he sat behind his desk, he was aware that he was suddenly quite tired. He could not afford that; the conference had not even begun! He wanted to pray but for the moment he could not, his head was too crowded with the kaleidoscopic impressions of the day. Instead he folded his hands on the top of the desk and waited deliberately for his mind to calm down.

Something caused him to look up; as he did so he saw Sir Cyril Plessey standing in the doorway.

Philip rose quickly. "Good evening, Sir Cyril," he said.

"Do come in and sit down. I was just reflecting on your incredible achievement — getting all of these people to come here for our meeting."

Sir Cyril came and sat, resting his hands on the top of his stick and looking across the desk. He remained silent for several seconds; when he did speak his voice lacked its usual bluster. "I wanted to talk to you," he said.

"Please do," Philip invited. "You came at a good time."

"I thought that might be the case. What I have to say is in a way a confession."

Philip raised his right hand and gave his sign that the seal of the confessional protected their conversation.

"I didn't mean that literally," Sir Cyril clarified, "but I don't want to be quoted in what I have to say now."

"Understood."

"Philip, there are some things concerning which I have no illusions. I'm in good health, my doctors keep telling me that I have the averages beaten completely, but I am perfectly aware of my years — and of the comparative few that remain to me. As far as money goes, I won't live long enough to spend what I've got and I have no immediate issue in need of my support. I continue to accumulate a little from time to time, more or less to keep my hand in, but I'm quite satisfied that I've got that one licked."

"Indeed you have," Philip agreed.

"Now the thing that has motivated my life from the time I was old enough to take myself to the pottie has been challenge. Knowing this, I don't want you to think that I set up this conference as some kind of supertoy to amuse myself; if you've had that idea, get it out of your mind."

"I never had it."

"Good. Now at home I support the local parish, but my pew gets cold from time to time — in fact that's its normal condition. One reason is that the Church isn't noted for its progressive tendencies. Dammit, man, the world is on the move and he who stands still not only loses his place, he's in danger of being buried by the avalanche!"

Sir Cyril stopped and reflectively wiped his upper lip. Then he recomposed himself and went on. "What it comes down to is this: there are two things which are commonly agreed to be the most hardheaded areas of human differences — politics and religion. Between them they account for all of our wars and always have. Politics is a tough nut, but it does crack sometimes; that's why the Labour Party gets in every now and then for a little while. But religion is a relentless rock; it has sent more ships to the bottom than any real shoal God ever created.

"Then you stood up in the pulpit and challenged the one most rigid and insoluble fixation that the whole race of two-legged creatures we call mankind has been able to dream up in all of the centuries since the Stone Age — perhaps even before that for all I know.

"I couldn't let that one go by; it was the supreme challenge, but also it was the single most urgent need. I wanted to know if a solution, any kind of one, was in any way possible. Because if it was, then we owe it to our posterity to find it if we can. That's all."

Philip answered simply. "God bless you, Sir Cyril; I mean that. I have a great hope too, a desperate one I know, but I don't want the conference to fail. I want it to accomplish *something*."

"It won't fail," Sir Cyril said. "I guarantee that."

Philip studied him. "How can you, sir?" he asked.

Sir Cyril arose to go. "Because I won't allow it to," he answered.

CHAPTER TEN

The preliminaries were over. The planning, the preparations, the thousands of details that had demanded attention were all in the past. Now over the campus of Maplewood College the sunlight blazed out of the sky as though it were some kind of celestial sign for those able to read its meaning. Arthur Gravenstine took his breakfast in the company of Janet Roundtree; as he ate he interviewed her concerning her reactions as the wife of the man who had brought all this about. He found the bishop's wife about as he had expected — happy that the conference had become a reality, but at the same time worried about what might occur.

When the early morning meal was over Gravenstine excused himself and checked in at the press room, where he obtained the last-minute details concerning the opening processional. The delegates would be gathering within the hour on the floor of the main gymnasium. The line of march had been very carefully worked out so as to slight no one, but also to keep delegations which might have a possible hostility toward one another well separated. The

Art Department had created a series of uniform standards bearing the accepted symbols of the major world faiths; it was a bit of window trimming that Bill Quigley had considered to be in good order. Fortunately when they were produced and shown to the respective delegations, everyone seemed to find them suitable.

On a raised platform outside the main entrance of the chapel auditorium four different television cameras had been set up; another crew was at work filming scenes of the college and its facilities for background use. The line of march had been marked out with tapes which, it was hoped, everyone would respect. As the temperature inched up from the early morning coolness, the activity on the campus seemed to respond; people hurried about more rapidly while a steady thin stream of sightseers flowed in from all directions.

The press room staff had worked most of the night finishing up an extended series of releases; each delegation of any size was described with the names and titles of the participants. General releases covered the smaller groups and those which were represented by single delegates. There were background releases on the college itself, a biography of the Right Reverend Philip Roundtree, and copies of the original sermon which he had delivered before the Convocation of the Church of England. There was only limited photo coverage, but Bill Quigley hoped to correct that situation in a matter of hours.

Traffic continued on the adjacent streets, many of the cars pulling up to discharge newsmen, photographers, and some of the city officials of Winnebago. A number of police vehicles had been parked at strategic locations; no one was quite sure how large a crowd might be attracted, so the proper precautions were in effect to guard against any incidents. Expectancy was everywhere.

On the floor of the big gymnasium Dr. Harley Poindexter went rapidly from group to group to be sure that all was well. He shook hands wherever it seemed to be indicated and made sure that the placement of each delegation was correct according to the plan that had been chalked out on the floor. At five minutes to ten he at last sought out his own position at the beginning of the line of march. Waiting for him was Philip Roundtree, attired in the scarlet Convocation robes of a bishop of the Church of England. Harley took one more look at him and was glad that he had, quite literally, put his money on this man.

"Two minutes, ladies and gentlemen." The words echoed from the public address system in the ceiling. In response there was a shuffle of movement, a general lining up of people in the exact places where they knew that they ought to be. Fifteen selected members of the Maplewood choir, in their robes, took their places at the head of the major delegations to carry the symbolic standards the Art Department had prepared. That simple arrangement eliminated any questions of protocol as to who would have the honor within each delegation.

When everything was finally ready there was a pause. For a single full minute everyone stood relatively still waiting for the signal to be given. Then, exactly at ten o'clock, the doors of the gymnasium were swung open.

Harley Poindexter turned to the man beside him. "All right, Philip," he said. "Here is your convocation. It's all yours and may God guide you."

"Amen," Philip answered. His features seemed almost fixed for a moment as though he was gathering himself, then Harley saw that his lips were moving very slightly. Presently he ceased and looked toward his host. "Thank you," he added.

The standard bearer ahead of him stepped out to be greeted by the bright sunlight. As soon as he was through the doorway he raised the cross he was carrying and moved forward at a measured pace. Behind him Harley Poindexter came, with Philip Roundtree beside him. As soon as the bright light of day surrounded them Poindexter sensed a change in his friend the bishop from England: confidence and resolution had taken hold of him. The campus was well filled with people, but the processional route, as far as he could tell, had been kept clear.

With the same pace that was being set by the standard bearer before him, Harley walked with Philip across the grass toward the chapel auditorium. He was aware of the many cameras that were being clicked in his direction, but he knew that the intended subject was not himself. As he passed one of the portable TV film units he turned his head and smiled his assurance half toward the lens. That was not for himself or for the college, it was for Philip.

Arthur Gravenstine could almost smell the ink on the front page once again, but to his credit he was thinking only of the great event that he was witnessing and his responsibility to cover it fully and in detail. This was real news; it could be news of overwhelming importance — but it would take a future generation to determine that. He had no illusions about the possible success of the meeting, but the physical fact of its existence was in itself a major achievement.

He stood at his chosen spot, one where he could see the full length of the procession but close to the doors of the chapel-auditorium so that he could be inside easily when the moment came. He was surprised that there was no music; then he realized the difficulty of finding anything truly suitable to play. *Pomp and Circumstance*, perhaps, but that had been worn threadbare long ago. He was still searching for an answer when the college carillon began to sound over the campus. That was the perfect solution, of course; the chiming of the bells fitted the occasion, the hour, and the purpose of the gathering. The rich tones came out in harmony, but he could not identify any recognizable melody. The strength and fullness of the reverberations were enough in themselves, they rang out a message in a universal language which no single faith could claim for its own.

He waited where he was until the head of the procession reached him and he could see how splendidly Philip Round-tree was leading the long assembly with the American college president beside him. Then he turned and hurried to the entrance to the auditorium. They knew him well by then and he did not have to show his press pass, although he already had it waiting in his hand. He went inside and this time he did hear music; the organ was being played, sounding its voice in preparation for welcoming those who were approaching and who were now almost within hearing.

He stood in the lobby, caught up despite himself in the drama of the moment, listening to the organ and waiting for the people who were coming. They were just people after all, with common hopes, needs, desires, passions, and aspirations. A shadow came into the lobby and a moment later the cross bearer entered, still at the same stately pace. With formal steps he turned toward the auditorium entrance, passed through, and started down the aisle. Then came Philip and Harley Poindexter, splendidly dignified as they too turned and passed into the auditorium.

Behind them followed a very long bloc of Christian congregations before the Star of David could be seen coming, and behind it another standard which was still too far away for him to make it out.

To the swelling music of the organ the delegates came in, some marching, others merely moving along, a few pausing to wait until the space immediately ahead of them had cleared. Superficially it was a large group of people ceremoniously entering a building to listen to some formal speeches, but it gained stature from the fact that its members came from all over the world and represented almost every major facet of humanity. To Arthur Gravenstine it was momentous, and that was how he proposed to describe it in print. As the Church of England four-man delegation passed slowly through the lobby, he noted that the Most

Reverend Frederick Danford-Sm th had seen fit to dispatch a bishop to give it added weight and dignity.

It was five minutes to eleven when the last of the delegates entered the auditorium to be followed by the remaining members of the Maplewood choir, who with proper dignity moved forward and took their places on the stage. When all was ready a baton was raised, the organ played a few introductory measures, and the choir in full voice began to sing an anthem of welcome which the Music Department had prepared especially for the occasion. It was not profound music, but when the singers had finished there was hesitant and then generous applause.

Dr. Harley Poindexter stepped to the rostrum and with a hundred and fifty words offered the formal welcome of the college. He then introduced Philip Roundtree.

In the balcony Janet leaned forward to hear what her husband was going to say. She sensed that this was the greatest moment of his life and she knew that he must be experiencing the feeling of inspiration that was reaching her too. Below, in a motionless parade of long rows of seats, sat the men and women who had come here from the far parts of the world in answer to the call that he had sent out, and now he was about to speak to them.

Then she heard Philip's voice, fully controlled but deeply imbued with unmistakable sincerity. "We have gathered here so that we may learn from one another and in so doing discover how better we may serve all of humanity. We have in common the knowledge that there exists a greater Power than we can see with our own eyes or experience with any other of our material senses. We seek to find and serve this Authority in many different ways, but inevitably we do stand together upon some common ground. To define it, and to magnify it so that our brotherhood may be enriched and solidified, is our mission."

He did not speak very long. For perhaps three or four minutes his words seemed to flow as though they were shaping themselves into a near perfect order of their own. When he had finished and the applause was over, Dr. Poindexter came forward once more and proposed the election of a permanent chairman for the convocation. He suggested that the delegates consider the matter until the next meeting, at which time nominations could be advanced from the floor.

There was a few seconds' pause when he had finished, then in almost the middle of the auditorium a slender dark-skinned man rose to his feet. One of the ushers hurried toward him with a cordless microphone. The delegate spoke in a soft sibilant voice characteristic of much of central India. "Such contemplation is hardly necessary," he said. "In coming here we have all expressed our confidence in the Right Reverend Dr. Roundtree. I propose that he is the only man we would wish to consider."

As he sat down there was applause; as it subsided a delegate near to the front stood up, accepted a microphone, and spoke in accented but well-formed words. "On behalf of the followers of Master Kung, I wish to second the choice of Dr. Roundtree."

Arthur Gravenstine was ecstatic. Roundtree had been nominated by a Hindu and seconded by a Confucian — both representing powerful non-Christian groups. When he heard the Southern Baptists also second the nomination he took note of it, but the news lay in the fact that the Church of England bishop had been given his due by some who, under different circumstances, might have wanted to advance their own candidates. From his seat in the rear he left the auditorium quietly and once through the door hurried toward the press room. He was too good a newspaperman to file before he was certain of his facts, but he lost no time in rolling paper into a typewriter and beginning his story. It would take him a good half hour to write it, and if the verdict wasn't in by that time, he could hold it until Roundtree's election was definite.

He was still at his machine when Philip Roundtree was

indeed chosen permanent chairman; if there were any who did not approve of the selection they did not make themselves known.

In that climate Dr. Poindexter read from the many telegrams, cables and other communications wishing the conference the best of good fortune. With a clear conscience he ignored the considerable number he had received that vented feelings from discontent to outrage. The majority of them stated that by entertaining any religious ideas other than those found in the Bible, the sponsors of the convocation had committed mortal sin. Mixed in with the general accumulation there were three threats of violent action, which had been turned over to the proper authorities.

The constructive messages took almost an hour to get through, but of those chosen to be read none could have been safely ignored. When it was at last all over, and a few announcements had been made, the first session was formally adjourned. It took another forty-five minutes for Philip to manage to get out of the auditorium; the number of persons who wished to speak with him seemingly was legion. True to his profession and his training, he greeted everyone with unabated enthusiasm and listened to fifty different suggestions — all of which he weighed as best he could on the spot. When at last he was able to go for a late lunch, he had the curious feeling that he was both exhausted and exhilarated at the same time. He was halfway to the Student Union when he was intercepted by Ames, who apparently had managed to locate him without any loss of dignity in the process.

"I beg pardon, M'Lord, Sir Cyril extends his compliments and suggests that perhaps you would like to take luncheon with him at his temporary residence."

"I'd be delighted, of course," Philip said.

"Excellent; the car is right over here, sir."

Barely five minutes later Philip was ushered into the presence. Sir Cyril rose to greet him and then led the way to a temporary bar which had been installed in a corner of the living room. "The facilities here are quite limited," he declared, "but the potables meet the requirements. Your pleasure?"

To have declined would have been out of the question and Philip knew it. "Perhaps a light whisky and soda," he suggested.

At a nod from Sir Cyril, Ames stepped behind the bar and functioned with smooth professional efficiency. As he was doing so, Philip put a question that had been in his mind. "Knowing the strength of your financial position, Sir Cyril, I have been wondering casually if you are related, so to speak, to the famous Plessey company back home."

"The aerospace people? No — a distant branch of the family perhaps, but I rather doubt it. Cheers."

Philip accepted the glass handed to him and found it more welcome than he had anticipated. He was only concerned that his breath might reveal his indulgence and he made a mental note to do something about it before he appeared once more on campus. His host seemed reluctant to engage in minor conversation; that being the case he remained quiet himself and reviewed in his mind the events of the morning. He was composed, but at the same time he was aware that the summons from Sir Cyril was for a purpose; his mind would be more at rest when he knew what it was.

Presently they sat down to eat. Philip did not know the source of the food and he did not speculate on it; it was of excellent quality, as he had expected that it would be, and that was enough. His host ate with a certain gusto until the first edge of his appetite had been satisfied, then he looked up and wiped his lips with his napkin.

"Philip," Sir Cyril began, "I wanted to talk with you a little about the session this morning. I was there, of course; Poindexter has been kind enough to arrange a permanent place for me in the front row of the balcony."

"By all means, sir," Philip said.

"It was all very fine and splendid in there and everyone behaved in a suitably civilized manner. They probably will continue to do so for another two or three days, then the lid will blow off and you had better be prepared for it when it does."

Sir Cyril glanced at his drink, which was slightly more than half consumed, and Ames removed it at once for refilling. "To continue: I know these people, not the various Christian sects which have largely come from other parts of the States, but the overseas crowd. I've lived with them, slept with them, caroused with them, eaten their food, and I understand them. There's an important difference and you ought to know it. I can put it to you in one sentence: we have a religion, at least most of us do, but they live theirs. Morning, noon, and night — they can't forget it for five minutes. It's bred into them until it becomes part of their being."

Philip nodded his understanding. His host paused while he was supplied with a fresh drink. He tested it and then resumed.

"Now it's got to change or we'll all end up eating each other and claim that we're serving God in the process. Things were relatively all right when the world was divided up into hundreds of different regions and traffic between them was at a minimum, but those times will never come back."

He ate a little from his plate with undisturbed relish and then returned to the topic at hand. "I know, Philip, that you're aware of much of this, but being aware of it isn't the same thing as sitting out in the middle of the desert with a bunch of Arabs and experiencing for yourself how much the Prophet means to them and how much their lives are wrapped up in their faith. It's an obsession. Or go to a Hindu temple and study the carvings — those that aren't too strong for your tastes. Visit the Buddhist caves at Ajanta;

you won't believe what you see. Tens of thousands of men labored there with primitive tools for three hundred years to complete the job. *Three hundred years*, Philip, twelve whole generations carving out the living rock to honor the Lord Buddha! Our people have built cathedrals, of course, but nothing like those. Imagine uncounted thousands of men, generation after generation, lying on their backs and hacking away at the living rock with chisels and hammers. With dust filling their lungs and the blackness of the excavations they were making all around them except for what elementary lighting they could rig with oil lamps or whatever else they had. A mob of them probably died of silicosis, but when one of them gave up the ghost they carried him out and someone else took his place. They kept at it because of unshakable religious determination and conviction. Their successors are out there now; they've come to your meeting."

"What do you want me to do?" Philip asked.

"Respect them, Philip, respect them! And allow for the depth of their beliefs. Treat them as they deserve to be treated and remember that if some of the things they do and believe in seem downright ridiculous to us, they don't understand a God either who is supposed to be all-powerful and all-merciful, but who still allowed His only Son to be put to death by frightful torture just so that a prophesy some soothsayer had given could be fulfilled. You wouldn't do it and they wouldn't either — not on those terms."

Philip did not answer. This was the man who had promised him that the conference would not fail, yet who perhaps more than anyone else understood the obstacles that blocked the way. He saw it all for what it was — a warning not to weaken when the barrage began. As he picked up his fork once more he inwardly renewed his private resolve that no matter what happened, he would keep his feet under him and try to find the way.

He was back in his office when, at shortly after three, a small delegation arrived to see him. He was not expecting anyone, but when his visitors were shown in he rose at once to greet them. A single glance told him that the three of them were Muslims; their headdresses indicated that. He searched his facile memory and found what he wanted.

"*Salaam aleikum,*" he said.

His visitors bowed in unison. "*Salaam aleikum.*"

Philip motioned toward chairs, but his guests elected to remain standing. The tallest of them, an imposing figure with a full white beard, spoke for the group. "You understand Arabic, Dr. Roundtree?"

Philip shook his head slightly. "I greatly regret I have yet to learn it. Please forgive me."

The spokesman looked down somewhat so that their eyes could meet. "There is nothing to forgive," he said. "We are honored that you greet us as brothers."

"Thank you."

The formalities for the moment concluded, the tall Arab came to the point. "As you may know, it is necessary for the faithful to pray at five stated times each day."

Philip nodded. "At sunrise, noon, during the afternoon, at sunset and two hours after sunset."

"I was misinformed," the spokesman said. "I was told that unbelievers knew nothing of Islam."

"We know very little, but we strive to learn."

For a moment the tall man seemed to be taken aback, then he almost visibly composed himself. "You have made our errand much simpler," he stated carefully. "As you will know, it is customary for the muezzin to sound the call to prayer from the minaret at the stated times. More recently we have become practical and have installed loudspeakers. It is much simpler, easier to hear, and some elderly men are spared a long climb several times each day."

"A very prudent idea," Philip said.

125

"Thank you. You will now foresee our request. We have inquired from Mr. Chalmers and have learned that the bell tower here is equipped with such a system; it can be heard through all of the grounds. We ask if it would be possible for us to make use of it; there is one with us who is qualified to summon to prayer."

Philip thought very rapidly. "I will ask Dr. Poindexter to try to arrange for this," he declared. "Unless there is some problem I know nothing of, I believe that it can be done."

The bearded man bowed once more. "You are most understanding. On behalf of the faithful of Islam, I thank you. What you have done will not be forgotten."

As Philip said the proper things and showed his guests out, he already had in his mind the possibility that others would be coming with individual requests of their own. Some of them might be all but impossible to agree to, but he would have to cross those bridges when he came to them. He realized that sunrise was a very early hour in the morning, but perhaps there was a little latitude in the requirement and the summons could be given somewhat nearer to the breakfast hour. He passed his hand across his forehead and hoped that everything would be all right.

The Reverend Aubrey Fothergill, for a man of his years, knew a reasonable amount about women; furthermore, he was not innocent of their more compelling potentialities. He had not always been a representative of the Church of England; during the days of his earlier youth he had had a normal number of sex experiences and had enjoyed them all. Consequently he was not particularly awed by the presence of Jayawardene Thiengburanathum or, for that matter, by her name either. She was a female very obviously, she was certainly attractive enough for any man who had eyes in his head, and her intelligence merited respect. So much for the factual inventory: the other ingredient, which he could not define, caused him to be more interested in her than would

126

have been the case if it had not been present. There was definitely something about that girl that had caused him to lie on his back in bed long after he had retired and stare up toward the ceiling.

In the morning the thought was still present. Since he was a thoroughly practical man, as he shaved he asked himself quite candidly if it was simply his ambition to take her to bed because of the exceptional promise she seemed to offer in that direction. If so, then he had better snap out of it. His present position required him to conduct himself in an exemplary manner and he had no intention of doing otherwise. Loaded as the United States was with most acceptable young women, some of whom already seemed to him to be approachable on intimate matters of mutual interest, it would have to be hands off as long as he was in the conspicuous position of being chaplain to the man who was the head of the entire convocation. Plus which, he had his position to maintain as an ordained priest. The only unfortunate thing was that the fact of ordination did not make him any less a man or take from him the basic motivations that had been implanted by the God whom he worshipped and served.

He completed his toilet, congratulating himself on having recovered his equilibrium; then he went to breakfast, saw her, and felt a peculiar pounding in his chest as he helped himself to scrambled eggs and bacon.

Damn the woman, what was it about her?

"Good morning," he said as he approached her table.

She looked up and smiled. It was not a very substantial action, but it startled him; he was suddenly aware that he had never seen her smile before. And as she did, it made her seem almost radiant.

He decided to put her to the test at once. He seated himself and then asked, "Do you mind if I ask a blessing for the food?"

"Of course not; I did."

127

That didn't make matters any easier. He bowed his head and silently spoke the words of gratitude; for the food and for all of the other gifts at hand, and then looked up once more. "Did you rest well?" he asked.

"Yes, very well. I have a nice room and a nice roommate — a girl from Taiwan." Her lips quirked a little impishly for a moment. "Not quite as interesting as the first roommate I was assigned."

Somehow that remark sent him soaring. He knew immediately that her English, while excellent, was a foreign language to her and therefore he must not read into it nuances that were not intended; nevertheless, it took him a few seconds to dismiss the provocative suggestion from his mind.

"What are you going to do today?" There was no session; for some religious reason he did not recall, one could not be held.

"I have no plans."

Aubrey considered for a moment, then he spoke with some caution. "Perhaps if I could get hold of a car from the motor pool we might drive around a bit. That is, if Dr. Roundtree does not require my presence. If he does, then of course . . ."

"Why don't you ask him? He is seated three tables behind you, with some people from India I believe."

Philip Roundtree thought it a very good idea for his chaplain to spend some time getting acquainted with those of other faiths who were in attendance. He knew that Aubrey had been working hard and a day off might be a good thing for him.

Aubrey thought so too. He returned to his place and deliberately tried a forkful of the eggs; they had turned cold, but for the first time he did not care. "I'm free," he announced. "If I can get a car, would you care to spend the day in my company?"

She studied him for a moment, then quite deliberately

she folded her hands underneath her chin. "It could make people talk," she said.

He was equal to that. "In our Christian theology we have a place called hell, have you heard of it?"

"Oh yes, I have."

"I think that it was designed, in part at least, as a home for those who stick their noses into other people's business."

She laughed, lightly and with real amusement. "This I admire about your religion," she said. "I shall accept your offer. Allow me, please, a little while to get ready."

As Harley Poindexter came to work early in the morning of that same day, he was in a cheerful and constructive mood. He had accomplished a considerable amount of thinking overnight and had reached certain decisions with which he was very much satisfied. Before he went to his office he stopped in to see the telephone operator and gave her some instructions. "Madeleine, I expect that we may be getting quite a few calls today regarding the conference."

"Dr. Poindexter — no doubt!"

"Try to get a line on the calls as they come in. I know you can do that very well. Those that seem to be general complaints or crank calls, put through to me. In particular, try to see that Bishop Roundtree isn't bothered with anything of that kind; he has enough on his mind as it is."

Madeleine flashed him a quick smile. "I understand, sir; I'll do my best."

That taken care of, Harley climbed the broad steps up to his office and from there phoned the mail room with similar instructions. By eleven, if he had been in any mood to do so, he could have congratulated himself on his foresight. The opening of the conference had been well covered in the press, so much so that the name of Maplewood College had been publicized more than at any time in its long history. That, of course, was to the good. But the press reports appeared to have inspired a near tidal wave of reaction from a variety of groups and individuals who held strong religious views of their own. There was a small deluge from the Bible Belt and, considering the fact that it was only Monday, much more could be anticipated.

A remarkable number of the mail communications came by special delivery. Some of them demanded that the conference be disbanded at once. The word "heathen" appeared with almost startling regularity, so much so that Harley Poindexter paused in his work to lean back and think for a few moments.

Technically the word had two meanings. First, it stood for any person who did not acknowledge the Christian and Jewish God, the God of the Bible. By that standard the Muslims were not heathens, but the Buddhists were. Secondly, it could be applied to any irreligious person. But that didn't hold water as far as the conference was concerned, because everyone attending was definitely interested in one form or another of religion. The atheists had asked for credentials, but he had politely declined on the grounds that this meeting would be entirely based on a pro-religious viewpoint.

There, was, therefore, a third meaning of the word, one which was probably not reflected in the dictionary. Being an educator, he took a moment to look it up and found that he had been correct. The third, invisible meaning was pure prejudice — someone who does not believe as I do. The Buddhists, on that basis, would have a perfect right to call the Christians heathens and perhaps they did.

His secretary interrupted him to inform him that a delegation was waiting for him outside. Her voice was expressionless as she delivered the message, but her face added volumes. Duly warned, he told her to invite the people in.

They came. There were, as far as he could tell, two families of them and they seemed to have come from some rural area, perhaps the Ozarks. They entered the long office a little as though they were in unaccustomed surroundings, but then came forward, and stood before his desk apparently fortified by some inner force.

Their spokesman was a tall, rawboned man who did not appear to have a spare ounce of flesh on his body. He was dressed in a suit, but every movement of his body betrayed the fact that it was not his accustomed garb. The faded woman beside him was obviously his wife; that was all that Harley had time to take in before the man spoke to him. "You'll be Dr. Poindexter?"

Harley greeted his visitors and indicated chairs. There were not enough to go around; a quick count advised him that he had eleven individuals — adults and children. Two women and a man did sit down, the spokesman remained on his feet. With instincts sharpened through years of practice, Harley Poindexter sensed that these were sincere people, that they were here on a peaceful errand, and that for the moment at least they were not mad at anyone. He offered the spokesman his hand and said, "Yes, I'm Dr. Poindexter."

"We come to see you," the lanky man continued, "because of this meetin' you're havin'. About different kinds of religions."

"I'm glad that you did," Harley responded. "Please tell me what I can do for you."

"Well, I'm Deacon Hobbs and this here is Elder Marcy. We come here all the way from Kentucky to tell you about the power of the Bible."

"It's a very great book," Harley said.

The response came quickly. "Oh, it's more than that! It's the guidepost for livin' and the cure for almost anythin' that can ail ye. And that's somethin' we can prove. We been provin' it for some time."

"I'm interested," Poindexter admitted.

"We call our church the Power of the Bible; maybe you've heard of us."

Slowly Harley shook his head. "I'm sure that I should have, but for the moment I can't recall. Will you refresh my memory?"

"Sure, if you want. You see the Bible can perfect you, or anyone else, if you believe in it enough. And that's what we prove. When we have a full service, that's when we use the snakes."

"Snakes?"

"Yep, rattlesnakes, and they ain't doped or nothin' either. When our meetin' is going good and we know that the Spirit is in us, then we bring in the snakes and play with 'em like they was family pets. We know that we ain't gonna get bit and we don't get bit. When our youngest was six months old we brought him to the church and put a rattler right there in the bed with him, and that snake he didn't do nothin' — we had the faith and that's all that it took. Mark sixteen eighteen, 'They will pick up serpents . . .' "

Then Harley Poindexter remembered; it had been in the papers or in one of the news magazines. "Now I recall your church," he said. "Pardon my asking, but didn't you have an accident a year or so ago? A child was bitten or something like that."

Marcy spoke up; he was a quiet man who seemed content to allow others to do the talking, but this time the response was properly his. "That was our daughter," he declared, "and she died for her sins. The snake tempted her like the snake did in the Garden of Eden — that's where we got the idea. She didn't believe; she got frightened and she cried and the snake he bit her. It was the Lord's will and a powerful lesson for us all."

"We know we got the truth," Hobbs continued, "so we came to help. We're all set to show everybody, even those heathens from across the seas."

Now that he was part of the conversation, Marcy took up his share. "We brought our snakes with us an' anybody can see that they're real lively ones. So whenever you're ready, we'll hold a service and learn the heathens to believe in the Bible. Either that or they git bit, and then it's good-bye heaven." He stopped because he had no more to say.

Harley Poindexter desperately needed time to think, but for once his agile intellect refused to generate an idea. He pressed the button for help. When his secretary responded he took the only way out that would come to him. "Please call Professor Moriarty and ask him if he can come over here right away. We have some guests who will require special attention."

"Right away, Dr. Poindexter."

A young man who might have been nineteen and who had been hovering in Elder Marcy's orbit cleared his throat and gave speech. "What'd ya say that guy's name was?"

"Professor Moriarty."

"Somehow I heard that name, an' as I recall it wasn't too good."

"Oh, Professor Moriarty is all right — he's been with us for some time."

"I guess if you say so."

When the head of the Political Science Department arrived, he had somehow been briefed. Without requiring further explanations, he ushered the representatives of the Power of the Bible out of the office and took them into his charge. When the room was once more clear, Poindexter for a moment regretted his own rule that distilled beverages were not allowed on campus. It was still morning, but he could have used a mild bracer.

He looked at his calendar and discovered that it offered him a respite — it was the day of his Optimist luncheon. With a quick surge of gratitude for the opportunity to be off campus for an hour and a half, he cleared away an additional detail or two and then walked briskly out of his office. Minutes later he was in his car and on his way downtown. His conscience pricked him slightly as he drove away from the scene of so much accumulating action, but there were

133

others well qualified to deal with the reasonable contingencies that might arise during his absence.

As soon as the campus area was well behind him he began to feel noticeably better. The pressure had begun to tell more than he had realized, he discovered, as he breathed in the good clean air and savored the thought of the pleasant summer that surrounded him. His spirits repaired themselves rapidly as he drove; within a few blocks he was almost back to normal. He parked by permission on the First Presbyterian Church lot and cut through the back toward the restaurant where the local civic leaders would be assembling to forget their own responsibilities as well. He emerged from the shortcut onto the main business street and almost at once detected something new.

For some weeks there had been a vacant storefront where a dry cleaner had been located. It was vacant no longer; a hastily painted sign proclaimed OFFICIAL SOUVENIRS in the largest letters that the available space would permit. The rest of the display area was devoted to such legends as *The Only Official Souvenirs of the World Religious Conference* and *Exotic Imports from All Parts of the World*.

Harley could not help himself, he had to look. One glance at the show window told him that the merchandise offered was almost all cheap and gaudy. There were some plaster statues of Catholic saints, an assortment of what appeared to be papier-mâché Buddhas in different sizes, and in the background a group of seminude female figurines made of some sort of flesh-colored plastic.

Dr. Poindexter stepped inside and was immediately confronted by a salesman. "Something for you?" he was asked.

"Yes," Harley answered. "Why do you advertise these as *official* souvenirs of the conference?"

"Because that's our name — we're the Official Souvenir and Import Company. We got a right to do business under our corporate name."

"That you have." He didn't like to say that because he

134

was endorsing a deception, or so it seemed to him, but unfortunately it was the truth.

"Then one more question: why are you offering those dolls?" He pointed.

The salesman shrugged. "This is a novelty store," he answered. "We give the public what it wants." His manner softened and he became a trifle confidential. "It's a nice little item — lots of fun. Put one on the bar. You see, you can lift up the apron if you want to and it's all there."

"Interesting," Harley said, "but hardly part of the conference."

Once more the salesman lifted his shoulders and let them fall. "So what, they move and they move good. And there's a tie-in. They got a lot of people up there from all over the place and these are made up to look like Arab dancing girls. We got some Chinese ones coming in. You like a good joke?"

"When it's funny, I certainly do."

"Then drop in early next week; we've got some 'Confucius say' booklets on the way and take it from me, they're rare. Picture of a long-bearded Chink on the cover so it fits. 'Confucius say: girl pilot who fly upside down have crack up.' Lots more like that. Only a buck."

Harley made a grim attempt to smile. "I'll be back," he promised, but even as he spoke the words, he sensed that he could do nothing and that this was, in all probability, only the forerunner of what was to come.

When he reached the restaurant he broke a long-standing rule and went immediately to the bar.

CHAPTER ELEVEN

The serious young Buddhist who had been looking for the Right Reverend Dr. Philip Roundtree found him in the Pit surrounded by half a dozen students who were paying him close attention. He hovered in the background until he was noticed and then delivered his message. "Bishop Roundtree, Your Grace, sir, the Venerable Kim would like to speak with you."

Philip got to his feet. "I hope nothing has gone wrong," he said.

"Oh no, sir, quite the contrary."

"Where is the venerable one?"

"He awaits you at our chapel; we have just completed it."

As Philip left the building he found the air almost winy; overhead a high moon hung above a pallet of drifting clouds that covered and uncovered its face with slow patterns of light and shadow. Then, out of the semidarkness, a perfumed, minor key sound began to echo around them, a sound made by a human voice, but it was disembodied, unseen, timeless, and ethereal. The intonations rose and fell, slow waves of strange cadence that might have come across the near eternal vastness of space.

The Buddhist stopped. "I do not understand," he said.

"It is the Muslim call to prayer," Philip declared. He had never heard it before either, but he knew it could be nothing else.

The Buddhist was impressed. "Do you also know the mantras, sir?"

Philip shook his head. "I still have much to learn," he confessed. With his guide he continued on into the Science Hall, where a classroom had been made available to the Buddhist delegation. He was quite sure what to expect, but when he was ushered inside, he was moved by what he saw. The people who had prepared the chapel had brought with them a surprising quantity of drapes, altar objects, and minor images. Sticks of incense that had been thrust into a sand pot sent up thin silent threads of smoke. All this Philip saw, but his attention was held by a compelling image of the seated Buddha a good seven feet tall. It had been placed on a kind of dais that raised it up until the top of the head was close to the ceiling. The face of the statue was hypnotic; the features seemed to be disassociated from the realities of place and time; instead they reflected an almost inhuman serenity and repose. The eyes looked at nothing, yet they saw everything. Before the compelling sculpture the incense smoke continued to drift upward, a silent homage of delicate eloquence.

For a bare moment Philip thought he ought to bow his head, then he was startled by the thought that he had almost paid homage to a graven image. A moment later he saw that an elderly man in saffron robes was there and waiting to speak to him.

"Good evening, My Lord Bishop, it is so kind and gracious of you to visit us." There was a liquid intonation to the words, but the language was flawless.

"I am honored by your invitation."

The Venerable Kim turned and picked up a stick of incense. "Will you honor us by lighting this?" He held it out.

To have refused would have given intolerable offense. Gravely Philip took the slender shaft and lit the tip by holding it to one of the already burning sticks. When it was ready and glowing, he pushed it into position into the sand, silently asking forgiveness as he did so.

"I shall this evening recite for you the prayer of Jesus," Kim said. "I was taught it many years ago by a missionary." He turned around and picked up a newspaper which he held for Philip to see.

It was one of the major papers of Midwestern America. In the very center of the front page was a large drawing done in the best style of journalistic illustration. Across the top was the heading *Great Religions of the World*; underneath, the artist had done a sensitively shaded drawing of a seated Buddha quite similar to the image which dominated the temporary chapel. The caption read: *Gautama Siddhartha (563–483 B.C.), the Buddha, in meditation.*

"We are so delighted," Kim said. "It is a magnificent tribute. The phrase *'the* Buddha' is incorrect as you know, but that is of no importance. And the hands of the Blessed One are not in meditation, but in the position of forbidding his relatives to quarrel, but the intent, the spirit, is a source of great joy. We are now most happy that we have come to attend your gathering."

Philip found the right words to say, then he excused himself and returned to the Pit. As he crossed the campus once more the spirit of good will seemed to abound and he was decidedly uplifted, even when he found that his little group was gone. Instead, his chaplain was there staring grimly into what appeared to be a cup of tea. Philip walked over and asked, "Did you have a pleasant day?"

Aubrey looked up, his expression somewhat mixed. "I did indeed, sir, I'd like to speak with you about it."

As Philip seated himself he realized that he had acquired

a taste for a purely American product available in the Middle West. When the waitress arrived he said, "I'll have a malted."

"Chocolate, strawberry, cherry, boysenberry, or vanilla?"

"You decide."

"Strawberry coming up."

When the girl had left Philip turned his attention to his chaplain. "You wanted to talk about your day," he invited.

"We had a wonderful time, really," Aubrey began. "Jaydene knows how to conduct herself — she is a very refined person."

"I thought so too."

Aubrey looked his superior squarely in the eye. "I found her more interesting than any girl I've ever met."

"She's undeniably very attractive; I'm not so far along life's path to be unaware of that."

"Thank you, sir."

"Then, Aubrey, she is a very exotic individual. Her features, her background, and her faith too contribute to a certain aura no one could miss." Philip leaned forward a little. "There is one more thing that I might mention entirely off the record. You are a young man in the full flower of virility and she is, I rather judge, a very potent female. Presumably all of them are, but Miss . . . I'm sorry, I just can't recall her name."

"Thiengburanathum."

"You just called her something else."

"Jaydene — it's her first name shortened. In Thailand they all go by first names anyway."

"Let's call her Jaydene then, I can handle that. As I was about to say, while Jaydene is obviously exceedingly well bred and mannered, she is still quite a superheated young lady — inevitably much of the appeal she undoubtedly has is biological in nature. No criticism is implied, of course. Your personal life is not my proper concern."

Aubrey chose to change the topic slightly. "Since we

were spending the day together, I tried my hand at a little missionary work. After I talked a bit she agreed to learn the Ten Commandments. I thought of the Beatitudes, but they might be too complicated for her at the beginning."

"That was very gracious of her, but did she suggest anything in return?"

"Well, yes — she proposed that I learn the Eightfold Path, which was a reasonable concession, I thought."

"How did it go?"

"The Commandments didn't take her five minutes — I have a suspicion she already knew them. When she asked about their origin, I explained that they came, through Moses, from God Himself."

"Which is true, of course."

"Yes, but then she asked me, if that was the case, why God wasn't a better writer. She pointed out that two of the Commandments are totally redundant, and surely He could do better than that."

The waitress arrived with the malted milk; Philip tried it and was refreshed. "I would be interested in knowing how you answered that," he said.

"I copped out — I suggested that she go ahead with the Eightfold Path."

"Did you?"

Aubrey nodded. "Right understanding, right purpose, right speech, right conduct, right vocation, right effort, right alertness, right concentration."

They sat in silence for a short while; then when he felt that the moment was right, Philip put a question. "Are you getting interested in this young lady?"

Aubrey took his time. "Let me put it this way: some day I want to be married, to have a home of my own and a family. I've only known Jaydene a very short while, but if the British girl I'm destined to marry is able to top her, it will take one helluva lot of doing."

Philip was not certain what if anything he should say. It

would ruin Aubrey's career in the Church if he were to take a wife of another faith, unless, of course, he converted her in the process. His chaplain was a very determined, not to say stubborn young man, but there was still a serious doubt that he could accomplish a complete conversion of Miss Jaydene Whateverhernamewas within a reasonable length of time. Unless — like a dawn flaming in the sky — the conference were to succeed completely. But the prospects of that, he already knew, were beyond attainment.

The first difficulties surfaced almost as soon as he opened the meeting the following morning. He had one even before he began; he had called the session for nine, but he was informed that the Sikhs were still engaged in their compulsory recitations from the Ad-Granth and would not be available to attend until they had finished.

Philip had planned to set up some committee chairmanships as a first organizational step, dividing the honors so that all of the major religions would be fairly represented. This had seemed safe and simple, but when the Sikhs finally appeared and he was able to start, he discovered some immediate roadblocks.

The first major committee on his list was the one on procedures; he announced the topic and then proposed that a Muslim be chosen to chair it. A few seconds of silence passed, then a white-robed delegate rose to ask him which of the two major branches of Islam he proposed to honor.

He had no ready answer for that and invited discussion. After ten minutes he was forced to cut it off; to pacify things he quickly suggested that a chairman be chosen instead for the committee on worship services. Because the followers of Gautama were notably tolerant, he suggested that a Buddhist might be an appropriate choice. The words were no sooner out of his mouth then he remembered too late that Buddhism had three major divisions and once again he had failed to specify.

This time the floor discussion went on for twenty minutes and he was all but powerless to stop it. He was rescued by a Methodist named Peasley, who moved that the matter be tabled for the moment.

Philip tried once more. There remained one major appointment; he proposed to the assembly that a Shintoist be chosen. Shinto, he was certain, was an undivided religion, and the Japanese had sent a liberal number of delegates to support his cause.

He had five seconds of peace; then someone from Jehovah's Witnesses rose and demanded to know why a Christian bishop was proposing for this important post a man who didn't believe in God. Before that could erupt a Jain rose to declare that the hour for morning prayer had come and requested a ten-minute break for the purpose of worship. With gratitude Philip granted the request and announced that coffee and doughnuts were available in the lobby; he quickly added that for the benefit of the Mormons, who were forbidden coffee, hot chocolate had also been provided.

He left the stage to find Sir Cyril Plessey waiting for him in the wings. The elderly nobleman wasted no time. "Philip," he said as soon they were together, "forgive me, but you're coming a cropper."

"I know," Philip agreed. "And it was my own fault."

Sir Cyril brushed that aside. "Allow me to make a suggestion. State your preferences if you wish, but then ask the delegations to get together and notify you of their choices. That puts the monkey on their backs."

"Good," Philip said.

"Also, you're showing splendid freedom from Christian bias, but they can't understand it. Don't be afraid to support your own faith, they'll believe in you more if you do. It's like graft — in the Far East if you claim that you never touch a farthing no one will buy it. Say that you only take a very little and you'll be considered fearlessly honest."

142

"I appreciate your guidance, Sir Cyril."

"Purely experience, Philip. I couldn't deliver a sermon to save my immortal soul, but I do know people. What's the next order of business?"

"I want to ask each of the major faiths to make a presentation of their beliefs, then we'll have a discussion to find in which areas we may have some chance of agreement."

"Fine, but let them do the choosing, with a little steering of course. Bring up the subject and then ask the assembly who they would like to hear first. It's your best bet." He stopped when a girl appeared with coffee and doughnuts for two. Philip took his portion and was grateful for the stimulation of the hot beverage.

Ten minutes later Philip called the meeting to order and announced that each delegation would be asked to select its own candidates. Things began to improve, the strain eased, and some progress was made. By the time the session was concluded Philip was in a much heartened frame of mind and his energy seemed to have renewed itself. As the delegates filed out of the auditorium he sensed that the banquet, at least, was going to be a success.

For further respite he collected his wife, and in a motor pool car drove her out of Winnebago to a country restaurant to which he had been directed. Janet had a letter from Geoffrey which assured them that everything was fine at home and that the dog was well. Thoughts of the conference were laid aside for a little while; it seemed like the old days when Father Roundtree used to find time, every now and then, to take his bride out for a meal or tea together.

When they returned to Maplewood, Karen Erickson greeted them. "Did you hear about the snake people?" she asked.

"No," Philip said. "Please tell me."

Karen filled him in. "It looked like a problem, but Sir Cyril solved it."

"I'm beginning to have a very high opinion of Sir Cyril."

"Join the club. Anyhow, Sir Cyril told them that he had heard of them and that his greatest ambition was to see their demonstration with rattlesnakes. But when he had tried to arrange it, he had found that there was an ordinance forbidding dangerous animals inside the city limits, so it couldn't be done. Of course a snake isn't an animal, but anyhow they went away happy and seemed to feel that they'd been well treated. Sir Cyril promised to send for them if he could get the ordinance changed and he promised to pay all of the expenses."

"Karen," Philip said, "I wish that there was some way that Sir Cyril could become the chairman of this meeting."

"Not a prayer, Bishop Phil, you're elected. It's your baby and you've got to rock it. But with Sir Cyril running interference and calling some of the signals, I wouldn't worry too much. We're all behind you, you know that."

The student committee in charge of the banquet arrangements put in a hard day's work with gratifying results. The rather barren dining hall in the Student Union underwent a considerable transformation. Paper streamers were tacked up to create an attractive pattern overhead. The standards which had been prepared for the opening processional were mounted around the walls, each one set off with some further crepe paper decoration to give it added luster. The plain wooden tables were covered with cloths rented from a linen service, the commonplace glass tumblers were replaced with goblets, and even the well-worn silverware seemed to have a fresh sparkle. When all the work had been done, the dining hall had been so altered it was scarcely recognizable.

In the kitchen the staff assigned to M. Henri Devereux worked with a fresh enthusiasm; the chubby little French chef had taken hold with style, revealing an unexpected gift for inspiring the best efforts from his temporary staff. He was a born teacher and the largely student staff was quite willing to learn. As a result conditions in the kitchen could hardly have been better.

After considerable consultation a menu had been agreed upon which would be acceptable to the maximum number of those expected to attend. A copy was posted on the kitchen bulletin board, which was quite unnecessary as everyone there knew it perfectly by heart. Nevertheless, it did look well on the nicely printed folder that had been prepared. It read:

DINNER

Cream of Celery Soup, Maplewood
Roast Leg of Spring Lamb, Sauce Alsatian
or
Soufflé Vegetarian Especial
Creamed American Corn   Pomme Frites
Garden Salad
Baked Alaska
Wines if desired   Kosher version available

Lunch for the kitchen staff was a highly impromptu affair, all of the major effort being expended toward the evening meal. When a break was called the refrigerator doors were opened and the student staff made up sandwiches to individual taste from whatever was available. An exceptionally pretty girl spread peanut butter thickly on buttered fresh bread, garnished the result with pickle chips and stuffed green olives, and poured a glass of ice-cold milk. She looked up to see that the master of the kitchen was watching her. Without hesitation she presented him with her creation and announced, "It's for you, sir."

It was then that Monsieur Devereux showed the stuff of

which heroes are made; he accepted the offering with a gracious bow and without hesitation took a bite. The peanut butter stuck somewhat to the inside of his mouth; he washed it away with a swallow of the milk. To his refined palate the taste was far less than captivating, but it was not as bad as he had anticipated. By the time he had finished the sandwich, he allowed to himself that as an emergency meal under desperate circumstances, it was edible. And the cold milk, surprisingly, was not half bad. It chilled the taste buds, but it had a certain texture that at a very cold temperature was actually inviting.

He also received an unexpected tribute. as he consumed the last bite and licked a bit of the overflow from his fingers the kitchen staff gave him an impromptu cheer. Then everyone went back to work.

Dr. Joe Hastings, the Dean of the Chapel, was carrying his share of the load with skill and diplomacy. Nevertheless, toward midafternoon he felt compelled to call Dr. Poindexter to clear up a point or two.

"Harley," he began when he had the connection, "they're still coming in. The Mennonites arrived a few minutes ago, and quite frankly I didn't think they'd attend. But four of them have showed up. The latest entry is the Doukhobors — three of them who came down from Canada have just left my office."

"Those are the undressing people, aren't they?"

"Yes, we touched on that subject as I accepted their registration. We have a gentleman's agreement that they will do nothing to disrupt the proceedings. I had to let them in because they are a recognized church and they've been in existence for more than two hundred years."

"Of course. How is the seating holding out?"

"Oh, we have plenty of places left, but there is the question of bed space and dining arrangements. Also I'd like to know how the money's holding out."

Harley dropped his voice to a lower level. "So far so good. With all of the student help the payroll isn't too big and the Bixby funds haven't been badly hit so far. Also, Sir Cyril put up a considerable stake and we have that to go on too. Don't take this as a wide-open carte blanche, but so far we're not in any trouble."

"Good, because the end isn't really in sight. This could go on for another two or three weeks."

"No problem. If the time comes when we have to cut things off, we can explain then that time has run out for registration and issue passes to the visitors' balcony."

"O.K. Next, the Jains have been in to see me; they have lodged a formal protest against the serving of meat at the banquet tonight."

"I understand that a vegetarian dish is on the menu."

"Right, it is, but they don't want to sit down to patronize a function where the flesh of innocent animals is to be consumed. That's their words."

Poindexter thought for a second or two, then made his decision. "Of course we can't act on that for obvious reasons, but we can make a concession. Offer to provide them with a special table at which no meat will be served as a mark of respect to their convictions. I don't think they really intended to kibosh the dinner, they just wanted to make their position known."

"The Muslims want to be assured that no lard is being used in the cooking."

"Check with Devereux, but I'm quite certain that you're safe on that."

"I will. That's all for the moment."

"That's enough. Good luck, and keep me posted."

Hastings hung up. Outside the window of his office the white-garbed, shaven-headed Hare Krishna group was chanting loudly as it made its way down the street. He got up to watch for a moment, just to satisfy himself that all was well. As energetic as always, the group, made up mostly of American young people, was half dancing to the drum beat which guided the incessant repetition of *Hare Krishna, Hare Krishna, Krishna Krishna, Hare Hare; Hare Rama, Hare Rama, Rama Rama, Hare Hare*. Since it was part of their doctrine that the chanting be taken to the streets, they had been granted permission despite the general ban on demonstrations in the vicinity of the college during the conference.

His secretary came in. "There are some gentlemen to see you," she reported, but neither her voice nor her face gave him any clue.

"Show them in," he directed, and sat down.

Moments later he was facing a very tall man with high aquiline features and a skin color that told of a lifetime of exposure to the out-of-doors. Like his two companions he was simply dressed; his trousers were blue jeans, his jacket a windbreaker obviously designed for use rather than beauty. The only distinctive feature of his appearance was his straight, jet-black hair, which was held in place by a headband worn without affectation. Hastings stood up.

When the man spoke, Joe was surprised to discover that his English, while adequate, was accented and slightly irregular. It was also very terse and to the point. "You register for the religion meeting?"

"Yes, may I help you?"

"You can." The visitor's dignity was immense. "I am John Whitewolf; we have come from Arizona."

Joe was equal to that. "From which nation?"

"*Diné*. In English you call it Navajo."

Gravely Joe shook hands. "You are very welcome," he assured. "Are you representing a religious faith?"

"We are. Native American Church, the traditional belief of the Indian nations. We come because today our faith growing very fast, maybe fastest in the whole country."

Outside, the chanting of the Hare Krishna group was growing fainter as the small procession went down the street. Standing motionless on the sidewalk watching them was an Orthodox Jew in his traditional black garments and headgear, the two required little ringlets of hair in front of his ears. He shook his head with an air of profound sorrow and turned away.

At seven-thirty the banquet hall had received its final preparations. After careful discussion it had been decided not to make specific seating arrangements, a device which kept any delegation from feeling that it had been deliberately put far in the rear. Signs on three of the tables read *No meat* for the benefit of the Jains, some Hindus, and any others who followed vegetarian rules. When the doors were opened precisely at eight the delegates began to flow in and, as Sir Cyril had predicted, they seated themselves with a minimum of confusion. Some clearly preferred to sit toward the back, the Catholics among them; others were not reluctant to take front tables. After twelve minutes, when the room was full, Harley Poindexter tapped on the microphone.

"It is most fitting," he said, "that we should begin this happy occasion with prayer. With fullest respect to all of the convictions represented here, I would like to ask that Dr. Roundtree say grace."

Philip bowed his head. "May the eternal Godhead, by whatever name we address Him, bless our gathering here together and the food we are about to eat. May it nourish our bodies and our spirits that our brotherhood may be enriched and peace be with us all. Amen."

As the sound of people seating themselves filled the big room, student waitresses began to come quickly out of the kitchen bearing tureens of hot soup. Quiet settled quickly, and as it did, through the open windows a plaintive chant could be heard — calling the faithful of Islam to prayer.

CHAPTER TWELVE

The guesthouse at Maplewood College was a pleasant facility in the Midwestern style, but it had not been designed to compete with the massive manor houses of England such as the splendid one owned by Sir Cyril Plessey. This did not cause Sir Cyril any concern; he could have set up housekeeping in an Indian hogan and found it suitable to his needs for the duration of his tenure. As for Ames, wherever his employer chose to tarry became his theater of operation and he carried on with unflappable aplomb.

The morning was bright and beautiful with the glow of approaching midsummer when Sir Cyril appeared for breakfast. Ames, as usual, was waiting for him behind the chair in which he was to sit.

"Good morning," Sir Cyril declared, offering it as a pronouncement.

"A magnificent day indeed, sir."

"As it happens, this is my birthday."

"I was aware of that happy fact, sir. Many very happy returns, sir."

"Thank you. Where is Miss Matsumoto?"

"I don't know, sir. For the first time she has failed to appear. Shall I make enquiry, sir?"

"No, give her a few more minutes. It allows me time to ask you a question that occurred to me this morning. What are you going to do, Ames, after I die?"

"I expect, sir, to be among those who will be welcoming you into paradise."

Sir Cyril seated himself with discreet assistance. "Not likely. Paradise, I understand, is reserved for those who lead notably virtuous and moral lives."

Ames unfolded a napkin and tendered it. "True, but I am certain that they will make an exception in your case, sir."

The doorbell sounded and Ames responded; he returned after a few seconds with a young lady who bubbled over with a kind of blond vitality that made her seem even prettier than she was. "Hello," she greeted. "I'm Denise."

Sir Cyril rose and subjected her to swift, detailed scrutiny. "Am I to assume that Miss Matsumoto sent you in her place?"

Denise beamed and returned the compliment by surveying him. "That's it, she just couldn't make it. You know how it is with girls sometimes. She caught it really bad last night — cramps and things like that. She was trying to get ready this morning, but I told her to stay in bed and I'd pinch-hit."

Sir Cyril motioned toward the vacant place at table. "I know very well how it is; every gentleman necessarily does. Sit down."

Denise sat. "I'm so glad you understand. The word is out that if you were forty years younger, this place would be in an uproar."

"*How many years?*"

Denise tightened. "Twenty . . . ten!"

Sir Cyril nodded. "That's better. There is something to

be said, young lady, for a man of experience." He paused while Ames set plates in front of them. "Now tell me, do you have a boy friend?"

"Sort of."

"Tell me about him."

"Well . . . he's quite nice — he has a nice car, and he's fun to be with."

Sir Cyril drilled her with a penetrating look. "Young lady, you don't have a boy friend — you have a temporary substitute, which is just as well. Now eat your eggs and tell me how you think the conference is going."

Dutifully she picked up her fork and went to work. When her mouth was again clear, she answered him. "I really don't know. Everybody loves Bishop Phil, of course, but he has been looking worried lately. Have you noticed?"

"Of course I've noticed. And today may be a very tough one for him."

"Why, sir?"

Sir Cyril tightened his jaw as he contemplated the immediate future. "Today the Orthodox Jews are to make their presentation. Which brings up a point of history. Religion has been more flexible over the years than most people realize; for example, Islam is modernizing to a considerable degree — it has to if it wants to survive in the present-day world. Its leaders know that and they are taking appropriate action. But throughout the centuries Orthodox Judaism has been the one totally indigestible religious belief. They've stuck to it through everything and they stick to it today."

Denise looked at him. "In other words, Sir Cyril, if they won't play ball, not at all, it could throw the whole show off the deep end."

Sir Cyril took time to consume a mouthful of his own breakfast before he answered that. When he spoke, his words had an air of finality that allowed of no question or debate. "There you have it," he said. "And since Philip has his heart set on getting everybody together, to some degree at least, today could break him. Unless someone prevents it, of course, which is why I shall make it a point to be present. *Ames.*"

"Yes, sir?"

"Send some flowers to Miss Matsumoto. Include a card stating that I regret her present indisposition and, even more, that I was not granted the privilege of forestalling it. Take care of it right away."

"At once, sir."

"Is the car ready?"

"It is waiting outside, sir."

Sir Cyril addressed his guest. "Denise, come along. You are ready now to begin learning how to deal with matters of human concern."

The high-backed chair that had been provided for Philip at the side of the stage was not very comfortable, but he had sat in many others of similar design before and had learned to endure the consequent discomfort with stoic calm. He was making a conscious effort to appear attentive and interested in what the speaker was saying, even though the thirty-nine-year-old rabbi, with a painfully dry voice, was sealing the doom of the conference as surely as Fortunato was encased, brick by brick, in his living tomb.

Philip swallowed and tried to fix his mind for a moment on all the good things that had taken place during the past four weeks. The Taoist presentation had been a model of dignity and intelligent effort; the Bahais had pointed out with great pride, when their turn had come, how they had been dedicated for years to the same objectives toward which the conference was now directed; and the Parsees had offered the best that their restricted membership could provide. All these and many others had shown themselves people of good will and understanding. All of them had had their own convictions, but they had indicated a flexibility and a willingness at least to discuss. The speaker he was listening to at that moment was making his presentation on behalf of Orthodox Judaism as had been requested, but in so doing he was systematically slamming every door of mutual religious understanding that might be considered to be even slightly ajar.

With no visible display of emotion he continued on with mechanical precision like a lecturer in mathematics whose premise and conclusion are absolute and beyond modification by any human agency. Without emotion he described the history of his people during the Middle Ages and the total resistance they had made against all efforts to convert them to a different form of belief. He told of the way in which Jew after Jew had faced death by torture rather than make the slightest concession to Catholicism or any other form of worship. When he had finished with that part of his presentation he turned another page in his manuscript and took up the topic of the conference and its purpose.

"It has been said many thousands of times," he continued with clinical detachment, "that it is very hard to be a Jew. This is a fully deserved comment; it is not generally known that each and every Orthodox follower of the faith must adhere to and observe a total of six hundred and thirteen unshakable laws and rules that are required of us. This means in essence that every true Jew devotes much of his entire life to the practice of his religion. When he rises in the morning his worship begins; the clothing which he puts on is predetermined for him. He may not shave. His is a life of devoted service to God. He has been ordered to follow this path since it was first laid down by Moses, who was God's servant and who knew Him face to face."

He paused and looked about the vast auditorium as a biologist might survey an ant colony. "I cannot therefore encourage you," he continued, "to expect any concessions from us. Our convictions are based upon the rock of God's own word and are supported by centuries of strict observance by generation after generation of dedicated Jews. We have endured persecution beyond that suffered by any other segment of humanity for the sake of our faith, and we have not yielded.

"There are those in the family of Israel who have chosen to follow other paths in what are known as the Conservative and Reformed factions. If they wish to do this, it lies between them and their individual consciences, but it does not concern us. Scattered as we have been for centuries throughout much of Europe and in other parts of the world, we have still maintained our total religious integrity. Nothing has ever been able to sway us from this purpose. Now, at long last, we have a homeland where we can gather together to pray at our sacred shrines, but there are those who would deny us this even now."

Once more he stopped and again he surveyed his listeners dispassionately. "It has been requested that each presentation of religious conviction made here end with some point of agreement with other faiths if such is at all possible. In complying with this stipulation we wish it to be emphatically understood that we are offering no compromise, no concession, since any such action is forbidden to us and would be a violation of God's own commandments."

He consulted his manuscript. "We are in agreement with the followers of Islam that the eating of pork is abominable and also that all males are required to be circumcised. We agree with Christianity on the identification of the Deity. We accept the brotherhood of man, but we have no desire to join in any common plans of worship. We shall continue to walk our own way; those who by deep conviction wish to join with us are welcome." He closed his manuscript and with total dignity left the platform.

Philip rose and walked calmly to the podium. He was far from calm inside, but he repeated over and over to himself that he had been listening to a man of God declare his faith; the fact that it was an indigestible one was simply a

155

reality that had existed for centuries. He could do nothing whatever to change it now.

"I would like to thank the learned Rabbi who has just addressed us for the clarity of his statement and for the information he has laid before us," he said. "We have a few minutes before this session is scheduled to conclude. Does anyone wish the floor?"

Someone near to the rear asked to be heard. A portable microphone was quickly delivered to him.

"Reverend Paul Marshall of the New Church of the Divine Light," he introduced himself. "Although I am the only delegate of our denomination, I have been in communication with all six of our congregations and we have now reached a momentous decision. I would like to announce it if I may."

"Please do, sir," Philip replied from the stage.

"Through prayer and careful examination of the facts, we have determined to our satisfaction that this meeting is being held under the blessing of God and that it is His will that it succeed. Therefore, in view of all of the great wisdom assembled here, we have agreed that we will regard any united church that comes out of these proceedings as the direct will of God and inspired by Him. We are, therefore, prepared to join this new church *en masse* and hereby pledge it our fullest support." The speaker sat down.

Philip's mind tried to appraise that at its fair value. It was the ultimate in what he had hoped for, and a magnificent gesture, but he was gripped by the knowledge that the source of it was a very new and very small sect that had hardly had time to formulate its own doctrines. The crushing weight of the Jewish denial pilloried him so that even the brave words he had just heard could not mitigate his inner anguish.

Holding himself in check, his outward poise intact, he announced, "With deepest appreciation to the Reverend

Pastor Marshall and to the very learned Rabbi Rabinovitch, I now propose that we adjourn for lunch."

He walked off the stage with his head high and his shoulders straight. No one was close enough to detect the moisture he was powerless to prevent from filling the corners of his eyes.

Arthur Gravenstine was too good a journalist not to report all of the news despite whatever personal feelings he might hold. He had a story and it was his duty to get it on the wire, but to give it the depth and solidity the *Times* expected he wanted to talk to Philip Roundtree and also to interview Rabbi Rabinovitch at some length. He tried the dining hall first, but the table where the small Orthodox Jewish delegation customarily sat was unoccupied.

The manager of the Union had the answer. "Sir Cyril has them all in tow in the smaller dining room. I don't know any reason why you wouldn't be welcome."

Arthur did, but he decided to try his luck anyway. He pushed his head inside the doorway where Sir Cyril was holding court and asked, "Excuse me, is this a private meeting?"

His countryman answered, "Yes, but you're welcome with the understanding that this is off the record."

Gravenstine hesitated: if he accepted that commitment, then he might handicap himself severely in digging out some of the data he was after. On the other hand, it would help greatly to know what was going on. He entered the room and by so doing pledged his word. He took a seat quietly at the round table and paid very little attention to the food that was placed before him, preferring just to listen.

"Now, gentlemen, let's get down to cases," Sir Cyril proposed as soon as the waitress had left. "At a meeting like this if there had been no representation by Orthodox Jewry, it would have been a conspicuous omission."

"We did not wish to refuse." The speaker was an older man of indeterminate age because of his full beard and flat black clothing, the yarmulke he was wearing effectively concealing the top of his head. Gravenstine noted that he spoke remarkably good English; officially he was from Israel, but it was quite possible he had grown up in an English-speaking nation.

"I appreciate that," Sir Cyril continued. "And another thing: I understand your point of view. No one can be in business in the civilized world for fifty years and not learn something about Jewish culture. I take it that the viewpoint expressed by Rabbi Rabinovitch this morning is common to you all."

Once again the older man spoke. "It is common to every true Orthodox Jew in the world."

"Then I have a suggestion: I think you should go home. Don't misunderstand my meaning, I am simply taking you at your word that you will never reconcile with any other form of religious belief. That being the case, I see no benefit in asking you to sit through presentations by a wide assortment of faiths — it will only tie you up most of the summer."

Although the older man had not given the address from the platform, he was clearly the head of the delegation and its spokesman. "Sir Cyril," he said, "we are aware that when some of our people were trying to reach our homeland and were denied the necessary travel documents, it was you who came to their rescue. You provided food and shelter, and through channels we shall never understand you arranged for the required permits. Our memories are long in such matters. We came here only to show our respect for you. If you wish us now to leave, we will go and no cloud shall cover the sun between us."

The elderly Englishman raised a hand. "A lot of merchandise is going to be on display here for the next several weeks, but since you aren't buyers I know you would rather be back making your devotions at the tomb of Rachel."

"You know about that?" Rabinovitch was mildly surprised.

Sir Cyril bristled. "Sonny, I knew about that before you were born. Now back to cases; I want to tell you something about Philip Roundtree. He's just as pious and God-fearing as you are, or anyone else you can name. You saw a dream of a homeland and you fought for it. He saw a dream of human brotherhood and he's fighting for that."

"And we are the specter at the feast," the older man commented.

"You are. Now I'm backing Philip just as I once backed your people and for precisely the same reason — because I believe that everyone is entitled to his chance in the world, not just to live, but to reach out and achieve great things. Perhaps impossible things. That's what Philip is after — something impossible. He won't get it, but I want to see him go as far as he can. This morning you gave it to him right in the eye. You were truthful, honest, and honorable, but you told him in uncompromising terms that his great dream is finally and absolutely impossible."

"That is a very severe statement, sir." The words were soft, but edged.

"You're damn right, but your man was like the shoe salesman who told a customer that one of her feet was larger than the other. He was right, but he should have said that one of them was smaller than the other."

The older man nodded slowly. "I cannot deny the truth of that, but I have a suggestion. There are four of us here; allow three of us to withdraw and return home, where we are badly needed. With your approval, I shall remain so that it may not be said that our delegation has walked out. That would cast reflection on Dr. Roundtree, who we agree is a most honorable and dedicated man."

Sir Cyril scooped up some peas. "I think that is very good," he declared. "We're drawing heavy press coverage; I don't want the *Daily Forward* to come out from New York and find none of you here. Your suggestion is excellent and I accept it wholeheartedly."

At that moment Arthur Gravenstine knew that was precisely what Sir Cyril had been aiming for from the beginning.

Rabinovitch spoke with care. "I am much relieved. It is, I believe, everything understood?"

The lapse of grammar was the first of which he had been guilty.

Sir Cyril nodded. "If you agree."

The senior delegate nodded as well. "We agree. As you know, there are less of us each year. Israel is increasing, but it is the more liberal congregations that are growing. It thus may come to pass that Dr. Roundtree's dream may yet be realized."

"I'm for the objective, but not at the price," Sir Cyril said. Then he turned to Gravenstine. "You remember your commitment."

"I do, sir."

"Good. Now for the record: because of the extreme pressure of critical duties at home, part of the Orthodox Jewish delegation, having made its presentation, has been compelled to depart. All of those going expressed their acute disappointment at having to leave Maplewood College and this inspiring conference. The greatest harmony prevailed and those departing spoke glowingly of the progress that had been made. Unquote."

The delegation spokesman looked at Sir Cyril. "If you were promoting our faith rather than other interests, perhaps we would be once more on the increase."

The elderly knight nodded briskly. "Thank you. I'm fully

engaged at the moment, but perhaps later I will be able to look into the matter."

As he arose the meeting was over.

When he stepped behind the podium to open the afternoon session, Philip was not aware that three of the four representatives of Orthodox Jewry were not present. His manner appeared unchanged and gave no hint of the setback he had received during the morning session. For the first half hour, if the adamant position that Rabinovitch had taken had discouraged the delegate body to any appreciable degree, it was not evident. Things moved forward according to the program and all seemed well. Then a lady representative of the Seventh-Day Adventists rose and demanded to know why, if the Orthodox Jews were so pious, they did not recognize the overwhelming evidence that their Messiah had indeed arisen, and from amongst their own people.

By the time that she sat down a dozen others were on their feet to be recognized. An hour later the discussion was still going strong. Some of the delegates had walked out of the hall, which was not a good sign. Others showed considerable signs of heat. When things broke down to the point where individuals on the floor began to shout directly at one another, Philip did his best to regain a firmer control. Unfortunately, it was too late — for the first time since the conference had begun he banged his gavel fruitlessly; no one seemed to be paying him any attention. A strong sense of alarm surged within him; if things went on like this, the entire conference could go to pieces literally overnight.

He rapped his gavel once more and asked that everyone please cease discussion for a few moments. He looked out in hope, but the shouting continued. Livid with rage, a Muslim leaped to his feet when he heard the words "false prophet" and understood them to be directed toward Mo-

hammed. Some of his fellows restrained him almost physically until it was made clear that the unfortunate reference
had been to Joseph Smith. Then the Mormons were on
their feet and the leader of the delegation so far forgot
himself as to shake his fist toward Philip Roundtree, who
was still vainly trying to restore order.

"Ladies and gentlemen," he shouted into his microphone. "Please be seated. This convention welcomes discussion, but I must ask and demand that you refrain from
any personal references. Joseph Smith was the founder of
the Church of Jesus Christ of Latter-Day Saints and he is
entitled to the fullest respect here!"

It was uncertain whether he was really heard or not. From
the balcony Sir Cyril issued an order; a few moments later
all of the lights in the auditorium went out. Individual
voices were heard cutting through the blackness, but they
died out quickly. When the power was restored, there was
a semblance of at least some kind of order.

Philip took command. "It is intolerable," he said clearly
into his microphone, "that any religious leader of sincere
intention and conviction should be referred to here in less
than a proper manner. I must ask you to remember this
throughout the remainder of our meeting."

That was enough to mollify the Mormons, and the delegation, which had already moved halfway up the aisle,
somewhat reluctantly returned to its assigned seats.

Philip waited, deliberately, letting things remain as they
were while calm gradually took control. He could sense
that he was succeeding when he became aware that toward
the right and well back there was a stir of some kind. He
could not see the area very well, but the incident, whatever
it was, had a different tone from the previous antagonisms.
Presently one of the ushers spoke into the portable microphone he was carrying: "A lady seems to have fainted in
her seat."

Then a pattern was visible: a dozen or more delegates of

varying faiths were clustered about someone who for the moment was hidden from view. Philip spoke into his own microphone: "Dr. Brady, would you be kind enough to attend this lady."

He could have saved his breath, the college physician was already hurrying down the aisle. The respite was in a way helpful; while the doctor was engaged discussion obviously could not continue and the bulk of the delegates fell quiet. A good five minutes passed in relative calm while tempers calmed down and the ecumenical spirit was given at least a small chance to revive. Then the doctor made use of one of the portable microphones. "I think it would be best to remove this patient by stretcher," he said. "Please send for an ambulance."

"Is she dead?" someone called out.

The doctor heard it and replied. "No, I simply want to take every precaution."

Knowing his duty Philip left the platform and went toward the area where the doctor was working. He arrived there just as two students appeared with a stretcher from the first aid room; they were accompanied by a matronly, middle-aged nurse who was hurrying as best she could. "What is it? he asked the physician.

Dr. Brady shook his head. "I think something internal; I'll check her over in the first aid room right away." Philip watched as the delegate was carried out, then he returned to the platform. "The doctor will have a report for us very shortly," he announced. "I suggest that we defer our further deliberations until we hear."

On that point, fortunately, there seemed to be a general agreement. A hum of conversation broke out, but it was subdued and there was no overtone of acrimony. Philip returned to his chair and sat down, content to leave things as they were for the moment. He did not have very long to wait: a young man came down the aisle, up onto the stage, and gave him the news. He listened gravely, then rose and took his place once more behind the rostrum. At that moment he sensed that the delegates, despite their many differences, had at that point in time a common interest.

"I am informed by Dr. Brady that his patient is showing signs of abdominal distress," he reported. "It could possibly indicate a sudden attack of appendicitis. The ambulance has arrived and she is now being taken to hospital; the doctor is going with her."

He paused and carefully read the reaction to his words. He could feel his listeners and knew that they were with him. "I am not a medical man," he continued, "but I am aware that cases of this kind can, under some circumstances, be serious. Most fortunately, expert care was immediately at hand."

Carefully he changed the timbre of his voice. "Since we are all, in our individual ways, people who acknowledge the power and authority of God, I would like to propose that we pause for five minutes so that each of us may, according to his own convictions, pray for the prompt and full recovery of the lady who is one of our number."

As his words died out, there was a rustle of movement. Some of the delegates rose to their feet, others knelt. The Muslim group moved into the aisle and on their knees bowed in the direction of Mecca. From the extreme rear there came the sound of soft chanting; in the front, a Jewish delegate donned a yarmulke.

Philip saw in front of him a scene perhaps unmatched in history. In a multitude of tongues, in various postures, and in a confusion of intonations, representatives of dozens upon dozens of totally dissimilar religious faiths were praying together — their differences forgotten in their common purpose. Emotion filled his body and a sensation he had seldom known ran the length of his spine; it was as though he had seen before him the Promised Land. In that moment of fulfillment he bowed his own head, both to pray and to give thanks.

164

An hour later he was passed a slip of paper. He read it carefully and then found a moment where he could interrupt the speaker who had the floor without giving offense. "I regret that I still do not know the name of the lady who was taken to hospital," he said, "however, I am most happy to advise you that the attention she received was just in time. Apparently she was suffering from a very swiftly developing case of appendicitis; there is reason to believe that a sudden attack of pain caused her to lose consciousness. After diagnosis at the hospital revealed her condition she was given surgery within minutes. I am now informed that it was entirely successful; there was no rupture and the danger is past."

He looked up. "Clearly our prayers were heard, and at the very moment they were most needed; from this we may all take new courage and inspiration. May I ask if anyone can inform me of the lady's identity? She is probably still under anesthesia and someone should be notified."

In the area where the incident had begun a man stood up. Even at a distance Philip could see that he was shaking with emotion. He accepted a microphone and then spoke in a voice fighting for control. "Her name, sir, is Mrs. Estelle Winifred Van Wyke. She came here in all good conscience to represent, through her great faith and demonstrated powers, the Christian Science Church. We sent a messenger at once to the hospital, but he did not arrive in time. By this unspeakable outrage, by taking advantage of an unconscious woman, and by refusing to listen to those of us who tried to protest to the doctor, you have forced us into an intolerable position. Can you comprehend, sir, what you have done!"

At that stunning moment Harley Poindexter appeared unexpectedly onstage. Gratefully Philip stepped aside and let the college president take over.

"I wish to make a further announcement," he declared in his best professionally dry voice. "As soon as Mrs. Van

Wyke was stricken we determined her identity; we were also aware of her church affiliation. Unfortunately, since she was unconscious she was unable to follow her religious training or apply its precepts. I therefore immediately called Judge Wettstein and asked for his advice."

He paused for a moment so that his words could be digested.

"Judge Wettstein informed me that he would issue an immediate court order authorizing emergency surgery in order possibly to save Mrs. Van Wyke's life and also to relieve her of any onus that might result from her receiving medical care."

The words were not out of his mouth before the man with the microphone challenged him. "And is that court order going to help this fine and wonderful woman when she regains consciousness and discovers that her profound beliefs have been ruthlessly violated?"

Poindexter retained his cool. "The point is, sir, that she now *will* regain consciousness. We respect her convictions, but she was unable to apply them in her condition — I'm sure you appreciate that. And we are not quite as unthinking as you seem to assume; we made some fast phone calls and were able to locate a practitioner who is on her way to the hospital now. This is the very best that we were able to do and I hope that you and your colleagues will find it acceptable."

From where he was listening in the lobby Dean Hastings was grateful that he had not been caught up in the middle of that one. He was reflecting on his good fortune when his attention was caught by something new on the campus. With admirable foresight he had stationed himself where he had a good view of what was going on in both directions, so he saw the lone figure that was approaching the auditorium while it was still some distance away.

The man had on a long robe which reached from his neck almost to the ground. It was tied in place at the waist by a

166

cord of soft rope, purple in color; his otherwise bare feet were shod in sandals. By far the most striking features of his appearance were the long staff that he carried and his immense beard which flowed in majestic white waves as though it had been created in sculpture by some contemporary Michelangelo.

He carried himself with great dignity as he mounted the steps to the auditorium and entered the lobby; as he did so Hastings came forward to meet him.

"Good afternoon," the man thundered in a voice that filled the area. "Is this the place where the great religious meeting is now being held?"

"Yes it is, sir," Hastings answered. "May I ask which denomination you represent?"

The bearded man transfixed him with his gaze. "I represent no denomination — and all denominations. You may announce me."

"And who are you, sir, may I ask?"

Once more the piercing look, one that spoke of a mind that did not walk in ordinary paths. The bearded man banged his staff on the floor. "I am astonished that you ask," he declared in his massive voice. "I, good man, am God!"

CHAPTER THIRTEEN

When the session was at last over, Philip lost no time in seeking the sanctuary of his office. He could not face the prospect of standing by the door conveniently available to anyone who might wish to speak with him; instead, all he wanted to do was get his mind back into order.

He sat behind his desk, his feet propped upon an inverted wastebasket, his head tipped as far back as it would conveniently go. He remained there, relatively motionless, letting his thoughts tumble as they would. He considered whether or not he ought to go to the hospital and inquire after Mrs. Van Wyke, or perhaps call on her after dinner as a gesture of consideration and regard.

A slight noise made him turn his head; he discovered Ames standing there, waiting to be noticed. Philip emphatically did not want another lecture from Sir Cyril; he wanted to be left alone. Still, he could not ignore a possible summons from his benefactor, so he made a moderate effort to gather himself and said, "Good afternoon, Mr. Ames."

"I beg your pardon, M'Lord Bishop, I perceive that perhaps you would prefer to rest."

Philip turned his chair around and put his feet back onto the floor. "What can I do for you?" he asked.

"Sir Cyril's compliments, sir, and a message of four words — the bar is open."

Philip thought of a whisky and soda and the relief and comfort that it might bring. "Why is it," he asked aloud, "that the Devil has so many good ideas."

"In this instance, sir, I would venture that it isn't the Devil as much as Sir Cyril, and despite some opinion to the contrary, there is a definite distinction."

Philip rotated his head to loosen the muscles of his neck, massaging them at the same time with the palms of his hands. "Have you seen my chaplain?" he inquired.

"I regret, sir, that I have not done so recently. If you desire his presence, I can make enquiries."

"I wouldn't know where to ask," Philip said.

"Perhaps, M'Lord Bishop, if you were to determine the whereabouts of Miss Thiengburanathum, that might be helpful."

"You pronounced that very well, how did you manage it?"

"It has been my great pleasure to accompany Sir Cyril on many of his trips to various parts of the world. These experiences have been very broadening, sir, and most educational as well."

"Of course. Upon due reflection, I believe that I will act on Sir Cyril's suggestion."

"Splendid, sir — I have the car just outside."

As he walked into the college guesthouse Philip was glad to note that Harley Poindexter was also present. He exchanged greetings and accepted a glass from Ames. Then he settled himself into a chair and let the world reduce itself to the room in which he sat and the three others who populated it.

"I have some encouraging news from the hospital," Harley reported. "Mrs. Van Wyke is not only on the mend, she seems reconciled to creating a minimum fuss. Perhaps she realizes what was done for her, I can't say, but there is no more sweat at the moment."

"Good," Philip said.

Harley turned. "Oh, by the way, did you hear about the arrival of the Almighty this afternoon?"

"Tell him," said Sir Cyril.

"It seems that the Santa Monica mountains of California have yielded up to us a gentleman who claims to be God himself. He has some followers who believe in him and I'm sure that he does himself. Fortunately Joe Hastings was able to persuade him that an appearance at this time would be so stunning that the whole conference would be thrown completely out of gear."

"Quite a harmless person," Sir Cyril added. "Also a very decent one. He simply has an illusion, and very few of us can claim to be free of any ourselves. He has returned to his sanctuary to await further results."

Philip visioned the dramatic appearance on the platform of a man claiming to be the Deity and inwardly shuddered. He tested his drink once more and found comfort in it. There was quiet for a few moments, then Harley Poindexter indicated that he had something to say.

"I have a confession to make," he began, "and right now is as good a time as any. I'm afraid that I haven't been entirely candid with either of you concerning our participation in this meeting."

"Go on," Sir Cyril said.

"I intend to. Here it is in plain and simple language. As you know, about fifty years ago we were left a sum of money by Mrs. Bixby to be used to find a common religious denominator on a worldwide basis. We have been sitting on those funds for half a century, rather helplessly watching them grow until they reached a point where their existence became relatively well known."

"I know the rest already," Sir Cyril contributed as he handed his glass to Ames to be refilled.

"I'm sure that you do. Philip, I assume that a good bit of your work, even on your level, has to do with fund raising in one form or another."

Philip nodded. "Definitely. The church is always poor, despite some popular beliefs to the contrary."

"Well, the same thing holds true for colleges, at least in this country. We are always trying to tap the till by every honorable means open to us. We don't hand out degrees in hope of bequests, but we do sponsor donors' dinners and things like that."

"And the Bixby funds proved a first-class embarrassment," Philip suggested.

"Precisely. Everyone knew about that very substantial bequest, but they didn't always understand that we couldn't touch it for any of our running expenses. The longer it went on, the worse it got. People asked me why I was soliciting donations when we had an unused kitty of over a million that wasn't part of the endowment."

He accepted a fresh glass from Ames and then continued. "So we had to do something to get rid of the damn money, we had no other choice. We considered the obvious thing — to hold a conference of our own and make sure that it was expensive enough to use up almost all of the Bixby funds. Then, Philip, we heard about your sermon and realized here was our out. So I'm afraid we urged you to come here principally so that we could satisfy the terms of that fifty-year-old gift and get our necks off the block once and for all. But I will add this: when you agreed to hold your meeting here, we determined to back you up to the very best of our ability."

"That you certainly have done," Philip said.

171

"Thank you. I'm telling you this for two reasons: one is to clear my conscience, the other is to ask you to keep going long enough so that we can unload most or all of the Bixby money as directed."

"Does Judge Wettstein know this?" Sir Cyril asked.

"He does, which is one reason, I suspect, why he was so prompt in issuing that court order this afternoon."

Philip took it calmly. "Harley, I appreciate your telling us this, but it wasn't really necessary. From our standpoint your embarrassment was our blessing, so let's leave it at that. And as far as I can see, the conference has a long time to run, perhaps even until your students are ready to return for the fall term."

"Splendid. Incidentally, I understand that Janet went back home for an interval."

"Yes, to look after our sons and to take care of some other matters."

"Fine; we'll be delighted to pay her fare."

At that moment the doorbell rang. Ames answered it and ushered in Aubrey Fothergill, who was closely accompanied by Jayawardene Thiengburanathum.

"I hope this isn't an intrusion," Aubrey said. "We have been looking for Dr. Roundtree and we were directed here."

Philip noted the two "we's" in the same sentence and wondered.

Sir Cyril promptly took over the role of host. "Anyone who comes here bringing a beautiful woman will always be welcome. Ames, see to them."

Ames was already providing chairs, but Aubrey appeared to prefer standing with the lady at his side. When the moment was appropriate he addressed himself to his superior. "My Lord Bishop, I ask your leave, and that of Sir Cyril, to announce our engagement. Miss Thiengburanathum has done me the great honor to accept my proposal of marriage."

Even though he had been partially prepared, Philip found

172

sudden thoughts cascading through his mind so fast he was hardly able to make a suitable response. Sir Cyril filled the void; he came forward briskly and shook Aubrey's hand, then to the surprise of no one he kissed the bride-to-be in a manner to which she had yet to become accustomed.

"My warmest congratulations and best wishes," he said. "Almost the first time that I saw the two of you together I noted the direction of the wind — and approved of it. Please sit down."

Aubrey and Jayawardene did as instructed.

"It is now necessary for me to make a speech," Sir Cyril began. "About people. Please to honor me with your attention."

He finished his drink and set it aside. "At present Dr. Roundtree, in addition to sharing your joy, probably feels a measure of concern because you two represent different religious backgrounds and Reverend Fothergill is professionally committed to the Church of England. He can't very well chant the mantras after dinner in public without inviting comment, and it isn't reasonable to expect that our bride-to-be is prepared immediately to set aside her own convictions in order to embrace Christianity. So we have the appearance of a dilemma."

"And we have a solution," Aubrey interjected.

"I anticipated that, sir, and I can guess what it is, but later. I shall continue. It is necessary at this juncture for you to become freshly aware of an overwhelming truth that is often politely neglected, and that is that people no matter what their origins come in only two varieties — male and female. The ideal combination is one of each and that is what we have here; the rest is superficial."

"Bravo!" Aubrey said.

"Now it is further necessary to note that people have an astonishing similarity in life and habits, regardless of origin or social environment. Everyone goes to bed, if he's fortunate enough to possess one, in order to repair himself with

173

sleep — newlyweds excepted for understandable reasons. Everyone has to eat and none of us can neglect the demands of nature when they arise; it would equally inconvenience all of the diverse personalities attending this conference if someone were to spirit away all of the toilet paper. These are essentials and no amount of ritual or protocol can change them a bit. The more we keep that in mind, the less we can go around with the mistaken idea that we are not all very similar to one another. We are so damn similar that only God himself could have accomplished the necessary engineering, and He's the one who handled the job."

He looked at Jayawardene. "Am I boring you?"

"Definitely not, sir."

"Very good. Now you may expect to run into a good many people who will try to tell you that you have too many differences. I have observed that when virile young military men on foreign duty take young ladies to bed with them, the so-called differences go down the drain as soon as the lights are turned off. If it is your joint decision to commit matrimony, then all you really have to do is pass the blood test. I trust that I make myself clear."

Philip had been listening, but he could not help doing some rapid thinking at the same time; the announcement presented him with several immediate problems with which he would have to deal. He waited until he was sure that Sir Cyril had finished speaking, then he asked his chaplain, "Are you planning to resign your orders?" He was careful to make it a simple question and no more.

Aubrey turned toward him. "No, sir, unless I'm compelled to. I believe that taking a wife is approved."

"It had better be," Philip answered, "or I'm in trouble."

"We are also permitted to marry," Jayawardene said, "and I am of a suitable age."

"In this case, what is suitable?" Sir Cyril asked.

"I am twenty-five."

174

There was a momentary impasse that was broken by Harley Poindexter. "You said that you had a solution to the apparent religious dilemma."

Aubrey put his arm across Jayawardene's shoulders. "Yes, sir, we do. We met because the conference was called — for the purpose of helping us all to agree on certain fundamentals. Based partly on our own experience, we both now think that it has a possible chance to succeed. So we are awaiting the outcome."

Jayawardene continued. "It's very simple — we want to be the first couple to be married in the new united church, whatever form it takes."

"So now," Aubrey concluded, "it's up to you."

Philip declined a ride back to his quarters; he wanted an opportunity to walk by himself and think about his new problem. He accepted the fact that the engagement of his chaplain was a very real one; if the young lady had only been of Christian faith and had had something a little closer to a conventional British background, there would have been no difficulties at all. He would gladly have married them himself if asked, but unfortunately the prospective bride was about as far from a well-brought-up English girl as she could be.

Or was she? He could not deny that Jayawardene was a young lady who knew her manners and her character appeared to be unassailable. She was certainly attractive enough, God knew! He admitted to himself that without downgrading the quality of the British product, there were very few girls to be found on the home islands who would fall into her league. She was also exceptionally intelligent and, from a purely biological point of view, her suggested potential was devastating.

Was that, he wondered, the main reason why Aubrey had chosen to ruin his future career in the Church? He considered his chaplain in that light for a few moments and then decided that while propinquity had undoubtedly been a contributing factor, the Reverend Aubrey Fothergill was too tough-minded a young man to have yielded to that alone. As to Jayawardene and Aubrey being the first couple to be married in the new united church, that was an attractive vision but no more.

He stopped dead in his tracks. He had just denied his own great purpose! If *he* didn't believe in the eventual success of the conference, then who would? Like Peter he had denied firmly the one thing he should have been the first to uphold and defend. He shook his head and wondered, almost fearfully, if he was destined to do it twice more. Good God, where was his faith?

At least his fault had been revealed to him, hopefully in time. He remembered the words of Byron:

> "He who shoots at the noonday sun,
>   Knows full well he will never hit the mark
>   Yet his arrow will go higher and farther,
>   Than his who aims at the bush."

It was so long since he had read that passage that he knew he was paraphrasing, but the thought was there just the same. The sun — he had declared his aim at the sun, therefore he would have to shoot toward it and with all the strength of his bow arm. He stopped, because he suddenly realized that someone was in front of him, waiting to speak. A man in simple clerical black who, unfortunately, he did not know.

"Good afternoon, Your Excellency."

That told Philip that the man was Catholic in all probability.

"Good afternoon, Father. We have been granted another beautiful day."

"Indeed we have, Dr. Roundtree. I am Father Heller, a member of the Catholic observing group." He held out his hand.

Philip took it warmly. "I'm happy to know you, Father. I hope you are enjoying the meeting."

"Indeed I am, but most unfortunately I am being replaced."

Philip was concerned. "Is anything wrong?"

Father Heller's smile reassured him. "Not at all, My Lord, on the contrary. I am returning to my duties at the archdiocese in order to make room for the new head of our party. Perhaps you know Bishop O'Hanlon. Sean O'Hanlon."

That was indeed news! So the Catholics were putting in a bishop; that was an excellent sign. "I have not yet had the pleasure," Philip said. "But I shall regret your leaving us, Father. Do come back if you are able."

The priest nodded. "Thank you so very much. May I say that you have certainly inspired many people with your leadership — and your patience. If we had not had that providential electrical failure this afternoon, even your powers might have been severely tried."

"I was frankly concerned," Philip admitted.

"In my judgment you had a right to be, but it was not in any way your fault. People sometimes forget themselves."

"Indeed they do."

Father Heller hesitated a moment, then he spoke more quietly. "Dr. Roundtree, there is a reason for this and I believe you should be aware of it in advance. It is my understanding that the Holy Father himself may be sending a message to this convocation. If this is indeed the case, then Bishop O'Hanlon will be delivering it."

"I understand, Father. And this is not to be made public prematurely."

"Thank you for your willingness, Dr. Roundtree, to keep it quiet."

"I shall do so. Do you have time to join me for coffee, Father?"

"I have an appointment to see Sir Cyril Plessey. If I may, later."

"By all means."

As Philip continued on, he decided to take his dinner in the main dining hall; it would give him a chance for further contacts with some of the individual delegates and that was most important to him. At the steps of the Student Union he paused to buy a newspaper from one of the vending boxes. He unfolded it to discover that once again the conference had been recognized by one of the splendid religious drawings that had so far honored the Buddha, Martin Luther, and Lao-tze. This time the artist had created an almost mystical portrait of the Virgin Mary holding the Christ Child in Her gentle arms. It was a beautiful Madonna and even on ordinary newsprint the picture had an immediate appeal.

The Catholics, Philip decided, should be very pleased; it augured well for the arrival of Bishop O'Hanlon, who presumably would be appearing shortly.

Philip took his dinner in the rear of the dining hall with a group of Protestant delegates, all of whom represented smaller denominations. In particular he was impressed by two men from the Salvation Army who told him about their work and by a Reverend Alvin Durham from the Christian Church whose quiet "country preacher" style had much to recommend it. The discussion was stimulating, and by the time the meal was finished Philip felt he had regained much of his composure and mental equilibrium.

In that mood he left the dining hall and went outside for a period of reflection. He sought the sanctuary of the campus, where he might be able, like the purloined letter, to be well concealed while still in plain view. He chose a bench under the inviting spread of a venerable tree where he could rest with his back protected by the wide trunk and look out toward the sunset. He composed himself and began to draw spiritual nourishment from the quiet scene before him. This was what he wanted and it was good.

"Dr. Roundtree."

Because it was a female voice Philip reluctantly rose to his feet to accept the inevitable; the tone of voice had warned him that he faced yet another complaint.

The woman who stood waiting for him to acknowledge her was quite normal in appearance — middle-aged, average build, and conventionally dressed. Philip put on his professionally pleasant face and said, "Good evening, would you like to sit down?"

His unexpected guest accepted, but she was careful to occupy only the front part of the bench. "I am Mrs. Philpotts, Dr. Roundtree. I'm sure that you don't know me, but I *am* a delegate at this conference."

"I'm delighted, Mrs. Philpotts," Philip said without a twinge of conscience. "What may I do for you?" He seated himself as though he were about to hear confession.

Mrs. Philpotts placed her hands formally in her lap and declared herself. "As a representative of Jehovah's Witnesses I think I may say that I know your true purpose in calling this meeting; we are very strong on missionary work ourselves. There is no more noble thing than helping to bring the light of the Bible to the benighted peoples of the world."

"Yes indeed," Philip said. He knew that God would understand.

"I was sure we would be in agreement; after all, you *are* a bishop. In view of this I shall speak clearly. I believe that the young man called Fothergill is your assistant?"

"Yes," Philip acknowledged.

"Dr. Roundtree, I am not alone in what I am going to say now; our whole delegation has discussed it, and so have the Adventists. We all feel that it is *most* unseemly for this young man, who is an ordained Christian minister of God, to be seen so frequently in the company of a foreign young woman who is an admitted pagan."

Philip felt a flash of anger, but he controlled it and replied quite calmly. "The young lady you refer to is not a Christian, but she is hardly a pagan. As you know, that means an irreligious person; she is representing the Hinayana division of the Buddhist faith, one of the most important in the world."

Mrs. Philpotts was unimpressed. "We aren't concerned how important it is; it isn't Christian and that's all that need be said. We all feel that you have been too tolerant in allowing all of these Oriental people to talk about their beliefs and superstitions. If you were to lay down the law to your assistant and remind him where his responsibility lies, it would do much to restore our confidence. May I have your assurance that you will take proper action?"

Philip kept his irritation hidden. "You do appreciate, Mrs. Philpotts, that the announced purpose of this meeting is to bring together different religious viewpoints, so it would be very difficult for me to go against this principle with a flat prohibition. Also Reverend Fothergill has been having some very rewarding discussions with this young lady according to his reports to me. As a matter of fact, he recently instructed her in the Ten Commandments."

Mrs. Philpotts let her mouth fall partway open. "I didn't understand," she said. "You mean that he is *converting* her?"

"I would prefer to say that he is instructing her in the Christian faith, and please consider that confidential for the moment."

Mrs. Philpotts rose. "I certainly shall, Dr. Roundtree. If you require assistance, we are prepared to help. Some copies of the *Watchtower*, if she is able to read English, might be most helpful, and we can supply them."

Philip was on his own feet. "Let me caution you not to expect too much too soon."

"No, we understand that these things take time. Good evening, Dr. Roundtree."

When he was once more alone Philip seated himself and tried to recapture his former mood, but it was gone and he knew it. A challenging thought came to him and he was forced to consider it: would it have been better if there were no formal religions at all? Then every man could have sought out God in his own way and all the multiple divisions and subdivisions, all the cross-purposes, all the persecutions and inquisitions, and all of the bloody holy wars would have died stillborn, unable to plague humanity with death, torture, dissent, and almost unceasing violence.

He bent down and rested his head in his hands, shielded by the beginnings of twilight, and wondered if he was ready yet to pray. He needed help, because he was only Philip Roundtree, who had gotten into a fearful mess at school when he was just twelve and who had once torn his very best pants hopelessly the very first day he had had them on. His father had calmed his mother's fury, but the years had not erased the memory or the feeling of impotent helplessness that had engulfed him then. Now he was a mature man, much better able to cope, but also burdened with far greater responsibilities. Janet, their boys, his whole diocese depended upon him, and now by God's will the whole conference depended upon him; he would have to find the strength to carry it forward.

Some sense that he could not define told him that he was again no longer alone. He raised his head and saw that a man stood before him, waiting with apparently limitless patience until his presence might be welcome. He could have been Japanese, but Philip was not sure. The man wore severely simple black robes and his head was shaven, which added further to the passiveness of his appearance, but it was in his features that Philip found something that attracted him. He was about to rise once more, but the man in black raised a hand to deter him.

"Do I intrude upon you?" The words came slowly, like something read from an ancient parchment; the voice, though accented, was gentle and subdued.

Instinct told Philip that this man was welcome; perhaps a different human contact was what he needed. "Please sit down," he invited.

The man sat where Mrs. Philpotts had been seated, his presence stilling the harsher vibrations that had emanated from that same spot a short while before. He did nothing for a few moments, letting the atmosphere settle quietly about him until an empathy seemed to hang in the twilight. Then he spoke again, slowly and quietly. "It is visible to me that your heart is troubled."

"There are many problems," Philip acknowledged.

"Indeed so — that has always been true."

The words were comforting, they suggested a companionship in misery and thereby provided a minute portion of euphoria.

"If you will allow me," the man continued, his words as calm as the last of the sunset that tinged the sky, "I too am a bishop. I am from Nagoya."

Philip knew that Nagoya was somewhere in Japan; beyond that he was out of his depth. He did not need to tell his visitor that — the man understood without his saying a word. He turned his head toward Philip and then spoke once more. "My name is Sumi. I am a Zen master."

His words were simple and utterly devoid of ego. "In times of stress, Reverend Dr. Roundtree, there is great comfort and peace to be found in meditation. Have you ever tried it?"

"I have never had the opportunity."

"I well understand. In Japan, at the Ryoan-ji Temple in Kyoto, there is a garden, one of the greatest of human creations. It is a garden of stones; a little moss grows, but nothing else. Fifteen stones rising out of a sea of raked gravel. If you were to sit and gaze upon it, presently it would begin to reveal many things. For five hundred years it has done this. It is believed to be without flaw."

"I would give much to see it," Philip said.

"To such a man as yourself it would offer great inspiration, for you would discern its purpose. We have no garden to offer you here, but we have arranged a meditation room where peace may be found. We would be greatly honored to have you visit it."

Philip had the impression that meditation involved a trance-like state that took years to master; it was an area unknown to him, but perhaps he should know something of it. "Is it open now?" he asked.

"It awaits you, if you so desire. Meditation, Dr. Roundtree, is not the possession of any single faith or culture. We of Zen understand it better than some because it is our main refuge. We invite you to share our joys."

It seemed to Philip that to refuse might be to give serious offense. "Shall we go?" he asked.

Like the Buddhist chapel that he had already visited, the meditation room was a classroom which had been converted into something else altogether. The plainness of the bare academic walls had been disguised by subdued hangings; scattered cushions relieved the starkness of the wooden floor. A kakemono scroll offered its subtle beauty.

Philip did his best to put himself into a receptive frame of mind, but wondered nonetheless if a middle-aged British clergyman could possibly fit himself into this picture and find in the room before him a new mental experience. It was a challenge and with it came the determination to try. As long as it did not violate any of the tenets of his faith, he was for it.

"May I suggest," Bishop Sumi said, "that you remove your shoes. You will be more comfortable."

Standing a little awkwardly on first one foot and then the other, Philip did as directed. The laces snarled a little, but he accomplished his purpose and at last stood in his stocking feet hoping that he would not be asked to sit on the backs of his heels — a position that he knew would be extremely uncomfortable for him.

His fears on that point were relieved when his guide arranged three of the cushions one on top of the other and then motioned for him to sit down.

"Please compose yourself however you would like," Sumi directed. "It is most important that you be entirely at ease."

Philip sat, and apart from the fact that his back was unsupported, he was at least moderately comfortable. He watched as his host seated himself on a single cushion before him, his legs folded under his body as though it was the most natural posture possible, and his hands lying easily on his lap.

"Now," his teacher began, "you may shut your eyes and remove from your vision, and your mind, all awareness of the outside world . . ."

For more than an hour Philip continued to sit there, oblivious of the passage of time, using the power of his mind to reach out and comprehend the things that were being told to him. He accepted it all as he might have listened to some great piece of music that he had never heard before. While the delegates of many widely varied and sometimes hostile convictions wove their separate ways about the campus, the Japanese Zen master and the British Anglican bishop sat together and passively formed another uniting thread in the brotherhood of man.

CHAPTER FOURTEEN

From the moment that it began, Philip Roundtree had to admit to himself that the Catholic presentation was the most impressive that had been made up to that point by any of the faiths which were represented. A great many additional people had come in for the occasion so that the weight of numbers alone was a factor. Beyond this was the richness of the vestments, the appeal of the music which filled the auditorium, and the candle-lit processional which seemed to compress past centuries into a single two hours of the present.

Bishop O'Hanlon himself was a man of impressive appearance and bearing; the authority of the Church seemed to exude from him as he made his grave way down the aisle surrounded by the other members of the Catholic group, which the day before had voluntarily asked to have its status changed from observers to delegates. Philip had attended to that with a great sense of personal satisfaction; it was another step forward in Christian unity. He had welcomed Bishop O'Hanlon personally and had found him a man greatly gifted in the difficult art of human relations. He was a powerful advertisement for his own church — considerate, gracious, dedicated, and profound in his conviction.

When they had had coffee together Philip had carefully refrained from giving any hint concerning a possible message from the Pope; if O'Hanlon wanted to talk about it he would in his own good time. O'Hanlon had greeted him as a colleague in Christ and then had been full of well-thought-out questions concerning the conference and how it was proceeding. Philip gave him entirely candid answers; his conscience would not have permitted anything else, and besides, if he had yielded to the temptation to paint the clouds a bit rosier than they were, O'Hanlon would undoubtedly have detected it even though he would have given no indication that he had done so.

To Philip it had been a rewarding meeting. O'Hanlon had talked a little about Christian unity and to Philip it seemed as though he might be in favor of it. A Catholic bishop was a personage within the Roman church, and judging by O'Hanlon's evident qualifications a cardinal's red hat might well lie in his future. Best of all, he was at the conference as a delegate and that was an omen of the best possible kind.

Sitting in his high-backed chair at the corner of the stage, Philip carefully watched and studied the dignified and impressive manner in which the Catholic delegation took command of the stage and captured the attention of the assembled delegates. Ever since Martin Luther there had been certain competition between the Catholic and Protestant divisions of the Christian Church, but insofar as richness of presentation was concerned, the Catholic Church had won in a walk. That did not diminish the fervor of the worship that might take place in simple clapboard churches scattered throughout the land, but the vaulting vastness of the great cathedrals and the mighty inspiration of music

186

and art that had been produced by centuries of effort formed a tradition that had been erected to endure.

The presentation of the Catholic faith that began as soon as the processional had been concluded was wholly professional and well planned. A team of four speakers alternated, dovetailing their remarks so that they all fitted together into a coordinated, integral whole. The history, the traditions, the inner church structure, the tenets, all were set forth with a lucidity and economy that set an unbeatable standard. In it there was an element of assumption, but that was common to many different faiths. The Muslims certainly regarded the Prophet in the light of a supreme teacher despite the fact that while on earth he had not learned either to read or to write. The Buddhists considered Siddhartha to have been the guiding light for all of humanity, and certainly they had going for them the fact that their founding prince had been a man of the utmost nobility of character and humanity. The wisdom of Confucius was a legend throughout all of the civilized world, so if the Catholics chose to assume that they held the true answers in their hands, they were not too far apart from much of the rest of mankind.

The presentation was a long one, but it was so masterfully done the attention never waned. A soloist with a magnificent contralto voice sang with an eloquence that completely transcended all barriers of cultural differences, and the choir was superb. When it was all but over Philip took comfort in the fact that the effort had been on behalf of the Man of Galilee and the vagrant thought came to him that perhaps Miss Jayawardene Thiengburanathum might have a fresh and deeper understanding of the Christian faith. He could not help himself, he daydreamed for a moment that the lovely girl was kneeling in a quiet church and it would be his precious privilege to lay his hand upon her head and say, "I baptize thee in the name of the Father, the Son, and the Holy Ghost. Amen."

Bishop O'Hanlon arose, majestic in his vestments, moved to the podium, and looked over the assembled delegates. When attention had focused to its highest power he produced a single-page document and laid it before him. "It is my very great privilege and honor to come before you, as one of your number, at this historic meeting," he began. "We too have read the inspiring words of Dr. Philip Roundtree delivered before the Convocation of his own church and we recognize in them the evidence of greatness. We do indeed live together in a new age, one in which the thought of all of the world's great men can be studied with profit by scholars everywhere. Never again shall we be separated as we have been in the past, unless God should cause a catastrophe which would force us to revert back to primitive isolation once again, deprived of all the benefits we have been permitted to attain."

He picked up the paper gravely and held it in his hand. "We have no reason to believe that it will be the divine will to so separate us again; rather, it seems destined that we shall move ever closer together. Therefore I bring to you, at this critical juncture in the evolution of humanity, a message of the utmost importance. It has been entrusted to me to deliver to you and comes . . . from the Holy Father himself."

He lowered his head and looked at the words written on the paper he held.

" 'May the blessings of God and peace be upon you all. At this great moment that God has ordered, our thoughts and prayers are with you that your deliberations may be successful and that the light of truth will be revealed to you all.

" 'From the moment that our Savior proclaimed Peter to be the rock upon which He would build His Church, we have, with human frailty but Divine guidance, carried forward our holy mission that the souls of men everywhere

188

may be saved. Our arms are open and our heart is filled with love for you all.

" 'To you has been given the monumental task of finding the true faith that leads to God and salvation. That which we have been given we ask only to share. May the lamp that we hold serve to light the path of all of humanity. Even as our Savior said, "Suffer the little children to come unto Me," so we with profound humility follow His teaching and welcome you all to join with us in the glorious company of those who have been redeemed by His sacrifice and infinite love.

" 'May the peace of God which passes all understanding guide and keep you all in Christ Jesus, Our Lord.' "

Bishop O'Hanlon paused and then carefully placed the document once more on the podium. "These inspired words," he said, "may not be directed toward today, or even tomorrow — they stand instead like a great lighthouse in an eternally stormy sea. Any and all of us who are privileged to serve in our Catholic delegation are at your service in any way that we can help."

Philip sat very still, giving no external sign of the thoughts that were passing through his mind. He remained that way while the Catholic delegation and the others who had joined with them for the presentation marched out in a recessional every whit as solemn and dignified as the entering processional had been. There was no visible change. And Philip, from where he sat, could not discover the slightest clue to tell him what the reaction was going to be.

Arthur Gravenstine sat in the Pit, a half-consumed malted milk before him, communing with his thoughts. The conference was now well under way, but apart from the fact that the Roman Catholics had decided to make their delegation official, there had not been very much in the way of concrete progress. He had filed a good story on the Pope's message, but he had nothing in sight with which to follow it up. He had known from the first that the conference would never be able to come up with any world-shaking decisions, but he had hoped, and continued to hope, for at least one good substantial achievement that he could sink his journalistic teeth into for the sake of Philip Roundtree and the rest of humanity.

He looked up to see that the bishop's chaplain had just come in with his Thai girl friend; lately when he had seen one of them he had seen the other. He presumed that they might be sleeping together, but that was none of his affair. He half rose and waved to them to join him; the Pit was crowded and they would need a place to sit, and besides, the young lady was very attractive.

He stood up to shake hands with Fothergill and say something polite to the Thai beauty. Up close she was even better-looking than at a distance, and every step she took inadvertently advertised that she was a female — a complete one. If the Reverend Mr. Fothergill was neglecting all that, it testified that he had one hell of a conscience.

"Thank you for inviting us," Aubrey said as he sat down. Before he was fully settled in his chair a student waitress was at his elbow. "Hi," she greeted. "Tea again?"

Aubrey pointed toward Gravenstine's malted milk. "I'm beginning to like those things," he said; then he turned toward Jayawardene. "How about you, dear?" he asked.

"Fine," she answered, "with some potato chips."

"Right," the waitress said, and left.

Arthur, of course, had noted the way in which the Reverend Mr. Fothergill had addressed his companion and he probed gently. "I take it that you two are finding a lot in common."

For answer Aubrey picked up Jayawardene's left hand and held it out for inspection. The diamond on her third finger was massive, there was no other word.

It was a surprise, but in the same electric moment Arthur

knew that it was news — perhaps big news. Good reporter that he was, he first made sure. "May I assume that means the same thing in Thailand that it does here?"

"You may," Aubrey answered.

"Then my very best wishes, and congratulations to you, sir. How long has it been?"

"Only a day or two."

Arthur's thoughts were gyrating. The significance of the engagement was obvious, but how did a bishop's chaplain manage to buy a ring of that magnificence? He looked at it again and Aubrey read his thoughts.

"We announced our engagement to Dr. Roundtree in the presence of Dr. Poindexter and Sir Cyril. Before I had time to buy a ring . . ."

"Sir Cyril insisted," Jayawardene said. "He demanded that Aubrey allow him to provide the ring. You see, he already had it, and it was the right size."

There was an awkward moment, then Arthur asked, "Have you set a date?"

"No," Aubrey answered, "that's up to the conference." Then he told the decision that he and his bride-to-be had reached.

Arthur's blood raced, for here was the story for which he had been waiting, the real news peg, and it had great human interest! He had all he could do to sit still, but there were details to be filled in. "I think your idea is wonderful," he said. "But what if the conference doesn't produce the results that you want?"

Jayawardene answered him. "We want to be married in a completely suitable manner, and we will be. But we don't want to wait too long."

"May I report this?"

"If you want to — it's certainly no secret."

Arthur blessed the fates that had brought this young couple to his table. "Since it is the bride's prerogative to choose the clergyman who will perform the ceremony, is there any possibility that you might have a Buddhist wedding?"

"We haven't discussed that," Aubrey answered.

"So you're going entirely on the expectation that the conference will score a major success."

Jayawardene took over. "You see, up to now the delegates haven't had any real incentive to do something. We can't provide very much, but here we are: two people who want to be married so that we can live together happily. When the word gets out, it may make them move — just a little."

"It's a start," Arthur agreed.

"It could be a mite more than that. We can't do very much by ourselves, but Sir Cyril has just announced that if the conference doesn't come up with something appropriate for us, he is going to blow off the roof. And when Sir Cyril gets on the warpath, if you will excuse the Americanism, something always happens. We may not like it, but there is certain to be some action."

The rich evening twilight had about it a certain wininess that offered Philip Roundtree solace of spirit. Sitting on the same bench where he had first met Mrs. Philpotts and the Zen master Togen Sumi, he considered carefully the matter of the engagement of his chaplain. The gentle warm air aided his thinking while the gathering darkness served to wrap up some of the confusions in his mind. He had a certain subconscious awareness that somewhat was amiss, but he could not define what it was. The thought disturbed him and he tried to ferret it out; then, quite abruptly, it came to him — the sunset Muslim call to prayer had not been given. It had become such a regular feature of the twilight hour that he missed it, perhaps because its haunting, unworldly, timeless sound seemed to symbolize the far-reaching nature of the conference and the vast span of cultures that it represented.

He wondered casually if the sound system was for some

reason out of order. That thought was still lingering in his mind when the gentle sound of chimes began to float across the campus. Since chimes were not normally rung at that hour, he wondered if he ought to go and investigate.

At that moment Ned Stone appeared quite unexpectedly in front of him and spoke with some urgency. "Bishop Phil, there's something wrong with the Muslim delegation and I think you'd better come immediately. All hell is breaking loose."

Philip was on his feet at once. "Have you any idea what it is?"

"No, sir, but please come now. Karen's getting Sir Cyril and we're trying to find Dr. Poindexter."

Philip hurried as fast as he reasonably could toward the North Dormitory, where the sizable Arabic delegation was housed. As he strode rapidly along, he weighed all the possibilities he could think of; if the whole delegation was upset, then the most likely explanation was a mix-up in the food service. The Muslim ban on all pork products was absolute; if something had been served to them in error, and had by any chance been consumed, then it would be a donnybrook and no mistake.

As he neared the North Dormitory there was no doubt what was taking place. Much luggage had already been carried out of the building and was piled up on the sidewalk outside. As far as Philip knew there was no transportation available at that hour, but even as he watched a young Arab came out with a bundle across his shoulder, from the top of the steps he literally threw it onto the other baggage. That was enough to tell Philip that the situation had not been exaggerated: something was indeed radically wrong.

As he hurried up he encountered, coming out of the building, the same tall, dignified man who had originally called on him to ask permission to broadcast the daily calls to prayer. Philip accosted him directly. "*Salaam aleikum,*" he said.

The man threw a piercing glance at him. *"Salaam,"* he returned, the minimum possible response. Anger was in command of his features and he was obviously controlling himself with an effort.

Philip met the problem head on — it was no time for half measures. "Please tell me," he asked, "what has happened?"

The tall Arab stopped, his immense dignity powerfully in evidence. "We are leaving," he declared. "We shall not return — now or at any time. Let the matter rest there."

By the way the words were spoken Philip knew that the hostility was not directed toward him. He liked the man he was facing, and whatever the problem was, he was determined to resolve it. He reached out his left hand and laid it on the tall man's shoulder. "Please," he asked, "let me share your problem."

The response he got was unexpected and startling; the Arab jerked himself away and his eyes flashed with indignation. "Keep your unclean hand off my body!"

Philip's muscles tightened and he could not help himself when he spoke. *"I am not unclean!"* Anger was in his voice, and the words were hard and cutting.

The Arab stopped, and for a single frozen moment Philip wondered if he was going to be subject to a physical attack. Then the tall Muslim took a very deep breath and slightly inclined his head. "It was not your fault," he declared. "You do not understand." He turned and marched back inside.

Philip followed him because he had to know what was wrong, and deal with it. If he did not, then it was all over and the conference was finished. Islam was too great, and too powerful in the world; no success could be possible without it.

When he reached the lobby the head of the Arabic delegation was still there speaking to a subordinate. When he had finished, he turned and faced Philip once more. "I ask your forgiveness," he said. "I have been unfair to you. We

194

are guests and it is written that we must be just in our conduct."

Philip was quick with his answer. "In turn, if I unwittingly gave you offense, *effendi*, I beg your pardon." He was not sure he had used the Turkish word correctly, but he knew he would be understood.

Once more the tall man inclined his head. "*Salaam aleikum.*"

"*Salaam aleikum,*" Philip returned.

"When you placed your left hand upon my body I forgot myself. Although you are an unbeliever, most certainly I do not consider you unclean."

Philip tried his best to find the right path. "Thank you for your forgiveness," he said. "At no price would I wish to give you offense."

The Arab lifted his right hand. "It is understood, let us speak of it no more. But we cannot remain."

Philip was very careful with his next words. "Will you honor me with the reason why we are to be deprived of your wisdom and counsel?"

For a long moment the Muslim surveyed him, then he reached a decision. "You show respect," he said, "and by so doing, you earn it for yourself." He turned toward the student room clerk behind the counter. "Show him the paper," he directed. "I will not touch the accursed thing myself."

In response the student laid out on the counter the front page of the powerful Midwestern paper that had given the conference a considerable amount of editorial attention. Again a very fine religious drawing covered four columns of the front page. This time it was the portrait of a bearded man clad in Near Eastern robes; his features radiated strength of character and deep conviction. It was another splendid effort by the artist whose work had found such great favor with all of the delegates. Underneath was the caption *Mohammed the Prophet* (570–632).

Philip knew. The drawing presented its subject with the

utmost dignity, there was even an allegorical touch as a rising sun in the background cast a flame of light into the sky. It had clearly been intended as a compliment and tribute to Islam, but it was total disaster.

The tall man addressed him once more. "We are fully aware that this was intended as an honor to us, but there is something you should know."

"Any representation of the Prophet is absolutely forbidden."

"Within our faith, no rule is more strict. It applies to *all* living things, but the sacred person of the Prophet is the most sacrosanct of all; to depict him is to give the most violent offense to all of Islam. To remain here after this has been done is impossible for us; we could never return home as respected members of the faithful. We would be literally in danger of our lives."

Philip swallowed hard as he knew the sharp sting of defeat. No words he could say would change things. At least he had been able to make a personal peace with this intelligent, devout man whose beliefs had been as outraged as his own would have been had Christ been depicted in a brothel. He saw and understood from the other's point of view, but even with this insight, there was nothing he could say or do.

He looked around to see that Sir Cyril Plessey was entering the lobby. With his walking stick he was as jaunty as ever and confidence exuded from him. Philip tried to flash him a warning, but if Sir Cyril caught it, he gave no sign whatsoever. Instead he approached the desk and spoke to the student behind it in his usual clear and incisive voice. "Phone over to the motor pool and ask for a couple of the lads to give us a hand here. There's a lot of baggage outside that's going to have to be brought in again and we can't expect our honored guests to do it themselves."

That attended to, he turned and found that he was confronted by the head of the Islamic delegation, who for the moment had deserted Philip. "Sir Cyril," the Arab declared, "we have told you before that we regard you as a brother among us, and we have not forgotten the great debt that we owe to you. But not even for you can we tolerate the incredible thing that has been done to us and to the great faith we represent. Already we face disgrace when we return home. To remain, under any circumstances, you must accept as impossible." His command of English was remarkable under the circumstances; Philip saw the flaring of the nostrils that told him how much the man was holding himself under control.

Sir Cyril's own composure was complete, as far as visible indications went. He leaned slightly on his stick and answered in a voice which had enough carrying power to be heard throughout the small lobby. "It isn't the Prophet," he said.

With a dignity that was nothing less than towering the Arab pointed one disdainful finger at the caption. "Despite my severe limitations, I am able to a small degree to read English."

Sir Cyril became gruffer. "It is not necessary to tell me that — I wouldn't for a moment assume less. But it isn't the Prophet. I've been in touch with the publisher of the paper; I called him the moment I saw it. The caption is wrong; the portrait is of Zoroaster. It's been corrected in all of the later editions. I have arranged to have some copies of the corrected version flown up here by chartered aircraft; they're on their way now."

In the momentary pause that followed, another member of the Islamic delegation dared to speak. "How can we believe this?" he asked.

Sir Cyril was spared from answering by the head of the delegation, who took it upon himself to reply. "The first and greatest reason is because we are told so by our brother, whose word is beyond all cavil. The second explanation I am presently also waiting to hear."

Sir Cyril obliged. "Please notice carefully the background

of the picture. You will note the flame rising from the edge of the sun."

The impressive Arab consented to look. "I do," he acknowledged.

"Fire is the symbol of the Parsees," Sir Cyril continued. "Eternal flames are kept burning in all of their temples; sandalwood is the usual fuel. You, of course, have heard of the fire temples. You will also recall that in the portrait of Martin Luther there was a cross in the background. In the one honoring the Buddha there was a swastika — a matter that had to be explained in detail to some members of the Jewish delegation. The flame you note indicates at once that here we have Zoroaster, the founder of the Parsee faith."

The tall Arab considered the matter. "Accepting this explanation without reservation, since it is you who offer it, then how do we account for the fact that the sacred name of the Prophet appears beneath the drawing of another man?"

Sir Cyril nodded. "The error came about because Islam is to be honored next week and an uninformed person had ordered this type set. Someone else, equally ignorant, put it with the drawing of Zoroaster and it appeared that way. The newspaper management, of course, is furious."

"Do you happen to know also in what manner Islam is to be honored?"

"As it happens, yes. I have not personally seen the artwork, but the publisher told me that it is a splendid drawing of the great Blue Mosque in Istanbul. At the same time I was informed that a letter of apology is being addressed to this delegation; it is coming on the same plane with the corrected papers."

At that juncture two young men from the motor pool came into the lobby and looked about for instructions. Sir Cyril nodded toward the tall Arab. Ten seconds passed that Philip Roundtree would not forget for the rest of his life;

then the distinguished Muslim made up his mind. "We have some baggage to be brought in," he said. "We would appreciate your help."

The tension broke and flowed away. Without undue haste Sir Cyril gathered up the offending paper and dropped it symbolically into a wastebasket. Then, after looking around to be sure that all was under control once more, he turned to take his departure. Philip was aware that his own presence would contribute nothing further, besides which a question lurked in his mind that he very much wanted to have answered. In the company of Sir Cyril he left the building, grateful for the opportunity to breathe the uncomplicated outside air. He had no fixed plan of action, he simply wanted to calm down and regain his full equilibrium once more.

"It was a fortunate thing that some of the students were still available in the motor pool," he commented.

"Yes, wasn't it."

"You arranged it, I take it."

"The matter was looked into. I had Ames stationed outside to send them in on my signal."

"I didn't see it."

"Precisely as intended."

The time was right for Philip to put the question that was in his mind. "Sir Cyril, *was* that a portrait of Zoroaster?"

The elderly knight appeared to reflect a moment before he answered. "Some time ago, in Germany, a statue was erected of a man who later fell from grace. The people who had it, being practically minded, put it up for sale. Some others bought it and set it up in their town square as the likeness of the splendid humanitarian who invented beer, or improved it at any rate. It has his name on it to this day, and everyone is happy."

"So it was a picture of the Prophet, after all."

Sir Cyril shook his head. "No, Philip. It may have been

intended that way originally, but it is now Zoroaster; the publisher and I agreed on that. Therefore I was able to tell the absolute truth to my Muslim friends — under no circumstances would I do less."

Philip considered the whole matter. "The Parsees should be very pleased when the revised papers get here."

"Undoubtedly."

"One thing I do not know," Philip said, "What is wrong with my left hand?"

"In your case nothing, but an Arab always uses his left hand when he urinates, which renders it unclean by their standards. Now, if you'll excuse me, I have an appointment to play table tennis with three very charming young ladies. You know the importance of regular exercise — of all kinds."

Philip in turn excused himself and turned once more toward the campus. He had some hard thinking to do, perhaps the most important since he had come to the New World. Only four more major presentations remained to be given; after that, discussion in earnest was due to begin. That would be the most critical part, and if he could bring even a modicum of success out of that, then the purpose of his life on earth would be more than fulfilled and he would truly have done the Lord's work.

Was there a magic touchstone somewhere, something to make the many men and women gathered at Maplewood truly want to reach at least a partial agreement? It was something he himself should have been able to supply, but so far he had fallen far short of that mark.

He was not even conscious of the fact that he was walking toward the meditation room and had no way of knowing that the Zen master, Togen Sumi, would be found waiting for him there. That profoundly wise man was fully aware of what was going on and he too wished to make his contribution.

Most of all, Philip Roundtree did not know that in the

200

press room, alone and completely immersed in the tools of his trade, Arthur Gravenstine was burning with a soul-seizing inspiration, and as his fingers thumped the type-writer keys he was creating the greatest story of his already distinguished career.

CHAPTER FIFTEEN

In less than five days Arthur Gravenstine's story went literally around the world. It appeared in the *Bangkok Post* on the front page, it was prominently featured in *Stars and Stripes,* and there was hardly a major paper apart from those behind the Iron Curtain and in other news-restricted areas that did not run it and comment upon it in the editorial columns. There had been a steady flow of news coming out of the conference at Maplewood College, but after the initial stories had been filed, interest had fallen off rapidly until the courtesy pieces that did appear had had to compete in interest with the food pages, the astrological forecasts, and the weather reports. In a single hour before a press room typewriter Arthur Gravenstine changed all that — and in so doing carved for himself a niche in journalistic history.

The story he had had to tell had been a natural and he had seized upon it with hot inspiration. For the first time in weeks he filed immediately without taking the time to think about what he had done and then rewrite. When he had finished he hardly had strength enough left to walk back to the Pit, where refreshment — of a sort at least — awaited him.

As he quaffed a glass of the ice-cold beer, he wished that he had been able to come up with a better head than *A Tale of Two People*. However, the boys on the rewrite desk would probably take care of that. It was out of his hands anyway. He had another beer and then fled from the sound of the jukebox to his quarters, denying himself even his usual pleasure of watching the young ladies in more or less minimum attire bouncing their spirited way at the Ping-Pong tables.

The first reaction that he got was in the form of a cable from Felix Wyeth, his colleague on the music desk: *Crime of the decade in Britain; you have stolen the front page.*

The story came back across the Atlantic almost as fast as it had gone. The *Philadelphia Evening Bulletin*, the *Cleveland Plain Dealer*, the *Chicago Tribune*, the *Los Angeles Times*, and almost every other major paper gave it prime display space and the editorial columns resoundingly backed it up. In hardly more than twenty-four hours an obscure young British clergyman and an unknown young lady from Thailand became international celebrities. America's mightiest magazine somehow secured a photograph of them together and put it on the cover, while in broadcasting studios across the nation commentators faced the formidable task of learning to pronounce Thiengburana-thum trippingly on the tongue.

Arthur read his own story and wondered if he had actually written it. He was well used to seeing his words in type, but this time his usual careful and precise recitation of the facts had given way to a different style altogether. Still, if they hadn't liked it they wouldn't have run it as written, so he saw no cause to worry. He reviewed his lead:

"And the Lord said, 'It is not good that man should be alone.' "

So it was that Adam came to behold Eve. He took her hand in his and with his new companion and helpmate set out to found the human race. He had no choice, but Eve was all that he asked and there was no other suitor for her hand.

It was very beautiful and totally uncomplicated.

Today something more than two billion of their descendants populate the entire earth and things have become enormously complicated indeed. But even now when a man beholds the woman that he loves, the glories of Eden can come again into being and they too can walk together in happiness through the flowers and under the trees.

If the rest of the world will let them.

Following that he had told the story of Aubrey Fothergill and Jayawardene Thiengburanathum in simple uncluttered prose. He had sketched in their backgrounds and had quietly pointed out how entirely suitable both of them were to enter into marriage. That done, he had let himself go a little bit, and had used some bolder strokes.

But the same basic world civilization that instituted marriage has shattered itself in an agony of religious division, and from the ruins have arisen the flames of intolerance, persecution, infused hostility, and war. On this pyre millions have died, but the agony of their consumed flesh and the crimson flow of their blood has purchased no precious peace, no closer understanding of the will of the Almighty.

Now in sober conclave eight hundred and twelve men and women, representing almost every organized form of worship currently existing in the world, are seeking at long last to find some precious fragments of common ground. And while they ponder and debate, two of their number have for themselves found much of the answer. It is only necessary for the very wise spiritual leaders who are assembled to find the proper path by which the Reverend Mr. Fothergill may lead his lovely bride up to the all-embracing altar of God.

"In the image of God he created them, male and female He created them."

204

So be it. Jayawardene and Aubrey have found each other; It remains for the rest of the congregation of mankind to do the same.

To the remaining delegates to this historic meeting we wish Godspeed, for time is drawing very short indeed.

Arthur Gravenstine realized that he could not rhapsodize like that very often, but he did not intend to. He looked at his watch. The meeting would be starting in a very short while and the Hopi Indian nation was due to explain to the assembly their historic prophesies which foretold the will of the Great Spirit. He didn't want to miss that, so he gathered up his note-taking materials and set off across the campus toward the auditorium.

The second reaction came from the small Winnebago post office, which was well set up to handle the considerable flow of mail that the conference had generated. As the full sacks came in they were taken up to the college as promptly as possible; deliveries were made two or three times a day as the volume required. This routine worked well until two days after the Gravenstine article appeared; after that the deluge began.

When the first overflowing truckload from the post office arrived on campus the mail room sent out a quick call for help. Many of the letters were addressed to individual delegations by name, but a truly massive quantity was simply directed to the conference generally. As soon as it became obvious that tabulation would be the only practical way to handle matters, Dean Hastings drew up some charts based on the first two or three hundred letters that were read. As many volunteers as could be located pitched in, but the task was monumental. When at last it appeared that the end was in sight, two more trucks appeared and began to unload a huge new accumulation. The drivers left with the cheerful information that a lot more would be brought up shortly.

When Harley Poindexter was notified of this new development, he promptly moved the mail operation to a much larger room and rounded up all available personnel to lend a hand.

In the offices which he had selected as suitable for his temporary use Sir Cyril Plessey was made aware of the situation. He promptly proposed a solution, and then without waiting for any official approval sent a message down to the press room. The power of his name, and the known fact that he could always produce something in the way of news, resulted in a turnout of all the newsmen who were on campus. Only five men appeared, but they had the right connections and that was quite enough for Sir Cyril's purposes.

"Gentlemen," he began in his best announcing manner, "Maplewood College and the conference are on the receiving end of what appears to be a tidal wave of mail. Literally thousands of pieces have come in today and the expectation is that by tomorrow there will be a flood. It was generated, of course, by Mr. Gravenstine, whose report on the engagement of the Reverend Mr. Fothergill and Miss Jayawardene Thiengburanathum has aroused the greatest international interest."

"What is the general tenor?" the AP man asked.

"I was just coming to that. The letters are being sorted on the basis of eleven categories at the present time, the eleventh being opposition to the proposed marriage on the basis of religious difference or national distinction, both of which are equally intolerable. I am happy to advise you that this last classification is so far distinctly the smallest. The other ten . . ." He paused and eagle eyed the others present. " . . . are very much in favor of the union. In various ways they all exhort the delegates and the conference generally to get on with the job of working something out."

206

"The voice of the people," someone offered.

"Precisely. Bahai has offered to have the wedding celebrated in their home temple, which is not too far from here. There is a growing list of churches, mainstream and otherwise, who are willing to lend their good offices and their facilities. If they wanted to these young people could spend the next several weeks getting married without repeating themselves, based on the returns already in."

"What do you think they will do, Sir Cyril?" the UPI representative inquired.

"The Reverend Mr. Fothergill," Sir Cyril replied, "is an exceedingly stubborn young man. He and his intended have agreed that they will await results from the conference. If none are forthcoming, it is my advice to them to live in sin until some are — one way or another."

"As a supposition, Sir Cyril, if the conference does not produce any results, and if the young people fail to accept your counsel, then do you think that the bride will choose a Buddhist clergyman to perform the ceremony?"

Sir Cyril tossed that one way. "Ask the bride. The point is, gentlemen, that from now on you can beat the drums on the theme that the conference has a new motivation. Not just to get these young people married, but to meet the challenge they symbolize. To some degree, at least, how much they will be inspired to get down to business will depend on you. Get on with it."

A representative of CBS closed the meeting. "We will," he promised.

High up in one of New York's major buildings, protected by full security and a confidential secretary unexcelled in the city, a man who was fifty-six years old had left his desk to stand at the window and look out over the Hudson River. He was not a conspicuous person except to the very observing; they would detect the quality of the suit that he wore, his handmade Italian shoes, and the flawless piece of

207

Burmese jewel jadeite mounted in the ring on his left hand. He had only to walk into a top-class restaurant to be shown to the best available table, despite the fact that few head-waiters would recognize him by sight. He avoided publicity because in his line of work it could be a serious drawback. His name did not even appear on the letterhead of the important international corporation he controlled.

Seated in a chair that yielded to every contour of his body was his trusted lieutenant, who in that capacity earned a six-figure salary because he was widely experienced, intelligent, efficient, and totally reliable.

The man at the window turned and, as he often did, expressed his thoughts aloud in the presence of his second in command. "When the whole thing was first announced I considered it to be insane; it was about as likely to succeed as a drive to erect a statue of Adolf Hitler in Tel Aviv. Consequently I dismissed it from my mind. Now, however, there is a very small possibility that something may come of it."

The seated man spoke. "Also don't discount the fact that Plessey is behind it. What his reasoning is only God knows, but that immediately takes it out of the league of just a bunch of churchmen having a guarded love feast. He's an old man, but he hasn't slowed up and he's sharper than sin."

The man at the window took time to light a cigarette. He inhaled once deeply and then continued. "Plessey has been a factor from the beginning, but this time he was clearly in over his head, despite his abilities. That was obvious — almost too much so. I assumed that he had found himself a new amusement and let it go at that. I didn't foresee this popular engagement. Hell, it's all over the world."

"J. R., how possible is it that Plessey cooked it up?"

"It's definitely possible, Jock, but whether he did or didn't, the net result is the same. When the public at large is stirred up over an emotional issue, any damn thing can happen. Remember Laika, the space dog? The Russians completely miscalculated the reaction to that one and they got caught in a very expensive backfire. It could happen again."

"And the time little Kathy Fiskus fell down the well."

"Or Floyd Collins was trapped in a cave. Those things happened years ago to unknown people, but their names are still remembered. I don't think we can afford to ignore this thing any more."

The man in the chair put an antacid pill into his mouth and crushed it with his teeth. He did not apologize for his action, and took his time as he swallowed the medicine. "If by any remote chance Plessey gets those people to reach any kind of an accord, no matter how flimsy, the net cost to us would be staggering."

The man at the window returned to his desk and accepted the comfort of the custom-built chair behind it. "Exactly. Death, taxes, and international religious hostility are foregone conclusions, but remember this. Not too long age we had the Siegfried and Maginot lines with billions poured into their construction. Now we have the Common Market and political union can't be completely discounted. Things change."

"What do you want me to do? Or have you decided?"

The man behind the desk was incisive. "I have decided; we can't let things drift any longer. Take whatever steps are necessary to see that the thing simply breaks up as expected. Set your own budget. Only one thing — stay out of sight."

The man called Jock got to his feet without visible effort. "If I have to lock horns with Plessey, it may take quite a bit of money."

The man behind the desk dismissed that with a wave of his hand.

Before the great religious conference had come to Maplewood College, Bill Quigley had found the job of being public relations director of that institution a relatively light task; then came the sudden opportunity to play in the big league, a challenge he accepted with unrestrained enthusiasm. That was before the Gravenstine piece had appeared; after that he felt like a man standing in the path of an avalanche.

Jayawardene was no problem; from almost any angle she took a ravishing picture and her behavior was a PR man's dream. For a short while it seemed that every television network and individual station in the nation wanted to get hold of her, as did all the talk show personalities who depended on guests to maintain their audience appeal. After a fast consultation with Harley Poindexter he pressed Karen Erickson into service and assigned her the job of handing the fissionable beauty from Thailand. That proved to be an inspiration and freed him to attend to other matters.

Up to that point the conference had gone reasonably well, but the honeymoon would soon be over. The last of the presentations had been given; after a three-day break to respect all the various sabbaths, discussions were due to begin, and that was where the danger lay. Not even politics could produce the same degree of ironheadedness and lack of concession as profound religious convictions. The Arabs were not about to like the Jews, the Greeks felt no brotherhood toward the Turks, and the Buddhists were not likely to forgive the Muslims for having destroyed so many of their shrines and defaced so many thousands of their sacred images.

To Sir Cyril Plessey the outlook was different. If anything constructive was to come out of the whole vast effort, it would not be easy, some friction was inevitable. He knew that he could not force an agreement, but he could referee the conflict.

He lifted his head and called out, "Ames!"

His manservant responded at once. "Yes, Sir Cyril?"

"Did you make the stock sale that I suggested to you this morning?"

"Yes, sir, immediately after you advised me to do so."

"How much profit did you realize?"

"Slightly over ten thousand pounds, Sir Cyril."

"Very good. I have never asked you this, but I assume that you are by now a millionaire."

"Definitely in dollars, sir, and very nearly in pounds. It is, of course, due entirely to following your advice at all times."

"I presume, then, that you will be leaving me one of these days."

Ames shook his head. "Not unless that is your wish, Sir Cyril. Sharing your life of extraordinary adventure is a privilege I value above almost everything else."

"But I make things very difficult for you at times. I create problems."

For the first time in many years Ames smiled in the presence of his employer. "None that I haven't been able to handle, sir. You must realize that I have had a great teacher."

"What do you think is going to happen to the conference? Your own real opinion."

The reply took a few moments. "I greatly fear that I see no hope whatever, unless you choose to pull off one of your customary miracles, sir. In that event, all bets are off."

Sir Cyril reflected. He tipped his head back and contemplated the ceiling. He remained motionless for some time, then his fingers began to tap against the arms of his chair. It was an automatic movement, as though his mental energies had chosen that manner of expressing themselves. "It would have to be a miracle, Ames, nothing less would do. The young couple has caught the public imagination, but their eventual marriage is a minor matter. However, it can be a useful one, as far as it goes."

"But it lacks the muscle, as you sometimes observe, sir."

"Quite right, Ames, quite right. Sentiment is a fine thing, but it has its own world to live in. This is another matter entirely."

"Have you any ideas at present, sir?"

Sir Cyril's fingers stopped their movement and seemed to poise themselves in midair, as though they were afraid to intrude on what was going on. "A fragment of one, perhaps. No more than that."

He straightened himself in his chair. "Where is Bishop Roundtree, do you happen to know?"

"It is my understanding that His Lordship is meditating, sir. He quite recently acquired the ability to do so."

"Splendid, that's some progress at any rate." He stopped and continued his concentration, putting pieces together in his mind until to Ames, who knew him so well, the process was almost visible. It was some time before Sir Cyril was ready to speak again. "It isn't going to work out by itself," he said. "There's just too much against it. Roundtree is magnificent, of course, but even he can't be expected to cope with plain flat-out insoluble prejudice and the fixations of centuries."

Ames nodded. "I greatly fear that I must agree with you, sir."

"But it isn't hopeless, Ames, not yet and not completely. Some very careful maneuvering will have to be done, and some highly important people will have to be moved about on the chessboard, to set the stage. They can only be invited with the fullest respect for their offices and convictions. But the game is worth the candle, Ames! In a sense it may be the greatest game of all. I don't wish to appear melodramatic, but the religious future of the human race is a large stake."

"I can think of nothing to exceed it, sir."

"I only hope that the Almighty will approve of what I may decide to do."

Ames waited a respectful moment. "You do have something in mind then, sir?"

The motio l ss fingers gripped the arms of the chair with the power of a decision reached. "Yes, Ames, I do. It's a very long shot, perhaps an impossible one, but there is one man in the world . . ." He did not finish the sentence; instead, his lips worked once more and the old determined look returned to his eyes. Then firmness came back into his voice and resolution hung in the air. "Fortunately, I know him," he concluded.

When Philip Roundtree had stood up to preach on that wintry Sunday morning before the Convocation of the Church of England, he had been fired by what had seemed to him an almost compelling urgency, but he had been too wise in the ways of the Church to expect anything more than a very gradual and slow process at the best. He had hoped, possibly, to see something actually started. Beyond that he had had no expectations.

Most certainly he had not foreseen the major conference over which he was presiding scarcely half a year later.

But Philip was far from an idealistic fool. He realized fully that to have the meeting come up with any sort of universally acceptable religious doctrine was a total impossibility. He had not expected that for a moment. So after taking careful aim at the noonday sun, he had given a great deal of careful thought to what might within the bounds of reason be set as a goal which, if achieved, would make the whole vast effort a success. His entire concern was for the welfare of the conference and of its members; personal aggrandizement did not interest him — he had had too much publicity already. After listening to the many presentations by the various faiths represented, he had turned his gifted mind to the task of finding the possible two grains of agreement in the two bushels of conflicting beliefs and dogmas.

In a week's time, after much profound thought, he drew up his thirteen points.

At first he kept them very much to himself until he was fully satisfied with their content. Then, because of the respect he had for the president of Maplewood College, and the stake that the school had in the meeting, he had shown them to Harley Poindexter. In consultation with Dean Hastings, Dr. Poindexter had approved them in full. "Philip," he had declared, "I will admit to you that I have been wondering how you were going to wind this all up. You're too competent by far to let it simply fall to pieces, and to have asked for a wide general agreement would have been an invitation to disaster. This is the answer. My hat's off to you."

That had been tremendously encouraging. Philip had debated whether or not he should go over his plan with Sir Cyril Plessey, but that unpredictable nobleman had momentarily deserted the campus on business of his own. He was reported to be in San Francisco, but he had not chosen to announce his whereabouts. Philip did sit down with his brother bishop of the Church of England and in somewhat less detail discussed what he intended to do. Here he found thinking very much like his own; John Duncan was also an experienced churchman with his feet on the ground, and when he could find nothing but praise for what Philip had in mind, a good sound glimmer of hope illuminated the way forward.

In addition to which Duncan had had an idea of his own. "Philip," he had begun, "I regard this as very good news. Now you have something that has an excellent chance of success in my opinion, and if you can pull off even a good part of it, you will have served God and the Church more than you may realize. In fact, all of humanity, if you will allow me that thought. It's an attainable goal, and that's what this conference has needed from the start."

Bishop Duncan had paused then while he had made up

his mind on another point. "Philip, I think you should know that Danford-Smith has asked me for a report, in some detail, as to how things are going here and how you personally are faring. I interpret this as a gesture of genuine interest, not as any questioning of your status or capabilities. With your permission, I'd like to convey these thirteen points to him. I believe they will do a great deal to put his mind at rest and gain his additional support."

Philip had agreed immediately. The whole plan would have to be made public in a few days in any event, and to advise his superior in advance of his intentions through Duncan was clearly most advisable.

He had hardly ushered his fellow bishop out of his office when another visitor appeared. Once again he did not know the man's name, but his attire, full beard, and the cross hung suspended on his chest all gave a composite image of the Eastern Church. Philip rose to his feet to welcome him. "Good evening, Father," he said. "I'm honored by your visit."

The Orthodox priest spoke without inhibitions. "Most kind of you. My name is Petris, and may I say at once that your meeting so far has been magnificent. We have all learned so much. Already I feel that I personally understand my fellow men far better than before."

Philip again felt the glow of good news. "Please sit down. And thank you for such wonderful encouragement."

Father Petris seated himself and declined an offer of coffee. "I have been waiting for this moment," he said, "when I would have the honor of meeting you face to face. For we are indeed brothers in Christ. And my errand is even more of a happy one, for I have some wonderful news to give to you."

"Please do." Everything seemed to be going right at that moment.

"I am sure that you know that this convocation is being watched with the greatest interest by all the branches of

215

our Church, even those that are attempting to operate in the Iron Curtain countries. Our delegation has been sending in regular reports, and I am pleased to inform you that you personally are held in very high regard by all of us."

"Thank you — thank you very much."

The visiting priest clasped his hands. "It is now my great privilege to tell you that as an indication of the importance we all feel toward this historic meeting, the Metropolitan himself is coming to attend the next two or three sessions. He cannot remain for long, I regret to say, but the impact of his presence, we know, will mean a very great deal."

He stopped and shook his head. "I am being much too formal — forgive me. More simply put, we are so confident of what you are doing, the Metropolitan is coming in person to demonstrate the strength of our support. It is our way of helping."

That was indeed news. Philip had had occasional thoughts about inviting some of the major religious personalities to visit the meeting, but he had not held out too much hope of success. The Metropolitan, he recognized, was a very important figure in the Orthodox hierarchy, probably at least the equivalent of a cardinal.

"I am quite overwhelmed," he said. "This is a totally unexpected honor."

"No more than you and this splendid conference deserve, believe me. The Metropolitan is a magnificent person, I am sure you will be most happy to know him."

"That is beyond all question; I shall be delighted."

"So kind of you, Dr. Roundtree. Now a small matter if I may venture . . ."

"Please, by all means."

"This is a possible suggestion, only that and nothing more, you understand."

Philip did not understand, but he nodded anyway.

Once more the Orthodox priest clasped his hands together. "You know, of course, that the rituals and services of our Church are perhaps the richest and most colorful in the entire Christian world. And the music that is heard in our cathedrals is sublime."

"They are both celebrated," Philip said.

"And very rightly so, if I may be allowed. The thought has occurred to us that our wedding service is of particular magnificence. We have available, not too far away, all the resources necessary to celebrate a wedding in the most splendid manner. And with the Metropolitan himself here . . ." He lowered his head. "It is just a suggestion," he concluded.

Philip was equal to the moment. "With your permission, I will convey this thought to certain people who should know of it. In the meantime, I would like to call in Mr. Quigley, the public relations director of Maplewood College, who is handling the conference publicity. The announcement of the Metropolitan's coming is of major importance and he will want to know of it at once."

As soon as his guest had nodded approval, Philip picked up the telephone.

As Arthur Gravenstine climbed the steps up to the balcony of the chapel-auditorium, his heart was pounding slightly, less from the exertion than from a certain sense of anticipation that he did not try to suppress. There had been three days of deceptive quiet throughout the campus, three days in which forces had been invisibly gathering themselves. Now the great discussion was about to begin.

Whatever was about to happen, one thing was practically assured: it would be news. As Arthur took his seat he glanced at the front row position customarily occupied by Sir Cyril Plessey. To his surprise, it was ominously empty. The action was about to begin, and if the elderly knight was not present there had to be a compelling reason. Arthur resolved to make inquiries the moment that he was free to do so.

Down below, on the main floor, the delegates had gathered as usual, but the normal hum of conversation that had preceded all the previous sessions had a different coloration — it was a little higher in level, a little less smooth in content. As Philip Roundtree walked to the podium to open the meeting it subsided, but an undertone remained and a certain sense of tension was already in the air.

Arthur noticed something else too: the almost self-effacing demeanor that Roundtree had been employing for the past several weeks was no longer in evidence. From this point forward the meeting would require a strong leadership, and clearly Philip knew that. Furthermore, he seemed determined to provide it. As soon as the level of sound had dropped sufficiently for him to be heard, he set some papers down on the podium and opened the session.

"From the start of our convocation until now I have learned a very great deal," he began. "I would like to thank personally all those who took part in the many presentations of faith and viewpoint; they were uniformly superb and collectively they constituted a great educational experience. I am happy to announce that one of the leading publishers here in America is negotiating to bring out all these addresses in book form, together with appropriate illustrations."

As he paused a small ripple of applause answered his words.

"We now come to what is in many ways the most critical phase of our meeting and one which I am sure we have all been anticipating. I have personally reflected upon it to a considerable extent and, thanks to my own advancing education here, I have also meditated. As a result of much mental labor, I have arrived at a reality which I should like to present to you now."

He took a sip of water. "With your permission. I would like to be brutally realistic for a few moments. We have all learned much about each others' doctrines and forms of worship, but I do not believe that we are collectively pre-pared to foresake our own convictions in order to embrace a common doctrine. Centuries of tradition and great learn-ing are not so easily set aside."

A murmur answered him; it was indistinct, but it was responsive.

"Yet I believe that most of us would like to foresee the day when all of the conflicts born of religious dissent will have been relegated to the pages of history. This, I believe, is an attainable goal — perhaps even within our own life-times."

This time there was quiet; they were listening to him, and that in itself was significant.

"As a means to this end, I have taken the great liberty of drawing up a proposal." He lifted a paper off the podium and displayed it. "I have set down thirteen points which, after a great amount of thought, I believe might contain the seeds of some measure of agreement. I ask your permis-sion to submit it to you at this time." He looked up and surveyed his audience. "If there is any other proposal — of any kind whatsoever — that any of you would care to ad-vance, I will entertain it with the greatest interest and enthusiasm."

He waited. When a hand went up, a microphone was quickly handed to the lady delegate who had asked for the floor. "Wouldn't it just be simpler," she asked, "if we all were to agree, as we all must, that Jesus Christ is God and King? Then we can go on from there."

Philip was very careful, for many reasons. "You and I can certainly agree to that, as can many others who are present here. But we also have with us distinguished men and women of other convictions whose great knowledge and wisdom is entitled to the highest respect. In deference to their viewpoints, I suggest that we look for some simpler areas of agreement first."

From the balcony Arthur Gravenstine noted that the

single remaining representative of the Orthodox Jewish faith nodded agreement with those words. So also did a bearded Sikh who was clearly the tallest delegate present.

Philip continued. "I know that it is presumptuous of me to advance my own proposal; I am only doing so in the absence of any others. I would like to submit it to you for a vote as to whether or not you wish to take it up. If it is your wish to do so, then each of the thirteen points that it contains can be considered separately. It we are able to agree on even some of them, we will have a firm accomplishment of a kind that as far as I know has never before been achieved."

Once again Philip paused. As he did so, Arthur Gravenstine knew that if the Right Reverend Dr. Philip Roundtree pulled this one off, he saw before him on the stage below the future Primate of the Church of England. This was history being made.

Without dramatics Philip read the preamble to his document. It was a carefully worded statement that after due consideration on behalf of all of the principal faiths being followed in the world, the delegates assembled had found agreement on certain important issues. The language was tempered with restraint, but it was also direct and notably clear. As he listened Gravenstine realized that in addition to being an eloquent preacher, Philip Roundtree knew a thing or two about putting words onto paper.

"The first point is as follows: *The universe in all of its complexity and grandeur is the creation of a sublime intelligence commonly called God whose authority is infinite and absolute.*

"The second point: *Most forms of worship now existing on earth are human inventions and therefore subject to error and misunderstanding of the divine will.*

"The third point: *Because of human frailty and lack of infinite knowledge, no set of existing doctrines can be regarded as infallible, and for the same reason none can be dismissed as untenable."*

There was still a careful quiet. It remained relatively intact as Philip read on, setting forth the remaining ten points of his proposal. As he did so, Arthur evaluated their chances of acceptance based on his own knowledge. It was difficult, particularly when he remembered on what small points of doctrine the Eastern Orthodox Church had separated itself from the remainder of the Christian body. Single words had, in the past, spawned religious differences that had gone on for decades.

When the reading was done, he had arrived at no decision. He only knew that the list in itself was an achievement and if the delegates had any real sense they would know that. Probably they did, but the question remained as to whether or not their individual convictions and prejudices would get too seriously in the way. If that happened, then chaos would be the most likely result.

He looked again at the place where Sir Cyril should have been sitting, but that notable gentleman was still absent. There had to be a reason for that, but Arthur had no idea what it might be apart from illness.

He got up quietly to leave. There was sure to be discussion for quite some time and he did not need to hear it. He had a good story to file, and if he knew Bill Quigley, copies of Roundtree's thirteen points would be awaiting him in the press room.

When he had finished his work he picked up his mail on the way to his room. It contained an unexpected copy of the *Times* which had been sent to him air mail, special delivery. A more careful look at the label informed him that his colleague on the music desk, Felix Wyeth, was the sender. He tore off the wrapper with a certain expectation.

He was not disappointed. Down in the corner, but still on the front page, there was a single column heading:

NEAR RIOT IN ALBERT HALL

Debut of new work marked by extraordinary conduct

BY FELIX WYETH

A well-thrown tomato, expertly hurled within the hallowed confines of Albert Hall, climaxed a series of remarkable events during the concert given there last evening. The occasion was the first British performance of a new work, "Xyonisis" by the well-known avant-garde composer Ossip Koskavinsky.

Mr. Koskavinsky's work was programmed immediately following the "Brandenberg Concerto No. 2" of Johann Sebastian Bach which began the evening. The Hall was well filled with followers of the new music who had come in the expectation of hearing another of the uninhibited musical explorations for which Koskavinsky is famous. The composer's fondness for almost continuous electronic and percussion effects is well known.

In a complete reversal of form, Koskavinsky offered a work of throbbing romanticism. In sweeping and occasionally brilliant harmonies the orchestra sang a splendid new song full of Viennese Gemutlichkeit and grandeur.

It quickly became apparent that this was not what the audience present had come to hear. In the midst of some of the most rewarding early moments of the piece, sounds of disapproval could be heard from the stalls. They grew in volume until it was all but impossible to hear the music being performed.

At this juncture a ripe tomato thrown from an uncertain location caught a particularly vocal protester who had risen to his feet full in the face.

The Koskavinsky work was not completed, a majority of the musicians in the orchestra being disinclined to continue. The new piece has been rescheduled for next Sunday afternoon. It will replace the "Nutcracker Suite" of Tchaikovsky which has already been heard once this season.

Arthur completed the article, reread it out of respect for his long-suffering friend, and then set himself down to compose a cablegram.

It took the assembly almost two full days merely to agree to consider the thirteen points which Philip Roundtree had proposed. The discussion several times came close to the brink of hostility, and only by the exercise of the maximum amount of patience, judgment, and diplomacy did Philip manage to keep reasonable order and some semblance of forward movement. When at last the issue came to a vote, a great many of the Christian delegates were close to bitter. It seemed to be their consensus that with a British bishop in charge of the meeting much more could have been done to steer the deliberations toward the goal of world acceptance of Christianity.

On the other hand, Philip knew that by regarding all the various delegations as exact equals he was taking the only possible path toward eventual success. The Asian faiths, in particular, were aware of his efforts in this direction, so that when the final count was at last taken, they voted for him and his proposals and by so doing provided the margin necessary to bring them to the floor.

It was a victory but a costly one. Philip had hoped for a general satisfaction with the document he had produced, but it had brought down severe criticism from the Christian bloc, in particular from the Missouri Synod Lutherans. That fundamentalist group had demanded that he declare his own convictions from the podium, that he give "Christian witness" just at a time when he was trying his utmost to appear a true and impartial mediator for the sake of God and mankind.

During the nearly two full days of debate over an issue which had required no declaration of faith or conviction, there had been few moments free of cross-currents, irreconcilable opinions, and a strong tendency to examine in detail each individual item. When it was all over and done with, the assembly had agreed by majority vote to take up the thirteen points which Philip had proposed, but the relative stability that had characterized the convocation up to that point was gone and feelings were running far too high to anticipate any success at all when the points themselves came up for discussion.

Then, at that critical point, the Metropolitan arrived, and Philip welcomed him as he might have an angel from heaven.

He seemed to be, literally, a Godsend. He was a huge imposing man, splendid in his clerical dress, but behind this sense of presence there was a brilliant brain and an enormous personal warmth. He was accompanied by several others who made up his personal retinue, but the larger than life aspect of the archbishop himself completely dominated the scene from the moment he stepped out of his car and surveyed the campus spread out before him. Philip was there to welcome him, of course, as were Harley Poindexter and Dean Hastings on behalf of Maplewood College.

The Metropolitan radiated good will. He shook hands with enthusiasm and bolstered Philip's cause by being equally cordial and outgoing to the three or four other delegates from the Eastern faiths who were also present out of the fine Oriental sense of respect for age and wisdom. Despite his size, the archbishop managed by some kind of magnetic personal alchemy not to appear larger than those with whom he was speaking. He was a man, Philip decided, who if he had been in the Church of England would have been a mighty voice in the land. When the formalities of greeting were over, the Metropolitan suggested to him in the manner of one peer to another that they confer as soon as convenient.

Gladly Philip led the way to his office, and once his distinguished visitor was seated and had been offered coffee, he shut the door. When he was himself seated he opened the conversation. "I am most grateful that it was possible for you to come here, Your Eminence. I don't need to tell you that your presence is an important event."

The Metropolitan sipped coffee and then waved one huge arm. "To begin with, my name is Nicholas and I ask that you use it. May I call you Philip?"

"Of course — please do."

"That is excellent. Now let us come right to the point as your time is especially valuable right now. I have been following most closely the progress of your meeting here. I have also read your thirteen points and consider them magnificent — it is the only possible way, of course, that you could bring anything concrete out of this meeting in less than, say, ten years, or a great deal longer."

"From your viewpoint, what chance do you think they have?" Philip asked.

The archbishop tossed his head back and consumed a few moments in thought. Then he took more coffee before he spoke. "I dare not say that they will all be accepted exactly as you have proposed them, although they deserve to be. Perhaps half of them stand a good chance of passage — that is, if they are properly promoted in the American manner."

Philip saw some beginnings of light. "Nicholas, is it too much to hope that you might consent to lend a hand here?"

"Not at all, Philip, not at all. I will now make a confession to you, for after all we are brothers in Christ. It seemed clear to me from the reports I mentioned that just about now this splendidly conceived meeting of yours could be heading into deep water. Therefore a little support might be in order, and it was with that thought in mind that I arranged to come here. And of course also I wanted very much to meet you."

"I'm grateful on both counts, believe me."

"First let us see what I may be able to do. Would it be possible, do you think, for you to clear a little time for me on the program tomorrow? I have a few words I would like to say."

Philip half lifted out of his chair. "Of course, absolutely.

It was my very great hope that you would consent to deliver an address . . ."

The archbishop waved him to silence. "Not an address, my dear Philip, just a few informal words that may in some small way assist in moving things along a bit. This is good coffee, by the way. Next, I am happy to inform you that our delegation will support you on eleven of your points with enthusiasm and at the worst we will abstain on the other two."

"That is tremendously encouraging, Nicholas."

"I do indeed hope so. Also I plan to remain here for three days and possibly part of a fourth sitting as a member of our delegation, if I may have that privilege. That should be interpreted as an indication of how important we consider this whole meeting to be."

Philip felt his body shaking; he recognized that it was a symptom of emotional tension and made a conscious effort to control himself. This promised aid from the archbishop, particularly one of a different branch of the Christian Church, was manna from heaven. "I'm so glad you came," he said simply.

"I wouldn't miss it, Philip — this is a great and historic event. By the way, I saw a mutual friend a short while ago and he asked me to convey his regards."

"Sir Cyril Plessey?" Philip asked.

"Yes. Remarkable man, isn't he? I met him first years ago, and at one time he did a great favor for the Patriarch of Constantinople himself — one which will be long remembered. I'm sorry that he isn't here so that I might greet him."

"Have you any idea where Sir Cyril is?"

The archbishop shook his head. "I really can't say. I only know that he has left the country."

Before Philip could respond to that the phone rang. He picked it up and then passed the instrument to the Metropolitan. "Dr. Poindexter," he said.

226

In a brief conversation His Eminence accepted a dinner invitation with expansive courtesy and quickly ascertained that Philip would be able to join the party at the president's home. Then he stood up and almost filled the office with his presence. "This will be delightful," he commented. "I understand that Poindexter is a remarkable man also — he'd have to be to keep a private college going successfully in these times. More power to him. He asked me to pass the word that he would like to ask your chaplain to join us and also a young lady whose name I was unable to catch."

Philip relaxed and smiled. "If you had, you would have been the first one," he said.

Dinner was a delight. The archbishop was a perfect guest and in his presence the party sparkled. Furthermore, he delighted Aubrey by approving magnanimously of his choice of a bride. "She is absolutely wonderful," he declared. "If I had a son, I would hope that he would find someone who even approached her. She's not only beautiful, but I sense an inner strength, a determination that will support and assist you throughout your married life." Then he addressed himself to Jayawardene. "Of course I would not be true to my convictions and my vocation if I didn't add that it is my hope you will some day discover the wonderful love of Christ for us all, but there is plenty of time. I believe very strongly that we who live in the world must learn to know and love one another as we were taught to do — by your faith and by ours. And loving you, my dear, for any young man would be very easy indeed." He raised his glass and offered her an individual toast.

Harley and Marsha Poindexter found themselves relaxing in the presence of this remarkable man, responding to his bigness of presence and of spirit. Philip was content much of the time just to sit and listen. It was his first close contact with a prominent member of the Eastern Orthodox Church, and he was finding a closer kinship than he had anticipated. He went to bed that evening genuinely looking forward to the next session of the assembly.

Nicholas did not disappoint him. The next morning was bright with optimistic sunshine and rich with a warm softness in the air. The Metropolitan and his party entered with suitable dignity and took their positions on the stage, then Philip introduced His Eminence as briefly as protocol allowed. After that his newfound friend took over.

"To you all I bring my warmest greetings and friendship," the archbishop began. "To those of you who, with me, follow the path of the Savior, I greet you from my heart to yours as brothers and sisters in Christ. To those of you who serve with devotion and wisdom in other ways, and with other convictions, I greet you as my fellow human beings and lovers of the combined wisdom which has guided mankind through the ages."

As he spoke he gestured, often flinging his great arms out in expansive emphasis. He was nothing less than superb, and Philip, sitting quietly in his chair at the side of the stage, silently praised God. Then, as the archbishop continued, a vision came to him — that some day this splendid man would indeed join with him to preach the same truths, labor in the same vineyard, and overcome together the testy differences in dogma that had racked the Christian Church almost from the reformation. And then to move on together to even higher ground and to help to bring the light of reason and of mutual understanding to everyone everywhere.

"I most profoundly wish," the archbishop declared, "that it could be my good fortune to join with you for the remainder of your deliberations. I may not do this, but I shall sit with you for the next few days, as a member of our delegation, so that I may have the satisfaction and happiness of knowing that I was, for a brief while at least, a member of this historic body. I say to you in all conviction that this meeting is one of the most momentous ever convened for

228

the purpose of religious discussion, and generations yet to come will study your achievements and learn what you accomplished here. I am honored to have addressed you; thank you for this great privilege."

As the archbishop sat down applause for him filled the hall. Philip did not know for certain whether it was for the man or for the words that he had spoken, but his great success was total and there was no question that the meeting had been revitalized. Philip stole a glance at his wristwatch and determined that the time was suitable for a midmorning break. He rose and announced it without disturbing the glow that the archbishop had left, and then watched as the delegates filed out toward the lobby where coffee, tea, and other refreshments awaited them.

That afternoon the Salvation Army moved the acceptance of the first of Philip Roundtree's thirteen points. The tension and the animosities that had been so much in evidence before were subdued and for the first time in many days the light of hope shone brightly ahead.

He only hoped, desperately hoped, that it would last.

CHAPTER SIXTEEN

Unfortunately, it did not.

It had seemed to Philip when he had originally drawn up his thirteen points that *any* religious convocation would be able to agree that there was a divine force of some kind, but almost as soon as the subject was opened to discussion, the Hindus objected to it. It was contrary, they claimed, to the Wheel of Karma, the inexorable force that controlled all of the universe. Brahma was not, they made it very clear, the same thing as God. As soon as they had stated their position at some length the Buddhists of the Greater Vehicle rose to concur.

The Muslims had argued right back that there was but one God, Allah, the Compassionate, the Merciful.

The Shintoists countered that with the argument that God was in reality nature and that after death nothing existed at all.

The Parsees, with considerable dignity, explained that it was against their principles and teachings to propagate their faith to any except those who were of Persian blood, but that the name of the Almighty was Mazda and those who sought further enlightenment could consult the teachings of Zoroaster.

By this time the Christians of almost every persuasion were on their feet demanding the floor. So also were the Jews, the Native American Church representatives, the Hare Krishna delegation, and the Taoists, all of whom were insistent on being heard.

Only by exercising the strongest control he could short of tyranny was Philip able to maintain some semblance of order and formal discussion. Twice he looked toward the archbishop to see if his powerful new ally wished to be heard, but he received no response.

He had asked for this, and now he had it — God give him strength. He rapped again for order and called on the representative of Unity.

Just before the meeting ended Peasley, the Methodist, raised his hand. Philip knew him for a man who could produce practical solutions to many problems and gave him the floor.

"It is now apparent," Peasley declared, "that for us to reach agreement on this very significant point is going to entail considerable work. May I therefore advance the suggestion that since the hour is already late we adjourn until tomorrow. Then we can, perhaps, have another reading of the thirteen points and see if there are any which present fewer problems. If we can find one or two on which we can all generally agree without extended debate, then we will have moved forward significantly. After that we can consider the others which may require more time."

Bahai seconded the suggestion and so did the Mormons.

"All those in favor . . ." Philip asked.

He had a majority and he took it. As the delegates rose quickly and moved toward the exits with more than their usual speed, he was suddenly overcome with fatigue. He waited until the hall was all but empty, then he left through a side door with a silent prayer that today no one would be waiting to speak to him. He could not remember when he had been so emotionally wrung out, when he had felt so dangerously close to losing control of himself.

On impulse he went to the meditation room. In the still bright light of day it seemed almost barren and uninspiring. It was empty and plain; there was no magic to be found.

He went on to his office, not because he wanted to, but because there would be mail waiting, and if there were any important visitors he could not afford to disappoint them. As he walked into the anteroom Bishop O'Hanlon rose from the chair where he had been sitting.

"You look very tired," the Catholic bishop said. "I know what a trying day you have had; would you rather that I came back later?"

Philip shook his head. "There is no need for that; please come in." Nevertheless, as he sank into his own office chair, he wondered how much longer he would be able to hold out. If the assembly could not agree on the existence of God, if they didn't believe in that, what else was there?

"I have some news for you that may help to lift your spirits," the bishop said. "I have just received the word myself and I hastened over to pass it on to you. The Apostolic Delegate has just announced in New York that he is coming here for a visit."

Philip stirred a little because he knew it was expected of him. "This is very good news indeed," he said. "I hope that he can be persuaded to address the assembly while he is here."

"I'm sure that he will if you ask him." O'Hanlon leaned a little closer. "I'd like to speak in confidence for a moment; is that agreeable to you?"

"Certainly." Philip gave a sign which his visitor understood.

"Very well. The delegate is a very learned man and an

232

altogether admirable one, but he is a very different type of personality from Archbishop Nicholas. He is much more reserved in his manner. Consider him as a scholar and you have the picture."

"I see."

"You understand, Philip, that from our viewpoint the invitation of the Holy Father is a momentous document. Of course the doors of the Church are always open to any and all who wish to enter, but this is an advance toward greater human understanding that His Holiness has instituted. It will take time, perhaps generations, but with no offense to your convictions, we feel that we are built upon a rock and therefore the passage of the years is not material."

"Then I take it that the delegate will be expanding on the Holy Father's message."

"I would imagine so. But the major significance of his visit lies in the fact that the Church is taking such a keen interest in what is happening here. And supporting it. It would be extremely difficult for us to revise our own tenets without profound deliberation, but we can indicate our support of your magnificent concept and the way in which you are carrying it forward. You have my fullest respect, Philip, and I mean it."

That helped quite a bit. "Can you tell me when the delegate will arrive?" Philip asked.

"I don't know yet, but it should be quite soon." O'Hanlon got up. "I realize how tired you are. Go get some rest and have a substantial meal." Without undue ceremony he nodded a cordial good-bye and left.

Philip sat by himself, too tired even to think clearly. When the phone rang he picked it up automatically, and discovered that Harley Poindexter was on the line.

"Philip, after what you've been through today you need something to reinforce the inner man. We are having a

233

standing rib roast this evening and you are expected. We usually cook our beef medium rare, but how do you like yours?"

It was a simple question and Philip answered it without thinking. "May I have the end cut?"

"It's yours. Come on over. For immediate encouragement, the bar is open."

Slowly Philip got up, turned out the lights, and carefully locked the door.

His feet complained as he walked the length of the carpeted corridor and his knees ached as he went down the steps. The fresh air outside failed to revive him; he was all but unaware of it as he crossed the campus toward the president's house. He did not need to ring the bell; his host had seen him coming and was waiting with the door open.

A whisky and soda helped; a second one actually made the world seem a little brighter. Poindexter offered him a third, but he shook his head without bothering to explain.

Professor Moriarty and Dean Hastings arrived together to join the party. Both were fully aware of Philip's state of body and mind; as a consequence, apart from the necessary greetings, they left him alone. When Marsha announced dinner he made an effort to pull himself together, and soon the good food and the presence of understanding friends made things easier. He did what he could to hold up his end of the conversation hardly noting that for the first time in a long while the convocation was not even mentioned.

As dessert was being put on the table the doorbell rang. Dr. Poindexter answered and ushered in Aubrey Fothergill and Jayawardene; they apologized for the intrusion. "We came too soon, but were looking for Dr. Roundtree," Aubrey explained. "We have some information for him. I hope you don't mind too much."

"Not at all," Marsha reassured, "but I hope it will keep until after dinner. This has been one of those days."

"We know," Jayawardene said. On behalf of Aubrey and

herself she declined the dessert being served, but accepted coffee. When the party had moved into the living room and settled down, Aubrey delivered his message.

"In Burma, in Rangoon I believe, they have a very famous school of Buddhist thought and philosophy. Jaydene can tell you more about this, better than I can, but it seems that the head of this school is a man of very great stature in the Far Eastern religious community."

"Don't tell me he's coming," Philip said.

"I have just been informed that he is, My Lord Bishop, and by his own wish."

Philip tried to think. "Of course he will address the assembly, everyone will want to hear him." He might have put that a little differently if Jayawardene had not been present.

The lady herself answered him by shaking her head. "I don't believe so, sir, because he doesn't speak English. He has several languages, but that isn't one of them."

"We could use an interpreter — perhaps you could do it."

Again the lovely Thai shook her head. "He doesn't usually make speeches. But he still wants to come and observe. So he will be arriving next week."

Philip passed a hand across his face. "I'm very grateful for his interest," he said, "but if he walks in on another session like the one we had today, I don't know what he will think. I've always regarded Buddhism as basically a peaceful religion, and we have very little of that at the moment to offer to him."

"It strikes me," Moriarty contributed, "that all of a sudden we are beginning to gather in the bigwigs. The logical conclusion is that we are attracting a great deal of attention of the right sort. Dignitaries don't come all the way from Burma to attend a wake."

Aubrey, who usually sat quietly at such meetings, spoke up. "Another thought has crossed my mind. Sir Cyril has been gone now for some while and the word is out that he is somewhere overseas. He isn't a man to sit idle while a meeting he is interested in is going on. And he has the reputation of knowing just about everyone."

"That could be," Harley Poindexter agreed.

"The high priest of the Parsees speaks English," Aubrey continued. "In this case the title is a little loose: there are about ten high priests in that faith. But the senior man is nominally regarded as the head of the church. He has his headquarters at a fire temple in Bombay."

"And he's coming?" Philip asked.

"Yes, My Lord Bishop, he is also."

"Then it's Sir Cyril and no mistake."

"Undoubtedly. But I also agree with Dr. Moriarty, we are getting a great deal of very good exposure in the press and other media. Jaydene and I have been the subject of some of it."

Philip managed a smile. "I'm certainly aware of that. I wish that I could think a little more clearly right now; I'm afraid that I'm not at my best."

Jayawardene stood up, quietly and easily. "Will you do something for me?" she asked.

"If I can."

"You can. Please take off your coat and collar."

"Why?" Philip asked.

"I will show you."

After a careful glance at his hostess Philip rose and removed his jacket. Then, after a moment of hesitation, he undid his collar in the back and released it from his neck.

He looked across the room and saw Jayawardene in subdued conversation with his hostess. Then Marsha nodded firm agreement. "I'll get a blanket," she said, and left.

Jayawardene came directly over to where Philip stood. "You have found merit in meditating," she said. "Now you will discover something else. Please take off your shirt."

"I couldn't do that, I'm afraid," Philip answered.

"Yes you can, sir. And Mrs. Poindexter agrees." She turned to the other men. "Help me," she asked.

236

"Go ahead, Philip," Harley said. "I have a great deal of confidence in this young lady."

"So do I," Moriarty agreed. "Off with it."

Still very hesitant, Philip complied. As he was doing so Marsha Poindexter came back into the room bearing a blanket; she smiled encouragement at him and then spread the blanket out on the rug. "Please do what Jaydene asks," she said. "It's a very good idea."

"Undressing in the parlor?"

"In this case yes. I assure you we're not at all disturbed."

"Now lie down," Jayawardene directed. "On your stomach, please, with your arms at your sides. Marsha, please could I have a pillow for his head?"

The pillow was supplied as Philip lay down, already regretting what he had done, but with his mind fixed on the rest he was about to have. That was the almost total need of his mind and body and it overcame everything else. He put his arms at his sides as he had been directed and then rested his head, a little awkwardly, on the pillow.

Almost at once his body wanted to yield to sleep, but it was prevented by the continuing protests of his mind at having had to remove so much of his clothing. The sole comforting factor was that no one present seemed to mind in the least.

Then, on her knees, Jayawardene knelt down beside him. She reached up and took hold of his deltoid muscles with sure fingers. She seemed almost to dig in, then she began a sort of gentle rubbing motion.

At first it hurt, but as the girl continued to work, an embryo sense of well-being began to creep in. Presently Philip was aware that she was manipulating the area at the base of his neck, but he did not seem to care. "He's as tight as a bowstring," he heard her saying.

For the better part of half an hour he lay still, forgetful of where he was, simply grateful for the comfort and release from tension that the girl from Thailand was giving him.

She was a marvel, there was no other word for it. He had never had such a body massage before; he had even entertained some reservations concerning the practice, but the experience he was undergoing voided all that. "Where did you learn to do this?" he asked.

"Almost every Oriental girl knows how, it is part of our upbringing," Jayawardene answered him. "We consider it very important. I have very often done this for my father when he was tired and exhausted. And for my brothers too. It is a definite part of our culture."

A glow of contentment filled Philip; he was grateful for it and blocked out of his mind the possible loss of dignity. It didn't seem very important to him at that moment, not important at all. The blanket was half folded over him, which was a further comfort. As he submitted to having the muscles of his right arm manipulated by Jayawardene's expert fingers, he found that he was looking directly at his chaplain. "Has she ever done this for you?" he asked.

"Yes, sir, she has. I had my reservations too, but now I know better."

The things that the girl was doing to his arm seemed to be pouring comfort into his whole body. His mind was eased too, and he had the feeling that as soon as he could get up and put the rest of his clothes back on once more, the world would be a far better place and the conference much less of a problem than it had been.

An impulse came to him and he responded to it. "Aubrey," he said. "You have my permission to marry this girl, and with it my blessing."

He had not meant it to be taken seriously, but it was. Aubrey leaned toward him and his voice almost choked as he replied. "Thank you, My Lord Bishop, thank you profoundly! You can't know what that means to us. Not only in terms of the Church, but of you personally."

Philip did not know what to say, but he felt something additional through the fingers of the girl who was now work-

238

ing on his lower forearm. Because he could not find any of the right words, he kept still — it was the only safe way.

"You see, sir," Aubrey continued, "you brought me here and in that way brought us together. I won't give up Jaydene, not for anything, but it's been tremendously important to both of us that you approve of our plans. Without your blessing — well, it just couldn't be the same. You understand, don't you?"

"Yes," Philip answered, "I do."

Moriarty ventured to intrude. "Isn't that what this conference is all about — people meeting each other despite long distances and varying backgrounds?"

"Of course," Dean Hastings agreed. "I'm certainly not going to intrude into the affairs of the Church of England, but Aubrey, I've been pulling for the two of you since you announced your intentions."

Jayawardene laid down his arm and shifted her position until she was opposite Philip's lower legs, then she began to work once more, seemingly without any fatigue in her arms and fingers. In a minute or two the tightness of the muscles began to give way.

He heard the sound of the doorbell, but he paid it little attention. When Harley Poindexter went out to answer he knew that his host would protect him from any embarrassment. His opinion was confirmed when he noted how carefully the college president closed the door behind him as he left the room.

The man who stood on the doorstep was someone whom Harley had never seen before. He was of slender build, past middle age but how far was uncertain. He was very conservatively dressed, with the clerical round collar that was so common on the campus it had almost become a uniform of the day.

"Good evening, sir," Harley said.

"Good evening, is this Dr. Poindexter?"

"It is. Would you like to come in?"

"Thank you." The visitor came as far as the entrance lobby and then stopped. "I trust you will excuse the intrusion at this time, but I am looking for the Very Reverend Dr. Roundtree."

Harley Poindexter's acrobat brain performed another of its deft maneuvers and he was on top of the situation immediately. "Dr. Roundtree is here, sir, but he is in the midst of a very important counseling session at the moment. Please step into my study, sir, and let me know whom to announce."

"My name is Danford-Smith. When he is free you might inform Dr. Roundtree that his archbishop has arrived and would enjoy seeing him."

CHAPTER SEVENTEEN

All things considered, Philip took the news with surprising calm. In well under two minutes he was fully attired and his composure was intact. He was still deadly tired, but the aches which had been plaguing his body were gone, he was far more relaxed, and he knew that he could cope. With his hand on the doorknob he turned and spoke to Jayawardene. "For your information," he said, "there are thirty-nine books in the Old Testament and twenty-seven in the New." Then he left the room.

The Most Reverend Frederick Danford-Smith surprised him with a greeting much warmer than he had expected; the archbishop actually reached out both hands and smiled in the bargain. "Philip, how are you?" he began. "I must say that you look well."

"I am very well, Your Grace," Philip answered. "This is a most wonderful surprise. I wish you had notified us so we could have arranged a proper reception."

"Entirely unnecessary, Philip, I dare say that you have enough on your mind as it is. But I had a few days free and it occurred to me that perhaps a little moral support might be in order. So I just came."

"How splendid of you, Your Grace. Please come in and meet the others."

"Certainly, Philip, certainly, but a word or two with you first if you don't mind. How are things working out with your chaplain? You understand what I mean."

Philip understood perfectly, but he chose to answer the question literally. "Fothergill is doing a splendid job, Your Grace, I can't speak too highly of him. He is a bear for work, which is fortunate because we have been receiving a barrage of mail and a stream of callers that never seems to let up. I would be lost without him."

"How good to hear. But what I had in mind, Philip, was this young lady. So much publicity, you know, all about a clergyman of the Church being engaged and all that to an Asian girl. They're a fine people, of course, but in our work you know the importance of a helpmate who supports you with her own profound convictions."

"True, Your Grace, but things are somewhat better than they may appear. She is, I'm very happy to say, a young lady of excellent breeding, high intelligence, and unimpeachable character."

"But by all reports, Philips, she is a Buddhist, and they don't even believe in God!"

"Perhaps that can be corrected, sir. I devoutly hope so."

"Do you see any light in that direction?"

"It is difficult to say offhand, Your Grace, but I was instructing her in the Bible just before I came to greet you. It may come about."

The archbishop gently shook his head. "But is it worth so much of your own time right now, Philip, when other matters are so pressing?"

"I am unalterably convinced, Your Grace, that all souls are worth saving, whatever the cost."

Frederick Danford-Smith was compelled to pause for a

moment. "Unquestionably right, of course. I put it badly. My thought was that such a conversion might be most difficult — perhaps even impossible. I was going to suggest that perhaps a bit of separation might be the answer. I have someone with me, an exceptionally fine and dedicated young curate..."

Philip shook his head. "If we did that, sir, the press would kill us. You perhaps have no idea how much interest there is in this country concerning these young people; they have become a *cause célèbre*. Come in and meet them."

The archbishop drew a deep breath. "It really is in the soup, then?"

Philip nodded and then opened the door to the living room. "I have wonderful news for you all," he announced.

At first Arthur Gravenstine was unable to decide whether the parade of VIP's scheduled to visit the conference would actually help the cause along or only postpone the inevitable. He leaned toward the latter conclusion simply because there was so much entrenched strength of tradition and prejudice on its side, but at the same time he had to admit to himself that some very important churchmen were suddenly displaying great interest in what was going on. Because something had never been done was no guarantee that some day someone *might* not do it. And Philip Roundtree was the kind of man who appeared once, perhaps, in a generation.

He left the matter open in his mind and then watched the developing events with the greatest interest. Good reporter that he was, he sniffed out every bit of additional news that he could and prayed for more. In particular he attempted to interview the archbishop of the Church of England who had so suddenly appeared on the scene, but despite the fact that he knew him quite well professionally, Danford-Smith was closely closeted with Philip and therefore was inaccessible.

As an alternative project, he called upon the Burmese

master as soon as that dignitary had arrived and had been shown to his quarters, but the language barrier proved formidable and there were other complications. For the first time in his professional career he was required to sit on the floor while the subject of his interview relaxed on a davenport before him. There was an interpreter, but Arthur had the maddening feeling that whatever questions he put, their translations were all coming out the same and so were the answers. When he asked about the Buddhist philosophy that was being followed in Burma, he was gently informed that he wouldn't be able to understand it. He did manage to ferret out a statement that if someone were to heed the Four Noble Truths and adhere to the blessed Eightfold Path, then more than half of his battle would be over. The subject of his interview was not hostile, but building a communications bridge was most difficult for Arthur, and when he took his departure he was more frustrated than ever. Most of all, he did not understand why this important personage had chosen to come so far when his participation in what was going on would necessarily be so strictly limited. But he *had* come, and that fact in itself was newsworthy.

Arthur went once more to the library to dig up whatever he could on Burmese Buddhism.

Three consecutive religious holidays suspended all activity other than isolated discussions, of which there were many. The appearance of the Most Reverend Frederick Danford-Smith before the assembly on the first morning after it reconvened was something of a surprise. The archbishop wore the full vestments of his rank and they did give his slender figure a considerable added dignity. As he stood behind the rostrum he seemed to be gathering himself; then in a carefully controlled voice he delivered his message. Leaning forward so that he would be in slightly closer communication with his audience, he talked a little of hope and what it meant in the hearts of people everywhere. He surprised Philip by citing certain of the teachings of the great Asian religious leaders and then related them to the tenets of the Christian faith.

He spoke for almost forty minutes, but he held the unbroken attention of his listeners. When at last he raised his right arm and asked for the privilege of blessing the assembly, Arthur Gravenstine had learned that this apparently very reserved man was in fact a mighty human being more than worthy of his high office. Frederick Danford-Smith might be normally very guarded in his words, but his heart was full and much of what it contained was greatness.

At the afternoon session the Church of South India voted to take up the seventh of Philip's thirteen points. It was restated from the podium: *Within every human being there is an immortal soul which infinitely transcends his existence on this earth.*

Before the discussion could proceed, it was necessary to define the word "transcend," which was not in the English vocabulary of many of those present. As soon as that obstacle had been cleared away, the Jains asked for the floor. When they received it, they explained at some length that *all* forms of life were sacred, which was why many of their members wore breathing masks and always swept the path before them as they walked so that they would not by accident crush out the life of any creature. They then asked that the restriction to human beings only be removed.

Jehovah's Witnesses came right back to declare that the Bible made human beings superior to the animals, the latter having no souls.

A gentleman from Ethiopia who represented that nation's ancient Christian Coptic Church rose to point out that all human beings were also animals and followed the same physical processes as their fellow mammals. He added that in this respect many animals were much superior to men, such as the dog in his ability to smell.

A Seventh-Day Adventist asked him to cite one instance of animals' *mental* superiority to man.

The man from Addis Ababa reflected briefly and then asked how many human beings possessed the cat's ability to find its way home even if dropped in unfamiliar territory a great many miles from its destination. Since its home was a matter of environment, instinct could not be given as the answer.

A Southern Baptist tried to put an end to it by stating that to compare animals with human beings was, on its face, an obvious absurdity.

Bishop Togen Sumi, the Zen master, rose to say that while he had an imperfect knowledge of the Christian faith, it was his understanding that Jesus was often referred to as the "Lamb of God."

Philip, who kept his composure as he gravely presided, had the private thought that his archbishop, who was present in the balcony, was getting a small taste of what he had been going through.

When the session reached its closing hour and adjourned, no conclusion had been reached.

Philip returned to his office to find the entire Parsee delegation waiting for him. He made the gentlemen from Bombay welcome and then waited to hear what they had to say.

"Most Venerable Bishop," the spokesman began, "we are calling upon you that we should make known to you our pleasure at this conference."

"That's most kind," Philip responded. "Thank you very much."

"We are different from the other major faiths because we accept no converts," the head of the delegation continued. "No outsider is admitted into our fire temples, and to be a Parsee it is necessary to be of Persian blood."

"So I have heard."

"Yet despite this, Venerable Bishop, we have been accepted here. We were especially honored when the portrait of our great teacher Zoroaster appeared in the mighty American newspaper."

Philip lowered his head for a moment. "I had nothing to do with that," he admitted.

"It is not necessary that you should. But we are very proud of our faith; we hope that you will visit us the next time that you are in India."

"I shall certainly try."

"You have been told that our most senior high priest is coming to be with us; it is a mark of our regard for you."

"It is a very great honor for us all. Does he by any chance speak English?"

"Yes, Venerable Bishop, he does — and quite well. He has to, because people are always asking him about the Towers of Silence."

"Why is there so much curiosity?" Philip asked.

"Because so much that has been said and printed is totally wrong. It is a beautiful custom, and it is most reverently done. All people must find ways to dispose of their dead — they put them in the ground, they burn them, and there are other ways. We prefer ours."

Another of the delegates, a quite elderly man, continued quietly. His English was better and he spoke it with greater ease. "People have written of the stench that comes from our towers," he said, "and it is a vast lie. There is no such thing. The towers, which only a Parsee may see, are in a beautiful park, with lovely trees and flowers. It is a peaceful and holy place, full of the spirit of Ahura Mazda. And there is no odor whatsoever — it is impossible."

"You may not see the ceremony," the spokesman continued; "it is against our law. But I shall explain to you. The towers, which are yellow, are only about five meters high. Those who place the bodies inside are especially initiated for this office; after that they may not mix with the rest of Parsee society. After the services have been held, and the prayers sent heavenward which will admit the newly departed into the seven zones of blessed light, the bearers carry the body down a winding path where they disappear from view. Then they open the door to the tower and carry the body inside, where there are three tiers in circles. The large outside one is for men, the second for women, and the inner one for children. The body is reverently placed in position facing the open sky. When this has been done, the bearers leave, close the door, and then one of them claps his hands. It is the signal to the birds, who wait until it is given."

"By birds you mean vultures," Philip said.

"Yes, Honored Bishop. It is all over very soon. By the time that those who have come to the service leave the park the soul is bathed in the heavenly light and the body is no more. There is no grief and sorrow, or sad thoughts when it rains."

"We find great peace and tranquillity this way," the older man added, "and we have no need of graveyards. We think of life and not of death. You know our principles?"

Philip was embarrassed. "I have read them, but I must confess . . ."

The man he was talking to raised a hand in forgiveness. "Allow me to state them, Most Venerable Bishop; I believe you will find them honorable: truthfulness, righteousness, loyalty, cleanliness, industry, peaceful disposition, and charitable activity."

"Speaking as a Christian," Philip said, "I can subscribe to them all — without reservation."

The head of the delegation bowed his head. "We are again most honored," he replied. "I know that our great Mobed will be honored too when he arrives."

He paused and took stock for a moment. "Ours is a very ancient faith, but we have always felt ourselves part of the world and not isolated. May we venture the hope, Most Reverend Bishop, that when you choose the path for all the world to follow, you consider our sacred string ceremony as a possible element. It has much virtue in it."

248

"I shall not forget," Philip promised.

"You are so good, sir. We have a small gift for you." He turned to one of his followers, who produced a package apparently from nowhere. The spokesman held it out. "It is a very fine copy of the Avesta, our holy book. Please accept it as a mark of our respect."

Philip stood up, received the gift, and spoke his warm thanks. When the small delegation had left he sat still, his mind turning on a new theme. Trying in some ways as the day had been, he felt a fresh strength. Whether the Parsees called God Mazda or not was immaterial, the point was that they had set for themselves standards no honorable person could dispute. And despite the bickering over minute points of doctrine, so long as men could agree on the basic principles of honorable human conduct, there had to be some hope somewhere. His great task, as of that moment, was to discover it while there was still time.

The great teacher from Burma was less of a success before the assembly, largely because he was far out of his element. A fairly short and quite stocky man, he did not create the same impression that Frederick Danford-Smith had done, and he was up against a formidable language barrier. He spoke only briefly and in French, the Western language in which he was most fluent. That imposed a considerable strain on his interpreter, who had to listen in French, think in Burmese, and then deliver up his results in English. He managed it for the necessary ten minutes, while his superior conveyed general greetings and a wish for inspiration for all those present. The Burmese master was not an orator; when he had finished there was proper applause, but clearly no inspiration.

Philip rose and expressed his thanks for the great effort the speaker had made in coming so far when his duties at home were heavy and continuous. He had hardly left the platform at the break when he found Aubrey waiting anxiously for him. For once, surprisingly, Jayawardene was not with him.

"My Lord Bishop," Aubrey began quickly. "The Apostolic Delegate will arrive on campus later this morning. Since you won't be free to receive him, I've asked Dr. Poindexter, Dean Hastings, and Dr. Moriarty to do the honors. Karen has lined up suitable quarters and has arranged a private dinner with the Catholic delegation this evening. I assume you will attend?"

"Of course."

"I'll take care of it, sir. That isn't all; I have just received word that the Grand Emir of Islam is on his way."

Philip drew breath and held it for a moment. "I wasn't aware that there was any such personage," he said. "There isn't any hierarchy in Islam — or I thought that there wasn't."

"Perhaps this is another case of the greatest among equals. Anyhow, we have a very VIP Muslim coming, which frankly astonishes me. I have gathered that this is one of those faiths which is strong unto itself and admits of no argument."

"Yes, Aubrey, but there are two main divisions and they hold different beliefs. Find out for me if you can which one the Grand Emir represents and get me whatever background you can on him."

"I will, My Lord Bishop. A number of other people are also coming, representing smaller Christian groups for the most part, who have read about what is happening and who seem to feel that they too should be here."

"I'm grateful to them all, Aubrey, but at this moment I'm not sure just what I should do. They can't all be invited to address the assembly." Philip paused and then shook his head as though to clear it by mechanical means. "It's *time*, Aubrey — time is running out on us and so far not one of the points has been accepted."

Aubrey ventured to lay his hand on his bishop's shoulder. "I know, sir, I too had hoped for much more. But at least we're getting tremendous press coverage now; there are three times as many reporters here and they're interviewing everyone."

"I know, they've been after me at all hours. And frankly, Aubrey, I'm beginning to run out of things to say." He stopped and for a moment pressed his lips together. "If they would just accept *one* of the points, that would help so much — it would show some definite progress."

"I'm sure they will, sir — they have to. Particularly with all of these important people coming on the scene."

"I hope so."

"And remember the mail, sir. It's still coming in in volume. The ordinary people, the ones who sit in the pews, listen to the sermons, and sing the hymns — they're with us because they aren't all tied up in doctrine."

Philip glanced at his watch. "Be sure that everything is done to make the Apostolic Delegate welcome," he directed. "Convey my warmest regards. I have to go back in now."

"God go with you, sir," Aubrey said.

The remainder of the week produced news if nothing else. The Apostolic Delegate gave a press interview in which he dwelt heavily on the Holy Father's message to the conference. His appearance before the assembly was correctly interpreted as a major recognition and received very good comments despite the fact that he had nothing new to say.

The high priest of the Parsees was elderly, reserved, but interesting nonetheless. He was asked at length about the Towers of Silence and exhibited considerable patience when he answered. On the question of why no one other than Parsees were ever admitted to the fire temples, he was definite; when the refugee Parsee colony had been admitted to India, they had given a promise that no attempt would be made to win over the Hindus. This obligation they had strictly observed, even though Hindus were not eligible to become Parsees even if they wanted to.

251

When asked if he thought that the various world faiths could be brought together into a common communion, he stated that he very much doubted it, but he had come to see what progress if any had been made. When asked for his conclusions he stated that he had not had time to formulate any.

The Grand Emir in flowing robes and beard cut a splendid figure and revealed a dynamic personality. His English was fluent though heavily accented and he had much to say. When he addressed the assembly he lectured on the vital tenet of the Sunnite sect that Allah helps each man to precisely the same degree that that man helps his brother. He took pains to point out that Christianity had correctly hit upon this same principle and called attention to the fact that Jesus of Nazareth is a most important figure in Islam. He surprised some by his declaration that Islam also looks forward to His second coming at which time He is expected to marry and to proclaim the teachings of the Prophet to the whole world.

He concluded his remarks by quoting the Prophet himself: "Difference of opinion in my community is a sign of divine mercy."

After hearing that, Philip decided that if Islam was indeed right, then a profound measure of mercy should be the lot of all those present.

Philip had dinner that evening with his distinguished visitor and enjoyed every minute of the meal. He did not experience the same kinship he had felt toward Archbishop Nicholas, but he was in the presence of another dynamic spiritual leader and he had to admit that much of what the Grand Emir stood for was beyond cavil. It was a tremendously stimulating dialogue and he knew that his guest was enjoying himself as well.

Then the parade of dignitaries came to a halt. After another three-day weekend to allow all of the necessary religious observances, the assembly reconvened and it was the same thing once more. The thirteen points were raked over and finally number ten was brought to the floor. Philip read it once more from the paper before him. *"Death as we know it is only a change in existence; the soul lives on and the body will be resurrected when God so wills."*

He had a four-second respite, then the Shintoists were on their feet to deny that there was anything beyond the grave in any form whatever. The whole session was spent debating the point: the Christians, Muslims, Parsees, Jews, Taoists, and the Native American Church supported it; the Buddhists, Hindus, and Sikhs accepted the principle only if rebirth fell within the definition of life after death.

When the meeting at last closed, there was reason to hope that point ten might prove to be the first basis of agreement. But the very strong opposition of the Shintoists would have to be overcome and the knotty problem of earthly rebirth also stood in the way, supported as it was by some very powerful and numerically strong faiths.

Philip ate his dinner with the delegates representing the Church of South India, that remarkable body which had virtually succeeded in uniting Christianity in its part of the world. It was heartening, but he could not escape a feeling of impending mental exhaustion. He went back to the president's home hoping to retire as soon as possible.

It was not to be. Poindexter met him at the door and invited him into the living room in a manner which was grave enough to foretell something serious. Without asking he mixed a whisky and soda for Philip and gave it to him, then he took one himself and sat down.

"I have news," he announced, "and I greatly fear that it isn't good. After a battle with my conscience, I've decided that you should and must be told." Harley glanced at him and then added quickly, "As far as I know, your family is fine."

"Thank God," Philip said.

Poindexter continued. "Before he left the campus a few

weeks ago, Sir Cyril revealed certain of his plans to me, but he swore me to secrecy on the matter. Don't take that personally, Philip — he had some very good reasons. He told me where he was going and what he hoped to accomplish. As you know by now, he did arrange for some very important people to come here and keep things moving. I can tell you very frankly that he wanted to kill any notions that the conference was dying or hung up hopelessly on disagreements."

"He succeeded," Philip acknowledged.

"He certainly did. Meanwhile he was on a mission which, if successful, could possibly have brought us something close to success. It was a very daring idea, but when he revealed it to me, I had to agree that it did contain a vestige of hope."

"Can you tell me what it is?"

"No, Philip, I cannot, I've given my word and I must stick by it. I'm sure that you are told many things you cannot repeat."

"That's a large part of my job, Harley; I understand your position."

"Thank you. I can tell you a little more — I have to, in fact. Sir Cyril has been keeping me informed. He was in New York briefly, then he flew to England, to Egypt, and on to India. I believe that he contacted the Grand Emir on the way and arranged for him to come here."

"Harley, pardon me, but a few moments ago when you were speaking of Sir Cyril's plan, did I understand you to use the past tense?"

Poindexter nodded slowly. "Yes, Philip, I did."

"He isn't . . ."

"As far as I am aware, no — thank God for that. I know of no death or serious accident. But I have just heard from Ames and the news is most disturbing. Sir Cyril has disappeared."

CHAPTER EIGHTEEN

In the humid heat of New Delhi the Oberoi Interconti-
nental Hotel stood like a magnificent oasis of European
luxury, its air-conditioning system keeping the various lobbies and dining rooms if anything somewhat uncomfortably
cool. A steady stream of vintage Ambassador taxis unloaded
guests at the front entrance, where they were waved inside
by a splendidly uniformed doorman with the customary
turban and beard of the Sikh. Many of the guests were less
than elegantly dressed and practically all of them were visibly wilted from their various sightseeing tours under the
blazing sun of north central India.

One middle-aged man with the unmistakable appearance
of a well-paid executive and dressed in a practical seersucker
suit entered the lobby, picked up his room key, and went
upstairs. Once in the privacy of his quarters he went into the
bathroom and splashed cold water over his face. When he
had dried and come out, he unlocked a case and took out
what appeared to be an electronic device about five inches
square. In a matter of seconds he unscrewed the mouthpiece

cap of the room telephone and fastened his interesting piece of equipment in its place. That done, he picked up the instrument and placed a call to an unlisted number in New York.

Fortunately the traffic load was light, so he did not have too long to wait until the connection had been made. When the ring in New York was answered by an executive excretary whose voice he knew, the man in New Delhi stated his business. "This is Jock. Put me through, please."

The girl had her standing orders on that. She pressed the intercom and within a few seconds the phone in the inner office was picked up. "Hello, Jock."

"Hello, J.R., I'm ready to scramble."

"Right."

The man in India clicked a switch on the device he had attached to the telephone. A tiny red light showed, indicating that the equipment was functioning. A synchronizing signal went out automatically, then a green light indicated that the circuit was ready.

"First of all," Jock began on the now scrambled circuit, "please bring me up to date. What's happening at the conference?"

"It's still alive, Jock. Plessey again; he's been getting a whole series of high dignitaries of various religions to come and give speeches. No agreements have been reached, of course, but there is a side effect: a lot of the various delegations are getting acquainted with each others' thinking and that in itself is dangerous. What progress have you made?"

"The Plessey problem has been solved, at least for the time being."

"How drastically?"

"No violence as per your instructions. But it seems that the old man may be showing signs of senility at last. He missed a local flight on Indian Airlines and since then no one has seen him."

"How good is security on this?"

256

"Excellent I would say; the only people he has seen are natives and they were imported from other areas for the job. They have him nicely cooped up for the duration. He has been given the impression that he is being held for ransom, which should flatter him and keep him relatively quiet."

"Where do you have him?"

"In the foothills of the Himalaya. He's not being tightly restrained, but he isn't going anywhere unless he wants to undertake several days of pretty severe climbing without food or equipment. And if he should get that idea, it will be discouraged."

"How will you get out of it?"

"When we're ready, we'll just turn him loose at some convenient place. He won't be able to tell where he's been or identify any of the people who are presently taking care of him. He will probably count himself lucky to be out of the scrape and that will be the end of it."

"Should we do anything more?"

"I'm on my way home to look into that. With Plessey out of the picture the expected outcome should follow as a matter of course. If it doesn't, then I can take further steps."

"Very well, Jock, I'm inclined to agree that you've handled the main problem. You can pass the word when to let him go?"

"Of course, and in a way that can't be traced."

"Good enough. Come on home and we'll see what happens next."

The Indian official was being considerate, but like all of the members of his department he was continuously harassed, overworked, and paid a bare living wage. He had heard the same story so many hundreds of times he could have supplied any of the missing details — granted that someone of Sir Cyril Plessey's importance was not the usual subject in the stream of missing person reports. "I shall notify the police authorities in the area where you last saw

Sir Cyril," he said. "I will also put out a general alarm so that if he appears anywhere, I will be notified promptly. For the moment, that is the very best that I can do, Mr. Ames."

"Thank you. I should like to add something to what I have told you previously: Sir Cyril is a man of very substantial resources and he is noted for his generosity. Anyone who helps him will be more than amply rewarded. I trust that you will allow him to express his gratitude to you also, and to any of your colleagues who assist."

The official did not deny that; in truth he lived to a large degree on the small informal fees he received for expediting certain matters, as did everyone else he knew. It was a way of life and it was also close to essential if he was to have any hope of putting his children through school.

"We will do our best," he promised. In that he was largely truthful, for any help rendered to Sir Cyril Plessey would be sure to be rewarded unless very powerful forces were in opposition. In that case a simple man only trying to do his best could be caught in the middle and crushed like a fly. Unfortunately, it happened all the time.

Ames arose. "I shall be available at any hour of the day or night." He laid an envelope on top of the battered desk. "There is some further information which may help you in your search."

The official looked and was shocked at the denomination of the rupee notes the envelope contained. It was almost too much and could put him in a very serious position if he was expected to earn it in full. But it was a tremendous addition to his slender assets and worth the risk. He slipped the envelope in the drawer where he kept a confusion of other papers and stood up to shake hands. "We shall try our best," he declared again.

"If you are successful," Ames said on leaving, "Sir Cyril will be most impressed. I understand that he is still searching for the right man to assume a very important post in one of his holdings here."

258

"Thank you." That was all that the official felt it safe to say. His promise to do his best was routine; beyond that, at the moment, he was not sure it would be safe to go.

During all of the long week, no word whatever was received at Maplewood College concerning the whereabouts of Sir Cyril Plessey. Meanwhile the assembly took up the matter of creation and it was like a string of Chinese firecrackers — endless poppings in all directions with almost no evidence of control. When at last Philip gaveled the Friday afternoon session to a close his outward composure was intact, but inwardly he was ready to throw in the sponge. He could not see that the week's work had accomplished anything at all, and in addition he was bone-tired in both mind and body. He and Harley Poindexter dined together at a small restaurant well away from the atmosphere of the campus where they had a frank and open talk. A few of the delegates had already left and they had not been replaced. Also almost all of the press representatives were unexpectedly gone. Arthur Gravenstine was on hand for the duration, but he seemed to be the only man with such an assignment.

In the cold, factual light of reality, there was no visible reason why the conference should be continued. It was by that time clear that none of the thirteen points was going to be accepted, either as originally proposed or in any modified form. Discussions which seemed endless accomplished nothing except for the possible wider understanding of various viewpoints. Any form of consolidation was beyond hope. Had Sir Cyril Plessey been on hand, he might have been able to suggest some face-saving way to conclude the meeting on a note of suitable dignity, but no such inspiration presented itself to either Philip or Harley Poindexter.

"I believe it would be the best plan," Philip said, "to announce on Tuesday that next week's sessions will be the final ones. I will try to say something about how much we have learned to understand each other's convictions — they can hardly deny us that — and then end without any special ceremony on Friday. That will give everyone suitable notice."

"Yes," Harley agreed, "and it will forestall the embarrassment of having a mass exodus that would force our hand. Sir Cyril may be upset, if and when he returns, but I honestly don't see what we can do about that."

Philip agreed. "Another thing, Harvey: I don't like to say this, but it isn't in character for Sir Cyril to absent himself after he agreed to keep in touch with you. Considering his advanced age, I am upset by the possibility that something may have happened to him."

"I'm afraid so, Philip; India isn't a place where the finest in medical care is always available either. I presume that sooner or later we will know."

Philip made a decision. "Harley, I've got to get away for a little while; I need a day or two entirely by myself. I have a place in mind. I'll be back in time to open things up on Tuesday morning, but in the meantime, will you cover for me? I'm not going far, but I want to be alone."

"Philip, I think that you should. I don't even want you to tell me where you will be. We'll manage, so don't worry. And now, since this is a business discussion, I shall allow our benefactress Mrs. Bixby to pay the check."

On Saturday morning Arthur Gravenstine could not find the Right Reverend Dr. Philip Roundtree. He consulted the bishop's chaplain, but he, for the first time since he had taken over his duties, did not know the whereabouts of his superior. In that critical situation he looked up Denise, the attractive blond who seemed always to know everything that was going on. When she had no clue, the situation was desperate indeed.

Aubrey stepped into the breach and took over all essential matters with considerable ability. He too knew that the conference was dead, but until Philip Roundtree said so publicly, he was resolved to keep his thoughts to himself.

He also made a private decision: with his fiancée's permission, he would ask his bishop to marry them with a minimum of ceremony or publicity. The splendid dream they had had of being wed in a new atmosphere of spiritual unity had been a palpable illusion to which he had allowed himself to succumb. He gave some thought also as to what he would do for a living if the Church refused to accept his bride, but that bridge he would cross when he came to it. Journalism appealed to him and he might find a career there. That more or less settled, he purged his mind of such speculations and got back to work.

That evening Bishop Togen Sumi spent some time looking for Philip, but he was unsuccessful. He went alone to the meditation room, sat down on the floor, and released his mind to the contemplation of Mu.

Arthur Gravenstine was of a different discipline: he got on the phone and checked the police department, the city editor of the local paper, all of the hospitals in the area, and the morgue. He too turned up nothing and was grateful that he hadn't.

Marsha Poindexter asked her husband where Philip Roundtree was and got an inconclusive answer. Being an intelligent woman, she did not pursue the subject.

Sunday morning was born as fine a day as the North Central United States could produce, but across the campus it lay in lassitude, heavy with inertia and infused by an all-prevailing sense of protracted failure. In the central part of the city various church services were being conducted according to traditionally accepted rituals, but there was little other visible activity. Even the air itself was still; the trees displayed their leaves in motionless splendor as though the very processes of nature were also coming to a gradual halt.

Dean Hastings did his best to make the worship service in the chapel-auditorium a significant event, but despite the fact that many of the Christian delegates faithfully attended he was not able to bring the fire of inspiration to his words or break the persistent mood of discouragement. It did not help that Philip Roundtree was nowhere in evidence and no one seemed to know where he was.

From a hotel room in Milwaukee, Jock phoned his superior in New York, reaching him at a private hideaway where he spent his weekends. He dialed directly with his scrambler device attached to the telephone, and reported. "You can stop concerning yourself about Roundtree's religious meeting. I've been in Winnebago for the past twenty-four hours and it's a wake."

"How about Roundtree himself?"

"He's gone — no one knows where. I presume that he'll be back, but it's far too late. Many of the people have left and I learned that another twenty-five or thirty percent are going to split this coming week."

"All right, that ties it up. I never had any doubts, but I still think we had to make sure."

"No question about it, J.R., we can't take chances — not if we want to stay in business."

"I think you can release your guest now. By the time he could get back on the scene, it's going to be all over anyway."

"Good, I'll pass the word. It'll take about a week before he can actually be let loose — communications are a little primitive back there. I'll also see that he gets the word that the meeting has broken up; that will send him home."

"Do that, then come back in; we have a good customer waiting for supplies in Africa."

"Look for me tomorrow." When he had broken the connection Jock disconnected the scrambler and put it carefully away in his bag. Then he phoned down to the transportation desk and asked for the first convenient reservation for New York.

262

Because of the quietness of the hour, and the fact that it had come by the back way, no one apparently noticed the powerful Lincoln Continental that came up the hill toward the college with hardly enough sound to disturb the still air. When Ames had pulled the great car up in front of the guesthouse that had been assigned to Sir Cyril for the duration, that venerable knight dismounted as Alexander the Great might have done in one of his better moments, looked about him, and then entered his temporary premises. As soon as Ames had closed the door behind him he laid down his stick, sniffed experimentally for a moment, and then remarked, "It strikes me that things are singularly dead around here."

"I have the identical impression, sir," Ames responded. "But of course it is Sunday."

Sir Cyril laid aside the Alpine hat he had chosen to wear. "Quite so, but one of the redeeming features of this country is the fact that the Lord's Day Observance Society is absent."

"The society's views are a bit archaic, I quite agree, sir."

"Embalmed is the word, I believe. However, it is now quite clear that there are things to be done, and with some degree of speed. As soon as you have prepared the restorative, arrange with Dr. Roundtree for us to confer as soon as possible. Also my compliments to Dr. Poindexter and suggest that I would like to see him too at his earliest convenience. If they can come together, so much the better."

"At once, sir."

"Then advise the young ladies that I have returned; I trust that they will be interested in the announcement."

"Unfailingly, sir."

"After that obtain an up-to-the-minute progress report on the conference so that I will have the overview, so to speak. Something may have broken loose without our having been notified."

"As soon as possible, sir."

"Finally, lay out one of those sport shirts we bought in Singapore. I rather fancy the patterns."

"Excellent, sir, I'm sure it will create an impression." He was already behind the bar preparing the necessary refreshment without a wasted motion; that done, he scooped up the telephone. Following three crisp conversations he was ready to give a preliminary report. "Sir Cyril, Dr. Poindexter is overjoyed to hear of your return; he will call on you here very shortly. I regret that Dr. Roundtree has been unaccountably absent for the past day and a half. No concern is felt, but his present whereabouts are unknown."

"Probably resting up, poor devil, but this is no time to spare the horses. Get some action going. I suggest that the young ladies be consulted; there is a feminine instinct for newsgathering."

"A profound one, sir, as I have noted myself. May I suggest that Mr. Gravenstine might be most helpful also."

"By all means, Ames, see to it."

The necessary calls were still in progress when the doorbell rang with authority. Since Ames was engaged, Sir Cyril himself responded and admitted the president of Maplewood College. He waved his guest toward a chair and signaled his man; within a few seconds the call in progress was concluded and shortly thereafter a drink perfectly made to Poindexter's taste had been placed in his hand.

Harley tasted it and then addressed his host. "Sir Cyril, we've all been somewhat frantic around here; no word from you came in for some time."

"I know, apologies and all that, but I couldn't help it. In a moment of weakness I permitted himself to be apprehended by some local hired hands in India. They tried to convince me that I was being held for ransom, but a senile cretin could have seen through that. I know who was responsible and they will be dealt with as soon as I have time."

"You mean that you were physically detained?"

"Briefly. Wretched food, and I got a bad case of heart-burn."

"How long was it before you were released?"

Sir Cyril glared. "I did not require to be released, I took care of that matter myself. Mountaineering has always been one of my pastimes and they gave me a splendid opportunity. No suitable equipment, of course, but it wasn't really necessary, not much more than a brisk workout. They tried to follow me, but obviously they didn't have any head for heights or knowledge of how to live off the land."

"I'm astounded."

"I see no reason for that; my experience in such circumstances is well known. Anyhow, I eventually reached a village where they were able to communicate. As soon as they announced my arrival things started to hum. The government people were most cooperative — they had reason to be. I would have cabled, but I considered it best to return here posthaste instead."

Poindexter consulted his drink and then changed the subject. "Sir Cyril, I would like very much to report to you that the conference is achieving a great success, but I very much fear that the reverse is true."

The titled Britisher nodded. "I'm quite aware of that and of course I anticipated it. I have taken certain measures, but now I urgently need to speak with Bishop Roundtree."

Poindexter was frank. "So do I, Sir Cyril, but I honestly don't know where he is. He left without saying a word."

"Since his manners are above any possible reproach, I assume that the severe mental strain he has been under has demanded a respite. When a man of his character requires solitude, it must be absolute. Now, however, we must dig him out. When is he due back on campus?"

"At the latest Tuesday morning, when the conference reconvenes."

Sir Cyril handed up his glass for a refill. "We can't wait until then; without alarming anyone, we must find him."

Ames ventured to interrupt. "That process has already begun, sir. The young ladies are going into action immediately."

"That's the kind of young ladies I like," Sir Cyril said. "Give them an hour or two and then get some reinforcements." He glanced at a clock. "It is now just short of three. If we have no results by five, I will want professional assistance in locating Dr. Roundtree. Make the necessary preliminary arrangements."

"Immediately, sir." Once again, without lack of decorum, Ames quickly swept up the phone.

Denise Ellen Applebaum was as female a young lady as any reasonable person had a right to expect. Her abundant blond hair and unmistakably ripe figure were assets of which she was fully aware; in addition she possessed a pair of slightly oversize blue eyes which she could manipulate with instinctive skill. All of this had been fully noted and her considerable popularity was a direct result. But over and beyond all of the visible blessings with which she had been endowed, there was another which at times served her even better. For Denise Applebaum, beneath her somewhat spectacular exterior, possessed a brain.

Since the day she had substituted for Yoshiko Matsumoto as Sir Cyril Plessey's breakfast companion, she had been waiting for the opportunity to prove her mettle. To her considerable disappointment that celebrated personage had offered her nothing in the way of a gentlemanly advance, a type of neglect to which she was wholly unaccustomed. Even at his age, she thought, he was far from unattractive and the possibilities were interesting. Breakfast had not been the ideal time, of course, and Sir Cyril's manservant had been in constant attendance, but he could have been sent on an errand somewhere. Or had the sense to invent one on his own. She had not expected that the titled visitor to the campus would try to bed her down, but she had a

266

quite natural desire to observe his technique. Having been disappointed in that, she welcomed a different way of attracting his favorable notice. Therefore she was glad to go out and look for Bishop Phil for him.

She got into the little blue car that her parents had provided for her and started the engine. As it warmed up she reflected on where he might have gone. The easy places had already been tried and he hadn't been at any of them. She drove slowly in toward the center of town pondering the matter. He wouldn't be too far away as he would have to be back by Monday night in order to preside over the session Tuesday morning. Of course it was possible that he could have flown to Florida or some place like that, but it wasn't like him. No, he would have to be somewhere within a reasonable radius.

His wife was back in England, which didn't help. With a sure instinct Denise knew that he had not sought out alternative feminine company — that simply wasn't his style. And he was all wrapped up in the conference.

He needed rest and also, if he could find it, some help.

Where would the help be? Since he was from England and had never been in the United States before, he probably didn't have any friends to turn to who were close by.

Except One.

She knew imediately that to him that would be the very best possible hope and consolation.

That decided, she began to take a mental inventory of all the places that she knew. The churches in Winnebago would be closed and locked except for the Catholic one, and he wouldn't be too likely to go there. He could have gone for a long walk just in the great out-of-doors, but not for a day and a half. No, he had gone somewhere, had had his dinner, and then after thinking for a while had gone to bed — alone. After getting up he would have had some breakfast, and then ...

Abruptly she remembered something. At the next major

intersection she turned south toward the edge of town while she sorted out the mental images that came back to her. She had been up and down the main artery to Chicago and the great commercial area that surrounded it many times. Occasionally the superhighway came close to the old road that it had replaced, and at one such near juncture there had been a sign that she seemed to remember had come up in the conversation during one of the sessions in the Pit. It had been an incidental item at the time, now it might be something else — at least it was worth checking out.

As the vast majority of the traffic flowed onto the new freeway she turned down the old road and kept her mind on her driving. Ten miles slipped behind her before she began to sense that she was getting close to her destination. A few more gentle curves in the well-worn pavement brought her nearer to the freeway and its incessant hurrying traffic; then, after climbing a slight rise, she saw a sign, a duplicate of the one that had been erected facing the superhighway:

THE CHURCH OF THE REDEEMER
(Nonsectarian)
ALWAYS OPEN
You Are Welcome — Come in and Pray
(Meals and Lodging Available)

Denise parked her car and walked across the gently packed earth toward the door which stood invitingly open. She entered quietly and waited until her eyes adjusted themselves to the much dimmer light inside. Then she tiptoed forward until she was opposite the pew where a man sat very still and alone. As he turned his head toward her, she laid a gentle hand on his shoulder.

"Bishop Phil," she said. "Please come back. We need you."

Although the party was gathered around the dining table in Dr. Harley Poindexter's home, it was Sir Cyril Plessey

268

who was the host in all but name. The illusion was aided by Ames, who stood behind his chair and aided with the food service with flawless skill. And it was also Sir Cyril who did practically all of the talking.

"Without being physically present," he said as soon as the soup had been served, "I had been keeping in touch with what had been going on here. Has anything dramatic occurred that I have missed?"

"Not recently," Philip answered.

"That is just as well. While I was absent, a delaying action was essential, therefore I provided one. I trust that you enjoyed the visit of Archbishop Nicholas."

"He brightened up the whole place," Harley responded. "A few more like him and we would be in clover."

"I believe that I fathom that. We are old friends and I took the liberty of prevailing upon him to come here. The same goes for some others whom I had chosen as too important to be ignored. In all cases they were most cooperative, in exchange for some past small favors I had rendered them."

"You do a lot of such rendering, don't you?" Dean Hastings inquired.

"From time to time I cast bread upon the waters. Among other things it's good business; greed has never paid off in the history of the world. I would say 'civilization,' but I have some doubts about that." He paused to consume some of his soup. "I relied upon these distinguished gentlemen to help hold things together pending my return here. There was to have been one more, but he was unavoidably taken ill and had to cable his regards. That's probably why things are a bit sticky right now."

Philip was listening patiently, but he had done a great deal of thinking during the preceding two days, so that his mind was both objective and clear. "Sir Cyril," he declared, "you have unquestionably served this conference in a manner that no other man alive could have done — I'm convinced of that. You have performed miracles, but there are human limits which even you cannot exceed. To put it very honestly, sir, we have now reached a dead end. Perhaps very unwisely I proposed some thirteen points on which I felt some agreement might be reached; they were all equally disastrous. I am now convinced that there exists no true common ground between the world's religions as they are presently constituted, and they are not about to alter their doctrines enough to allow any. We have explored this to the utmost and the results have been nil."

He turned to Harley Poindexter. "This is a good moment," Philip continued, "for me to tell you that for every remaining day of my life here on earth I shall be grateful to you and to everyone at Maplewood for the splendid help and support you've given to me. Words aren't adequate to express my true feelings, please believe that."

"Of course," Harley replied. "It was our pleasure and we'd do it again in a minute — right?"

Dean Hastings nodded quick agreement; so did Denise, Ned Stone, Karen Erickson, Marsha, and Professor James Moriarty.

Sir Cyril calmly resumed control of the discussion. "Excellent sentiments, but definitely premature. You were kind enough to remark, Dr. Roundtree, that I have performed miracles — that is incorrect. Miracles are successful. I recall the 'miracle' of a faith healer who cured a patient of cancer. She was duly rewarded for her achievement although the patient died two weeks later. However . . ."

He stopped and took his time, looking around the table. "We have a goodly company here, so this is perhaps the moment for me to offer some guidance." He looked at Philip. "I have your permission, I presume?"

"Absolutely, sir."

"Very well. We shall now proceed to haul the chestnuts out of the fire. You may recall that some weeks ago I gave my personal guarantee that this conference would not end in failure because I wouldn't permit it. I am not in the habit of making careless statements. We are about to have a success." He stopped and calmly gave his momentary attention to the food before him.

Aubrey Fothergill was not the kind of man to hesitate. "I would be intensely interested, sir, in knowing how you propose to pull that off."

Sir Cyril studied him sharply for a small fraction of a second. "I imagine so, but it's quite obvious. I'm going to take personal charge. Assuming that everyone is willing, of course." He did not wait for a response to that. "Also, before the dust settles I'll have you safely married to that captivating wench you have beside you. If you have altered your views and she is again on the available list, I desire to be notified at once."

"Not a prayer," Aubrey answered. "She's mine — for this and all future incarnations."

"Fothergill . . ." Philip admonished.

"I know, My Lord, but we're here to consider all viewpoints — meditation included.'

"Your thoroughness is to be commended," Sir Cyril said. "Now the plan of action includes your entering into more or less holy matrimony, something which I may even do again myself some day."

"Name the date!" Denise invited.

Sir Cyril nodded toward her. "Thank you. Now, time is short and we have to pace things exactly right to accomplish what I have in mind. We are already off schedule, and I'm afraid that the lapse let things get a bit out of hand — too many opinions from the floor. This must be corrected. On short notice there is only one immediate solution, so with proper reluctance I shall address the meeting Tuesday morning."

"I think you should," Harley agreed. "Philip willing."

"Of course."

"Then that is all set," Sir Cyril continued. "Following my

remarks there will be a different atmosphere, I anticipate, and the ground will be fertile for plowing."

"Could you give us a clue as to your plans?" Hastings asked.

Sir Cyril shook his head. "Not at the moment, except in part. I agree that we require a miracle and I have one tentatively scheduled one week from tomorrow. Some final arrangements, however, remain to be concluded. I shall attend to them promptly."

Harley Poindexter recognized the awesomeness of the moment. "I think we should leave matters in Sir Cyril's hands and get down to the serious business of eating," he proposed.

No one contested that suggestion. Ames began smoothly to serve, and before long there was a sound of contentment about the table.

"Dr. Roundtree," Sir Cyril said. "Based on the strength of years and what I may describe as profound experience, I am going to venture to advise you."

"Do," Philip invited.

"When you introduce me, don't let any implication creep into your remarks that would suggest a ringing down of the curtain. Putting me on, as it were, before everything falls to pieces. You have been anxiously awaiting my return in order to do this while things are at their height."

"I understand," Philip said. "Don't worry."

"I won't. Let's go, whenever you're ready.'

Philip opened the meeting with every evidence of full energy and strong confidence. He made a few minor announcements and then expressed his great pleasure that Sir Cyril Plessey had at last returned. Knowing that everyone would like to hear from him, he had prevailed upon this great humanitarian and benefactor to say a few words.

As Sir Cyril walked on, some of the delegates rose to their feet. Others followed until the entire assembly was paying tribute to the man to whom so much was owed by so many. After basking for an appropriate interval in this recognition, Sir Cyril gestured that he was about to speak and the delegates sat down.

"Although my name has attracted some public notice from time to time," he began, "I have never been especially distinguished as a religious man. It isn't that I disavow God, it is simply that I haven't met Him yet, and I am not sure of His pleasure. In that we are all to some degree on common ground, for while we are confident of our views, we can't be positive. The fact that we differ amongst ourselves is proof of that."

Five minutes later he was in complete command of the situation, the conference, and in a position to pronounce on future developments. He proceeded to do so with unshakable authority. "In a few days your deliberations will be coming to a conclusion because time is a factor and many of you have important responsibilities to discharge. I offer the opinion that this assemblage is now in the position of a swimmer who has been crossing a long and dangerous channel. The opposite shore remains shrouded in mist, so that the encouragement of seeing the attainable goal is absent. But the swimmer is closer to his destination than he knows; already the deep waters are yielding to the rising ground beneath and ahead lies his success. The swimmer cannot see this, he cannot as yet sense it, but it is true nonetheless."

He paused and looked up, taking his time.

"I am in a position to know whereof I speak. Something very close to triumph lies immediately ahead of you all and it will become a reality sooner than you may now believe possible. On this I ask that you accept my assurance — there are those among you who know that my word on such matters is not to be questioned. In fact, should you so desire, you can discount it at the bank. I wish you all good morning."

There was business and discussion to occupy the rest of the session, but it was conducted in a new atmosphere. Sir Cyril had done his job; the conference clearly was reacting to a fresh injection of vitality. The new feeling continued throughout the afternoon, and when it was all over, it seemed to Philip that some tiny amount of progress might actually have been achieved.

On the following day the press descended once more, but Sir Cyril had nothing to tell them. Even to Arthur Gravenstine he remained mum; his sole statement was to reaffirm what he had said from the platform.

The great Midwestern newspaper which had been giving the conference notably good coverage resumed its picture series and ran the portrait of John Wesley. That evening an extraordinarily good meal was served in the dining hall, the result of a special effort on the part of the kitchen staff and M. Henri Devereux — an effort inspired by a request from Sir Cyril. Following the dinner there was a concert by way of entertainment; Wings Over Jordan sang to a full house and the rich heritage of the spirituals resulted in a standing ovation when the program was over. Philip had heard spirituals before, but never delivered with such authority and depth of understanding; it was to him a moving experience and he had renewed thoughts about the brotherhood of man. He was not alone in this — which was precisely the effect that Sir Cyril had desired.

On Thursday one of the world's most eminent actors appeared before the assembly and in a cultivated British voice of almost incredible richness read selected passages from the Koran, the Bible, the Book of Mormon, the Rig Veda, and other major religious works. With distinguished art he delivered some of the quotations from Confucius and then concluded with part of the Sermon of the Lights by the Lord Buddha. He literally made the words live, and when he had finished he received an ovation. A spirit of unity *was* beginning to pervade the atmosphere, and in addition the event was good for some fairly extended press coverage.

Philip perceived that some extremely skillful stage setting was being done. Beyond that he had little to go on other than Sir Cyril's reassurance, but that came very close to being enough. He trusted in the Lord and Sir Cyril in that order, and he considered it possible that the doughty knight was also serving as an instrument of divine intention and will.

Just before the Friday session Aubrey delivered an envelope which contained an announcement to be read. Philip reviewed it and then delivered it just as it had been written. As he spoke from the podium he had good attention, because the assembly had been expecting something.

"I have just been advised," Philip said, "that our meeting next Tuesday will be of extraordinary importance. I must confess to you all that I have not yet received any further details myself. However, since this information comes from our mutual benefactor, Sir Cyril Plessey, I most certainly give it full credence."

He then turned to another matter. "It has been proposed that a uniform edition of the world's greatest religious books be issued for the benefit of scholars, libraries, and interested individuals. This proposal, which was introduced by the Taoist delegation, has met with success. It is my very great pleasure to tell you that a most responsible publishing concern has agreed to undertake this project. I have been advised by the editor-in-chief that the initial edition will consist of eight volumes, with others to follow at periodic intervals until all of the significant literature has been covered. The sole exception at present is *Science and Health with Key to the Scriptures* by Mrs. Eddy, which is under copyright and which has not been made available by the owners. There remains a question as to which are the definitive versions, but this, hopefully, can be resolved by the proper authorities within each of the major religious communities."

He allowed himself to smile. "We seem to be meeting with unusual success lately. I take pleasure in noting that here is something very specific that has come out of our convocation; I understand that more is to follow."

For once there was not a single dissenting hand raised from the floor; no one stood up and asked to be recognized.

Then a Japanese Christian signaled and received a microphone. "In this same spirit," he said, struggling slightly with the three s's, "could not each delegation prepare a pamphlet which could be printed uniformly and exchanged between ourselves by mail later when they are available. They could also be given out to anyone interested."

That, for a happy wonder, was approved in less than an hour. The only problem lay in the fact that the conference was almost over and there was hardly time to take any action. But it was another indication of at least some kind of cooperation and as such Philip welcomed it eagerly.

The head of the Bahai delegation rose and stated that his church would be honored to produce the first edition of the pamphlets provided that some copies could be sold at a modest price to defray part of the expenses. He promised that all texts would be reproduced unaltered in any way and that the printing and binding would be entirely uniform.

Philip could hardly believe it — people were being reasonable and, what was more, they were being constructive. He very much doubted that Sir Cyril had managed this, but it was happening nonetheless.

A Billy Graham delegate rose to move that the offer of Bahai be accepted. There was some limited debate, but the outcome was clear from the first — by a substantial majority the motion was carried.

The luncheon break was the most encouraging one in weeks; instead of sometimes sullen silence there was talking as the delegates came out of the chapel-auditorium, and even the fact that it had started to rain did not spoil the atmosphere. It was a warm summer shower which brought on repeated remarks that it was needed and would be good for the crops. No one seemed to be discouraged by the overcast sky.

The Friday afternoon session was not quite as successful, but it went well enough. At the conclusion the housing desk was not surrounded by those who were announcing their plans to check out and go home. Only two actually left and both of them made it clear that they would have stayed had they been able.

The weekend settled in with an aura that all was well. Philip was fully aware of it, but he knew also that in a way it was an illusion, one created by the promise of something spectacular to occur in three days' time. If a disappointment came instead, then the whole atmosphere could be reversed in a matter of minutes. Therefore, as soon as he had concluded his necessary business, he picked up the phone and called Sir Cyril.

He did not need to announce either himself or the purpose of his call. "You have rung up, of course, to ask what is on the docket for next Tuesday," he was informed.

"Correct."

Sir Cyril wasted no time. "My trust in you is complete, of course, but in this instance you must forgive me for not informing you. It is a moral matter — I have given my word."

"That is sufficient," Philip said.

"Thank you. If convenient, I would much appreciate your holding yourself in readiness to join with me on Monday evening — I cannot set the hour as yet."

Philip was reasonable. "Can I expect any information before then?"

Sir Cyril hesitated, which was rare for him. "Possibly, but I don't wish to guarantee it. If I may, I will."

Philip hung up with the full realization that it was now a matter of faith. Faith in God, of course, but more immediately, faith in Sir Cyril Plessey. He went for a walk to turn the whole matter over in his mind. Then, without self-consciousness, he went to the meditation room, where he was delighted to discover that Bishop Sumi was present. He was learning the knack of turning his mind inward, and the tranquillity that it brought helped to renew the flow of his spirit.

On Sunday evening Philip called Sir Cyril once more to see if there had been any developments. When he hung up he had learned little other than the fact that things still seemed to be under control. Once again he divested his mind of the matter and spent the evening in the company of Professor Moriarty at the latter's home. The professor displayed a dry wit that he liked and his wife produced a strawberry shortcake that was a triumph. The time with the Moriartys passed rapidly and most agreeably; they proved delightful friends who had a most comfortable home complete with a striking portrait of Sherlock Holmes which adorned the wall above the fireplace.

On Monday morning he went firmly to work. He still trusted in Sir Cyril, but he had no intention of walking in to conduct the meeting on Tuesday morning without a clear plan of action in case the promised miracle had failed to materialize. He scheduled two or three matters, none of which were of great moment, that he could take up; when he had done that he drafted an announcement that the conference was concluding. Anticipating that he might soon have to deliver a short speech of thanks and farewell, he prepared that also.

It was past four in the afternoon, and there was still no word. He closed his office, and desiring a walk in any event, he determined to call on Sir Cyril without announcing his intention of doing so. It was time for him to know what was going on, for the responsibility was still his.

Sir Cyril was not at home. Philip was received by Ames, who welcomed him with genuine cordiality and asked him to be seated.

"Sir Cyril has gone to the airport, M'Lord," he reported. "It is my understanding that a special flight he arranged is due to come in. Normally I drive him, but this time he arranged for Mr. Ned Stone to do so."

"I presume, then, that someone is arriving," Philip said.

"Undoubtedly, sir. I would even go so far as to say a group — at least I gathered that impression."

Philip remained for a few minutes and then left. Something at least was happening, but he did not like being kept in the dark, and for the first time in many weeks he began to feel slow anger. It was a weakness, he recognized that, but he could not help it. True, Sir Cyril had given his word, but it would have been thoughtful of him to have included a proviso that would have avoided his own present embarrassment. Suppressing his irritation as best he could, he tried to turn his mind to other matters.

He was at dinner when the Lincoln Continental came up the hill once more, leading a small caravan of other vehicles from the motor pool. He was with a gentleman from Africa who proved to be a remarkably interesting companion. He had known Schweitzer and was an encyclopedia about missionary work in that part of the world. He was so interesting, in fact, that Philip was able to forget for just a little while the anxiety that had taken hold of him; he ended by inviting his dinner companion to come to England and deliver a series of addresses in his diocese when the conference had been concluded. He was still absorbed in the conversation when he was called to the telephone.

Sir Cyril himself was on the line. "I shall begin," he declared, "by apologizing to you for not having communicated sooner. There was an unexpected delay and I was as upset as you must have been."

"I quite understand," Philip said. During most of his ministerial life he had been called upon to "understand."

"Very kind of you, but it is not my practice to treat distinguished people shabbily — or any others. I shall now proceed to make it up to you."

Philip felt a sudden surge. His mind and body were hungry for something to grasp and to hold — something to fill the vast void that inaction and frustration had created. Something within him declared that this remarkable man, who had a formidable reputation for surmounting all obstacles, was about to do it once again. "I am all attention," he said.

"Excellent. I desire to meet with you as soon as you find it convenient. Could you please come to the Science Building where the temporary chapels are located?"

"Of course."

"It might be well to bring your chaplain. If his intended is with him, she may be included."

Philip had a very good idea where his chaplain would be — in the Pit. Jayawardene had cultivated a taste for ice cream desserts which could be supplied there at any time. "Shall we say twenty minutes?" he asked.

"Fine, Philip. I suggest the second floor." Sir Cyril broke the connection.

Aubrey was indeed in the Pit, and in the process of reducing what had obviously been a sizable ice cream concoction to oblivion. Jayawardene, of course, was with him. As Philip came up to their table, the girl looked at him and said immediately, "You have news."

"Yes, I have. Sir Cyril has requested that the three of us meet with him. I believe it to be important."

Aubrey stood up at once. "It had better be," he declared.

"It will be," Jayawardene said. She allowed herself one more mouthful of ice cream and then picked up her purse.

The three of them crossed the campus without speaking. There was little to say and they each knew what thoughts they held in common. Philip had one of his own: that the girl his chaplain had chosen would make a superb mate for him — the religious question only excepted. He had no desire to delve into that thorny problem now — only to meet with Sir Cyril and finally have the mask removed from whatever that venerable conjurer had prepared.

Aubrey held open the door as they entered the Science Building. Having learned that it was expected of her, Jayawardene went first, climbing the steps to the second floor with a natural grace that invited admiration. When they had ascended two flights Ned Stone met them with a face that was curiously wooden; obviously he was keeping himself under careful control. "This way, if you please," he said, and turned.

They walked past the meditation room, which was occupied; three persons were sitting silently, oblivious to the outside world. The Muslim sanctuary, which was next, appeared deserted, but the light inside was so dim it was not possible to be sure. At the Buddhist chapel Ned gestured toward the door.

Sir Cyril was waiting for them inside, leaning on his stick, his penetrating eyes sweeping those of Philip and his little party. There were others present also, a number of the brown and saffron-robed monks who stood out so distinctively on the campus.

"Good evening," Sir Cyril said. "You have been laboring long and hard in the vineyard and I promised you that it would not be in vain. By the profound generosity of a very great personage, I am pleased to provide you with your miracle."

Philip did not understand as he surveyed the small chapel. Then he noted that one of the monks was very old, and was aware immediately that he was a newcomer to the conference. And his cast of feature was distinctive — unfamiliar and a bit baffling to a British bishop.

At that moment, Jayawardene sank to her knees, and placing her hands before her, bowed to the floor. Suddenly an awareness of a benign presence seemed to Philip to fill the room as some rare perfume might have done. Then he looked into the face of a man who, though he was surrounded, stood alone. Garbed exactly like the others, and shaven headed, he nevertheless in his well-molded features revealed a deep and unique spirituality. Physically he might have been somewhere around forty, and the glasses which he wore gave him an unneeded touch of gentility, almost of nobility.

As Philip looked at him he smiled and held out his hands. It was then that the barriers of sect and tradition were swept away and doctrines crumbled to dust, for Philip knew and understood that he was in the presence of a saint. Goodness and compassion radiated from the man and they would not be denied.

"Sir," the voice of Sir Cyril Plessey declared, "I am honored to present to you the Right Reverend Philip Roundtree, Doctor in Divinity, whose great achievements you already know. My Lord, His Holiness the Dalai Lama."

CHAPTER NINETEEN

At precisely nine-thirty in the evening the public relations agency that had been engaged by Sir Cyril Plessey distributed releases to all the major news media informing them that the legendary Dalai Lama had left his Himalayan retreat for the United States and had arrived at Maplewood College. Included in the package were photographs of His Holiness and an assortment of background materials. All of this was intended for use on the eleven o'clock nationwide news broadcasts, which allowed an hour and a half for digging into the morgue files and rewriting.

It all went according to plan, apart from a few of the more enthusiastic reporters who rushed on the air to declare that the god-king of Tibet had appeared. That inaccurate description was promptly corrected when the major newscasts went on at eleven. In the lead story it was accurately stated that His Holiness was the head of state of Tibet and its absolute ruler prior to the invasion of the Chinese communists of this most peace-loving of all of the nations on earth.

The dramatic story was retold of how His Holiness and a small group of his followers had made their escape at the last possible moment across the most terrible mountain barrier in the world, but only after his people had literally forced the decision upon him. A few of the existing film clips of His Holiness were shown and some of the more resourceful commentators quoted passages from his book *My Land and My People.* He was correctly identified as the fourteenth in his great succession, vastly respected as the living incarnation of Chenrezi, the god of mercy, and a Bodhisattva of the Buddhist faith.

This was all summed up admirably by an Asian expert who appeared on short notice before the cameras to supply additional information.

"In terms of Christianity," he told his vast audience, "it would be almost exactly as if His Holiness the Pope were to be regarded not simply as a cardinal who had been elected by his peers to the highest office of the Catholic Church, but rather as St. Peter himself returned to earth to serve both as a monarch and a definitive spiritual guide.

"There will be, of course, those who will resist such an idea, but an integral part of the Christian faith is the belief that Christ will return to earth as stated in the Bible 'to judge the quick and the dead.' The Second Coming is, in fact, one of the cornerstones of Christian theology. Since this is the case, it should not be too difficult for the Christian majority of this country to comprehend a closely similar doctrine held in the vast Buddhist world. Buddha himself was a man of great nobility and splendid character whose life set an example for the ages. Now, by the standards of a major segment of the church he founded, a living saint has been granted to us and he is paying us the great honor of his presence.

"His Holiness the Dalai Lama occupies a unique position since he is both a supreme personage and spiritual leader within his faith and the absolute head of state of his country. In recent years certain political entities for reasons of expediency have tried to support the fiction that Tibet is part of China. If this be true, then Ireland is properly part of England, Canada belongs to the United States, Korea has no right to exist, and the state of Israel should never have been permitted in the first place."

After the newscasts and the commentaries were over, Sir Cyril retired early. He was expecting a full day on the morrow and he wanted to be fully prepared to meet it.

He was not disappointed. Before breakfast had been completed more than fifty reporters and other press people had descended *en masse* on the campus of Maplewood College and they were only the vanguard. The reception facilities were swamped; Bill Quigley had foreseen what was in store, he had had no time to prepare for it.

Due to the degree of confusion that prevailed, it was almost impossible for Philip to conduct a meaningful morning session. For reasons with which he was forced to sympathize, the delegates were not really concerned with the business at hand. Shortly after ten Aubrey appeared and passed him a note. He read it and then made an announcement which he knew would be popular.

"I have just been advised," he reported, "that His Holiness the Dalai Lama will address us this afternoon at three. This being the case, I deem it expedient to adjourn this session so that the television people may set up their equipment and other preparations can be made. We shall meet again here at two-thirty."

The exodus was prompt, and for once it was not the result of either heated tempers or plain discouragement. When Philip left the building himself he had a clear path to his office and no one detained him, despite the fact that the campus was crowded. As he made his way across the inviting grass he was not sure whether he should regard this remarkable change as a miracle or not. Whatever it was, it was off to a good start. Even the weather was cooperating — the rain was gone and the clear sky was warm.

As soon as Philip was alone in his office, his phone rang. Somehow he knew who it was; he picked up the instrument and said, "Good morning, Sir Cyril."

"Good morning, Philip. As you can see, phase one is moving ahead strictly according to plan. Now if you can spare the time, I would appreciate your joining us here at Dr. Poindexter's residence. I am about to outline the next moves."

"I shall come at once, Sir Cyril."

"Excellent."

At the home of the college president the air crackled. As soon as Philip had been admitted he found gathered there Sir Cyril, Harley Poindexter and his wife, Dean Hastings, his chaplain, Jayawardene, and a young Buddhist monk he had not yet met. As soon as they were introduced he discovered that the younger man, who was a member of the Dalai Lama's party, spoke fluent, effortless English.

As would be expected, Sir Cyril held the floor. "A suitable processional is now being organized to welcome His Holiness to the assembly," he reported. "The entire Buddhist delegation is taking part and the matter is entirely in their hands. His Holiness himself is resting at the moment, for he has had a very long and tiring journey."

Harley Poindexter turned toward the monk. "Forgive my asking this," he said, "but does His Holiness speak English?"

The young man nodded. "He does. He acquired it without taking any formal instruction; he has a great gift for languages."

A thought persisted in Philip's mind and he felt that he had to express it. "I realize that all of the reporters and television people are here," he began, "but isn't it asking too much of anyone to travel so far and then to speak so

286

soon after his arrival? He might appreciate some additional time to rest and to prepare his address."

His Buddhist colleague answered. "That is most considerate of you, Dr. Roundtree, but the thoughts which His Holiness brings have been in his heart for weeks. Although he had not planned to come here, he has been following the progress of this momentous meeting with great interest; since it began he has given it much thought and he has prayed. He is prepared."

"Then we must not deprive ourselves any longer of the privilege of listening to his wisdom," Sir Cyril declared crisply. "We must also agree on certain plans for the rest of the week and the closing of the meeting. Today we all will have the great honor of hearing the address of His Holiness. I anticipate that the press will wish to meet with him at his convenience, which will probably be tomorrow after he has had some additional rest."

He looked toward the man who was the Dalai Lama's English-language secretary and received an answering nod of approval.

"I didn't get your name," Sir Cyril said.

"Tenzin."

"Thank you. The deliberations of the delegate assembly have now gone about as far as is possible under existing circumstances, and despite certain appearances I am personally convinced that a great deal of progress has been made — not all of it on the surface."

"Amen to that," Dean Hastings contributed.

"To continue, there is one major piece of unfinished business which, if everyone agrees, will serve to bring this conference to a fine and dignified close." He turned and focused his penetrating eyes onto Jayawardene. "Is it still your intention to give up your fascinating eligibility in order to marry the Reverend Mr. Fothergill?"

"Yes," she answered him.

Aubrey was next to receive the eagle's scrutiny. "And you,

sir, are still rejoicing in your good fortune that this lady has accepted you?"

"Totally."

Sir Cyril brushed his upper lip. "This being the case, I venture to recommend that the wedding be celebrated on this coming Friday as the final event of the meeting. I have some excellent reasons."

He rose to his feet, planted his stick before him, and assumed the role of commander-in-chief. "This is to be a solemn and beautiful religious occasion." He turned to the bride-to-be. "Have you given thought to who will be your choice to perform the ceremony?"

"Yes, Sir Cyril," Jayawardene answered him. "Since our dream of being married in a united church is clearly impossible, we hope to have a very quiet private ceremony as soon as this conference is over. And we plan to ask Dr. Roundtree to officiate."

Philip had not expected that, and for a moment he felt sudden emotion well up within him. Since the bride was a Buddhist, he had fully expected her to select someone of her own faith to preside. It was a major concession for her to choose him; furthermore, it took away one of the lesser worries that had plagued him — the image of a Church of England clergyman standing up to be married before someone very far removed from his own convictions and dedication. His appreciation of Jayawardene went higher still; for the first time he felt an easing of the strain of this inter-religious union and he praised God for it.

"Now," Sir Cyril declared, putting the full force of his dynamic personality behind his words, "I am going to ask something of you. I am asking it for the benefit of this whole great effort on the part of so many, and for the future possibilities which it portends. I am asking your consent to be married publicly before the assembly this coming Friday."

Dean Hastings spoke. "Sir, understand what I mean

when I say this, but I don't believe that a sacred occasion should be manipulated for purposes of publicity."

It was quiet for a moment, the air hanging thick in the room. Only one man could break that silence, and when he did so he spoke with the accumulated strength of many decades. "I would neither suggest nor permit that; my reasons lie elsewhere. As you are aware, the eyes of almost the whole civilized world have been turned toward this young couple and there is a great awareness of their somewhat unlikely romance. I am personally persuaded that they are entirely sincere in their intentions."

"I don't doubt that," Hastings said.

"This wedding," Sir Cyril declared, "is to be in every way an earnest religious ceremony in the presence of God and man. I believe the setting to be appropriate, and if we cannot have a united church we can settle for something else . . ."

He paused and looked around the room. "Think of the *witnesses!* Think of the men and women gathered here representing all of the world's major faiths, and most of the lesser ones as well, united in the celebration of a joyful sacred occasion. If we cannot have a united church, we can instead have a united congregation — and I regard that as not too bad a substitute."

Again, for a few moments, it was quiet.

Then it was Harley Poindexter who spoke. "I am not a churchman, but from my lay viewpoint, I must say that what you are proposing is a master stroke. I never thought of the united congregation, and of course that's absolutely true. I would question if there has ever been a time in history when so many people of so many different convictions have ever assembled for a religious occasion."

"Assuming that the principals are willing," Sir Cyril concluded, "it could represent a most successful termination of this meeting, and at the moment I cannot see how anyone could take exception to it."

"No reasonable person, surely," Poindexter agreed.

Philip saw that his chaplain was looking at him, waiting for him to speak. He understood, and chose his words with great care. "I have accepted the fact that Aubrey Fothergill has chosen his bride from outside our own Church and even our faith, but since we all came here to understand one another better, we necessarily must abide by that principle —and that conviction. I must now add that since I have come to know this lovely young woman better, I cannot deny that my chaplain has made a superb choice and I most sincerely congratulate him."

He looked at Jayawardene, and the smile she gave him was radiant.

"If it meets with the approval of the bride," Philip continued, as carefully as before, "then for us to bring the meeting to a close with a happy spiritual occasion is as much as any of us dare hope for. I trust Sir Cyril implicitly that the dignity consistent with the circumstances will be maintained."

"I guarantee that," the venerable nobleman said.

Aubrey Fothergill reached out and took Jayawardene's hand. "I believe that we should," he said.

Jayawardene looked up at him. "Then we shall," she responded.

"But there is so much to be done!" Marsha protested mildly.

Sir Cyril shook his head. "Perhaps not. The guests have already been invited — so to speak. M. Devereux can handle all of the necessary culinary arrangements with ease. The legal requirements are simple and can be complete today. The hall has been secured. One other matter remains and that is the bride's wedding dress. As it happens I have a very good eye for female proportions and I am quite aware of Miss Thiengburanathum's near perfect dimensions. While I was in Paris recently I took the liberty of ordering an appropriate outfit for her from the House of Dior — I trust that it will be satisfactory."

"Can they get it here on time?" Marsha asked.

Sir Cyril answered her. "It has been on hand in my quarters for the past three weeks."

By two-thirty in the afternoon the chapel-auditorium of Maplewood College was filled as it had never been before in its history; every seat in the sizable auditorium was occupied, and the three walls were completely lined with standees. Frank Chalmers was well aware that the fire regulations were technically being violated, but that fact did not disturb him unduly; he was more concerned in trying to figure out where he could put any more people without resorting to chairs in the aisles.

Even the back and the sides of the balcony were packed with people, and there were more waiting to be accommodated. Frank did the best that he could; he had a hundred additional chairs brought into the lobby and arranged to have the sound system piped through.

Even more than the people, expectation filled the vastness of the assembly chamber. It could be felt and it could be heard in an unaccustomed quiet. There is a certain manner in which people behave when the occasion reaches a level of importance that is beyond their ordinary experience; that influence had taken hold of all those gathered and the remarkable quiet was almost uncanny.

At ten minutes to three there was a slight stir, a subdued movement as positions were shifted a little to relieve cramped muscles, but it lasted less than a minute and then passed away. Although no clock was posted in the auditorium, the hour and the minute seemed to be known to everyone present.

At five minutes to three the monk Tenzin appeared on the platform with a group of five others, all identically garbed. It was clear at once that there would be no procession, no ceremonial introduction of the legendary religious personage about whom everyone present had heard repeatedly but whom none of them, apart from the members of his own party, had ever seen.

Philip Roundtree came onto the platform and conferred for a few moments with the young Tibetan. He was in his usual clerical dress without any added vestments in honor of the occasion. It was understood that this was in accordance with the wishes of His Holiness without anything being said. Philip himself would probably have turned out in the ensemble commonly called "magpie," but he was secretly relieved that that had not been necessary.

The brief conference over, Philip glanced at his watch and then for a few moments studied the auditorium. He too noted the remarkable stillness; even Sir Cyril Plessey in his accustomed seat in the balcony was uncharacteristically quiet.

He took a deep breath and held it to steady himself. It was indeed close to a miracle that people of so many different persuasions were waiting to hear one man from behind the Himalayas on the other side of the world.

As he turned back he discovered for the first time that there was a banner displayed at the rear of the stage, one which appeared to be a sunburst in red and blue with two lions crouching below in a white triangle. He did not know exactly what it was or who had put it there, but he surmised correctly that it was the national flag of Tibet.

The time stood at two minutes to three.

More people appeared onstage: Bishop Sumi and the other members of the Zen delegation, the Thai Buddhists, the two delegates from Cambodia, and three representatives from the Republic of China. Following them four more saffron-robed monks came in a group.

Peasley, the most conspicuous member of the Methodist delegation, was the first to rise to his feet in the auditorium proper; as soon as he had done so there was a wave of movement until everyone was standing. A smattering of applause started, but Philip raised his hand to stop it, and the speed with which his request was heeded made it evident that the delegates agreed with him.

Tenzin caught his eye and nodded. Philip looked once more at the last little group that had come in and saw His Holiness there smiling at him, his features composed behind his glasses. Silently and carefully Philip cleared his throat as he stepped behind the podium and rested his hands on the slanted top. He did not need to wait for silence, it was already there.

He motioned for the assembly to be seated and delayed ten seconds while it was done. In that brief interval he took note of the two television cameras that had been set up as much out of the way as possible, and he knew that a very large audience would be listening and watching.

Once more he made sure that his throat was clear and then he spoke. "Ladies and gentlemen, I have the great honor to introduce His Holiness Gejong Tenzin Gyatsho, the Dalai Lama." Quietly he turned and then stood before his own uncomfortable high-backed chair.

Even though he was perhaps fifteen feet away, he could almost feel the charisma of the man who came quietly forward and took his place behind the speaker's podium. He was a perfectly mortal human individual, but that reality was submerged by a feeling of grace so profound that Philip felt a tug of conscience that in experiencing it he might be compromising his own Christian convictions. Then he realized that the man before him transcended all that as, in an infinitely greater way, Christ had when He was on earth. Philip had often thought that the late Mahatma Gandhi had come very close to being a saint, and had wondered if that elevation of a human individual was necessarily restricted to the Christian faith.

He did not know, but he wanted to listen. He riveted his whole attention as His Holiness began to speak.

"My friends and my brothers, I am profoundly grateful that the path ordained for me has allowed me to come here and to stand before you. From the first occasion that you met, I have been following with the greatest interest the reports of your deliberations, both those which have appeared in the public press and those which were sent to my office for my added enlightenment."

His voice was a well-controlled instrument, notably accented, but that became insignificant in the light of the words he was speaking.

"This great adventure in human understanding surely will find its place not only in religious history but also in the more general accounts of the significant happenings of humanity. It is my feeling that you have come much closer together here than perhaps anyone realizes. As one meets a new person unaware that he is to become a great and dear friend, so it is, I believe, true that you have found more together than appears or can be understood until you have gone your separate ways once again and then discover that a new element has been added to your lives. As I have said before, no other pleasure can be compared with that derived from spiritual practice. This is the greatest pleasure, and it is ultimate in nature. Different religions have each shown their own way to attain it."

Philip turned his head just enough to look out over the assembly. At that moment those who were crowded into the chapel-auditorium were substantially of one mind, and that was a realization he had never hoped to see.

It was as close to a miracle as he was likely to witness in his lifetime.

Then he shut his eyes and consciously listened as the voice of the Dalai Lama cut through the barriers and obstructions to reach the minds of men and women who were united at least in their desire to find the path to peace, to rest, and to salvation.

Philip did not hear the words as separate entities within the English language; he listened instead to the thoughts that they conveyed and pondered them. For a little while the whole packed auditorium receded from his consciousness and he was in spirit alone with the man who was yielding up the fruits of his lifetime dedication to the One who had sought to banish suffering from the world. He listened, and to his widened outlook the words he heard were timeless in their truth — truth unhampered by doctrine or the minute specifics of individual beliefs. And as he listened, gradually the burden that he had been carrying for so many weeks seemed to ease and to evaporate.

One thing he knew for sure — no other human being could have worked this magic. The world was, thanks to God, filled with men of great vision, inspiration, learning, and stature — but this man from Tibet was a special creation and there was none other like him.

"Although our country and our people have for centuries maintained a strict policy of nonintervention in the affairs of the world beyond the mountains that surround us, we have grieved nonetheless that so many times conflicts and bloodshed have broken out over religious issues. While other factors have been involved, it has mainly been religion and differences of religious viewpoint that have brought about such unhappiness as the hostilities between Egypt and Israel, between India and Pakistan, between China and India, and between two different Christian groups in Ireland. The history of holy wars is a long and terrible one, and none of them have ever brought to humanity any real benefit.

"It is here that we may recall the words of a man whose greatness reached far beyond his own country, or his own hemisphere. It was Mahatma Gandhi who taught us, 'It is not nonviolence if we merely love those that love us. It is nonviolence only when we love those that hate us.' And this universal love has been taught to us also by the Blessed One and by Jesus, who forgave his persecutors and prayed for them even as they were nailing Him to the Cross."

Philip glanced out to read the reaction to that. It was indefinite, but it was there. From his own recent experience he knew that some of the more conservative Christian delegates would not expect someone so far removed from their own doctrines to be familiar with the passion of Christ. It was good for them to find out.

As though he too understood that point, the Dalai Lama paused and allowed a few moments for his words to be received. When he continued, his voice seemed, within itself, to carry enlightenment.

"There are very few, I think, who would not agree that in many different ways we have been directed toward this path, and at many different times. It is stated by Bahai, 'Ye are all the fruits of one tree and the leaves of one branch. Walk, then, with perfect charity, concord, affection, and agreement.' This, I know well, you are all striving to do.

"This same call to charity and understanding is found in the Bible, in the New Testament. In the tenth book of Acts, Peter says, 'Truly I perceive that God shows no partiality, but in every nation anyone who fears Him and does what is right is acceptable to Him.'

"I am myself pleased that Arnold Toynbee has written, 'Who are . . . the greatest benefactors of the living generation of mankind? I should say: "Confucius and Lao-tze, the Buddha, the Prophets of Israel and Judah, Zarathustra, Jesus, Mohammed, and Socrates." ' "

His Holiness stopped for a moment and looked at the manuscript before him. His shaven head was bowed, and as he stood there Philip wondered at the near miracle that had raised this wonderful personage from the simple village

296

where he had been born to his present great position. If it had been an act of God, he was prepared to accept it as such.

"I would now like to speak to you about the thirteen points which were laid before you by the very wise and good man who sits beside me now. It is an almost impossible task for one person to lay down precepts that every faith throughout the world will accept, but it is my opinion that the truly great Bishop Roundtree very nearly accomplished the all but impossible task. For while none of these points, I am told, was fully acceptable to everyone here, they did provide much discussion, and when that takes place we all learn from one another.

"I have myself thought a great deal about all of these points, and I find in them evidence of a great faith and personal dedication. Many years from now I believe that men and women of good will and spiritual orientation will still be discussing them and learning from them."

The Dalai Lama stopped at that point and searched the faces of his listeners. There was no shuffling of feet, no intrusion of sotto voce conversation.

When the pause had extended for a few seconds, he continued his discourse with a slightly altered tone. "Over the course of many centuries we have all been shown the path in one way or another, and we have listened to the voices of many great teachers. Out of all this a great complexity has arisen, and sometimes we find ourselves in what we believe to be direct conflict. But it is not so, we have only made it appear so because we have unconsciously emphasized differences of viewpoint rather than seeking out what it is that we all share. For there *is* something upon which I believe that we all may agree — without hesitation or reservation. It is, if you would like to call it that, a fourteenth point, or you may consider it as standing by itself. It is one thing in the whole field of religious study and observance which unites us all: Buddhist and Christian, Muslim and Jew, Jain and Hindu, Taoist and Shintoist, Catholic, and Protestant, even the most devout teacher of any faith and the agnostic."

Philip drew a long breath and held it. God knew that everyone had been searching for such a thing, himself most of all, and that it had not appeared. His mind leaped into a familiar path and he uttered the shortest prayer of his life — that, God willing, the Dalai Lama did have such a wondrous gift to offer. It was very late in the day, but humanity would go on long after the conference had been formally concluded.

His Holiness bent over his manuscript and then looked up once more. "Let us go back in time to the founding of perhaps the most ancient of the living faiths of the world, to the prophet and teacher Zoroaster. In the Dadistan-i-Dinik there are certain words we may listen to and heed: *'That nature only is good when it shall not do unto another whatever is not good for its own self.'* "

He once more surveyed his audience. "Who is there here that can dispute this principle? I do not believe that there is anyone.

"I turn now to the Analects and the profound wisdom of Kung Fu-tse. He was asked by Tse-kung, 'Is there one single word that can serve as a principle of conduct for life?' To this Confucius replied: *'Perhaps the word "shu"'* — reciprocity — *'will do. Do not do unto others what you do not want others to do unto you.'* "

Philip gripped the arms of his chair while his mind seemed to spin inside his head. The Golden Rule! He had not once thought of it since the conference had begun, but he remembered, now, that it had appeared in many forms in many parts of the world. He felt like a child who had misunderstood his lesson and was being patiently corrected by a sympathetic and understanding teacher. And he, a bishop of the Church of England, the devoted servant of Christ Jesus, had not remembered the words of the Man of Galilee!

For Christ had taught it too.

The Dalai Lama looked up once more from his notes. "It is fitting also to turn to the Talmud, that book of ancient wisdom that has guided Israel through the centuries. Within its pages the statement is made with great strength and authority: '*What is hurtful to yourself do not do to your fellow man. This is the whole of the Torah and the remainder is but commentary. Go and learn it.*' "

Once more Philip looked at the huge auditorium crammed with listeners and his peculiarly sensitive instincts told him that an invisible, soundless, yet overwhelming change was taking place. For the stubborn, ingrained differences that had plagued even the most placid and noncontroversial meetings were being uprooted at that moment by a legendary Buddhist monk from literally the most remote part of the world. It was difficult to credit and to believe, but he had to because it was there before him.

"At the present time," His Holiness continued, "I and many of my people are very much indebted to the great nation of India for shelter and help in many different ways. It is therefore most appropriate that I quote to you a statement from the Hindu faith that is found in the Mahabharata: '*This is the sum of duty: do naught to others which if done unto thee, would cause thee pain.*'

"India is also the land most closely associated with Sikhism, a path which merits respect through all of the civilized world. In the Kabir it is stated: '*As thou deemest thyself, so deem others. Then shalt thou become a partner in heaven.*' "

Philip knew then, knew that whatever its source and whatever its shape, he had his miracle. He was content with that and ceased upbraiding himself that he had failed to find the light that was being shown to him now. Neither he nor any other man had the right to question the ways and workings of God — he could only be profoundly grateful for them with all of his being.

"I realize that here in the Western world not too much is known about many of our Eastern faiths, because for about two hundred years colonialism was very strong in Southeast Asia, and people who consider themselves to be masters often overlook the opportunities they have to gain added wisdom and understanding. Therefore not all of you may be aware of the T'ai Shang Kan Ying P'ien and the teachings of Lao-tze, but from this source we are admonished: 'Regard your neighbor's gain as your own gain, and regard your neighbor's loss as your own loss.'

"The faith and doctrines of the Jains are also little known here, apart from the fact that they venerate all forms of life and go sometimes to great lengths to be sure that they do not unwittingly destroy any living creatures. Those here who are of that faith and who are familiar with the Yoga-shastra will recognize these words: 'In happiness and in suffering, in joy and grief, we should regard all creatures as we regard ourselves, and should therefore refrain from inflicting upon others such injury as would appear undesirable if inflicted upon ourselves.'

"So it can be seen that there is much accord on this principle. The whole life of the Blessed One was a continuous demonstration of this wonderful rule of conduct, and in the sacred writings of Buddhism you will find it set down many times. The Udanavarga states it: 'Hurt not others with that which is painful unto yourself.'

"The teachings of the Enlightened One and of the Prophet of Islam do not always agree, but upon this point they stand united. In the holy Koran are the words of Mohammed: 'None of you is a believer when he does not wish for his brother what he wishes for himself. Whoever believes in Allah, and the Day of Judgment, should speak only good, or remain silent. He should honor his neighbor and his guest.'

"Although all of the great religious systems of the world are represented here, I am aware that the largest single group is made up of the many divisions of the Christian faith. But whatever path each of you has chosen, and there are very many within the Christian community, all of you will know the words of the Man who is the Savior to whom you all turn. And you all know that He too taught this principle. You will find it in your Bible in the seventh chapter of Saint Matthew: '*So whatever you wish that men would do to you, do so to them; for this is the law and the prophets.*'

"So I believe you can see that every great leader whom we revere and follow here taught us each in his own words the very same thing, and this, surely, is something against which no man can raise his voice. For if he does so, he must first turn his back on the wisdom of the ages and also on the greatest forces for good that this present world has ever known.

"I ask that you consider this and see if it is not possible for you to find here the common point of beginning, the place where we can truly all stand together.

"I ask you now to allow me to offer my blessing to you all and to the great and wonderful purpose that has brought us all together." His Holiness shut his eyes and raised his hands.

As Philip stood, his eyes were wet, and he was not ashamed. As he bowed his head, he saw that throughout the whole auditorium there was a wave of reaction; he could not define it all, but when he caught a glimpse of the Jewish delegation, he saw that the men who comprised it were placing yarmulkes on their heads.

In Philip's heart there came a feeling that his mind had not implanted there, and to his silent lips there came a prayer that he had not consciously shaped. He spoke it silently, but hearing it for the first time as he offered it: "Thank you, dear God, thank you, for truly I have with my own eyes seen Lazarus raised from the dead."

Because the auditorium was so very full, and because there had been a demand for every possible place, some of the careful and diplomatic seating arrangements had had to be set aside in order that every possible person could be accommodated; it was for that reason that the learned Rabbi who had agreed to remain on to represent the Orthodox Jewish faith found himself next to a tall Arab whom he had seen many times with the Muslim delegation, and whom he understood to be its head. Ordinarily the proximity would have been at the least a mutual embarrassment, but both men were highly intelligent and understood the circumstances. They had, therefore, politely ignored each other and the fact that they had sons in opposing armies. For the sake of the dignity of the faiths that they represented, they had each made the necessary concession knowing that in all probability others were doing the same.

The rabbi was not, therefore, with the rest of the Jewish delegation as was normally the case; one of the most distinguished leaders of American Judaism had appeared unexpectedly and he had willingly yielded his place in order that his distinguished co-religionist might be given the best possible seat.

For most of the discourse of the Dalai Lama he had remained very quiet with his head bowed. Although the speaker was two decades his junior, he was aware that wisdom is not confined within the bounds of seniority just as virility and courage is not solely the property of the young. He listened very carefully, and not long after the discourse had begun he knew that he was hearing a very wise man indeed.

Well before the quotation from the Talmud had been given he had thought of it by chapter and verse, but he had momentarily doubted that the devout Buddhist from the other side of the high Himalayas would know of it. When it was revealed that he did, the equally devout rabbi yielded a point in his own mind — any man of such wisdom could not be the head of a faith that totally lacked merit.

The rabbi had never read the Koran; therefore the words of the Prophet came to him as something of a surprise. He had understood the doctrine of Islam to be primarily "an eye for an eye, a tooth for a tooth, a life for a life." Despite the fact that he was no longer young, and very senior in his calling, he was not past the time of learning and, what was vastly more important, profiting by it. Learning, to the rabbi, was something that became a part of you and shaped your whole being. And if he had confidence in what was being offered, he was not disturbed by whatever form the teacher might take. In the Dalai Lama he recognized greatness and he listened humbly.

When the discourse was over and His Holiness raised his hands to offer his precious blessing, the rabbi reached into his pocket and drew out his yarmulke. He placed it on his head and then thanked God for the presence of this human being.

He did not, of course, understand the words that His Holiness spoke in Tibetan, but their import reached him nonetheless. A blessing was a definite and universal thing — it required no rote or formula. At that instant he remembered a story told about a former Pope. A group of sailors had gone for an audience with the Holy Father, and at the conclusion of the brief meeting they had knelt to receive the papal blessing — all but one. "I am Jewish, Father," the sailor had explained. "Come anyway," the Pope had said to him. "There has never yet been a young man who was not better for an old man's blessing."

The rabbi, whose heart was in a war-torn land, wished for all of the blessings he might have. He understood the words though never in his long life had he ever heard that language spoken. And he responded to them.

Because he could not escape doing so, he turned his head

slightly and out of the corner of his eye surveyed the tall Arab who sat beside him. Their eyes met, for the Arab was looking at him.

For an indefinite number of seconds they looked at each other, somewhat parallel thoughts racing through their separate minds in widely diverse languages. Then the rabbi saw, or thought he saw, the Arab incline his head very slightly in what might have been interpreted as a fractional greeting.

The hallowed words of the Talmud came before the rabbi once more and told him what God expected of him. He had served the Almighty all of his adult life and he knew that now too he was called upon to obey. Consciously he blocked all other thoughts from his mind and remembered only the Covenant to which his mortal life was dedicated. Because God asked it of him, he held out his hand.

Because of the will of Allah, and the words of the Prophet, the Arab steeled himself and took it.

CHAPTER TWENTY

Sir Cyril Plessey sat back quietly in a rare mood of reflection. For an unstated reason Ames was not present; as the late afternoon sunlight slanted in through the windows only the venerable knight and the dedicated British bishop were present in the living room of the guesthouse. Sir Cyril had prepared refreshments at the bar and then had composed himself for a few moments of relaxation.

"I am strangely at peace," Philip said. "I haven't felt this way for years."

"I well understand, I have somewhat the same reaction myself. Thanks to an insight which I venture to say neither of us possessed, we are out of the woods. And it was the thickest and deepest forest I have ever known."

"Nothing in my experience matches it," Philip agreed. "At this point there are many things that I could say to you, but you already know what they are and the words themselves seem superfluous. And," he added, "totally inadequate."

Sir Cyril stretched his weatherbeaten fingers along the

armrest of his chair. "Jointly we have a great many people to thank, going all the way back to Freddy Danford-Smith, who had a little more to offer than I had suspected. I have a confession to make here."

"Don't bother," Philip said.

Sir Cyril consulted his glass and then tilted his head back. "I want to. You see, Philip, I had felt that if I could persuade His Holiness to come here, the very charisma of his presence would have a favorable impact. And, of course, it was news — something to get us out of the doldrums. Then, in the afterglow of the appearance of the most legendary religious personage there is, we presumably would have been able to fold our tents and conclude the meeting on at least a hopeful note. That was frankly all that I was aiming for. My error was in underestimating the Dalai Lama — and I have always held him in very high regard."

"You knew him, then?"

"Yes, I did — I had had three audiences with him previously. I was personally concerned with the Tibetan refugees — people of enormous courage who like the Jews under Hitler are the victims of twentieth-century savagery. In a small way I was able to render some assistance and His Holiness expressed his gratitude. Now he has taught us all a lesson."

"And a very sound one," Philip agreed. "I've taken certain steps, Sir Cyril, which I believe you know about. I have passed the word informally that the conference will conclude this weekend. Everyone knows it by now. Tomorrow, if the present mood prevails, and I believe that it will, I am going to try to get the assembly to agree on the fourteenth point."

"Have you someone set up to so move?"

"Yes, Bishop O'Hanlon is going to do it on behalf of the Catholic delegation. Bishop Sumi will second for the Zen branch of Buddhism."

"Philip, I hesitate to make reckless predictions, but I

think that you are in. If the assembly agrees on that, and I fail to see how it can miss, then you will have a triumph."

"Sir Cyril. *If* it passes, and I detect any leftover good will, then I am going to make a proposal of my own." Philip tightened the muscles of his body as though he was gathering his resources. "I'm going to propose that we meet again. Time and place unstated, but consider the impact if that motion can be accepted. It will mean that a bridge has been formed over the bickering that has characterized much of this meeting."

Sir Cyril considered that. "If you leave the matters of time and place entirely open," he said finally, "it might go. Possibly because it would be difficult for anyone to vote against it."

"That is exactly how I see it," Philip responded.

"Now we come to another matter . . ." Sir Cyril began, but he was interrupted by the doorbell.

He rose to answer it and ushered in Aubrey Fothergill, who was surprisingly alone. "Would you care for a drink?" Sir Cyril offered.

"I need it," Aubrey admitted.

He dropped into a chair with no trace of the careful manner he invariably used in the presence of his superior. When Sir Cyril placed a glass in his hand he sampled it almost eagerly and then rested his head far back against the cushion. That was the first time that Philip had ever seen him indulge himself in such a manner, but he did not mind. The strain and tensions of the conference had affected everyone and Aubrey had had his full share.

"Has anything gone wrong?" Philip asked.

Aubrey bestirred himself and after a second consultation with the refreshment Sir Cyril had prepared he pulled himself up in his chair. "No, M'Lord, not exactly."

"Unburden yourself," Sir Cyril directed.

"I don't know if I can," Fothergill answered him.

Sir Cyril penetrated him with his eagle's eye. "Son, if

you can tell me anything that I haven't heard before, you will appear in the next edition of Guiness' *Book of Records*."

"I can," Aubrey threatened.

"Then do so by all means!"

The young clergyman looked up at him, then he turned his attention to Philip. "Your lordship," he began, "I ask your forgiveness in advance for this . . ."

"Granted," Philip responded.

Aubrey had one more go at his drink and then came out with it. "Sir, I am getting married on Friday as you know. And you have done us the great honor to accept our invitation to officiate."

"Indeed my pleasure," Philip said. As soon as he had spoken he caught a glance from Sir Cyril and understanding swept over him. "Wait a minute, Fothergill," he interjected. "Let me try to fit a few pieces together. Your lovely bride-to-be is a Buddhist. And . . . " he thought carefully . . . "His Holiness is here."

"That's it — exactly," Aubrey confessed.

Sir Cyril was about to speak, but for the first time Philip ventured to cut him off. "The situation is very clear in my mind, and I understand it fully. I am entirely sympathetic with Jayawardene's wishes to have His Holiness perform the ceremony, and it is the bride's choice. I withdraw gladly in favor of His Holiness and I am honored to do so."

Aubrey was still not out of his agony. "But My Lord. . . ."

This time Sir Cyril was not to be denied. "In order to handle this matter in the most efficient and diplomatic way possible, I suggest that you turn it over to me," he declared. "I will make all the arrangements."

"There is nothing to arrange," Philip told him. "My feathers aren't ruffled in the least. I am completely sympathetic and I am in no way miffed."

"There are certain other considerations," Sir Cyril persisted. "Including the future career of the Reverend Aubrey Fothergill. Leave it to me, I beg of you!"

Philip surrendered. "It's yours."

Sir Cyril nodded emphatically. "Good."

During the following twenty-four hours the performance of the titled Britisher was an awesome thing to behold. He first managed to secure a prompt audience with the Dalai Lama, assuming correctly that His Holiness had not been approached on the matter of the wedding. While Philip Roundtree had been the clergyman of record, to have done so would have been impossible.

The matter did not prove to be as simple as might have been the case. His Holiness was of the opinion that Bishop Roundtree should be the man and in support of that position he raised gently but definitely the question of legality. Surrounded by his attendants His Holiness pointed out that it was probably necessary to be licensed under American law, not to mention the state concerned.

An interview with Judge Wettstein resolved that; that resourceful jurist offered to appoint His Holiness a temporary officer of the court with the necessary privileges. After several other minor matters had been disposed of, a careful talk with M. Henri Devereux assured that artist's fullest cooperation. No other person, it was explained, could possibly meet the requirements — the success of the occasion rested in his hands alone. The prospect of baking a cake which would feed upwards of eight hundred people did not disconcert him in the least. By this time he was served by a near-adoring staff and the challenge was one they welcomed.

Sir Cyril, in the midst of everything else, found time for a conference with the groom-to-be. "My boy," he declared, "like every man, with the exception of Franz Liszt, you would much prefer a simple quiet ceremony with a minimum of fuss and feathers. I am totally aware of this, and as I recall you so expressed yourself."

"I did," Aubrey declared.

"Unfortunately, to get this girl you will have to go through the agonies, but in my well-qualified opinion she is worth it. What you are up against is the fact that your romance has been so widely publicized, you will cheat the public out of their eye teeth if you don't allow them the satisfaction of a full-fledged wedding. We could play it down if the bride were as homely as a bat, but such is not the case."

"Definitely not," Aubrey agreed. "Incidentally, Liszt never married."

"I am aware of that, and in his case that was probably the wiser decision. Matrimony would have cramped his style and he was richly endowed with that. A man of many gifts. Now back to the case in hand. As far as the wedding goes, remember that you only have to endure it once in the normal course of events unless you find that you have made a bad choice. If you come to any such conclusion, I shall personally regard it as evidence of advanced insanity. So stand up and be brave, you'll have her all to yourself shortly thereafter."

"And I will have to look for another job."

"I don't think so. If Freddy Smith were to attempt to persuade you to give up your calling, the walls of Jericho would come crashing down on his head. You and your wife-to-be are a symbol of what this whole conference is about and you are carrying the ball on behalf of tens of thousands of others in a similar position, but in relative obscurity."

The Reverend Mr. Fothergill was a stubborn man and even the fearsome Sir Cyril Plessey did not silence his argument. "That's well and good and so far I agree with you," he said. "But there is another thing to be considered. After the dust has settled and we are just man and wife, where in England is there a congregation likely to call a priest who is widely known to have a Buddhist wife? I don't think that the Ladies Missionary Society is likely to be enchanted, to give an example."

Sir Cyril eyed him and he withstood the blast. "On the contrary, let me inform you that you have yet to learn about people. If you want a congregation, so long as you stay out of the intellectual wilderness areas, you can probably have your choice."

On Wednesday afternoon Bill Quigley released the information that His Holiness the Dalai Lama had consented to officiate at the wedding with the understanding that the Right Reverend Dr. Philip Roundtree would also participate. The next paragraph in the release conveyed the news that Dr. Roundtree had also consented. Since the ceremony was a sacred religious occasion, at the request of the bride only a single press photographer would be permitted in addition to the man whom the college had engaged. A limited number of seats would be available to the press. When Arthur Gravenstine went to claim his, he discovered that he had been invited as a guest.

By Thursday noon the preparations were complete; the license had been issued, the other legal requirements had been satisfied, and the bride had tried on her gown. It fitted perfectly.

While all this had been taking place, Philip had been fully engaged with the conducting of the final sessions of the conference. They were almost anticlimactic despite their serious tone. Bishop O'Hanlon moved the acceptance of the Fourteenth Point. When he had done so, Bishop Sumi offered his second. As he sat down a rabbi rose to his feet, and with him two Buddhists and the leader of the Jains.

When Philip opened the question to debate, there was no response. He waited for a full interval and then asked if it was the will of the assembly to vote. The tally was solemnly taken, and when it was over the count revealed that there had been no one willing to go on record as opposing the universal principle of equity to all. It was so easily done, it seemed to Philip that if he were to wait for a few moments the roof would fall in just to keep things relatively normal.

But the structure stood intact and the thing was done. Since there remained plenty of time, Philip risked his triumph in the interests of a greater cause and proposed the suggestion that they meet again.

The motion was made and accepted, then the amendments began. Islam proposed that the next meeting be in five years' time. Bahai favored two years; the Catholics, well aware of the long history of their Church, proposed ten years.

Peasley, the indefatigable Methodist, proposed that instead of setting a definite time, the assembly name a committee to consider the matter and call a meeting when, in its judgment, the time was right. If any member was unable to serve out his term, his faith would be empowered to select a suitable person to occupy his chair.

That was seconded by the Parsees with the addendum that Dr. Philip Roundtree chair the committee.

Philip declined, giving as his reason his belief that someone of a different persuasion should be named.

Upon being asked to reconsider, he refused.

A Seventh-Day Adventist, who had been spending some time in the meditation room, proposed the name of Bishop Togen Sumi. Not everyone knew the Zen master, but enough did so that he was elected without an opposing candidate being named.

Then, suddenly, it was all over. Philip could not quite realize it, but the fact was before him. For a moment or two, even as he stood before the assembly, his mind turned back toward that wintry morning when he had mounted the pulpit and had called for this meeting. He had known then that he was inviting disaster and he had expected it. The outcome, however, had been very different.

He glanced at his watch. "If I may," he said, "I would like to share with you my feelings at this moment. And my profound gratitude. I have myself learned so much during the progress of this meeting. I have made many friends of faiths other than my own, and from them I have gained inestimably. I have discovered how little I truly knew about other beliefs and the great accumulated wisdom that is to be found in so many of them. Tomorrow my chaplain is to marry a young lady he never would have met except for this gathering, and to some extent their union is a symbol of your achievement."

He could not say more. He wanted to, but the words eluded him.

The tall Arab who headed the Islamic delegation slowly rose. When he had received a microphone he moved that the assembly express its gratitude for the inspiration and leadership that the Right Reverend Dr. Philip Roundtree had so liberally provided.

For the third time in the final sessions the assembly was of one mind and the formal resolution passed without dissent, even from the few factions that had given Philip the greatest amount of trouble.

"Thank you," he said humbly when the vote had been taken. "Thank you very much. I believe now that we should stand adjourned."

Ten minutes later the delegates were filing out of the auditorium. Philip waited until most of them had passed through the rear doorways, then he turned to go. He was in a strange mood he could not define: his conference was behind him and it was a success, the vast load of responsibility had been lifted, and he should have been mildly elated — but he was not. He was even slightly depressed, and he had no idea why.

As he stepped out into the sunlight he noted that the trees were beginning to show the first signs of the approach of autumn; that made him think of home, and of Janet and the boys. And of the familiar diocese he had missed without knowing it. He had been unduly prominent for some time; it would be good to return to the relative obscurity he had so much enjoyed. Almost subconsciously he heard the Muslim call to prayer that had become so much a part of the campus life and he had an odd desire to respond to it in some way. Without pausing to think about it any further, he began to walk toward the meditation room. Peace awaited him there, and at that moment it had an almost irresistible appeal.

As he stood quietly waiting, thoughts swept through the mind of the Reverend Aubrey Fothergill in a tumbling cascade of recollection. He lived again the first time that he had met Jayawardene and had been amazed that Thai young women could be so stunning. That was before he had learned that Her Majesty the Queen of Thailand was herself a celebrated world beauty.

Back to him also came the time, early in their acquaintance, when the radio had been on in the lobby of the dormitory playing some sort of strange and unusual music. Just for him she had raised her arms, turned her hands back at an amazing angle, and then had gently begun to dance. It had been utterly, totally captivating. And when she had finished and he had expressed his admiration, she had smiled and said, "We aren't barbarians, you know."

There was an odd thing about people: if you were with someone often enough, and watched carefully, sometimes a certain expression, or shift in the light, would reveal how that person would look in twenty years' time. He had had that happen with Jayawardene, and he had been sharply impressed with the fact that she would be even lovelier then; maturity if anything would enhance her beauty.

314

He brought himself back to the present and glanced down once more to see if his shoes were still properly shined. They were. He did not feel flustered; he had been to many weddings and he had officiated at several, so the experience would be nothing new to him — except that this time he was to be the groom.

He had often thought about it in his imagination when he had been younger. No particular girl had figured in his fantasies, but she had always been a typical English beauty with the fair skin and hazel eyes so much a part of the British Isles. That was all erased now; his bride-to-be had raven-black hair, dark eyes, and came from a land famous for its klongs, its incredible temples — and its lovely women.

It could be no one else; if he could not have Jayawardene, then he didn't want anybody. But by the grace of God, in a few more minutes she would be his, and for that reward he was willing to pay any price — even that of his chosen career.

Having communed with his own thoughts he turned to Dr. Harley Poindexter, and received a warming smile even before he spoke. "It's very good of you to stand up for me," he said.

"On the contrary," the college president answered him. "I wanted to get into the act the worst way, and this was my only chance."

The organ was playing; at any moment it would break into the Wedding March. "I would feel better if we had had a rehearsal," Aubrey said. "I have no idea what His Holiness is going to do, or in what language."

"Don't worry," Poindexter advised him. "Everyone else is in the same boat, and if you did make a mistake no one would know the difference. But you won't, you'll manage."

"The British gift for muddling through? By the way, is the Wedding March Christian or pagan music?"

Harley had the answer immediately. "It's Christian.

Lohengrin was the son of Parsifal; they were knights of the Holy Grail."

The voice of the organ paused in transition, and then in an almost triumphant manner began the familiar strains of the Wedding March.

Very quietly dressed in his clerical garb, Aubrey Fothergill bowed his head for a moment, not in prayer but in thought, and then with his best man at his side walked slowly into the chapel-auditorium to be married.

It was packed as he had expected that it would be, but he thrust that reality out of his mind. Far toward the rear the procession had started down the aisle, but he could not yet catch a glimpse of his bride; he turned instead toward the people who were awaiting him on the stage. His attention was riveted by Philip Roundtree, dressed in the full formal vestments of a bishop of the Church of England, his miter crowning his head with the authority of his office. As he looked at his superior he received a gentle but reassuring smile. That washed from Aubrey's mind the last reservations he had had concerning the acceptability of his soon to be wife in his bishop's eyes. Philip was with him, and that meant a very great deal.

He turned his head slowly, aware that a great deal of attention would be focused upon him before the bride appeared, and saw His Holiness the Dalai Lama awaited him also. He was dressed as before in his brown and saffron robes, but now he wore in addition a yellow hat which, while of simple design, seemed to give him a vastly greater aura of authority. He saw the monk Tenzin on the stage in attendance on His Holiness, and another whom he did not know, but he had no more time to think of them at the moment; he wanted, almost desperately, to see Jayawardene.

The procession was still coming down the aisle, close enough by then so he could begin to distinguish faces. The first person he truly saw was Denise Applebaum, lovely in

316

her rose-pink bridesmaid's dress and smiling just enough to enhance her blond beauty even more. She was pacing herself precisely to the music as she led the procession down the aisle, moving forward a step, pausing momentarily, and then stepping forward once more.

Behind her, separated by a few feet, was Yoshiko Matsumoto, poised and exquisite in pastel blue, holding her bouquet with consummate grace. Her features were composed, but she still drew every eye.

Behind her, in yellow, Karen Erickson followed, trying her best to be appropriately solemn, but obviously suppressing a certain feeling of triumph. The fingers that held her bouquet were wet, but her emotions did not cause her to miss a step or slacken the careful way she poised her shoulders.

After a longer space the bride herself appeared, on the arm of Sir Cyril Plessey. From where he stood Aubrey could not yet see her very well, but even at a moderate distance he could not mistake the regal bearing and style of the venerable knight whose every step forward was a triumph of British tradition. When Aubrey at last could see Jayawardene clearly, his tensions ebbed in her approaching presence. Of course she was utterly lovely, but that he had expected and he kept his composure. When at last she stepped beside him, fulfillment flooded through him and he no longer cared if he knew what to expect or not.

When all was ready Philip came forward, an open book in his hands. "Dearly beloved, we are gathered together here in the sight of God, and in the face of this congregation, to join together this man and this woman in Holy Matrimony, which is an honorable estate . . ."

Aubrey listened to the long-familiar words and wondered how his bride was reacting to them. As far as he could tell, she was entirely motionless beside him, her head slightly bowed, listening.

"Therefore if any man can shew any just cause why they may not lawfully be joined together, let him now speak, or else hereafter forever hold his peace."

In the pause that followed Aubrey wondered with tightened jaw muscles if any of the representatives of the many faiths in the vast auditorium would take that invitation literally. *Someone* could object on religious grounds and then . . .

By the grace of God nobody did.

"I require and charge you both, as ye will answer at the dreadful day of judgment when the secrets of all hearts shall be disclosed, that if either of you know any impediment why ye may not be lawfully joined together in Matrimony, ye do now confess it . . ."

For some reason those words triggered Aubrey into a sudden sense of inadequacy. He was getting much much more than he deserved and he knew it. Then he forced himself to pay attention to what was going on.

Philip was addressing him. "Wilt thou have this woman to thy wedded wife, to live together according to God's law in the Holy estate of Matrimony? Wilt thou love her, comfort her, honor and keep her, in sickness and in health? And, forsaking all other, keep thee only unto her, so long as ye both shall live?"

Aubrey drew breath and said, "I will."

He listened while Philip addressed Jayawardene and then held his breath for a moment as he listened for her answer. She was, after all, of another faith and even at the last moment . . .

He heard her say, quietly, "I will."

"Who giveth this woman to be married to this man?"

Sir Cyril Plessey stepped forward and placed Jayawardene's hand in Aubrey's in a manner that kings would have envied.

Philip continued, "Repeat after me: 'I, Aubrey, take thee, Jayawardene, to my wedded wife . . .' "

Aubrey turned and recited the lines, for which he required no prompting. Then he stood motionless while Jayawardene repeated her own vow; he did not miss a syllable of it.

Dr. Poindexter produced the ring and laid it on the book that Philip held. To Aubrey's relief, so far everything was on the rails and he knew what to do; he placed the ring on his bride's finger and spoke his piece: "With this ring I thee wed . . ."

When he had finished, Philip stepped back and to one side. The Dalai Lama came forward flanked by his attendants; as he did so his first act was to reassure Aubrey with a quiet smile. Then he indicated that he should kneel. As Aubrey did so he told himself that if His Holiness would continue to provide cues in that manner, all would be well.

He heard the voice of the Dalai Lama in a language he could not recognize, but assumed to be Tibetan. It was presumably a prayer and lasted perhaps half a minute. When it was over he looked up and understood that he was to stand once more.

His Holiness carried no book and he required none. "Since you have exchanged vows here before this congregation and have sealed them by the giving and receiving of a ring and the joining of your hands" — he lifted his own before them — "by the authority that has been granted to me, I pronounce that you are man and wife."

With his hands still raised he spoke once more in Tibetan. As he did so Aubrey knew that he was a married man, and that he was probably sharing with his wife the crowning blessing of their lifetimes. Then he heard Philip adding the ritual of the Church of England in the formal words that had stood for centuries. His soul expanded and he tightened his grip on Jayawardene's fingers.

The voice of the Dalai Lama demanded his attention once more. "I am aware that it was the wish of this young couple to be married within the authority of a new and united church. This is an achievement we shall probably not see in our lifetimes, but they symbolize the hope that it may at some future time become a reality. As we learn to know and to understand one another, and as we exchange our ideas and philosophies, we shall inevitably draw, degree by degree, closer to each other.

"We are united now in wishing them the best of good fortune, the blessing of children, and the opportunity to live together in happiness and in peace. When you have returned to your own countries and to your churches, your temples and synagogues, your mosques and your pagodas, remember them and pray for them. Pray for them as two people and for them as representing the meeting of persons who are different in small respects, alike in all of the greater ones. Please join me in giving them your blessing."

Aubrey felt, when the Dalai Lama had finished, that that had been a very fine statement and a marked improvement over the sermonettes on matrimony that so many of his own colleagues usually delivered at that point. He was unaware that behind him, on the center aisle end of the third row, a man dressed in black had risen to his feet.

He first sensed that something was taking place when he saw that His Holiness, by gesture, was inviting someone to speak.

"If your Holiness will permit," the man said, "may I bless them now?"

Aubrey looked quickly at Philip and saw an expression he could not quite read. His bishop's features were composed, but they also had another cast, one which defied analysis.

Then Philip looked at him and he knew that he had to speak. It was in the middle of the wedding ceremony and improvisations were not in order; he saved himself by a one word response that could mean almost anything: "Please."

Aubrey watched as the man from the congregation came almost hesitantly onto the stage, his manner suggesting that he already regretted having interrupted the ceremony, but that he would do so again nonetheless. Then Aubrey recognized him: he was the rabbi who had consented to remain and represent Orthodox Judaism when the rest of that delegation had left.

With the manner of a man of God long accustomed to his calling, the rabbi stepped before them, adjusted his yarmulke, and raised his hands. He spoke briefly in Hebrew and then repeated the words in English: *"Love thy wife as thyself, says the Talmud, and honor her more than thyself. Be careful not to cause a woman to weep, for God counts her tears."*

The rabbi lowered his arms. "Forgive me," he said softly, "but I wanted to so very much."

Philip and His Holiness exchanged glances, then Philip spoke, addressing the congregation. "Are there any others?" he asked.

For a full five seconds no one dared; then the tall Arab who headed the Islamic delegation stood up. When Philip nodded he came forward, stood before Aubrey and Jayawardene, and in Arabic bestowed upon them the blessing of Allah.

Behind him the even taller Sikh, mighty in his beard and turban, came, and at that moment Aubrey awoke to an unexpected and dazzling truth.

He and Jayawardene were receiving something that had never been previously given. There was no united church, but there was something close to a united humanity.

Despite his aching knees, he remained on them gratefully while the union he was entering into was blessed, and blessed again — in many languges, according to many different beliefs, but with a common objective. For every major faith in the world believed in marriage, and they were all there.

When at last it was over, and the signal was given to him to rise, he stood up suspecting that he was the most fortunate man who had ever come forward to be married.

When he looked at Jayawardene and prepared to kiss her, he was certain.

It had not been prearranged, he knew that; not even, for once, by Sir Cyril. He did not care, nor did he dwell on the fact that this was a historic occasion — he was just grateful. He kissed his bride, hardly feeling the touch of her lips, then he looked toward the eleven men who still stood upon the stage and remembered that he himself was also a priest.

If others could do it so could he. "Gentlemen," he said, "may I?"

He did not wait for an answer. He looked once more quickly at the respectable line that had formed: the rabbi, the Arabic emir, the turbaned Sikh, Bishop O'Hanlon, the chief Parsee, the priest of the Jains, the Confucian, the Taoist, the high-ranking Hindu, his own bishop, and the supreme living Buddhist; then he raised his right hand and spoke in a voice strong with his own authority and conviction: *"The Lord bless you and keep you, the Lord make his face to shine upon you; the Lord lift up the light of his countenance upon you, and give you peace, now and forevermore. Amen."*

Sir Cyril Plessey's presence of mind was complete; with a quick gesture he signaled to the organist. Almost at once the mighty voice of the instrument was raised in the wedding recessional. Fully in possession of himself, Aubrey tugged one more time at the hem of his coat and then turned to offer his arm to his bride. He led her up the aisle proudly past the hundreds of delegates, through the lobby, and into the outside air.

There he paused to take stock. First he looked at Jayawardene, the only real chance he had had to do so since the ceremony had begun.

"I'm your wife," she said.

He wanted to kiss her then, but others were coming out behind them and they could not remain there.

"You always will be," he promised her, and then with her still on his arm he headed toward the Student Union and the dining room where the reception would be held. Outside the building the press people and photographers were waiting *en masse*, and they would not be denied. For almost ten minutes Aubrey and his bride were compelled to face this way and that, to look solemn, to smile, and then to kiss. When that gauntlet had been run and they were at last safely inside, the guests were beginning to gather.

A certain controlled confusion took over. While more and more people came across the campus and into the Union, the food was uncovered and the small college orchestra began to play. When Philip came Aubrey was genuinely relieved to see him. "I hope you approve of my actions, M'Lord Bishop," he said.

Philip beamed on him. "You were superb. But not everyone was looking at you, you know."

"I'm very much aware of that, sir. Is it your intention to kiss the bride?"

"I was about to ask your permission."

"She will be disappointed if you don't."

The arrival of Sir Cyril Plessey was creating a stir behind them. Already the crowd was thick and the food servers were busy. The formalities were finished and done; the holiday mood had fully taken over.

It was three quarters of an hour later that a young man, very plainly dressed in a simple robe of monk's cloth, came hurrying into the building. With obvious determination he made his way through the busy lobby and into the main dining room, where a few people noticed him but gave him no real attention. There were many others present in various forms of religious dress, so that his normally distinctive appearance was all but absorbed into the background.

He did not seem to care. As soon as he was safely inside

he paused momentarily to look about and assay the situation. The bride and groom were still present, well surrounded as he had expected. By means of the bishop's vestments he located Dr. Philip Roundtree and then, after searching a bit more, he spotted the place where, surrounded by his attendants, His Holiness the Dalai Lama was graciously greeting the guests.

Against one wall there was a table which had been placed there to receive used punch glasses. The young man walked over to it, examined the underside, and satisfied himself that it was sturdily built. At that moment the orchestra stopped playing. Flipping back the tablecloth to give himself a clear spot, the young man swung himself up onto the table and then stood there, looking over the whole assembly. That done, with a strength and presence surprising for his age he called out loudly, "May I have your attention, please."

Philip, Harley Poindexter, and Sir Cyril were conferring together at that moment; it was not until the young man had called loudly for the third time that they took notice of him.

"Who is it?" Sir Cyril asked.

"I don't know," Philip confessed. "I don't recall ever having seen him before."

"Listen, listen to me!" The voice of the young man, powerful and persuasive, once more cut through the noise of the room.

"He probably wants to propose a toast," Harley Poindexter suggested, "but that isn't the way to do it."

"*Please, please!*" The young man's voice was intense — demanding. As the room began to fall quiet, even from where he stood Philip was able to see that here was someone of unusual fiber. Intensity seemed to radiate from him, fueled by determined purpose. He stood awkwardly on top of a table, but that meant nothing to him as he held up his arms and turned slowly so that he swept every part of the

324

huge room with his attention. He had presence too, and bearing. But Philip could still not recall having ever met him.

"I have news!" the young man shouted. "Great and wonderful news!"

At last the hubbub of the reception was stilled; Aubrey stood with Jayawardene beside him waiting for whatever was to come.

When, finally, he had the attention of everyone, the young man held out his arms, projecting a considerable personal force over the assembly. "Listen, listen to the incredible news! *The Messiah has arisen again!*"

"Good God!" Sir Cyril said.

"*He is with us, he lives!*" the speaker declared. "*From the mountains of Mexico he has come to us, and he is performing miracles!*"

He surveyed his listeners, measuring them and their attention to him and his message. "*He is called El Milagroso, and he is God!*"

"Get him out of here," someone called.

If the speaker heard it, he paid no attention. "He has healed the sick, he has brought forth water, and he is the king of mankind!" As a truly great actor might have done, the young man held out his palms, pleading for and demanding belief. "Already he has chosen his disciples and congregations are being formed."

He stopped, clasped his hands, and looked over the heads of all those assembled. "*This* is the universal faith. *This* is what you have been seeking. *This* is your salvation!"

He drew a deep breath. "Come, come, all of you, and join with us. For although he is only seventeen earthly years, he has the eternal wisdom. Come and be received, for the new world is at hand!"

AUTHOR'S NOTE

The preparation of this book was made possible through the great generosity of many religious dignitaries who gave most liberally of their time and help. So much was done by so many in England, Italy, Greece, Egypt, Israel, India, Burma, Thailand, Singapore, Turkey, Ethiopia, Iran, Malaysia, Nepal, the Republic of China, Cambodia, Bali, Indonesia, Ceylon, Korea, and Japan, individual acknowledgment is impossible.

The Reverend Dr. Evan Williams made a major contribution, particularly through his extraordinary knowledge of the Church of England and its modes of operation.

In Bombay, Mrs. Lily P. Jayasinghe earned the author's particular gratitude for arranging an appointment with the ranking high priest of the Parsees and also a visit to the beautiful park which contains the Towers of Silence.

The remarkable abilities of Mr. Tyler Tanaka, the president of Japan-Orient Tours, need to be acknowledged; repeatedly he brought all but impossible destinations into focus and somehow made the necessary arrangements despite often formidable obstacles.

Finally, and with the utmost respect, the author is honored to acknowledge his great indebtedness to His Holiness the Dalai Lama for granting him the unprecedented permission to include him in the present work. His Holiness is precisely as depicted here and the world is vastly richer for his presence among us.

JOHN BALL

Printed in Great Britain
by Amazon